D1522395

even if he ran it, because he was carrying dead weight."

"So, say twelve minutes there, he could sprint back, maybe round trip you're looking at twenty plus times three," Roy said, staring in the direction where the three women had been found lying side by side.

Mitchell nodded. "Plus it was dark. He probably couldn't use a flashlight because his hands were already full."

"Right. It might have taken him even longer." John pointed to the woman a few feet from them. "This last victim…he adjusted his plans because he knew he was running out of time."

Mitchell eyed him for a moment. "Of course this is all based on the assumption that they're decomposing at the same time."

"Of course," John conceded. Although he knew in his gut he was right, he also knew the CSU tech would follow procedure and waste time.

"Good theory, but after the bodies have been removed, I'm still going to have my people do that search. You never know." He shrugged then walked off toward the embankment to one of the CSU vans parked alongside the road.

Roy motioned him to do the same, but John stopped him, and scanned the highway again. "Sheriff, how many truckers do you get through here?"

"Quite a few, but my deputies, Ed Young and Dan Malvern would be able to tell you more on that. This is the area they're assigned to patrol."

"Are they here?"

"Both of 'em. Ed's the one who'd found the first body. Hang tight." Roy pulled out his cell phone, and punched his speed dial. "Ed, grab Dan and meet me at my cruiser."

John followed Roy up the embankment leading to the sheriff's car. "Who found the others?"

"That'd be Deputy Lloyd Nelson. He was that big guy working with the CSU techs down by the three vics."

The Viking. He remembered the man now. As tall as Roy, only trimmer, leaner, and more muscled, with a shock of white blond hair drifting from beneath his department-issued tan hat.

"Do you want me to call him in?"

A deputy, who looked like a mustachioed Howdy Doody on steroids, approached Roy's county squad car. Another man, big, lean and looking as if he'd just watched someone run over his dog with a tractor trailer, stood next to him.

Tractor trailer.

John viewed the highway as if for the first time, then turned to the sheriff. "I'll talk to Nelson later. Young and Malvern?" He thumbed to the two deputies.

The sheriff nodded.

"How many truckers do you get through this area?" he asked them.

"Plenty," Ed Young said, bobbing his head, a bit of color returning to his pale cheeks.

"They like this run because it's a fast detour to the interstate. Considering how short staffed we are, there aren't many deputies to patrol the area so they can speed on through," Dan Malvern said, his red mustache twitching as he curled his lips.

"How often do you pass through here in a night?"

"Every two hours or so," Dan said. "Sometimes longer if we're held up by a speeder or maybe a DUI."

"Hell, John, that would fit right in the time—"

"Thank you. Give us a moment." John waited until the deputy walked away, then turned to Ed Young. "So you were the one who found the first victim?"

"Yeah, I traded shifts with Dan. He didn't have anyone to look after his wife last night. I was making my last run, and had to take a leak..." His cheeks reddened. "And that's when I...I found." He shut his eyes. "I found the body."

"You didn't touch anything?"

"Nothing," he said with vehemence.

"Thank you, if we need anything else—"

"Roy knows where to find me," he finished, his blank eyes on the CSU team working the crime scene. "Am I dismissed, Roy? I need..."

"Head home," Roy told the deputy.

As the deputy walked off, John noticed a rusted, silver minivan pull up behind the road block. "Are you expecting company?"

"Dammit," the sheriff bitched as a man slid out of the van. "That's Mathias Boysen. His family owns *The Chippewa Gazette*. It's a weekly of no more than a dozen or so pages with nothing but local gossip, garage sale ads, and the occasional police blotter. We'd kept radio silence to avoid the *real* media, but this is such a small town, Matt probably saw all the cruisers and smelled a story. He's nothing to worry about."

"In my experience, anybody with the media is something to worry about. Have one of your deputies stop him before he starts snapping pictures. Promise him the first interview if he can keep his mouth shut."

Roy called over Jesse Peterson, the deputy who had picked him up at the Eau Claire airfield, and told him to take care of Boysen. Once the deputy ran off, the sheriff smoothed his mustache. "Okay, John, let's not pussyfoot around here. You work for Ian, and he says you're one of the best criminalists out there. I need to make this go away, so gimme your best guess."

John turned and studied the sheriff. Less than two hours ago, Ian had him flying off in CORE's private jet to Eau Claire with no information about this case other than the sheriff's name, that four women had been found dead just outside of Wissota Falls, Wisconsin, and that he was to follow Roy's lead and instructions. The only other thing Ian had mentioned was that DCI wasn't involved. John knew better than to question Ian, he had always been one of those "need to know basis" type of guys, and for whatever reason, he hadn't felt John needed to know. But he wanted to.

Most local law enforcement agencies who didn't have the capability or capacity for this type of murder investigation would have asked for assistance from their state departments, or even the FBI before they called CORE. Why would Roy call Ian first? What was their connection? And his gut told him there definitely was a connection. John had known about Ian's private line—a number none of the other agents had been given. Roy had called him on that line, which meant this case might be...personal.

He'd find out eventually, either on his own, or when Ian deemed the time right. Releasing a smug smile when Boysen climbed back into his van, red faced, waving his arms and swearing a litany of curses at Jesse Peterson, John turned to the sheriff. "Without the ME's report on the victims' autopsy? Best guess? You're looking for a long haul trucker, maybe one running a trailer with a refrigeration unit. I'm betting this guy didn't do all four women in one night. I'm betting he *froze* them, then when the bodies built up and he had a load to haul...he dumped them."

Roy whistled. "Makes sense. Ed and Dan were always bitchin' about the truckers that passed through here. Like Dan said, though, we just don't have the manpower to ticket them."

John understood. Roy's county covered many miles, with only a smattering of small towns popping up here and there like zits on a teenager. "I'm also thinking owner/operator. The killer owns his own rig. But again, that's my best guess until the ME does the autopsy."

"It's good though." Roy nodded, then paled, his eyes focusing on the embankment.

John turned, following the sheriff's gaze, and clenched his jaw. A couple of members of the Eau Claire CSU team were hauling a black body bag up the slope. Four dead women. Brutalized, raped, and murdered. One in a bag, three to go. And one sick, twisted bastard to find.

"You got a place to stay?" Roy asked as he continued to watch the CSU team load the body into their van.

"CORE made the arrangements. I'll be at the Chippewa Inn." The only hotel/motel in the area. Lucky him. He'd love nothing more than a Marriott with room service and all the amenities. But this was Small Town, USA, so the Chippewa Inn would have to do.

"It's not a bad place. Arthur Foley and his wife own it."

Roy kept his gaze on the body bag. "Good coffee, clean rooms."

"I'm sure it will be fine," he replied quietly, as another body bag was hauled up the embankment.

They stood in silence as the third victim was loaded into the van, then Roy scrubbed a hand down his face. "I gotta go talk to the mayor. When the media catches wind of this, I'll handle them, or let the mayor. So you know…Ian wants you to keep a low profile."

John wondered what else Ian wanted out of this. "Understood. I'd like to come back here later, though. Do another walk through while we're waiting for the ME's report."

"Me too. I'll have Jesse drive you into town. Bev, our receptionist, said there's a rental car waiting for you at the Sheriff's Department. I gotta hand it to Ian, he works quick when needed."

Yeah, and why was that? What was the history between Roy Hauserman and Ian Scott? The connection and tie to Wissota Falls?

Roy looked at his watch. "It's twelve-thirty now. Meet me at my office around two. That'll give me enough time to talk with the mayor and grab a sandwich. While you're at it, you might want to do the same. Check out The Sugar Shack, it's on the way to the Chippewa Inn. The food's good..." Roy's voice trailed off as the last body bag was hefted into the CSU van. "If you have an appetite."

John climbed into Jesse's cruiser. He had an appetite, all right. A hunger for information. Who had killed those women? And what exactly was Ian keeping from him?

He clenched his jaw as he stared at the woods, the CSU vans, the cruisers, and controlled the rage, the betrayal coursing through him. Garrett had gone behind his back. He'd killed without him.

Without him.

Worse yet, he'd dumped bodies out in the fucking open where anyone could find them?

When his vision blurred with hatred, causing a kaleidoscope of oranges, reds and yellows as he stared at the trees, he quickly reined in his temper. He needed to keep his cool, not allow his judgment, his instincts to be warped with vengeance against his brother. He'd deal with Garrett later.

Despite the anger surging through him, he fought a smile. If only that cocky son of a bitch knew he'd had a little fun of his own. His dick hardened as he pictured the fifteen-inch hunting knife stowed in his workshop. Garrett had called him a pussy one too many times in the past, but in reality that asshole was the pussy. He couldn't handle the sight of blood, the idea of gutting a woman, ripping her flesh with the sharp edge of a steel blade. But he could, and he did. The thought of going back to using a cord to snuff the life out of a whore no longer interested him. Before their last two kills, he'd graduated, from a cord to a knife. From whores to the girl next door.

While slicing that debutant had been exhilarating, intoxicating, he'd missed having Garrett with him. Missed staring into his gray eyes as he'd taken that mouthy bitch.

He shifted, wishing he could rub his arousal. At the same time, he cursed himself for allowing his disgusting, immoral thoughts to continuously invade his mind.

He'd take care of his sexual urges in the shower later. Right now he needed information. He needed to know what the sheriff knew, and what part the outsider, who looked like an agent, played in this. He needed to make sure they didn't mess up what he and Garrett had, because if they did, he'd make them pay. Four dead bodies in the woods would be nothing compared to what he could and would do.

CHAPTER 3

"CELESTE, PHONE," RICK Stanock, The Sugar Shack's short order cook griped, as he dropped a couple of plates, piled high with burgers and fries, under the hot lamps.

"Who is it?"

He slammed a few more plates. "It's the middle of lunch rush, don't know, don't care."

She stuck her tongue out at him, making him grin, then grabbed the burgers, and headed off to deliver them. After making sure the couple didn't need anything else, she headed back to the kitchen and grabbed the phone receiver Rick had left dangling against the wall. Realizing she really needed to bring the diner into the twenty first century and buy some cordless phones, she yanked the receiver up by the curly cord.

"Hello, this is Celeste, how can I help you?" she asked, businesslike. She hoped the call came from either Booker Foods, who owed her a credit to her account after they'd screwed up the order she'd placed last week, or from Sam, her bus boy who hadn't bothered to show up for work today.

"It's Roy."

She leaned against the wall, and flipped through her notepad, itemizing what table needed what and when. "What's up? We're in the middle of lunch rush and you know how the meatloaf sandwich draws a crowd when it's on special."

"I do, so save me one."

"Okay, will do. I'll drop it off on my way home."

"Why don't you come by around two instead? I've been looking over the notes you gave me, and I thought maybe we could talk a bit. Do you think Will could cover you for the rest of the afternoon?"

She glanced around the kitchen, where her brother *should* be helping Rick or at least the two other servers. While she adored her brother, his mind was always on his paintings, not their livelihood. He might not be happy about having to stick around this afternoon, but he owed her.

"Don't worry about Will. I'll see you in a bit." She hung up the phone. After she made a quick round to her tables and the customers at the counter, she went in search of her brother, knowing exactly where he was, and where he liked to hide.

"Hey," she said, and leaned against the doorjamb of their stock room.

Will looked up from his clipboard. "How's it going out there?"

"Busy."

"Meatloaf sandwich on special?"

"Duh, it's Tuesday."

"I know what day it is."

"Then you should also know now isn't the time to do inventory." Irritated at how obtuse he could sometimes be, she pushed off the doorjamb. "I mean, you do realize we're in the middle of lunch rush." She eyed her brother and waited for his next brilliant excuse to avoid dealing with the hungry customers keeping their business alive.

"I...I...hell, you know I hate waiting tables." He cringed and held up his hands.

God, he acted like she was forcing him to wear a g-string rather than an apron. "I know," she said, softening her voice and offering him a sympathetic smile. Will embodied the dark, brooding artist who'd rather sit on the sidelines and observe than place himself at the center of attention. "I don't need a server, but I do need a bus boy. Sam never showed today."

He tapped the clipboard against his leg. "I don't have to take any orders or mingle with the customers?"

She fought an eye roll. While her brother inherited their father's size and brawn, his strength lay in his art, not his social skills. He hated working at the diner, and hated living in Wissota Falls even more than she did. Small town life had never agreed with him. Until he could survive on his paintings alone, he was stuck here, helping her run the diner while her dad was *finding* himself in Florida. Finding himself my ass, she thought bitterly. He was golfing, dating again, and now that he'd bought a condo rather than rented one, she doubted he'd ever return to Wissota Falls.

"Nope, you don't have to talk to anyone." Shoving the bitterness aside, she tugged an apron off the hook, then tossed it at him. "Now, how about it? I can really use your help. Pretty please," she added, widening her eyes and batting her lashes in a pathetic attempt to guilt him into doing his job.

Will narrowed his eyes, and twisted his mouth into a droll smile. "Don't bother with the 'Oh my, I'm so in the weeds, I need your help' act." He'd hitched his voice and mocked her by batting his long, thick eyelashes.

"Snot." She grinned, and swatted him with her notepad. "You've got eyelashes like a girl."

"You're just jealous," he teased as he gave in and put on the apron.

"Oh and before I forget, I've got an appointment at two, so you'll have to watch the diner after lunch." She dashed out of the stock room and headed toward the kitchen, her brother's protests muffled by the crowd in the diner.

Several plates of The Sugar Shack's signature sandwiches, piled high with golden brown, hand-cut fries, greeted her under the hot lamps. She pulled the ticket and the plates then made her way to the counter.

"Here you go, boys. Your usual." Both Glen Anderson and Stu Clemens' eyes bulged as she set the sandwiches in front of them. She'd known these local cranberry farmers for years. Every other week they came into town for a supply run and

31

always stopped by the diner for a couple of roast beefs on rye with horseradish mayonnaise and cheddar, one minus the tomato.

"Geez, Celeste, you've outdone yourself." Stu salivated.

"I'll say." Glen tore his gaze away from his sandwich. "Before I forget, can you pack up a couple dozen of your chocolate chip cookies? Ya' know, for the wife."

"Uh-huh. For the wife, is it?"

"Yeah and the kids, too. They love 'em. Don't know what you put in 'em."

"Oh, and the kids too. Aren't you thoughtful."

"He's full of it," Stu said around a mouthful. "Those cookies won't make it home. He'll have 'em—umph." He rubbed his ribs. "Whaddya do that for? She knows you eat them all and—umph—ouch, cut it out."

"Then shut your trap, she don't need to know about my addiction to her cookies."

"Boys, please." Her heart swelled with pride. She did make a damned good cookie and knew these guys were putting on a show for her. "Tell you what. I'll throw in a few extras, on the house, and they better make it home." She pointed an accusing finger at Glen. "Don't forget, I know your wife."

They chuckled as she turned away, giving her a couple of "yeah, yeah's." They were always suckering her into a few extras here and there. She didn't mind, they'd be harvesting soon, and always gave her the best cranberries at cost.

A full coffee pot in hand, she eyed the diner, pleased at the number of customers crowding booths, tables and the counter. After her mom had died and her dad went off to grieve and find himself in Florida, he'd turned over all responsibilities of the diner to her and Will. She'd worried they'd lose business. But with her degree in accounting, not to mention her knack for baking, she and Will had managed to not only keep the diner alive, but helped it grow, even if it was a continual bane to her and her brother's own aspirations.

Rather than frown at that last thought, she smiled when she caught Will efficiently busing tables, especially when he went out of his comfort zone and greeted several patrons. If it wasn't for the nightmares, life would be…just as boring and unfulfilling as it had been for the past three years.

With a sigh, she refilled empty coffee mugs and joked with the regulars sitting at the counter. The bell on the front door chimed, and sunlight spilled into the diner. When she glanced up from the mug she'd been filling, she nearly fumbled the scalding coffee pot as she caught her breath and stared at the man strolling through the door.

Very male, very hot, and certainly not from Wissota Falls. If he had been, she would already have known every detail about him. Who needed to be psychic when the diner was a regular gossip factory?

Tall, dark and sexy glanced around the busy diner, then chose a vacant stool near the wall at the end of the counter. If a man that big could move with such a fluid, commanding grace by simply walking, she'd bet he had even better moves in bed. She startled herself with the thought, then even further when she pictured him in her bed, naked and between her thighs.

"Can I get a little more coffee?"

Her cheeks burned. Good Lord, she was fantasizing about a complete stranger when the diner was hopping with customers needing attention. "Sure, Russ, need anything else?"

He grunted a refusal, which gave her a chance to lose the coffee pot before she did some serious damage. She wrung her hands on her apron, then reached for her notepad and pencil.

He's just a man like any other, she told herself. No big deal. So what if her fingers tingled and itched to touch his thick black hair? So what if she'd already pictured him naked? It had been a long time since she'd had sex. Too long, she supposed, based on the sudden desire to touch and be touched sizzling through her body. She stuffed any notion of having sex with the stranger in the back of her mind, like she did with any thoughts or memories she wasn't sure she could control. This time, though, it didn't work.

Images of his large hands caressing her bare skin forged

past her mental barrier. Thoughts of his firm, kissable lips exploring her mouth, breasts, and between her thighs where she now throbbed and ached took over and made her body hum with urges she hadn't experienced in a long time.

In an effort to control and hopefully hide the pure lust and attraction this complete and total stranger had evoked, she plastered on a smile as she approached him. "Hi there. What do you want me to do to you?" She winced, realizing her gutter mind had taken over her tongue when a few of the regulars sitting nearby snickered. She narrowed her eyes at them. "I meant, what would you like me to *get* for you?"

He shifted his gaze from the menu. His dark chocolate eyes, heavily fringed with long lashes, swept up, and briefly settled on her breasts before finally meeting her gaze. Thank God for her stiff, uncomfortable apron and the way it hid her hardening nipples. If she hadn't been in lust before, she sure was now. His gaze alone set her body on fire, and she could only imagine what his mouth and hands could do. And she had a very vivid imagination.

When he cocked a brow, she shook her head, but couldn't shake the thought of him touching and caressing her. Damn, Roy was right. She really needed to date more. "I'm sorry, I was distracted. What did you say you'd like to order?"

"I didn't say anything." He sent her a crooked grin, his deep voice holding a hint of amusement. "But an iced tea would be great."

She made the mistake of glancing at the regulars sitting at the counter watching her make an ass of herself. Stu and Glen were grinning like idiots, and Russ sent her a wink and a nod. Rolling her eyes at them, in an effort to act as if she wasn't a lust-struck fool, she left the counter to grab his iced tea.

When she returned to take his order, she kept her head down and her eyes off his mesmerizing gaze. She didn't want the guy thinking she was some sort of small town girl easily flustered by a handsome city slicker. City slicker? God, now she sounded like her neighbor, Mrs. Turner. Next she'd be using words like whippersnapper and scallywag.

"Okay." She scribbled on her note pad. "One turkey, bacon ranch with fries. It'll be out in a few."

"Wait." He reached out and touched her arm.

A powerful jolt rocketed through her body. She jerked as if electricity coursed through her, surging along every nerve ending, every pore. A split second image of the stranger emerged.

He rocked his naked body against hers, hovering his mouth inches from her lips. His eyes darkened, his face tensed, strained in passion. Skin against skin, the friction, the heat, the overwhelming desire, she arched her back and groaned...

He snatched his hand away. While the vision immediately dissipated with the loss of his touch, the erotic image remained seared in her mind, igniting a passion and desire that went beyond lust.

He glanced at his palm, then up at her, his eyes questioning, probing. "I...ah..." he began, his voice thick, husky before he cleared his throat. "I wanted to add a cup of soup to my order."

She nodded slowly, unable to tear her eyes away from his. "Right. A cup of soup," she echoed, then forced her feet to move. After placing his order with Rick, she ladled the soup. His stimulating touch still distracted her, still sent sensual tingles across her skin.

Something was definitely wrong with her. Most of her psychic visions came to her through her dreams, and over the years she'd learned to retrieve images from inanimate objects. She'd never understood how or why, but she'd also never had a vision that included *her*. Then again, she'd never had vivid nightmares before, either.

As her mind tried to grasp what had just happened, she glanced back at the man with the electric touch and caught him rubbing a hand down his face. He looked tired, worn and as lonely as she'd been feeling lately. She wanted to ease the tension from his shoulders, erase the worry from between his brows, kiss the grim line from his lips...

Damn. She needed a serious grip on reality. What had

happened was probably her body's way of telling her it had been way too long since she'd experienced any form of intimacy with a man. Her state of exhaustion probably didn't help, either. Add on the stress of the nightmares...

She placed his soup in front of him, then kept herself busy. Fluttering from one customer to another, she moved on auto-pilot, the stranger never far from her thoughts, his touch still humming through her body.

She couldn't wait for him to finish his meal and leave. She didn't want to deal with his distracting aura, his hypnotic eyes or the desire he'd awoken. His touch had left a small imprint on her, had her longing for intimacy, affection...sex, had her facing a feeling she'd denied for years. Loneliness. The need to run from the responsibilities that had been dumped on her was stronger than ever, leaving her longing for the freedom to live her life, her dreams.

The bell at the front door chimed. She looked up from her notepad. The sun haloed the stranger's body. He paused, looked over his shoulder and met her gaze, then with a curt nod he left. She closed her notepad, and instead of going to the kitchen to check on the food she'd been waiting for, she went to the end of the counter where he'd sat.

A twenty dollar bill sat on top of his nine dollar and twenty-eight cent check. Although pleased with the tip, a part of her wished for a business card. Stupid. She shook her head and gathered his money. Would she have called him anyway? Nope. She wouldn't have had the nerve, and besides, she didn't do one-night stands. Instead of allowing ridiculous disappointment to fester, she looked at his departure logically.

The good news, she ticked off in her head, he wasn't local, just a stranger, probably a traveling businessman stopping in for lunch. The bad news, she would never seem him again.

Damn. That was *supposed* to be the good news.

CHAPTER 4

WHAT THE HELL was that all about?

John burst from the diner, dragging in a deep breath. The unusually balmy late September air only intensified the unexpected sensual heat pumping through his veins.

All he'd wanted was a freaking cup of soup. Instead, he'd ended up with a full-blown erection. He stood on the sidewalk, clenching and unclenching his fist. A strange pins and needles sensation still tingled through the hand he'd used to touch the sexy waitress. Touching her had dazed him with needs he'd never experienced. Lust. Primal, animalistic and possessive. His dick began to harden again as he relived the rush of arousing sensations she'd evoked, then his chest tightened as heartburn set in, which he deserved. He'd shoveled his sandwich into his mouth too fast in an effort to leave the diner and the waitress behind as quickly as possible. He didn't mix business with pleasure, not anymore.

Without another glance at the diner, and knowing he still had some time to kill before meeting Roy, he set off in search of a store that sold antacids. A couple dozen short, brick buildings lined the entire town square, twelve foot lamp posts stood at attention every thirty feet giving off an antiquated air. Some shops had awnings, others boasted the American flag. Each had their business name centered above their store.

Nothing flashy. No bright lights or gimmicks to draw the customer in, just good old-fashioned hometown simplicity.

A peaceful setting, and from what he'd read about Wissota Falls on the flight over, a tight knit community, very family oriented, with low crime and a good school system. Unfortunately the four dead women found this morning would put a huge blemish on the town's image. The thought of the bodies he'd stared at only an hour ago had indigestion weaving its way into his chest, and his feet moving to find those antacids.

The R & P Grocery had what he needed. He popped a few antacids into his mouth, then headed for his car, his mind still on the waitress from the diner, and his body still throbbing with the need to have her.

"Ridiculous," he mumbled to himself as he climbed into his rental and turned the key in the ignition. He just hadn't had sex since...Renee.

He hardened his jaw. He'd thought he'd buried his memories of her, of her betrayal, the day she'd been buried six feet under. Since he'd worked with the Chicago FBI Field Office on the serial pedophile/murder case, he hadn't been able to ignore those memories. Although he'd been exonerated from anything having to do with Renee and her death, agents he'd known for years, had worked with, trained with, had still looked at him as if he'd been the one to pull the trigger. If they only knew the truth.

He drove into the Sheriff's Department parking lot the same time Roy did. As he climbed out of his rental, he nodded to the sheriff.

"I'm glad you're early," Roy said as he led him through the double-wide doors into the building. "I got a call from the ME right after my meeting with the mayor." He turned his attention to the receptionist. "Bev, did you get a fax from Carl?"

She gave him several papers. "Just a few minutes ago."

"Here are those copies you asked for." Jesse Peterson came out of a back office and handed them to Bev, who in turn handed them to the sheriff.

"The originals?" Roy asked.

"On the bottom," she said, her worried gaze trained on the sheriff. "Did you remember to take your blood pressure medication?"

He released a deep sigh. "I...no."

"Thought so, here." She plucked a pill bottle from her desk drawer and handed it to him.

"Thanks." He nodded to Bev, then motioned for John to follow him. When they reached the sheriff's office, Roy popped the pill Bev had given him and dry swallowed. "Don't get old," he said, taking a seat.

John hid a smile as he took in the sheriff's office. Paul Bunyan liked color and a cozy atmosphere, and apparently art. Several paintings hung between large maps of Chippewa County and the state of Wisconsin, standing out against the yellow walls. One painting of the town square and the other...well, it was a chaotic display of colors, sort of abstract, he supposed—not that he knew anything about art. But he did know something beautiful when he saw it, and damn if that waitress didn't pop into his head.

"Okay." Roy drew his attention away from the paintings and thoughts of the woman who served an excellent sandwich. "Carl Saunders is the ME working on the victims. Dean Atwell, his assistant, ran all four of our victims' prints through AFIS and we got a hit on two of them. Ruby Styles and Colleen Kelpick both have records for prostitution in Indiana and both had been known to work at truck stops, which might confirm your trucker theory."

Roy continued to scan the fax, then his green eyes lit up with excitement. "And apparently our guy wasn't as thorough as he thought. Dean found a broken necklace with a heart-shaped charm tangled in Ruby Styles's hair. Oh this is good. Real good."

He frowned not understanding what good the necklace would do them. They already had an ID on the woman, but if Atwell had found the necklace on one of the other two Jane

Does, it might have helped link them to someone who knew them, and maybe been able to help give them an ID. "He washed the bodies, and didn't leave a stitch of any of the victims' clothes behind. I'd say he was not only thorough, but that he knew what he was doing, and probably has done this before."

Roy looked up from the fax, the earlier excitement fading from his eyes. "I can't believe...I should have paid better attention. Those women were in bad shape, there should have been blood on their faces, on their..." He cleared his throat, his face paling, the lines of worry and anxiety deepening around his eyes. "I should have paid better attention."

"How many murders do you get around here?" John asked, softening his tone. "Don't beat yourself up over it. What you saw today, most law enforcement officers will never see in their lifetime. Now, back to Ruby Styles and Colleen Kelpick, if we can pinpoint their last whereabouts, it might help us link them to this guy." Adding now might be the time to ask for DCI's assistance was at the tip of his tongue, but Ian had expressed, vehemently, that he'd wanted no outside help. Again, why?

"I'll have Bev pull both victims' arrest reports and make calls to the local PD. I'll get Indiana State Highway Patrol involved, too. I know a few guys from way back when." The color in the sheriff's face had returned to normal as he jotted notes on a pad of paper. "Do you think the other two vics are prostitutes, too?"

"Probable, based on Styles and Kelpick. The Jane Does appeared younger, though. Maybe they just hadn't been on the job long enough to get busted."

"But you think our killer has been."

"On the job? Oh yeah. Let's go back to his dump site. I want to do another walk through while the ME does the autopsies." Let his mind go to work, momentarily become the killer.

Roy looked at his watch. "I'm waiting on a third party."

"The deputy who'd found the body? Did he remember

something else?"

"No, not Ed." The sheriff released a sigh. "Now, don't get all shitty with me, but I'm close friends with a psychic—"

John laughed as he started to rise. "Sorry, Sheriff, I don't do psychics. I'll head to the dump site alone."

"Ian said you'd give me full cooperation," Roy reminded him, "and, well, here's the thing." He paused. "Would you please sit back down?"

He did, although reluctantly, while wondering if Ian had any idea about Roy and his personal psychic hotline.

"She—"

"Your *psychic*?" He released an impatient sigh, wishing he were on that golf trip to Scottsdale right now, even though he couldn't play the game worth shit. He didn't want to deal with a psychic, he wanted hard evidence.

"Over the past week, she's had visions of four murders, and I asked her to meet with us. I want her to tag along to the dump site, and see if she gets...I dunno what you call it."

"A reading?" Oh, this was just too much. What the hell was Ian's connection to the sheriff that he'd made him promise to follow along with *whatever* Roy wanted during this case? Psychics. They were a load of shit. If they could predict the freaking future then every last one of them would have hit the lotto and been living like kings.

"See, now you're getting shitty with me on this."

"I *am* getting shitty. I don't want to waste valuable time on a bunch of BS that..." He stopped mid-sentence. The aroma of freshly baked cookies wafted through the room. The air around him seemed to charge with an electrical current. His skin prickled with a strange, sensual excitement, setting him on edge and once again reminding him how long it had been since he'd given into his baser needs. His cravings.

He caught the sheriff's line of vision and swiveled in his chair.

Her. The waitress from the diner stood in the doorway with her hip propped to the side. Her faded jeans riding low on her curvy hips, and wearing a tight pink t-shirt with the words

"Got Sugar?" emblazoned across her full breasts. She smiled at the sheriff, a big, broad, dimpled smile. Dark blond curly hair fell just below her ears. It looked downy, silky and sexy. His fingers tingled to touch it, to feel the softness run though his hands.

Her smile faded when her blue eyes met his. "Hey. Sorry I'm a little late. We were busy today and I had a few things to wrap up before I could leave."

She kept her gaze on him as she spoke to the sheriff. John swore the room vibrated with her electricity, licked at his skin, touched him in a way he had no words to describe.

"Not a problem. Come on in. Are those cookies in that bag?"

She pulled out a Styrofoam container. "Plus the meatloaf sandwich you'd asked for," she said with another dimpled grin. Dimples he'd like to run his tongue along just before he kissed her.

"Thanks, I'll save it for dinner." Roy took the container, then nodded to him. "This is John Kain. John, Celeste Risinski. She runs The Sugar Shack, is the best baker in three counties, and the psychic I was telling you about."

As Roy turned his back to stow the sandwich into a mini refrigerator next to his desk, the psychic offered her hand. He looked at it, then to her face. Her eyes snared his. Challenging him.

The sexy blonde had him in knots. With reluctance, he shook her hand, then was both relieved and disappointed when he didn't experience another sensual jolt like he'd had at the diner. Still, he felt a deep connection. Sexual urges that he'd never experienced before, that were, even now, causing his dick to harden again. But those urges needed to remain dormant, especially if Roy planned on partnering her with him. He couldn't allow himself to become involved with a partner. Renee's image flashed in his head. Been there, done that.

"I had lunch at the diner," he said to Roy's back, as he released Celeste's hand, even as the urge to keep touching her ran strong. Damn it. What was wrong with him? He had a case

42

to conduct, not the time to fool around with one of the locals, especially a psychic who'd sent his libido into overdrive .

Celeste rocked on her heels, and shoved her hands into her back pockets. Since he'd walked out of the diner, she hadn't been able to push him or the longings he'd awakened from her mind. While she hadn't had another sensual vision when they'd touched, she had felt a connection. Something deep, and disconcerting. Something that made zero sense. Something she needed to pretend didn't exist.

Over the years, she'd become very good at pretending things didn't affect her. Her best friend Mary, a career student, who'd taken courses from art history to psychology and everything in between, called her aptitude for purposeful forgetfulness a defense mechanism. Mary was probably right, even if she didn't have a psychology degree.

Keeping her mind clear of upsetting or unexplainable emotions and thoughts had kept her sane.

"Good food, huh?" Roy took a seat. "Ain't nothing like The Sugar Shack for miles."

She couldn't help the genuine grin. "I swear. You're a walking advertisement. I should double your freebies." Her smile fell when she caught a glimpse of her handwriting scribbled on top of a stack of papers in front of him. "Are those..." She swallowed hard as the anxiety that had been with her for four days made her knees weaken.

"Yeah, honey, these are your notes. Take a seat. I think you'll need to."

She sat, dread gripping her. She'd only seen Roy this serious and disturbed once, and that had been when her mother died. Like then, the laugh lines that normally crinkled around his eyes seemed deeper, more somber. "You found the women," she whispered, and gripped the edge of the chair.

He gave her a solemn nod. "We did. John is here to help with the investigation."

"FBI?" she asked, running a shaky hand along her forehead.

"No, ma'am. I'm with CORE, a private agency which

specializes in all types of criminal investigations."

Her mind was too muddled with the fact her visions were real to care who Kain worked for. Right now, her head was full of the memories of her nightmares. Brief glimpses of women during their final moments, before a cord had been wrapped around their necks and the life squeezed out of them.

"Celeste, look at me." Roy's rough, stern tone refocused her attention. "That call I'd gotten from Ed this morning...he'd found one of the women. When we got there, we found three others. While John is here to help, I'd like your involvement as well, but only if you want to."

She met his gaze. "Of course, whatever I can do." She'd do anything to make the nightmares stop before they drove her insane.

He grinned, though the smile didn't meet his eyes. "That a girl," he encouraged. "John and I are heading to the dump site now. I was hoping you'd join us, look around, see if you can, I dunno, *see* something we can't."

"Yeah, sure." She stared at her lap, then raised her eyes to Roy as she had a horrifying thought. "None of the bodies...victims, I mean, are—"

"No, honey, CSU took them to the morgue in Eau Claire." He played with his mustache, a nervous habit she'd picked up on a long time ago. "They were able to ID two of the women."

"And?"

"Well, one of them had a necklace tangled in her hair."

"Sheriff." Kain's censuring tone had her whipping her head in his direction. "You're revealing pertinent information that if leaked could—"

"Celeste won't tell anybody," Roy snapped, irritation flushing his face. He kept his eyes trained on Kain for a moment before turning his gaze back to her.

She wanted to cry. Roy looked as if what he was about to say had him tortured, mind, body and soul. "I know you can sometimes get a read off of objects. After we check out the dump site, would you be willing to try to get something off the victim's necklace?"

"This is a murder investigation," Kain said before she could answer. "And I don't think there's any need to rely on her *special powers*." He gave her a sidelong glance. "Let's leave it to the professionals. Really, Sheriff, she's out of her league."

"*She* is sitting right there." Roy rose, and stabbed a finger at Kain. "Celeste is a strong woman. There's nothing out of her league, and I trust her with my life. So lose the attitude or I'll call—"

"Enough." She turned to Kain. "I honestly don't want to be involved in this, but I do want to put an end to my nightmares. If you're worried I'm going to gossip, don't."

His dark eyes softened before he shrugged. "I'm just the hired help. If Roy wants you on board..."

"I do, so let's go. It's about thirty minutes to the dump site and at this time of year, the sun fades fast. Celeste, you can ride with me, Kain, you go with—"

"Roy, Matt's here, demanding to see you," Bev broke in on the phone intercom.

"Shit. Okay, tell him to hang tight."

"Boysen, the reporter?" Kain asked.

Roy sighed. "The one and only. Okay, change of plans. Jesse and I will meet you. Lloyd has been keeping the area secure, and Dan's meeting us there. Both can show you around. Now go on and head out the back door. I don't want Matt knowing we're using Celeste on this." He handed Kain her notes. "Read these when you have a chance."

"What about my car?" she asked, although more concerned with the papers in Kain's hands. She had seen the disbelief in his eyes regarding her abilities, and while it had ticked her off, for the second time today, she wished she were normal, not psychic. She'd rather have the heated gaze Kain had sent her earlier at the diner, than the one he was giving her now. Once again the loneliness set in, wrapping itself around her and making her shiver as if this were another dreaded Wisconsin winter rather than an Indian summer.

"Everybody knows that if you're not at the diner, or baking in your basement, you're here, BSing with me and Bev. Don't worry, I'll handle Matt. Besides it'll give you two a chance to talk."

The last thing she wanted to do was talk to someone who looked at her as if she were a complete nut job. Except, as she followed him to his car, his broad shoulders and ass caught her attention. Her body instantly hummed with the remembrance of his touch, making her crave more. Something about this man had her longing for freedom, and passion, and searching for an answer to the loneliness and restlessness plaguing her.

Not that she'd necessarily find those things with him. Besides, she couldn't be with a man who didn't accept or believe in her abilities. But a girl could dream...without nightmares.

CHAPTER 5

JOHN PULLED OFF of Main Street and onto the two lane highway leading them to the dump site. The minutes stretched. With Celeste staring out the passenger window, ignoring him, the silence grew unbearable. So much for talking.

He hadn't meant to come off like a total dick, but damn it, he didn't do psychics. Okay, he'd like to *do* this particular psychic, spread her out on his bed and find out if she tasted as delicious as she smelled.

Bad idea. She was now officially his unofficial partner, and the past had taught him a deadly lesson in that regard. You just don't mix business with pleasure. Besides, Roy had an obvious fatherly affection toward her, and a strong connection to Ian. Those were two men he didn't want as enemies. Ian was his boss, he respected him, admired him...owed him for giving him a second chance after he'd left the FBI. Roy? Well, even though he was probably twenty years younger than the sheriff, and had a tremendous amount of combat training, the man still resembled Paul Bunyan, and he didn't believe in *the bigger they are the harder they fall* bullshit. Been there done that, too many times.

Still, he couldn't disregard that touch back at the diner. Just thinking about it, how his body had exploded with the need to possess her in every way possible, had him wanting to know more about her. Which was stupid. He had no interest in becoming involved with a woman claiming to be a psychic.

47

Besides, other than his body, he had little else to offer her. What was left of his heart, he dedicated to his family and CORE. His soul...his soul was too tarnished, blackened by a past he couldn't seem to put to rest. Renee's image flashed in his mind. Not her pretty angular features, or her dark eyes, but what she'd looked like the last time he'd seen her. Her thin lips, held wide with the barrel of a gun shoved down her throat.

Holding back a wince and clearing his head of a memory that had continued to haunt him for nearly two years, he gripped the steering wheel. He'd do his part in Wissota Falls, keep as much distance as possible from Celeste, then take Ian up on the trip to Scottsdale. While he hated golf, he hated the unfamiliar territory he treaded on with the sexy psychic even more. His career was on track again, and he had no room for a relationship. A one-night-stand maybe, but just picturing Roy's beefy fist bouncing off his nose had him eliminating that idea before it could take root.

So he was stuck with the psychic beauty for the time being. He'd had worse partners, but at least they'd talked to him. Glancing over at her, he wished she'd say something. Tell him to go to hell or better yet joke around with him like she'd done with the customers at the diner. It appeared, though, that she carried a stubborn streak. "It's unseasonably warm here," he said lamely, breaking the ice.

"Mmm-hmm."

"So you run the diner?" He'd try that route.

"Yep."

Minutes ticked, then she released a dramatic sigh.

Shit, here it comes.

"Kain, I—"

"John."

She swiveled and stared at him.

"I'd prefer if you called me John." For whatever reason, Kain sounded cold, and he didn't like the idea of any coldness coming from her lush, kissable lips, even if he couldn't taste them.

She furrowed her dark-blond brows. "Okay, *John*. Look, I

don't care if you believe in my visions."

"Yes, you do."

"No. I. Don't." She twirled a curl around her finger. "But Roy asked for my help, so maybe I should just tell you about these dreams I've been having."

"You mean the *nasty* little nightmares keeping you from your beauty sleep."

"Please don't talk to me in that condescending tone. I'm tired, exhausted, actually. I haven't slept much in the past four days." Her voice trembled and guilt niggled at him.

She did look tired. Like the sheriff, she wore a smile in public, but the telltale signs of weariness were there, etched on her face. He glanced at her and for the first time noticed pale purple smudges under her stormy blue eyes.

"I'm sorry. I didn't mean to sound condescending."

She looked out the window. "Yes, you did."

He chuckled. The little smartass busted him. "You're right, I did. Sorry." When she didn't say anything he looked over at her again. "I really am sorry. Please don't pout."

"I'm not pouting," she told the window. "I'm…wondering."

"About?"

She turned and stared at him with a probing gaze. "Did you feel anything when you touched me at the diner?"

There was no way in hell he'd admit to the erotic connection that even now was ready to blow his dick through the roof of the car. Even if she'd enchanted him with those intelligent eyes, lush lips, soft curves, and the aroma of fresh baked cinnamon rolls on Sunday morning. What would be the point? He'd do his job and leave.

"I don't know what you're talking about," he lied. "Let's stick to your visions."

Narrowing her eyes, she stared at him for a long moment, then waved her hand. "Fine, whatever. The first vision happened four nights ago." She leaned into the leather passenger seat and closed her eyes. "I remember being agitated that day. Not for any particular reason, just edgy, bitchy. I came home from the diner and worked out."

That perked his interest. No wonder she had such a hot body.

"When I finished, I felt better, but after I showered I couldn't keep my eyes open, so I went to bed." With her eyes still closed, she drew in a deep, shaky breath. "I fell asleep right away, which is unusual for me. I like to watch some TV before I go to bed or sometimes I lie there and think about what needs to be done the next day, you get the idea."

He nodded and refrained from telling her to move along with her story. He didn't want to imagine her lying in bed, maybe wearing a t-shirt and panties or nothing at all.

"It was a drugging sleep, like someone snuck cold medicine in my coffee..." She trailed off for a long moment.

"Okay and then what happened?"

When she didn't answer, he glanced over, and nearly jerked the car toward the embankment. She stared at him, her eyes no longer sparkling blue, but lifeless pools of murky gray. They spoke of disillusionment and horror, and caused a sickening sense of dread to ripple through him.

"Celeste? Are you okay?" he asked, and locked his gaze on the road.

She remained silent so he chanced another glance, then did a quick double. Her face had grown disturbingly pale, beads of perspiration collected on her brow and upper lip. Either she was one hell of an actress or in a state of psychosis. He'd place his bet on the latter. Four years ago, he'd worked a case where a Bible-thumper had killed his entire family. His delusions and hallucinations had him believing his wife of twenty-two years and their three children were plotting against him with a satanic cult. Later, they'd learned he'd had a brain tumor, which doctors believed had caused the psychosis.

Not fully versed on the subject, and treading on unfamiliar ground, he pulled off the highway, then threw the car into PARK. As he reached for his cell phone to call the sheriff, she arched her back. Agony contorted her face as she released a scream that sent his skin crawling.

Dropping the phone, he moved to reach for her, but she slumped into the seat, her head lolling from side to side. "I ache all over. Everywhere." She raised a shaky hand to her face, tenuously touching her cheek, then her eye. A sob tore loose. "My face, I could have taken his fists, but the knife...I hate him." She gnashed her teeth. "I hate you," she screamed over and over, then shuddered. "Oh no, he's coming back. I've got to get away. Let go of me." She pulled on the seatbelt, kicked and pivoted her body. Her knee connected with the glove box, then she went still.

Stunned, he weighed his options. He could try shaking her out of the hallucination, but she could cause injury to him or herself if she thought he was the one with the knife. He could also try hauling her out of the car, but he worried she'd run. With neither option feasible, he reached for his cell phone again. As he was about to hit the sheriff's preprogrammed number, she began panting as if she'd just sprinted a forty-yard dash.

"I'm free," she blurted, then the contorted smile shaping her mouth fell and her brows furrowed. "But there's too many trees. I can't figure out where to run, can't tell which direction to go." Sobbing, she clutched her stomach, and heaved in gulping breaths. "Oh God, shut up you sick fuck. Shut up." Celeste pressed her hands to her ears and squeezed her eyes shut. Rocking in the passenger seat she started mumbling. "Come out, come out wherever you are."

The eerie melody made his gut coil. The heartburn he'd thought he'd taken care of earlier returned. "Celeste, you have to—"

She groaned and clasped her shoulder. Pain and confusion twisting her face, making her almost unrecognizable to the women he'd met at the diner. She darted her eyes around the front seat. "I...I fell into a, I don't know what it is, but it's metal. Cold. Big. Like a combine or...Shit, he's coming. I can't move fast enough, he's right behind me. Gaining. Almost there, almost..."

She gasped. Tears streamed down her pale cheeks, as she

raised a trembling hand to the back of her head.

"He split my head open, the skin's torn. So much blood." She looked down at her hand, then grunted. Her head shot back, and she arched her neck. "Let go," she wailed. "Oh God, why didn't I cut it, I should have listened to Judy and cut my damn hair." She swung her head from side to side, blocking her face with her wrist, as if warding off imaginary fists. "Make him stop. God, please make him stop."

His stomach tightened, his concern intensified. He grabbed the cell phone, but it slipped from his sweaty hand and landed on the floorboard in the back seat. As he reached for it, his eyes locked on the notes Roy had given him before they'd left the Sheriff's Department. While he was convinced she was experiencing some sort of psychosis-induced hallucination, a small part of him wondered if maybe this *was* a psychic trance. Although skeptical, he decided he'd take a chance. He didn't want to miss out on catching the man who'd killed four women, even if he held no belief in the supernatural.

"Who's after you?" he asked gently, and while he wanted to hold her, erase the pain and horror from her beautiful face, he fisted his hands instead, worried touching her might pull her from whatever was happening to her. "Can you see his face?"

"No, no, no," she cried. "He has on a ski mask. Oh God, he stinks." She wrinkled her nose and gagged.

He frowned. "Stinks?"

"Like bleach. I can't take anymore," she sobbed. "The smelly bastard...I need air. Fresh air. I need to smell my Mama's prized gardenias and my Daddy's Old Spice. I can't breathe. I can't..." Her mouth gaped open as she gasped and clutched her stomach. Face ghostly pale, eyes wide, her body jerked up, once, twice before she released a gurgled moan.

Tears streamed down her cheeks as her eyes rolled back. "So much blood," she murmured, her lips barely moving. "My poor parents, I should have listened to them. I should have stayed home. I should never have left. I'm so sorry Mama. Why didn't I listen?"

"Shhh, it's okay, Celeste," he soothed.

Her sobs ended. She blinked, then parted her lips. A long sigh escaping as she closed her eyes. "I can't feel my body anymore. Red. So much red."

"Blood?" he prodded.

She shook her head and smiled. Not the shy grin she'd flashed him at the diner, or the beautiful dimpled smile she'd laid on Roy. Without mirth, without life, she thinned her lips. "No. Teeny, tiny balls of red. I'm swimming in them. They're everywhere, my nose, mouth. It's getting dark, they're fading...fading..."

Her breathing grew alarmingly shallow and her body went slack.

Panicking, and no longer caring about how she'd react if he drew her from the hallucination, he grabbed her shoulders and gave her a hard shake. When she didn't respond, he placed his ear to her mouth. Christ, she wasn't breathing. "Celeste," he shouted, and jerked her body again. "Wake up, damn it."

She gasped and panted, clawed at him, punched her fists against his chest and arms.

"Stop, it's me. John. Calm down, you're okay."

She blinked several times, her eyes changing from gray to blue, as she released a sob and wrapped her arms around his neck. Aftershocks of fear trembled though her body. Wanting to ease her fear and give her comfort, he embraced her and cradled her against his chest. Inhaling her sweet cinnamon and vanilla scent, he wished like hell he could hold her under different circumstances, even if he knew he'd be in for trouble.

A minute passed. She composed herself, then scooted toward the passenger door. She wiped at her tear-stained face with the back of her hand. "You wouldn't happen to have a tissue in this car, would you?"

He nodded and opened the glove box, and offered her the napkins he'd found when he'd first checked the rental.

"Thanks," she said, drying her face, then blowing her nose. "God, I'm so embarrassed. I've been so tired lately. I must have dozed off and had another nightmare." She frowned. "Although I don't remember dreaming." Crumpling the napkin in her hand, she frowned and looked out the window. "Are we here?"

"Not quite."

The color that had returned to her cheeks began to fade. "Then where are we?"

"Based on the mile marker, about a mile from the dump site."

She glanced to where he'd nodded, a frown furrowing her forehead. "What happened to me?"

"What do you remember?"

Twining a curl around her finger, she shook her head. "I was telling you about my first vision, and then something about cold medicine, but that makes no sense."

"You'd mentioned the stuff just before you..." He trailed off, not wanting to admit what he'd seen, what he didn't understand. "Before you seemed to become another person."

She released a nervous chuckle, and shook her head. "C'mon, what are you talking about? I'm not a medium." Staring out the window, she pursed her lips. "At least I don't think I am." She sighed. "Who knows, lately I can't seem to control it."

"How so?"

"The nightmares, for one. Usually if I don't want to dream about something, I simply will it. The same goes if I'm trying to get a reading."

"Like?"

"Like, if you lost your wedding ring, I'd think about it over and over again before I'd fall asleep, then hope I have the dream necessary to find it." She momentarily drifted her eyes to his left hand, where no ring existed, and likely never would. Love and marriage came with trust, and after Renee, trust wasn't something easily earned.

"What else has changed? I mean as far as your *abilities*."

"*Abilities*," she mimicked, lowering her voice and exaggerating the pronunciation with a few bobs of her head. "I hate the way you say that word. I mean, I get it. You don't believe in me. You're not the first and won't be the last. Trust me, I'm used to it."

"Meaning?"

"Meaning I've grown thick skinned, and have learned to ignore the snide remarks and whispers behind my back. Most people around town don't have a problem with me, but there are some, like you, who can't comprehend my capacity to envision events. That the human mind holds more power than any neurologist, even those with a bazillion degrees gracing their walls, could even begin to comprehend."

He stared ahead, the sting of her words bothering him. He didn't like being grouped with the nonbelievers, even if he was one. As much as she'd sloughed off those people, the way she frowned while twisting a curl around her finger had him thinking she wasn't as thick skinned as she'd like him to believe.

Shrugging, she dropped her hand in her lap and looked out the window again. "Anyway, back to my *abilities*," she said, stressing the word with the same mocking, sarcastic tone. "I've never been prone to sleepwalking, yet I've been waking up in different parts of my house after my nightmares. And, um, there was what happened at the diner today. With you."

"Static shock," he said, quicker than he'd meant.

Arching a brow, she let a smile play across her lips. "If you say so." She waved her hand. "I'm sorry. I know you don't want to talk about the diner incident."

"It's not that." He ran both hands through his hair. "This isn't about whether or not I believe in you or what happened at the diner. Damn it, didn't you hear me? You seemed to have *become* another person." Blowing out a frustrated breath, he asked, "Have you heard of psychosis? Where a person—"

"Has unreal beliefs, hallucinations and delusions, which could be caused by drugs, alcohol, brain tumors, epilepsy...shall I continue?"

"This isn't a joke."

"Who's joking? Look, John, I've never been checked by a neurologist or psychiatrist, but I can tell you I'm perfectly healthy. What I have is normal in my family. My mom had the gift, so did her mother, and her mother and, well, you get the idea."

He wiped a hand down his face. "I can only imagine what your family reunions are like."

"You need to have family around for those," she said, her tone turning somber. "And rather than pick apart my family tree, why don't you tell me what I'd said instead of looking as if you'd just eaten liver and onions."

A smile touched his lips. God, he hated liver and onions. "Tell me you don't serve that crap."

"I don't." She returned the smile. "But I do need you to tell me what happened. It could be important to our case."

"Our case," he muttered. Not for long, he hoped. A call to Ian should have her out of this situation. Chances were he wasn't aware of exactly what Roy was up to...or was he?

A horn blared. He checked the rearview mirror and caught the sheriff climbing out of his cruiser.

She gripped his arm. "Don't tell Roy until you tell me. I don't want him worrying. He has enough on his mind."

No way would he say anything to Roy about any of this. Hell, at this point, he wasn't even sure where to begin. "Trust me. My lips are sealed." He rolled down the window. "Roy, how'd it go with the reporter?"

The sheriff rested his arms against the roof of the rental and leaned into the window. He flicked his wary gaze from Celeste, then to him. "Fine, for now. Got rid of him with another promise of an exclusive." He jerked his chin. "Everything okay?"

"I thought I was going to puke," Celeste said before John could answer.

The sheriff's eyes softened with concern. "Honey, you don't have to go to the dump site. No one's forcing you."

"No, I'll go. It's just nerves, that's all."

He tapped the roof of the sedan. "Okay then, daylight's wasting. We're just a few minutes out. Lloyd called and said Dan's just arrived, so let's do this."

"I'll follow you," John said, then closed the window.

"Why do you two keep calling it a dump site, rather than a crime scene?" she asked.

"A crime scene is where the crime had taken place. The bodies we'd found were placed there after the fact."

"Gotcha," she said, and looked back out the window.

When Roy pulled his cruiser ahead of them, he turned to her. "Maybe what happened could be your mind's way of coping or maybe protesting going to the dump site."

"Doubtful, but I'd know better if I knew exactly what happened while I was under."

He shifted the car into DRIVE, then eased onto the highway. "Under?"

"You know, like a trance. I'm assuming that's what happened, but until you tell me—"

"Exactly what happened," he finished for her and nodded. "Not right now. I'm still trying to digest it myself. Besides, we're here." He slowed the car, then eased off the highway, parking the sedan behind Roy's cruiser.

He turned off the ignition, and clutched the keys in his palm. "We do need to talk about this," he assured her with a deep sigh. "Just not right now, okay?"

"But later?" she asked, her eyes hopeful, pleading.

"Later." He moved his hand to tuck a loose curl behind her ear and stroke the softness. Realizing he'd momentarily lost his mind, he quickly opened his door, rounded the front end, then opened the passenger door. After she climbed out of the car, he asked, "Are you sure you want to do this?"

She drew in a deep breath, her gaze moving along the tree line, and likely to the yellow police tape. Paling, she nodded. "I'm fine. Really."

"Let's go then."

"Wait. No bodies, right?"

"No bodies." He eyed her pale skin, the alarm widening her eyes. "Celeste," he said, and moved closer. "If at any time you want to leave, just let me know, and we're out of here."

"You've got my back, then?" A bit of sarcasm, mingled with apprehension, and maybe a need of reassurance, filled her voice.

"Yeah, I've got your back."

She offered him a nervous half-smile. "Thanks, but I'm sure I'll be fine."

He wasn't, but kept his mouth shut and led her to where Roy stood with Dan Malvern.

"Hey, Dan," she said, then leveled the deputy with a sympathetic smile. "Sorry to hear about your day."

Dan adjusted his mirrored sunglasses, then ran a finger along the brim of his hat. "All part of the job."

"And Miranda? How's she doing?"

"Havin' a good day, thank the Lord."

"Glad to hear."

"Are we done? I'd like to get things moving before we lose daylight," John said, not bothering to hide his impatience, especially after the joy ride in his rental. He looked to the sheriff, who nodded.

Roy offered Celeste his arm. "C'mon, honey, let's see if being here jogs anything."

As they moved down the embankment, despite what had happened in the sedan, he couldn't keep his eyes from diverting to her ass, until they broke through the thicket. Neon yellow redirected his attention, and he once again took in the dump site. The area appeared serene, peaceful, and nothing like the earlier makeshift graveyard.

"We found the first body here." Roy pointed toward the first area sectioned off by police tape and approximately twenty feet from the road. "The other three were found deeper in the woods. Lying nearly side by side."

She nodded and rubbed her arm where goose bumps rose along her skin. "A clearing?"

"The nearest clearing isn't for another hundred yards or so." A deep baritone came from behind him, and he pivoted.

Deputy Lloyd Nelson, the Viking. He glanced to Celeste. Her eyes softened as she gazed at the deputy. "Hey, Lloyd."

The Viking blushed. Who would've thought, considering he looked meaner than cat shit? "Hey."

"John, you remember Deputy Lloyd Nelson."

He nodded. "We weren't formerly introduced. Roy said you were second on the scene and found the other three victims."

"Unfortunately," the big man grunted.

With sympathy in her eyes, she moved away from the sheriff, then touched Lloyd's arm. "You okay?"

An intimate look passed between them. John bit the inside of his cheek as an uncharacteristic spark of jealousy twisted his gut.

"I'm fine. Just doing my job. But, I don't like you being involved in this," Lloyd said, and glared at the sheriff with disdain.

Interesting. Lover? Boyfriend? Not that he gave a rat's ass. Once he did his part in Wissota Falls, he'd either head back to Chicago, or on that Scottsdale trip Ian had offered him.

"Let's just get this done," Roy said to the deputy, his tone stern, but empathetic. "Starting with the area you found the three victims."

Forty minutes later they were back at the side of the road. Nothing new discovered, and nothing helpful from the psychic, who leaned against his rental, twirling her index finger around her curls. She'd given them nothing to help with the investigation. No surprise there.

He hadn't expected her to look at the dump site, then hand over their killer on a psychic silver platter. A part of him had wanted her to, the part that lusted, he supposed. But the other part? That egotistical "man of science and evidence" part he held onto tightly, relied upon, and had at one time bitten him on the ass, needed to be right. After Renee, he'd been second-guessing himself on every case. His partner had snowed him, clouded his judgment, and almost cost him his career.

As Dan climbed into his cruiser and sped off, the Viking moved to Celeste and rested a meaty hand on her shoulder. He said something as he leaned in, sending that spike of jealousy into full alert. Again, stupid. He had nothing to be jealous of and nothing at stake where she was concerned.

"You didn't get anything?" Roy asked. "Nothing that

matched those visions you gave me?"

She dropped her arms and pushed off the sedan. "No. It's weird, too. I really thought I'd get some sort of connection if I came here."

The Viking squeezed her shoulder again. "Don't beat yourself up."

"I'm not, but I'm wondering if it's because this isn't where he killed them." She offered the giant a helpless smile, then looked to Roy. "What about that necklace you mentioned?"

The sheriff nodded. "It's at the ME's in Eau Clair. You have time or do you need to get back to the diner?"

"Will's covering things."

"Good enough. Any objections?" The sheriff looked at him, and the narrowed-eyed, *you'll do as Ian says* look had him refraining from *any* objections. After all, he was just the puppet, but the puppet master would be answering some serious questions once this case ended.

CHAPTER 6

JOHN PULLED ONTO the highway and followed Roy's cruiser. According to the sheriff, they had about a thirty minute drive to the coroner's office in Eau Claire where Carl Saunders had been autopsying Ruby Styles this afternoon. He hoped the ME had found some evidence they could use against their guy. Although doubtful considering how clean the dump site had been, and how the killer had likely washed the victims' bodies. But he had made a mistake by leaving behind Styles's necklace.

Remembering the necklace, he still couldn't believe Roy had bought into all this psychic nonsense. Ever the good little puppet, though, he'd sit by and watch Celeste try to gain a reading off the jewelry. Ian expected him to fully cooperate, and once she came up blank again—like at the dump site— Roy would hopefully dismiss her from the investigation.

While a part of him wanted her to fail, another part wanted her to prove him wrong. Especially with how forlorn and confused she'd looked after not gaining any images or visions, or whatever she might call it when they'd been traipsing through the woods. There was also what had happened in his car on the drive over to the dump site. Logically, he could dismiss it as a psychosis-induced hallucination, but emotionally, he wasn't certain what to think. Psychic phenomena? God, what the hell had Ian gotten him into?

"You're quiet," she said, her voice soft, thoughtful, as she stared out the window.

"Just thinking."

"About?"

Glancing over, he grinned. "You're the psychic, you tell me." For whatever reason, he liked messing with her. He had a sneaking suspicion that beneath the sweet as sugar act she played for her customers, the sheriff and even his deputies, she was nothing but pure hell cat. After all, she was certainly quick enough with the barbs and sarcasm.

She sent him a droll smile, and rolled her eyes. "Har, har. You're a real riot and—hey, isn't that Matt's minivan?" She pointed and turned, looking over the headrest.

He checked his rearview mirror. Boysen. So much for Roy taking care of the reporter. In seconds he called the sheriff's cell phone.

"I saw him," Roy answered. "I'm about to get on it, although I'm not too worried. Lloyd is still there waiting on Mitchell and his boys. I'll have him get rid of Boysen. Fucking prick can forget his exclusive now."

"No shit. But you know this means he'll probably run the story."

"It was bound to get out sooner or later. No worries, the mayor will handle it. And hey. Maybe our girl will give us a new lead off the necklace."

Before he could respond, Roy disconnected. John slipped his cell phone into the center console and banked his irritation.

"So Matt's determined to get his story?" she asked.

"Appears so. Considering your car was parked outside the Sheriff's Department, don't be surprised if he hits you up for an interview. You better hope your name doesn't go public, because when the media swarms Wissota Falls, reporters will hound you at your doorstep and at your diner, too."

"Well, they'd be stupid to try. My next door neighbor would probably turn her garden hose on them if they so much as stepped on her lawn, and as for the diner, maybe we'll make some money off them. I do make a mean cheesecake."

"Don't be so flippant about all of this, Celeste." He gripped the wheel and stared at her for a moment before looking back to the road. "Four women are dead, and thanks to Roy, you're now involved in a murder investigation."

"I'm not being flippant. I'm trying to ease the tension. And don't blame this on Roy," she said, her voice rising, defensive. "Blame it on the guy who killed those women."

"That's still no excuse to use you on this investigation."

She crossed her arms and settled in her seat. "Roy believes in me and I'm sorry you don't. Just because you can't comprehend my abilities, don't disregard them. From where I'm sitting, it appears you could use all the help you can get."

"No, what I need is solid evidence." He ran a hand through his hair. "Look, I've made it obvious I don't believe in the use of psychics."

"*Very*, according to the way you chalked up my psychic trance as a simple state of psychosis."

"Now you're calling what happened earlier a psychic trance?"

"Sure, what else could it be? Although it would be helpful if you'd clue me in on what exactly had happened."

The city of Eau Claire loomed ahead, not a metropolis, but when compared to Wissota Falls it seemed like one. "We don't have time to get into it, and I promised to tell you about what happened later." Much later. He didn't want to feed into her delusions, like Roy had, because when she failed again, the reality check would likely hurt her.

Besides, *if*, and that was a big fat if, she really had gone into a psychic trace, he wanted no part of it. Ghost, demons, poltergeists and anything supernatural creeped the hell out of him. He'd rather deal with the human boogeyman any day of the week. He could understand those types of predators, whereas the occult or anything affiliated with it held no logical explanation. He needed logic. He needed facts and evidence.

"I'm holding you to it," she said.

"I always keep my word. I *am* curious about your dreams, and I'm not talking just about the ones you'd had about these women."

"Okay," she said with a cautionary tone.

"When you have your psychic visions, are they about what happened, is happening or about to happen?"

"I...uh, I'm not sure."

"Not sure?" He hated pressing her, and as much as he didn't want to do it, he wanted to put doubt in her mind. About her visions, about her ability. If she questioned herself, she might walk off the investigation on her own and make his job easier.

"You'd better be," he said, "because I have a feeling, not based on a hunch or *psychic* intuition, but based on evidence. I guarantee the ME will confirm that those women were decomposing at the same time, meaning they'd been frozen, until the killer chose to dump them. Also meaning that your dreams, the nights that you'd had them, make no sense. How could you have four different visions, four nights in a row, if the women, let's say, were killed four weeks ago, then dumped last night?"

"How do you know they were dumped last night?"

"Didn't you folks get some rain yesterday?"

She slowly nodded. "Around the dinner rush it poured for about twenty minutes, then the sky cleared."

"Every victim was bone dry, other than the still-damp mud splatter on their bodies. You saw the crime scene. Their bodies had left an imprint in the mud. Plus, I saw little to no insect activity on their bodies, and based on the times Ed Young reported patrolling that particular stretch of highway, I'd guesstimate that the bodies were dumped sometime between two and four in the morning. *Last night.*"

"Is this the point where I give you a round of applause?"

He half-laughed. "Psychic and sarcastic. Got any other hidden talents?"

She didn't reply, instead, she stared out the passenger window, wringing her hands. As he parked the sedan alongside Roy's cruiser, he couldn't see her face, but based on her rigid posture and the way she tortured her fingers and knuckles, his words must have hit a chord and planted some self-doubt.

Pleased, he pulled the key from the ignition. "You ready?"

"No, I don't think I am."

"Why's that?"

"Gee, I dunno, are my dreams related to these crimes or are they just good old-fashioned nightmares?" She turned and leveled him with such a questioning, probing gaze filled with so much indecision, and yes, doubt, that a punch of regret hit him square in the gut.

"Look, I'm sorry. I'm just trying to be realistic."

"Funny, you have no idea what a realist I am." She shrugged and the disillusionment in her eyes made him ache. He hadn't meant to hurt her. He'd only wanted her off the case so they could focus on whatever evidence they had.

"This isn't a good idea." She waved a hand toward the ME's building. "I should skip this and head back to the diner. I've got some paperwork to look over, payroll to do and—"

"Celeste." He turned in his seat and took off his sunglasses. When she met his gaze, he had the sudden urge to believe in her. Maybe because of the strange connection he'd felt the moment he'd touched her at the diner, or maybe it was the way she stared at him. So trusting, so unsure. Whatever it was, he couldn't stop himself from saying, "No one is making you do this, but if you don't, won't you always wonder?"

"I would," she answered, "but what if I'm wrong? What if I can't get a reading off the necklace?" She shook her head. "I'd look like a fool, make Roy look like one, too, and waste valuable time."

She drew out her cell phone from her purse. "I'm going to call Lloyd and see if he could give me a ride back to my car."

The fucking Viking. A splinter of jealousy fissured, and before it could completely crack his judgment, a thought occurred to him. If she quit now, Roy would question him, or her for that matter. Either way, the sheriff would figure out that he'd been the one to plant the seeds of doubt, then rat him out to Ian. Who knows what would happen from there. He sure as hell didn't because he hadn't had time to piece together the connection between Roy and Ian yet.

At the same time, despite his disbelief in the supernatural, he wanted her to walk away from this feeling as if she'd made a difference. Something told him that she'd need the reassurance. To know that she mattered.

"What if you *do* pick up something by touching the victim's necklace?" he asked, even as his mind screamed *you had her right where you wanted her*—doubting. Ignoring logic, he spoke from the heart, encouraged by the way her eyes began to brighten. "Think about the families, heartsick and devastated by their loss. What you may or may not see might not solve this case, but it could give us an insight into the killer or the victim herself. It might lead us to something the evidence doesn't."

She searched his eyes with suspicion. "I thought you didn't believe in using psychics."

Smiling, he said honestly, "I don't, but if you have this gift, then use it. Prove me wrong. Don't run away just because you don't understand why the pieces of the puzzle aren't coming together." He broadened his smile at the irony of his own unsolved puzzle with Roy and Ian. "If I did that, I wouldn't have a job. I might have to come work for you at The Sugar Shack. Maybe do the dishes for a piece of that cheesecake you were telling me about."

Celeste studied him for a moment. He had her head spinning in circles. First he made her doubt herself, now he encouraged her to prove him wrong. If she walked away, she *would* always wonder if she could have helped with the investigation. Especially if they ran into a dead end and the murders were left unsolved. Knowing she had a tendency to over think, if she did as she'd suggested, and had Lloyd cart her away, she'd stew. She'd regret. She'd always wonder.

"So?" He raised his shoulders, then jerked his head toward the building. "Are you in?"

Encouraged, yet still confused by his turn around, she nodded, and opened the door. "Yeah, and by the way if you did the dishes, I'd throw in a cup of coffee, too."

He climbed out of his seat, and met her around the front end of the car. "Aren't you generous?"

"I'm a fair boss," she said, then drew in a shaky breath, as she hesitated at the bottom of the concrete steps leading to the double wide doors of the morgue. She didn't want to do this. She didn't want to look like a fool.

He grasped her elbow. "Prove me wrong," he whispered in her ear.

She turned. His touch gave her comfort and confidence. His woodsy scent filled her senses. She flicked her gaze to his lips, only a fraction of an inch from her own, then back to his eyes. They challenged her, and if she wasn't mistaken held a hint of...admiration? Couldn't be. Then again, who knew with this man? He had her confused, intrigued, and despite what they were about to do, turned on. Could her week become any more weird? "I plan to," she finally said, then pulled away from him, and took two steps at a time.

Jesse held the door open for her. Roy walked in next to her as she stepped inside, while John trailed behind. A faint trace of his scent still clung to her, reminding her of the desire he'd awakened. She needed to rein those emotions in and stay focused, which wasn't hard once she stepped into the foyer.

Dean Atwell greeted her, his expression grim and devoid of the normal, shy grin that usually tilted his lips when he visited the diner. "Hey, Celeste. Roy, Jesse."

She'd known Dean all her life. He'd grown up in Wissota Falls. While he now lived in Eau Claire, he was always visiting his family, and was considered a regular at The Sugar Shack. "Hey, Dean."

Roy shook Dean's hand. "Lookin' good, kid. That crabby old bastard must be treating you right."

"He goes for the gut where the bruises can't be seen."

Roy chuckled. "I bet he does," he said, then nodded to John. "This is John Kain, he's part of the investigation. John, this is Dean Atwell, Carl Saunders' right hand man."

After the two men shook hands, Dean led them down the hallway. He stopped, then angled his head through the only open door. "They're here," he said in a voice that reminded her of the little girl from *Poltergeist*.

Jesse snickered, and both John and Roy shrugged. She couldn't believe Dean could make a joke when he and Carl had been performing an autopsy all afternoon. Although she supposed even twisted humor helped ease the pressure of dealing with death on a daily basis.

"What the hell are you waiting for?" Carl groused. "Bring 'em in, goddammit."

"He's in rare form today," Dean whispered. "Dead bodies tend to get to him."

"Aren't dead bodies his job?" Jesse whispered back.

"I might be old, but I still have my hearing," Carl griped as she trailed behind the others into his office. "To answer your question..." He squinted at Jesse's name plate. "Deputy Peterson, I'm used to old people crappin' out at the old age home, or in their own homes, or at the supermarket. Not young women bein' strangled and ra—oh hey there, Celeste. I didn't know you were going to be here."

She stepped inside the small, cramped room, filled with too many filing cabinets, too many chairs, and not an element of order. But she knew Carl. He was a methodical man, and seemed to thrive on organized chaos, both at work and at home. "Hi, Carl. Don't mind me."

Apparently he did. He glared at Roy, who raised his hands and said, "Carl, I asked Celeste to join us, not to look at any of the victims, but to maybe get a reading off that necklace Dean found in Ruby Styles's hair.

Carl shifted his gaze to her. His eyes softened. "Couldn't hurt. She did help find my wife's antique diamonds."

"And your prized Labrador Retriever, if I do recall," Roy added.

That Lab, which had cost Carl over a thousand dollars to purchase, then another five hundred to train as a hunting dog, had gone AWOL last summer. The dog might have been able to catch the scent of pheasant, but he couldn't find his way home even if Carl had lined a trail with dog biscuits.

"How is Lucky?" she asked.

"Stupid is what he is, goddammit."

She held back a giggle. Carl really was a softy, once you got to know him.

Carl jerked his silver head toward John. "Who's this guy?"

"John Kain. He's part of the investigation."

"Looks like FBI. Smells like one too."

John sniffed. "Really? And here I thought I'd gotten rid of the stench."

She shifted her gaze to him. *Former FBI?* Interesting.

Carl's chuckle drew her attention away from John. "Okay, enough of the chitchat, I've got three other women to autopsy. So let me give you the rundown on Ruby Styles." He rested a pair of cheap, black framed reading glasses at the tip of his nose.

"Wait," she interrupted. "I don't want to know any of this. It might interfere with my reading."

Roy nodded. "Whatever you say."

John didn't roll his eyes like she'd expected him to. Instead he suggested they let her sit in Carl's office with the necklace, while they stepped into the corridor to discuss the details of the autopsy.

Carl handed her a sealed sandwich bag. "Have at it. The only prints on the charm are the victim's, so you're free to touch it with your bare hands. Let's let Celeste do her thing." He rose, nodding to the others, and headed out the door.

They all followed, except for John. "You need anything?"

"You mean like my crystal ball?" Lame joke, but her nerves were working overtime.

He smiled without mirth. "Seriously."

"Nope, I'll be fine. Would you please close the door behind you?"

Although he nodded, he lingered.

"Go, shoo," she said, and waved her hand.

Shaking his head, he moved into the hallway, closing the door.

When silence filled the room, she unsealed the plastic bag, then drew the gold heart-shaped charm and broken chain into her hand.

"What happened to you, Ruby?" She closed her eyes and clutched the charm. The pointed part of the heart bit into her palm. She winced and clutched the charm closer to her chest. She regulated her breathing and stared at the tile floor.

Concentrating on the black and white mosaics, she felt a pull, a slight tug to her psyche as her mind began to fall into that familiar tunnel she'd been down before when trying to gain a reading from an object. Her mind spiraled and pitched from side to side. Rapid movements, flecks of images lined her peripheral vision, but it was what was at the end of the vortex she wanted to see, needed to be a part of to gain the vision she needed. Swirling, colliding, a kaleidoscope of colors...

There.

She gasped. Crystal clear. She blinked her dry eyes, focusing...focusing...

"You lookin' for some company, honey." Ruby used her best sultry voice to command his attention.

He leaned against his rig, one booted foot crossed over the other, while he smoked a cigarette. "I don't know," he drawled. "Are you?"

Ruby released a low, husky laugh. "Honey I'm always lookin' for company."

He appraised her, seemed to drink in her shiny black hair, her skimpy hot pink tank top, ultra short denim skirt and spiky black heels. "I bet you are," he said and tossed the cigarette onto the asphalt. The red hot ember sparked as it hit the blacktop, then crashed and burned.

Oh, she had a hot one tonight and might even enjoy this ride. He wasn't hard on the eye, with his sexy smile and dark beard. She liked a guy with a beard. It made him look rugged, masculine.

She cocked her head to the side and batted her lashes. Not too much, though. She'd perfected the look and didn't want to overdo it. Sauntering over to the rough cowboy, she settled a manicured hand on his hard chest, inhaled his cologne and smiled.

"Mmm-mmm, you smell good." She flattered him with a sensual smile. A little something she'd picked up from one of the other lot lizards who worked the truck stop. "I love a strong man," she said in a sultry tone as she tip-toed her fingers across his muscular chest.

He grinned and settled his gaze on hers. His silver eyes seemed to assess her worth. "Come on, I know of a place we can go."

She hesitated, then jerked her head toward the old motel opposite the truck stop. "I've got a place here."

He shook his dark head. "Uh-uh, baby doll. I'd like to go someplace a little more private. Away from this. I don't like folks knowin' my business."

She understood, yet wasn't too keen about climbing into his rig and driving off into the night. One of the first rules she'd learned: never, ever get in the cab unless it's parked for the night.

It had been a slow week, though. More like a slow couple of weeks. She needed the money and he seemed all right. "Okay, cowboy, but it'll cost you," she teased.

"Worth every bit, I'm thinkin'." He bent down and nuzzled her neck. "Come on, climb in."

"Where we headin'?"

"Just to the next rest area, 'bout five miles down. Shouldn't be too many cars there at this time of night. And I've got a bed in my cab, so we can have a good, private time." He winked and grinned.

His smile reassured her and she caved. He really was a good looking guy. If the opportunity came up, he could have gotten for free what he was about to pay for now.

He drove his rig for a few miles then slowed and turned off the exit heading north. Her stomach somersaulted. The rest area was south, and he was heading north. She gripped the door handle and shouted, "Hey, where are you going? This isn't the way to the rest area. Turn around and take me back."

He ignored her, never taking his eyes from the road. Panic clawed at her insides. She broke into a cold sweat. Oh God, why didn't she turn him down? Why didn't she stay in the safety of her motel room where one scream sent her pimp crashing in, guns blazing? She had to get out. Had to run.

He started to pick up speed and she realized now would be her only chance. Open the door and jump. Open. Jump. At this speed she might break her neck.

He might break your neck anyway, she reminded herself.

Okay, ready, one, two, three...

"What the fuck do you think you're doing?" He grabbed her by her

upper arm, his grip strong enough to bruise her flesh and maybe break the bone. "Uh-uh, baby doll, I'm paying for this ride and you'll give me what I want, where I want it."

He yanked her closer to him, hard enough that she saw stars. She cried out and clasped her shoulder, gasped for breath and fought the pain. "I...I can't move my arm," she sobbed. "Why are you doing this? Why?"

He sneered. Gone was the rugged, handsome cowboy. In his place sat a lecherous, vile creature with the strength of a bull and the bite of a rattlesnake.

He shrugged. "Because I can."

She didn't understand, didn't get the enigmatic remark. Widening her eyes she tried to talk him down. "Okay, whatever you want. Just don't hurt me. Please," she begged.

"What I want is for you to shut the fuck up and enjoy the ride."

He punched her in the jaw. Her head shot back and smacked the window. She tried to stop the second blow with her good arm to no avail. He rained punch after punch. Blood seeped into her mouth, the metallic taste reminding her she was still alive. Still conscious. Then she watched in horror as he cocked his fist back again.

"No!"

"No! No! No!"

"Celeste, shhh. Wake up. It's John. Wake up."

She gasped for air and clung to John's shoulders. "Oh God, it was so bad," she sobbed into his chest. "John...you don't understand. He's evil. So...Oh God." She buried her face into his crisp button down shirt, and soaked it with her tears.

"Shhh." His soothing voice worked magic on her muddled senses. His touch, both reassuring and protective, calmed her. "Take your time. Breathe deep." He turned toward the door.

Over his shoulder she watched as Roy, Jesse, Carl and Dean all gaped at her. They looked concerned, anxious and lost.

"Get some tissues and water," John demanded.

Jesse and Dean both bolted, which seemed to satisfy John. He turned his full attention back to her, cupped her face, searched her eyes, and rubbed his thumbs along her jaw. The alarm and trepidation in his deep brown eyes made her heart ache and wish that for one moment, he was hers. That he could erase what she knew. What they didn't.

An involuntary shiver ran through her. He ran his hands up and down her arms, as if to warm her. She wasn't cold. Even if she was, every one of his stimulating strokes left behind a trail of heat. His touch strengthened her and gave her confidence, control.

She slipped her arms away from his shoulders. Still not ready to relinquish her hold on him, she reached for his hands, her lifeline, and tried to suppress her emotions.

"John, I..." She took another deep, gulping breath.

"Take your time. Did you see something?"

Oh, she'd seen something all right. "Yes," she whispered. "I saw the killer and Ruby."

Roy stepped forward, worry lined his face. "Could you give a description to the sketch artist?"

She nodded, keeping her eyes locked on John's.

"What is it?" he asked. "Tell me."

"I know you don't believe...you're not going to believe..." She trailed off not knowing how to put what she'd seen and what she'd *felt* into words.

"Believe what?" he coaxed.

She drew in another breath. "I *did* see the killer. I know he murdered those women. I can *feel* it. But...he's not the one from my nightmares."

He searched her eyes and wrinkled his brow. "What are you saying?"

She tightened her grip and drew his hands closer to her pounding heart. "What I mean is. *This* killer and the one in my visions are two different men. There's more than one killer. More bodies. You just haven't found them yet."

CHAPTER 7

IN THE PRIVACY of his workshop, he rummaged through the alphabetized disposable cell phones he'd kept hidden in the bottom drawer of his tool chest. When he found the phone log he'd been searching for, he scanned the page.

For years, he'd used similar phones to contact Garrett. He'd even bought a few from a local Kmart with minutes already attached. They'd been untraceable, safe and an excellent mode to communicate. Once the rest of the criminal world had caught on—not that he'd group himself with lowlife drug dealers and gangbangers—the phones had been taken off the shelf. The only way to buy a disposable phone was through the Internet, with the use of a credit card, making it possible for the authorities to trace the owner of the phone. He'd found an easy loophole, though. With the age of technology came the age of identity theft.

Sitting on a stool, he glanced at the log again. According to his list, he'd placed twenty-two calls to Garrett since the beginning of the year, meaning he'd used all but two of the phones twice. Also meaning he could use either phone M or phone N to make tonight's call.

Should he? Should he confront him? He wanted to. He wanted to rant and rave, call him the mother fucker he was, and then rub his little tryst with the debutante in his face.

Thinking about that little Deb had him unlocking another drawer on his tool chest. He pulled out the knife he'd used on her. Unsheathed, the blade gleamed under the fluorescent lighting. The handle seemed to almost melt into his palm and become an extension of his hand. Like Captain Hook, he thought with a small smile. Only better.

He'd used the fifteen-inch knife on that pretty little Deb as if he were one of those Japanese guys in a Ginsu Knife commercial. Slicing and dicing. Stabbing and gutting. Fucking her had been one thing, but when her hot blood had coated his skin...?

Raw anger suddenly burned inside of him, and he returned the knife back into its leather sheath. He wouldn't have a chance to use the fucking thing for a long while, thanks to Garrett. The risk was just too great, and while he'd always been prepared to run if necessary, now wasn't the time. There were too many loose ends he needed to take care of first.

His digital watch released a series of beeps. The alarm he'd set earlier, reminding him he didn't have much time. In a split second, he stowed his anger and rationalized the situation. Garrett needed to be contained. He needed to know the bodies had been found. As much as he wanted to berate him over dumping them practically in his own backyard, he'd refrain. Garrett fed off his anger, used it against him.

But *he* had the upper hand now. He had knowledge and the means to find out what the authorities knew. A new sense of control had him searching for phones M or N. When he found N, he dialed Garrett's cell phone without hesitation.

After ten infuriating rings, Garrett finally answered. "Now why you botherin' me? Hang on." Loud music and laughter filled his ear, then he heard Garrett say, "Yeah, give me another, and add this pretty little lady's drink to my tab."

Shit. He needed him sober. He needed him aware. "Damn it. Pay your fucking bar bill, we need to talk."

"What's got your panties in a wad? It ain't our time."

Our time. Those two little words had always been their signal when it was time to play. Unfortunately, playtime was over for a while. "They found them."

Except for the background noise from whatever bar

Garrett had stumbled into, the phone went silent. Then he heard him say, "Hang tight, honey, and enjoy your drink. I'm gonna catch me a smoke outside. Keep my stool warm." A giggle, then a squeal of laughter followed, until blessed silence.

"Found what?" Under other circumstances, Garrett's husky drawl would have sent a pulse of pleasure straight to his dick. Tonight his tone, laced with innocence, angered him.

"This isn't a fucking game. You know exactly what I'm talking about."

"Maybe I do, maybe I don't. Regardless, I don't give a shit. I've got a sure thing waiting for me in the bar. A real party girl. I've already sampled some of her *and* the coke she's carryin'. So get the fuck on with whatever you got to say."

Drunk and coked up. Not good. Garrett was arrogant enough sober, combining alcohol and drugs into the mix had always made him think he was invincible. "Don't play stupid. What were you thinking? You couldn't have done it in another state, hell, another county?"

"Okay, calm yourself, *Toby*," he said, his voice low, hushed...damn it, sexy.

He grit his teeth, controlling his need, his lust. "Don't use my name, and don't tell me to calm down. Others are scattered around the outskirts of the county. Didn't you *think* about that? Didn't it *occur* to you that they might look? Do you have any idea how fucked we could be?"

"You're just pissed I went behind your back. I didn't mean to. Honestly." His voice was so soothing, so apologetic, he almost lost focus. Then the Deb, her hot blood, her virginal ass, flooded his memory.

"I've had a little fun of my own, but at least I'd been smart about it."

"Ho, lookie here, Toby's grown some balls. 'Bout time."

"Fuck you," he uttered, "and listen close. The sheriff brought in an outsider."

"FBI?"

"Don't know what he is, but he has me worried. Just stay low for a while. Damn it, stay sober. If shit goes down, I'll call, and we'll meet where we'd arranged."

"That bad? Or are you just fired up 'cuz I had some fun without you?"

He was more than fired up, he was seeing fucking red. Garrett had gone behind his back, betrayed him and their pact. Killing those women also had him wondering how many other times Garrett had done this before without his knowledge. Right now, though, he needed to keep his head clear and focus on what needed to be done.

"Just do what I say, and if you get caught—"

"They gotta catch me first, which they won't. I'd left things clean as a friggin' whistle." The arrogant chuckle Garrett released had him grinding his teeth.

"Don't be so sure of yourself. It looks like the sheriff has Celeste, that psychic I told you about, involved in this, too."

"Get the fuck outta here. Don't tell me you're paranoid over some batty-assed fortune teller. Christ, Toby, sometimes I worry about you."

"I'm paranoid. Period," he snapped, running a hand down his face to rein in the rage. "You should be, too. You should be running scared, and laying low."

"Pull your tighty-whities out of your frickin' ass and settle down. You know I've got a job lined up and I'm leaving in a few days for the West Coast. I'll be gone about four weeks. Can't think of a better way to lay low, can you?"

Our time had been back to back because of the job Garrett had taken. Neither of them had been able to go for more than a month without the rush of the hunt and the kill. Although those women were spread around the county, and their limbs were likely torn apart and scattered by coyotes, he still worried. While he doubted the others would be found in the near future, if at all, the discovery of the whores Garrett had killed could complicate things and leave an additional loose end. *Garrett.*

Not wanting to consider Garrett a loose end, he took a positive approach. Garrett would be gone for a month, maybe more. Without having to worry about him, he could focus on what the sheriff and his new partners knew. "No, I can't." He looked at his watch. "I've got to go. I'll call you at this time in two days."

"On what phone? D or maybe K," he laughed. "I can't keep track with all your cloak and dagger bullshit. Dude, you need to relax."

Relax? Garrett had dumped four bodies in his backyard. He couldn't risk being caught. Not yet. Not when he'd waited, bided his time for all of these years in this shitty town.

"Just stay cool, and sober," he said again.

"That's a ten-four good buddy. Then when all the shit dies down, we'll have *our time*."

Our time.

Those two words aroused him, especially the way Garrett had said them. Low. Husky. He rubbed his dick. "Can't. We had *our time* too close together, and now this..."

"We've been through this before," Garrett reassured him. "Maybe it's time for a change of scenery? I'm sick of these winters around here."

"I just need a few more months to tie up loose ends, and then we're gone."

"Those loose ends could have been tied up a long time ago," Garrett snapped, all traces of amusement gone. "But what the fuck do I know."

The phone line went dead. Just as well, he thought as he dropped the disposable cell into the drawer, then locked the tool chest. Garrett might have thought he knew what those loose ends were, and in some regards he did. But there were still some secrets he'd kept to himself, secrets that he'd eventually let Garrett in on when the time was right.

That is, if Garrett didn't become one of those loose ends.

Ian Scott sat at his desk, nursing a Scotch. The evening news ran on the flat screen TV encased in the bookshelf of his office, the volume muted. He wasn't interested in the news.

His focus remained on the unopened manila folder in front of him and the call he expected at any minute.

He stared at the folder filled with thirty years of notes, pictures, and letters all worn from age and the many times he'd handled them. He hadn't opened the folder in six months. Progress, considering he'd tended to review the file on a monthly basis. Why he'd tortured himself, he couldn't answer. Regret?

Could be, he thought, then picked up the watered down Scotch. His private line rang before the glass touched his lips.

He glanced at the clock. "Right on time," he said as he set down the drink, then picked up the phone. "How are things?"

"My cholesterol is up, I'm about fifteen pounds overweight, and I've got four dead women at the morgue. How'd you think?"

Smiling, he thought back to the last time he'd seen Roy. Four months ago on their annual fly fishing trip to Canada. Roy had aged well, and he'd appeared as fit as a forty-year-old. "I don't know about the cholesterol, but you could stand to lose a pound or two," he joked to ease the tension.

"Unlike you, I don't have access to a fancy gym. Besides, you'd be thickening up, too, if you had Celeste dropping off her baked goods all the time."

Another jolt of regret, along with jealousy, had him reaching for the Scotch. What would it be like to sit with her, maybe over a cup of coffee and a slice of pumpkin roll, as he listened to her talk? About her day, about her life. Bypassing the drink, he touched the closed folder. "How is she?"

"Something went down tonight that had left her pretty shaken up. When I took her home though, she kicked me out the door because she said she was tired of me acting like a worried old woman." He released a chuckle. "She's a strong one. Stubborn, too."

She sounded so much like her mother. Janice had been strong and stubborn. She'd also had an issue with over analyzing, and not letting things lie where they should. Did Celeste share those traits? God, he didn't know. He stared at the folder again, which only gave hard facts, not the emotional connection he sought.

"What happened?" he asked, now questioning how sound his judgment had been when he'd allowed Celeste to be part of the investigation. He'd witnessed the heart-wrenching turmoil, the emotional and physical exhaustion Janice had endured while working cases for the FBI. Some of those investigations had left her raw, her mind scarred with the memories of her visions. While he wanted to see Wissota Falls cleared of a killer, Celeste's safety, both physical and emotional, came first.

"I'll get to Celeste. Let me bring you up to speed first. Of the four victims, we've ID'd two. Both were prostitutes known to work truck stops, and John suspects the others are, too. He also thinks the killer is a trucker, likely an owner/operator, and his recent contract was with a company where he used a refrigerated trailer, which could explain why all the victims were decomposing at the same time. Hell, he even managed to pinpoint a window when the bodies had been dumped. He's as good as you'd said," Roy added, a hint of admiration in his tone.

Yes, John was very good at his job. Recruiting him to CORE had been a decision he'd never regretted. One he'd made years before John even knew that Ian had been watching him, waiting for the right moment to make him an offer he couldn't refuse.

"The autopsy done on one of the victims revealed she'd been raped, beaten, then strangled," Roy continued. "The ME is currently working on another as we speak. He'll have the other two finished tomorrow, but he's suspecting he'll find the same results. He also hopes to have their toxicology reports within the next few days."

"Excellent, if you have any issues getting them sooner, let me know. I have—"

"Connections. Yeah, I know. Anyway, there's more. A necklace was found tangled in the hair of one of the victims."

"Let me guess," he interrupted Roy. "You had Celeste try to gain a reading from the necklace."

"You said to use her, and she was willing. She didn't get anything from the dump site and was eager to try with the necklace."

"And?"

"I gotta tell you, I haven't seen anything like it since Janice. While she wasn't able to pinpoint the location where the woman had been taken, she saw the killer's face."

Ian raised a brow. "Do you need me to send a sketch artist?" He could whip one up in a second if need be. His resources never ran dry. Money, influence, and power were sometimes a beautiful thing. *Sometimes.* Because none of those things could give him what he wanted most. A cup of coffee with Celeste.

"No. State Highway Patrol out of Eau Claire had one. Celeste was able to give her the description, and I've already sent it out on the wire. That man's face is now plastered on the wall of every county and city police department across the country."

Pride seeped clear to his bones. "Can you scan a copy of the sketch and send it to my email?"

"Already done. But, Ian...there's more. Celeste is convinced the four women we found aren't the same ones from her dreams. She thinks we're going to find more bodies, and possibly another killer."

Ian flipped open his laptop and let it warm up, as another thought occurred to him. "How did John handle that?"

A chuckle filtered over the phone line. "When he first learned I was pairing him up with a psychic, I thought the boy would blow a gasket, but by the end of the day... Put it this way, he damn near growled at anyone who tried to come near her. I'm a little worried about him becoming involved with Celeste, which is why I sent him back to his motel and took her home myself. I don't want him sniffing around her. Celeste doesn't date much, and John will be gone once his job here is done. He breaks her heart, and I'll break him in half. I don't care if he's your guy or not."

Ian smiled at Roy's threat. "You won't be breaking anybody

in half. John's nothing to worry about. Trust me. I know the man better than he knows himself."

"You didn't see the way he looked at her after she finished performing that reading on the victim's necklace. I'm telling you, he—"

"Doesn't become involved with witnesses, partners, victims' families, etcetera. Especially while working on a case. He's too bent on control."

After what John had endured during his last days with the FBI, Ian doubted he had anything but ice running through his veins. He'd changed. He'd become edgy, distrustful, an asocial workaholic. When he'd joined CORE, he'd volunteered to take on the worst cases, almost as if punishing himself, pushing himself. He'd showed no emotion, no attachment. He would work one heinous case, then move on to the next.

"If you say so," Roy said with a sigh. "I gotta run. The mayor's waiting on me. I'll call you when I have something new to report."

After hanging up the phone, Ian finally flipped open the folder on his desk. A snapshot of Celeste, one Roy had sent him six months ago, stared back. She stood in front of the diner, with her brother, Will, who had his arm draped over her shoulder.

She truly was a beautiful woman, with wavy blond hair, a wide, beautiful smile, and sparkling blue eyes. So much like her mother's eyes. He slammed the folder shut at the memory and the regret he'd carried for thirty years.

He downed the warm, watery scotch with one swallow, wishing in his youth he could have been more like John. Detached, unemotional, and able to resist temptation.

John eyed the organized chaos he'd created across the old, lumpy motel bed. Files and photographs stared back, mocking him. The blur of papers and pictures made it difficult to concentrate, to put the pieces together. Damn it, *she* made it difficult.

He couldn't stop thinking about Celeste. How anxiety and horror had reflected in her eyes after the reading she'd performed in the ME's office. She'd been so pale, so scared. She'd trembled in his arms, and as she'd clung to him, or maybe he'd been the one doing the clinging, her fear had crawled under his skin. That fear had made him want to erase whatever horrors she'd seen and protect her from the boogeyman they were after. No, make that boogey*men*, he amended.

As much as he didn't want to believe in her abilities, he couldn't discount one huge fact—she'd known that Ruby Styles had a dislocated shoulder. Carl Saunders hadn't revealed that information in front of her, but in the hall outside of his office. Could she have heard him? Or had she actually *seen* what had happened to Ruby?

Curious, he reached for the notes Roy had given him earlier. Celeste's visions. He'd been avoiding them for nearly two hours. He hadn't wanted to read her nightmares, to know the fear she'd been living with these past four nights. Even though he still wasn't exactly sold on the whole psychic phenomena, after what had happened in his car, and again at the ME's office, he decided maybe it was time he opened his mind. See if there was anything in her notes that might help their investigation.

As he was about to open the folder, his cell phone chimed indicating a text message. He quickly read the text from Ian. *Spoke with Roy. No need to talk tonight.* Irritated, actually downright pissed and perplexed, he tossed the phone onto the bed.

During the two years he'd been working for CORE, Ian had never once taken a report on a case from someone outside of the agency, yet he'd taken Roy's over his. Was the sheriff somehow part of CORE? Was that his connection to Ian?

Frustrated and edgy, he reached for the folder again, then flopped into the wobbly chair in the corner of his small motel room. As he skimmed the pages from her first vision, certain words stuck out at him. Trees, running, bleach, pain, and red. Lots and lots of red.

Blood? Or maybe the tiny balls she'd mentioned during her "trance" in his rental.

He reread the vision, this time not skimming or skipping around the page, and when he reached the end, he sucked in a deep breath. "She'd been stabbed to death. Not strangled," he murmured. This killer, the one from her dreams, had a different MO compared to the four women discovered in the woods. Was it possible Celeste was right? That there were more bodies out there? Another killer on the loose?

The memory of Celeste in the passenger seat of his car came back to haunt him. The way she had clutched her stomach, her body jerking upward as if an imaginary force had been...

He dropped the folder onto the floor, then rushed to the bed where he'd left his cell phone. Needing to see her, to know she was safe, that she was...all in one piece, he punched in her number.

"Hello," she answered, sounding out of breath.

Alarmed, he gripped the phone tight. "Celeste? It's John. Are you okay?"

"I'm feeling *much* better," she panted.

His fear quickly turned to jealousy. What had he caught her in the middle of that was making her feel *much* better?

The Viking's image came to mind. He'd seen the way Lloyd had looked at her, the way she had looked at him. There was a connection, an intimacy between them. Was he with her now? Enjoying her body, easing her tension? Disappointed, he slumped to the lumpy mattress and drew in a deep breath.

"Whenever I'm stressed, working out always helps," she continued, her breathing now closer to normal.

"I understand," he said. "During some of my worst cases, I've been known to run for miles, even during the middle of the night, just to blow off some steam and clear my head." The relief over knowing the Viking wasn't the one giving her the workout must have affected his brain. He *never* shared personal information. Not that what time of night he'd gone for a run was all that personal, still, it was more than his counterparts at CORE knew.

"Um...is something wrong?" she asked. "You sound, I don't know, upset."

"No, nothing's wrong. I just wanted to see how you were doing. We didn't have a chance to talk after the, uh..."

"Psychotic vision?"

"Don't you mean *psychic*?"

"Yes...no." She released a heavy sigh. "I don't know. I'm feeling a little mixed up right now."

"Understandable."

"I suppose."

"You've had a strange day, even for a psychic."

Her soft laugh warmed him and made him wish they were face to face. He wanted to see her beautiful smile, to see if that smile reached her eyes. In less than twelve hours, he'd been bombarded with a bunch of emotions and uncertainties he hadn't experienced since...never. Not even with Renee. She'd been as blasé about relationships as he'd been. Sex had been a way to release the tension, a quick fix. There had been no dating, no romance. The only pillow talk they'd shared had been about their cases.

Celeste stirred a longing he hadn't realized he'd wanted, and he didn't understand the connection he felt toward her. The deep protectiveness, the need that went beyond pure desire. A need that made him ache, made him wish he had more to give.

"Yep, even for a psychic," she said with a sigh.

"I know it's late, and maybe you've already predicted this," he teased, "but do you want some company? I thought we could talk."

She laughed again, and he couldn't help grinning like an idiot at the sound of it. "Really? I'd like that. Give me a half hour to shower and change. Okay?"

"Sure, see you then." He kept his tone neutral, even as his heart hammered and anticipation roared through him.

After ending the call, he cleaned up his motel room, then

hopped into the shower. Thirty minutes later he pulled the sedan into her driveway. He momentarily admired her large, brick colonial, as he stepped out of the rental. Lit by an array of solar lamps and the moon's bright, dazzling beam, her house, like all the others in Wissota Falls, was beautifully landscaped. Neat and trim with no overgrown hedges, no weeds in the beds, no—what the hell?

As he strolled along her brick walkway, tiny plaster men stared at him, their rosy, cherub faces smiling while their lifeless eyes danced. He did a quick double take. There had to be at least a couple dozen ugly garden creatures guarding her house.

He ignored the eerie plaster eyes watching his back, took a deep breath and rang the door bell, wondering if this was a mistake. He never paid personal visits to witnesses during a criminal investigation. Although technically, she wasn't exactly a witness, she was his partner. The sober reminder had him gritting his teeth as Renee's image flashed in his head.

His chest tightened, not in a good way, and he wished he'd left the antacids he'd bought earlier in the car. He might be able to overcome Celeste's belief that she was psychic. Hell, at this point a part of him was almost a believer. But he couldn't, not after Renee, allow himself to become mixed up in a physical relationship with a partner. No matter the unexplainable attraction.

He should have waited, voiced his fears about her safety to Roy and ordered a cruiser parked outside her door. But the sheriff didn't have the manpower for that, he reminded himself, giving him another excuse, another reason to see her.

The gun barrel lodged in Renee's throat filtered past his reasoning. Clenching his jaw even tighter, he decided he'd check on her then leave. Looking around the yard again, he caught the accusing glances from her ugly garden creatures. Then the door opened.

He drew in a deep breath and forgot about every reason he should *not* be here, and quickly tried to come up with an excuse to never leave again.

***

Dr. Alex Trumane stepped onto the sidewalk and into the balmy night. The air was thick with humidity and the threat of rain as he bypassed his Lexus, and did what he'd done every week for the past two months.

He tested himself.

Looking in the distance, not more than two blocks away, he focused on his destination, Dudley's Diner. Unfortunately, temptation stood between him and the diner. Three bars were scattered among a pawn shop, a small-time, family-owned electronics store, an all-night laundromat, and an apartment building. As he approached the first bar, The Office Lounge, he quickened his pace.

Neon lights advertising Heineken, Budweiser, and Corona reflected off the bar's front window, beckoning him to stop in and sit for a spell. While he preferred gin or whiskey, a cold beer on a hot night sounded damned good.

His mouth watered, but without pausing he kept moving. He passed Reliable's Pawn Shop, then a small alley, until he came to the next temptation. High and Dry boasted the same neon lights. Only the bar's door stood wide open, the sounds of laughter and people talking drifted to the sidewalk and had him longing to step inside and erase the loneliness. He had acquaintances in there, as well as at The Office Lounge. He'd learned, though, that sobriety meant not only a change of lifestyle, but a change in the people he'd associated with regularly. Barflies didn't make the greatest friends for a recovering alcoholic.

Forcing himself not to run, he kept his focus on Dudley's Diner. He passed the laundromat and then the next bar without wavering, until he finally stood in front of the diner. Eight weeks he'd tempted and tested himself, and once again he'd done so with triumph. Breathing a sigh of relief, he stepped inside, then took his usual seat at the counter.

Kira, a middle-aged blonde he'd suspected was only a few years younger than himself, approached. Her pink uniform clung to curves he'd fantasized about way too much over the past two months. "Coffee?"

He nodded. "Decaf, please."

"How'd it go tonight?" she asked as she filled his mug.

When Kira had learned he'd been stopping by the diner after attending his weekly Alcoholic Anonymous meetings, she'd proudly confessed that she too was a recovering alcoholic and had been sober for more than ten years. A bond had grown between them, and while he suspected she might be romantically interested in him, he wasn't ready to date. Hell, as it was, he couldn't even work up the nerve to visit her any other time but after a meeting. Before he could even consider a relationship, something he hadn't had since his wife divorced him six years ago, he needed to work through AA's Twelve Steps first. He'd made it through the first seven, and was now on step eight.

"The meeting went well," he said, and poured creamer into his mug. They talked for a while, not about the meeting, but about life in general.

He loved this time with Kira. Before he'd sobered up, he wouldn't have given her a second glance. His drunken ego had lured him to twenty-something women, who, he'd realized once sober, had only been interested in him for his doctor status and money.

What a fool he'd been. Thanks to his lack of self-control, he'd allowed booze to ruin his life. He'd lost his wife, his kids, and nearly lost his license to practice medicine.

As Kira spoke, he stared into her smiling hazel eyes and realized how much he needed to stay on the wagon. Failing in front of Kira was not an option. He had too much respect for her. Hell, he was in love with her.

The door swung open and a group of laughing couples stumbled to an oversized corner booth. Kira sighed as she eyed the new customers. "Looks like the bar crowd has the munchies. I gotta run. Give me a wave if you need a refill."

He kept his gaze on her full bottom as she walked away. Urgency ran through the new and improved sober Dr.

Alexander Elliott Trumane. He wanted his life back, and he wanted Kira in it.

Drawing a pen from his pocket, he flipped over the paper place mat and stared at the white canvas that would eventually lead him to atonement. He'd hurt many people over the years, and it was time to make amends.

As he began to write, he wondered if he should have skipped the decaf and gone for the high octane stuff. Listing every person he'd harmed during his years as a drunk could take all night.

CHAPTER 8

CELESTE TIGHTENED HER grip on the doorknob to keep herself from falling into John's arms. She knew they were strong, heavily muscled. He'd held her in his car when she'd woken from her trance, and again at Carl Saunders' office after that awful reading. Right now, she needed to feel his protective strength again. Since leaving the ME's, the ruthless visage of a killer loomed in her every thought. If she closed her eyes now, his bearded face would be there, fist cocked, ready to release another painful blow.

An involuntary shiver ran through her body.

"Cold?" John stepped into the front foyer.

"A little." She closed the door. "The days have been so unseasonably warm, but the nights are getting chilly."

He stared at her, his concerned gaze dark and penetrating. Worried he'd see past her fight to control her emotions, her fears, she looked away.

She couldn't let him know how badly she ached, how badly the case was affecting her. As much as she wanted no part in the investigation, she had to pretend everything was a-okay. Otherwise, Roy would pull her off the case, and she couldn't have that happen. She needed closure. She needed to do her part to help find justice for those women. If she didn't, she worried the nightmares would remain seared on her soul forever.

"Come on in," she said, and moved toward the living

room. "Roy mentioned you're from Chicago. I bet you're seeing the same kind of weather there, too, huh?"

He snagged her hand, and drew her to him, gently bracing his other hand at the small of her back. She stared at his chest, only inches from her face, her heart pounding at the nearness, her body tingling from his touch. She desperately wanted him to hold her, soothe her, erase the nightmares, and the memory of Ruby Styles's murder from her mind. But she couldn't, just as she couldn't bring herself to look up at him. She couldn't let him see—

Cupping her face, he tilted her head. "Look at me," he demanded in a hushed, coaxing tone.

When she did, tears instantly blurred her vision. The concern, the tenderness, and the heat in his gaze made her want to bury her face in his chest. She wanted to cry so bad. Curl against him and vent. Tell him her fears, her anxiety, how her emotions were raw, ravaged, and tearing her apart.

He caught a tear with his thumb, then traced it along her cheekbone. "I don't want to talk about the weather. I want to talk about what happened today at the ME's. I'd ask if you're okay, but I think I've already gotten my answer."

As he continued to stroke his thumb along her cheek, the tears threatening to fall subsided. His simple, gentle caresses calmed her, *soothed* her, and helped her regain control of her emotions.

Feeding off of his strength, she forced a smile. "I'm fine, just tired. It's been a long day."

"Celeste, you don't have to put up a false front for me."

She pulled back, regretting the loss of his touch, the strength he offered. "I'm not. Can I get you something to drink?"

"Whatever you're having," he said with a deep sigh.

"Chardonnay it is then."

He followed her into the kitchen. "Look, I really think we need to talk—"

"Did you have any trouble finding my house?" she interrupted. Needing more time to compose herself, she pulled the bottle of wine from the fridge.

He took the bottle. "Here, let me. Wine opener?"

She reached into the drawer, then handed him the corkscrew. As he worked on the cork, she stayed close to him, wishing they were back in the foyer. She wanted him holding her again, needed the comfort his caresses offered, the security, the protectiveness. She wanted to lose herself in his body, forget how lonely her nights had been before the nightmares had begun, and how miserable and frightened she'd become since they'd started.

It had been so long since she'd been with a man, kissed, made love. She'd missed the intimacy, and as she stood next to him, inhaling his purely male scent, she wished she could throw caution to the wind and be spontaneous. She'd caught the way he'd looked at her. Admiration and heat had lit his dark eyes several times throughout the day. How would he react if she made a move on him? Offered a no-strings affair?

Duh. He's a man. Of course he'd jump at the offer.

And she'd regret her impulsiveness. As much as she wanted him to hold her, she knew herself too well. She didn't have sex for sex's sake. Considering he'd leave once his part in the investigation was over, she knew sex was all he'd be able to offer her. Right now, she didn't need another person leaving her life.

When her mom had died, their family had unraveled. Her dad moved to Florida and seemed to enjoy golf more than talking to her. Her sister rarely called or visited now that she was busy with her career in Chicago. Even Will wanted to leave. When he did, she'd be stuck here, alone. Running a diner she didn't want, and leading a boring, dismal existence.

No, she couldn't afford to become attached to John or the idea of a relationship with him. He'd leave, like everyone else.

The cork popped. "Freed at last," he said. "Glasses?"

She grabbed two and placed them on the counter, then watched as he poured the chardonnay. His hands seemed huge next to the delicate wine glasses. He had nice hands, big, strong and lean.

"Thank you." She took the glass from him.

As he brought the glass to his lips, very nice lips, he stopped and cocked a brow. "Mind explaining the little man staring at me?" He nodded to the gnome perched on her kitchen windowsill wearing an apron and chef's hat.

Grateful for something to distract her from his hands and lips before she started studying his other body parts, she reached for the gnome. "Don't you like my little buddy?"

He looked around the kitchen and into the dining room. "Don't you mean *buddies*? You've got these guys everywhere."

After replacing the gnome, she reached for her wine. "I'd like to tell you that I keep these guys around because I believe the mythical little creatures provide luck."

"But?"

She shrugged. "I bought one for my garden when I moved in. It was cheap, and I don't know, it was so ugly it was kinda cute. So I put it in the front flowerbed. That afternoon, the old woman who lives next door, Linda Turner, came banging on my front door. She told me she hated my gnome, how ugly it was, and that it gave her the creeps." After taking a sip of her wine, she smiled. "She also told me what flowers I should grow, how to arrange them, that my music was too loud, which it wasn't by the way...she just kept nitpicking at me. So I went out and bought a couple more just to terrorize her."

"You're vicious," he chuckled.

"Aren't I though? I mean, I had to get back at her in some way without being nasty. Anyway, the next thing I knew, everybody started buying me gnomes. You know, for Christmas, birthdays...I guess they thought I collected them." She eyed the chef gnome again. "Now I do."

"How many are around here?" he asked as he topped her wine off, then his.

"Outside? I think I'm up to around twenty. Inside? Maybe three dozen or so."

He kicked up his brows. "Wow, that's a lot of gnomes."

She rolled her eyes, and tried to hide her embarrassment. First the psychic thing and now the bazillion gnomes. He had to think she was an over the top eccentric. "I know. I have no idea where to put them anymore. Maybe I should call Matt Boysen and ask him to put an ad in his paper announcing I've reached my full capacity."

Running a finger along the gnome cookie jar, he frowned. "Boysen's a piece of work. Remember what I said about him and other reporters once the murders are leaked."

Damn, just when she was relaxing, he had to bring up the investigation and remind her exactly why he'd stopped by tonight. He might have showed concern, but this wasn't a social call, this was business. "And I told you that I could handle it."

"Really?" He faced her. "Have you ever had a reporter follow you around? Shove a microphone in your face? Harass you when you're at the grocery store, or at work, or in the privacy of your home?"

"You know I haven't, but apparently *you* have."

"Apparently. Let's talk in the living room," he said with a tight smile, then grabbed the bottle of wine.

And apparently that was the end of that, she thought as she trailed behind him. It didn't take a psychic to know when someone was hiding something, and John, she suspected, had a few skeletons in his closet. She hadn't missed the way he'd tensed, or how his eyes had narrowed before he'd masked his emotions with a forced grin. He'd said he worked for a private investigation firm. Now she wondered what line of work he'd been in before joining CORE. Carl Saunders had made an off-handed comment about him smelling like FBI. If that were true, why had he left?

Curious, and nosey as hell, she was prepared to ask him more about his job, rather past job, when he suddenly stopped. He stared at the large painting she'd hung on the wall opposite her brick fireplace, his gaze riveted on the beautiful collage of colors.

"This is good. Where did you get it?"

"My brother."

"You wouldn't happen to know where he got it from. I've

been looking for something like this." He glanced back at her, and she swore he blushed. "For my mom. Christmas isn't that far away and with my schedule I shop early and whenever I can."

For his mom? Good lord, the man did have a sweet side. "Actually my brother *is* the artist."

"Really? *Your* brother painted this?"

"Mmm-hmm. He sculpts too, although I'm partial to his paintings. You can see more of his work all around town. They're in a lot of the local shops, the county library. Even Roy has a few in his office."

"Yeah, I saw those. Maybe I could look at any extras he might have."

"Trust me. He'd be happy to sell a painting to you. He's trying to get his name out there. Actually, he has a showing at some new gallery in Chicago at the end of October."

"I'll have to check it out."

Right. Because that's where he lives, and that's where he'll be heading when the investigation is finished. "I'm keeping my fingers crossed for him. He's desperate to leave Wissota Falls, but until he can earn enough money from selling his paintings, he's kinda stuck here."

He moved toward the bookshelf lined with pictures and memories. "What about you? Does small town life agree with you?"

Standing next to him she let her gaze drift over the framed snapshots. "So-so."

He cocked a brow.

"I mean, yeah, it's okay. Like with any place, though, it's not always peaches and cream. Know what I mean?"

After studying her for a few seconds, a smile tilted his lips. "I do. While I love Chicago, I used to think small town simplicity seemed more appealing."

"Now?" she prompted, curious and eager to learn his take on where she lived. Did he think they were all bumpkins? Most visitors did. Wissota Falls sponsored many annual festivals. Tourists would come from big cities, and then act as if they'd time traveled in their Mercedes or BMW's into another century. She didn't resent the tourists, they were good for the town and for The Sugar Shack. She resented that she couldn't leave with them.

Wissota Falls had become stifling. She'd wanted out the moment her mom died, but she hadn't been able to leave. Her dad's grief had weighed on her. She was a fixer, and he'd needed fixing. Only she hadn't anticipated the fix she now found herself in three years later.

Living a life she didn't want.

"Well," he began. "Let's just say I think I like the anonymity I have in Chicago."

No shit, hovered on the tip of her tongue, but she refrained with a false smile. She understood more than he could ever comprehend. "Well, it's not for everyone." She shrugged, and sipped her wine.

After setting his glass on the bookshelf he picked up one of the photos. Her favorite. It had been taken the year before her mom had been diagnosed with cancer, when she'd been healthy, beautiful.

"Your family?" he asked, as he caressed the frame with his thumb.

"Yep, and that's my mom and dad. My brother Will and my sister Eden."

"She's pretty."

Was he blind? Eden was gorgeous, exotic, and the total opposite of her. Black hair, green eyes and olive skin, then there was her body. Eden was one of those women who had a natural, runway model physique. She was tall and slender, while Celeste was short and curvy. Sharing clothes had never happened when they were growing up, no matter how many miles Celeste ran.

"She looks familiar...not because of a family resemblance, you two don't look anything alike."

Her brother and Eden had similar coloring, and favored their dad, while she looked more like her mom. "You probably recognize Eden from the news. She's changed her name, and is a reporter at WBDJ-TV in Chicago. She does—"

"Investigative reporting," he finished for her. "Eden Risk, right?"

She nodded.

He shook his head. "Please tell me you didn't contact *her* about this. No offense, but your sister is as bad as those reporters I was telling you about."

Bristling, she moved to the couch. "No, I didn't tell her, and she's nothing like those leeches."

He dropped to the opposite end of the couch. "Really? Then why haven't you told her?"

"Because she's based in Chicago, and I doubt anyone around there would be interested in what's happening in Podunk, Wisconsin." And Eden didn't believe in her psychic abilities, just as she hadn't believed in their mother's. As much as she loved her sister, and knew Eden would foam at the mouth over this story, she worried about the spin Eden would put on the investigation.

"No one but Boysen knows about the murders yet. This case could be a coup for her career. Why are you really holding back?"

She stared at her sister's photo. "Put it this way. I love my sister, and I want her to be successful, but what's happening around here, what's happening with me, isn't something she needs to know about."

"She doesn't believe in psychics," he said, not a question, but a bitch of a reminder.

Eyeing him for a second, she smiled. "You're perceptive."

"That's my job, and I'm wondering about yours. Have you always worked at the diner?"

"No. After high school, I went to the University of Wisconsin for a degree in accounting. After I graduated, I stayed in Madison and worked at a firm."

"If it's so-so here, why'd you come back?"

"Anybody ever tell you you're nosey?"

He shrugged. "All the time."

A grin tugged at her lips. "I can see why."

They sat in comfortable silence for a few moments, then he shifted and set his glass on the coffee table. "So are you going to tell me how you ended up back in Wissota Falls?"

"You're relentless," she chuckled.

"That's why I'm good at my job."

She eyed him and decided to take the opportunity he'd given her. "How long have you worked for CORE?"

"Not talking until you answer me first," he said, and cocked a dark brow.

She shook her head. "Why do you care? It's not like I'm all that interesting."

"A psychic accountant, who's a baker, runs a diner, and owns more gnomes than should be legal? I'd say you're interesting."

"Hardly, but since you can't let this go, I moved back three years ago. My mom was diagnosed with cancer and it was too much for my dad and brother to handle. Eden was already in Chicago, so I came home to help. I wanted to anyway." She drained her glass, then cleared her throat.

"My mom passed away six months later and my dad...he couldn't stand being here without her. Too many memories I suppose. It started out that he was going to Florida for a few months to clear his head, but he ended up buying a place and left Will and me running the diner."

He leaned forward with genuine sympathy in his eyes, and caught her hand in his. "I'm sorry for your loss."

She curled her fingers around his, relishing his touch. Holding hands shouldn't have caused the longing coursing through her, or the ache to be held, but it did. In that instant a hunger settled in the pit of her stomach, a need so fierce, and nothing she'd ever experienced before. She wanted him. She wanted to do more than hold hands despite what her head told her.

She closed her eyes and remembered the quick image she'd had when he'd touched her at the diner. Picturing them naked, writhing and moaning, had her inner thighs growing damp and her nerve endings humming with need and anticipation.

"Celeste?"

She opened her eyes. Her face heated to the point that she wanted to fan herself. "Sorry, my mind was wandering."

"To where?" he asked, and inched closer.

"I...you probably don't want to know."

Keeping his gaze on her, he murmured, "The diner."

"I'm sorry, it's just...when you touched me, I had a vision that *included* me. That's never happened before, and I'm wondering if you'd felt...forget it." She sighed, wishing she'd kept her mouth shut. "It was probably my imagination."

"I..." he began, then drawing away from her, stood. "Maybe we should talk about what happened today."

Grateful he'd changed topics before she made a fool of herself, she nodded. He obviously hadn't felt what she had at the diner, and considering he didn't believe in psychics, there was no reason to bring it up again despite the need he stirred in her.

"Good. Let's start with the car ride over to the dump site."

Although curious about the trance she'd gone through, a part of her was now afraid to know exactly what had happened. After all, when he left tonight, she'd be alone. Again. With nothing but her nightmares.

"You know, before we get into all of that..."

He turned away from the mantle and eyed her.

"I understand your reluctance in using psychics. Not everyone is a believer, but I was wondering about your experience, as an investigator or whatever your title is."

Shaking his head, a slow cocky grin spread across his lips. "You want to know my qualifications?" he asked, as if shocked she'd have the audacity.

Her curiosity in him multiplied. "Yes, that's what I meant. You're not a cop or a government agent. How did you and your company end up part of a murder case—"

"In Podunk, Wisconsin?" he teased. "Honestly, I have no idea. I go where I'm told. But, as for my credentials, I joined CORE two years ago. And I'm not just an investigator, I'm a criminalist. I trained with the FBI for ten years before I left."

"Why'd you leave?"

"Anybody ever tell you you're nosey?" he asked with a smile.

"All the time," she echoed his earlier reply. "Honestly, I'm surprised you didn't just tell me to look into my crystal ball if I wanted answers."

"Welcome back, Miss Sarcasm," he said, and although he smiled, she caught a hint of regret in his eyes. "Besides, didn't I use that line earlier today?"

"If you did, I missed it."

"If I did, I'm sorry I was stupid enough to say it." Rubbing the back of his neck, he turned to the painting again. "You have to understand my line of work. I do believe in hunches and gut instinct, but I have a hard time believing in psychics. During an investigation, solid evidence is what I rely on, and what will hold up in court. Hell, even then, it can sometimes be difficult to convict. The wrong person can be put on trial and sent to prison for life, while the other..." He turned to her. "Look, I'm not going to discount what you said in my car, or at the ME's, but I need more to go on."

"Thank you. And I promise not to interfere in your investigation. Honestly, John, I only want to help."

"I know you do." His dark eyes softened. "But I'm, um, hell, I'm worried about you."

The aching loneliness, the misery of the nightmares was suddenly overshadowed with a ridiculous sense of pleasure and relief. Warmth and hope spread through her. He might not believe in her, but he wasn't looking at her as a kooky fortune teller, either. And he cared. She suspected as much with how protective he'd been today at the ME's, but to hear him say it out loud? Then again, maybe she was reading too much into this. All he'd said was he worried about her.

"I'm fine. Really," she said, stressing the last word when he shook his head.

He pushed away from the mantle, and moved toward the couch. Kneeling, he gripped her hands. "I don't believe you."

"You don't believe in much, do you?"

She caught the regret in his eyes before he looked away. "I honestly don't know what to believe anymore. I came here to do a job, and ended up…"

"Ended up what?" she asked.

Heat simmered in his eyes as he moved closer. "You said you had a vision when we touched at the diner. Tell me about it."

"I told you, it was probably my imagination."

His breath quickened, as he dipped his head. His mouth, those lips she'd admired, only inches from hers. "I don't think so."

"W-why do you say that?" she asked, drifting her gaze to his tempting lips.

"Because you made me feel something I've never felt." He moved impossibly closer. His masculine scent enveloped her, his warm breath, laced with the sweet remnants of wine, caressed her mouth. "You made me feel alive," he whispered, then captured her lips.

She gasped into his mouth as their lips melded and fused. As he eased her against the couch, her body exploded with need. With pure hunger, she held onto his broad shoulders and kissed him with all the desire bursting through her pores. Their noses smashed together, teeth collided, as their tongues mated. She'd considered herself a good kisser, but finesse had no place here. Not now. Not when all she wanted was to be closer to him, crawl into him, show him exactly what she wanted.

He didn't seem to care, either. Instead, he deepened the kiss, speared his hands through her hair and held her head in place. Drawing in a deep breath, he tore his mouth from hers, peppered her jaw and neck with opened-mouthed kisses only to cup her cheeks in his warm palms as he drew her back to his lips.

This time, he slowed the pace. He nipped her lower lip, pressed a kiss to the corner of her mouth, then ran his tongue along where he'd bitten her. "You taste so good." He untwined his fingers from her tangled curls, then moved his hands over her body.

His large, warm hands plundered and took. Slid under her shirt, caressed her bare back, then ran lower over her hips and bottom. He gripped her there, and pressed her against his muscled thigh. Too many layers of clothes prevented her from the contact she desired. Unashamed, she pushed her heat against his hard thigh, the friction of his jeans against her sweatpants stimulated and rushed through her. Close...so close. God, she needed more.

"You're so hot," he whispered, then took possession of her lips again. She lost herself in his passion. Hushed gasps and quiet groans echoed throughout the room as she hung onto his shoulders and rode his thigh.

He shifted and settled his erection between her legs. "I haven't been able to stop thinking about you, about touching you." He nuzzled her ear, his hot breath puffed at the curls framing her face.

"Then touch me." She took one of his hands between their bodies then placed his palm to her breast. Releasing a soft moan, she urged him to massage her, to take what she offered.

Through her cotton t-shirt, he rolled her stiff nipple between his fingers, then muffled her cries with a hungry kiss. She tore her mouth away, delved her hands through his hair, cupped his head and urged his mouth lower.

He took the cue, shoved her shirt over her lacy bra then lowered his head. His soft stubble teased her flesh as he opened his mouth over one, lace-covered peak.

"Oh, John," she gasped.

He kissed her taut nipple, cupping her breast with his hand. Liquid desire flooded between her thighs and she couldn't stop herself from grinding her heat against his arousal.

Through the lace, he tugged and pulled at her nipple. She longed to feel the contact of his hot, wet mouth on her bare skin. Reaching between them, she grazed her palm along his hard shaft. His cock surged. She rubbed him through the rough denim, wishing they were naked. Naked and in her bed, or on the floor...at this point it didn't matter. She wanted him, plain and simple.

The doorbell rang.

Breathing hard, he raised himself above her. "You expecting someone?"

Damn. Damn. Damn. "No."

She stood and began rearranging her shirt and sweatpants. "It's probably Will. He lives in the room above my garage, and uses it as his studio." She blew out a frustrated breath, then gave him a half-smile. "Sorry."

He tucked in his shirt. "Don't worry about it."

Don't worry about it. Yeah right. She was about to orgasm, possibly have ultra hot sex, and now the mood was ruined. She stomped to the foyer then swung open the door.

"Hey, saw your lights on. Hope you don't mind my dropping by so late." Deputy Dan Malvern stood in her doorway wearing an uncertain grin on his freckled face. He poked his head around the corner, keeping his hand on his gun belt in that casual police stance he liked to use. "Bad timing?"

Duh. "No. It's okay, what's up?"

"Jesse told me about what happened at the coroner's and I thought I'd do a drive by before logging off for the night. When I saw the car...well, I just wanted to make sure you were all right."

"She's fine," John answered, as he moved to the foyer.

Dan straightened. "That your car?"

"I'm sure you recognized it from earlier."

Dan kept his hand on his gun. "Roy know you're here?"

"Planning on telling on me?" John asked and folded his arms across his chest.

"Knock it off, both of you," she scolded them like the children they were acting, then offered Dan a smile. "Thanks for stopping by, but as you can see, I'm okay. But since you're here, why don't I save you a trip to the diner tomorrow and give you your order of kalachkis now."

Dan relaxed his hand, and eased it off his gun belt. "Really? That'd be great. My wife loves 'em, and we were just about out of the last batch you'd made."

"What are kalachkis?" John asked her with interest, while

still frowning at Dan.

She adored a man with a sweet tooth, and hoped John had one. She loved baking and experimenting with recipes but Will hated sweets and made for a bad guinea pig. "They're cookies, filled with either fruit preserves or cheese."

"Don't forget the powdered sugar," Dan added.

"You know I wouldn't since you're always asking for extra." Despite the tension and testosterone radiating from both men, she offered Dan a smile. Dan had been caring for his sick wife who suffered from some rare disease—she couldn't remember the name except that it had more consonants than vowels—but wished she could do more than give them a free box of cookies. Especially after how she'd cared for her own mother. "They're already boxed. Just let me run to the basement kitchen and grab them."

When she returned with a dozen strawberry and lemon kalachkis, she rolled her eyes. Since when did her house become Grand Central Station?

"Hey, Will," she said.

Her brother didn't respond. He darted his eyes between John and Dan, then raised a questioning brow at her.

"Celeste." John turned to her. His eyes were unreadable, distant. "Looks like you've got a houseful. I'm going to head back to the inn."

Nodding, she tried to keep the disappointment from her face. She didn't want him to leave, not yet. Not without more of his kisses. Then again, maybe this was for the best. His kisses could become addictive.

She followed him off the front porch, then onto the brick pathway leading to where he'd parked his car. When they reached his rental, he stopped and turned to her. The light from the porch and solar lamps cast shadows across his face, but she still caught the desire, the raw, hot passion in his dark eyes.

"Maybe we could pick up where we left off tomorrow?" he asked, his tone husky, promising.

She hugged herself, warding off the cool, night air, and him.

Although she wanted to finish what they'd started, she knew where it would lead. Another dead end. He'd leave, and she'd be stuck where she was, dreaming of more. "Sure, sounds good."

"I, ah," he sighed, and looked over her shoulder toward the opened door where Will and Dan stood. "I meant, we never had a chance to talk about your trance, and your other visions."

"Right." Stupidly disappointed, she dropped her gaze and focused on a gnome in a perpetual state of mooning someone. Of course this was business. Dan's arrival had doused cold water on a huge mistake. While her body didn't think kissing and maybe even sex were bad things, her mind knew better. Apparently John did, too.

He raised her chin and forced her to meet his gaze. "Don't, Celeste." He caressed her jaw. "I *will* see you tomorrow. Sleep tight."

She watched him climb into his car then drive away. "With you by my side, maybe," she mumbled, then headed toward her house filled with unwanted guests.

CHAPTER 9

THE ONLY DECENT thing about the Chippewa Inn was the free cable TV, John thought as he absently flipped through the channels. Reality shows, infomercials, news programs and B movies blurred together. None of them worth settling on, none of them enough to distract his thoughts from Celeste.

That kiss still had him hard. Hungry. Edgy.

He wanted more. He wanted her moans, her soft curves filling his hands, her hard nipples against his tongue. He stroked his arousal hoping to alleviate the pressure. He wanted to strip her naked and bury himself between her firm thighs. Feel her heat, her slick desire as she screamed his name and burned with the same hunger he couldn't seem to control. He would have, too, if Dan and her brother hadn't shown.

Releasing a frustrated sigh, he turned off the TV, then glanced at the clock. Nearly two a.m. He needed to crash. Tomorrow would be another busy day.

Horny and restless, he tossed on his side, trying to find at least one part of the mattress that didn't have a lump or a spring. But as he lay on the shitty bed, he couldn't stop his mind from racing or his body from aching for her.

Damn if she hadn't nearly made him come in his jeans like a teenager copping his first feel. Never in his life had he experienced anything hotter than kissing Celeste. As their lips had met, as their mouths had fused, he'd tasted her hunger, her raw, naked need. Her…trust.

He'd denied believing in her psychic gift, yet she trusted him. If only she knew how much that meant to him.

During his last months with the FBI, his reputation had been in shambles. Close friends and coworkers had taken the deeds of a dead woman and lost faith in him.

Yeah, trust had become a bitch of a thing.

Muttering a curse, he shifted on his side again and stared at the clock. Maybe he was reading too much into this. Maybe his body still hummed and ached with need because he hadn't been with a woman since Renee. That's what this had to be about, that's what made sense. He was reacting to a beautiful woman, a trusting woman who had been as greedy and hungry as he'd been to have sex. Just like Renee.

He'd never loved her, and she hadn't loved him. They'd been friends, partners, who shared the same job, the same day-to-day bullshit. Sex between them had been more of a way to blow off steam, because neither of them had time to find a real relationship. But he'd trusted her, and she'd betrayed that trust.

He pushed thoughts of Renee where they belonged—six feet under—because he knew deep in his bones whatever was between him and Celeste was different. Renee had manipulated him, used him. Although he didn't know Celeste well, and he'd like to hold onto the logical assumption that his attraction to her was solely based on sex, he knew it was a lie. She wasn't like Renee in any way, shape or form. Literally. The two were polar opposites. Renee had been hard, her body, her mind, where Celeste held a softness that had him thinking of puppies, babies and a frickin' white picket fence.

She was unconventional. A psychic accountant and baker who had a plethora of gnomes surrounding her should have had him running in the opposite direction. Instead she had his head spinning and his body craving.

And where would it lead?

Nowhere.

He doubted she was the blasé affair type, and he wasn't,

either. But he wanted her. The touch of her lips had given him a perpetual hard-on and had made him want to claim her, protect her, keep her all to himself.

But he had no right to even consider pursuing anything with Celeste. He'd leave when his time here was finished. She needed a man who'd stick around, and he wasn't that guy. He had a life in Chicago, his work. While Wissota Falls offered a simplicity he sort of liked...what the hell was he thinking?

Christ, one kiss and he was contemplating a relationship?

His cell phone rang, and the tension coursing through him turned to dread. At—he glanced at the clock—two-twenty in the morning, this couldn't be good. Without checking the caller ID, he answered, hoping to God it wasn't Celeste calling about another nightmare.

"We got him," Roy said, his tone tired, but excited.

He sat straight up in the bed and was already reaching for his pants. "You're sure? How?"

"The sketch. I sent it over the wire yesterday afternoon and apparently our suspect overindulged last night. State Highway Patrol picked him up on a DUI, just south of Eau Claire. After they finished booking him, one of the officers happened to see the sketch. He said it was uncanny. I guess our girl got it right, huh?"

Our girl. "Yeah, I guess she did." He didn't know what to feel, pride in Celeste for the hit, regret for not fully believing in her, or disappointment that his time in Wissota Falls was nearing a fast end.

"Get dressed and I'll pick you up in fifteen."

"I'll be ready."

He cleaned up, dressed, then waited for Roy outside of his room. The moon had sunk a little lower, its strong beams filtered through the swaying tree tops. He stood with his back against the motel door and instead of thinking about the suspect being detained in Eau Claire, his thoughts focused on Celeste. Deep melancholy settled on his soul. For what could have been, for what might have been. Time to explore the rattling emotions she'd evoked. Time to ensure that what he'd experienced in less than twenty-four hours wasn't his body playing games with his mind.

Headlights illuminated the parking lot. When Roy's cruiser came to a stop, John pushed off the motel room door.

"Helluva wake up call," Roy said as John settled into the passenger seat. "I had Bev whip us up some coffee." He nodded to the two travel mugs on the center counsel. "It's black, hope you don't mind."

"No, this is good, thanks. I could use some caffeine." He reached for the mug and realized what Roy had said. *Bev made the coffee?*

"Does Bev always work this late?"

"Um...no." Roy blew on the rim of his travel mug. "I...she...oh hell."

He held up a hand to stop him. "Enough said, Sheriff. It's none of my business."

Roy released a hearty chuckle. "Yeah, tell that to the rest of this town. You take a crap and everyone knows about it. That's small town life for you."

"I wouldn't know about that."

"Of course not, you grew up in Richmond, Virginia, lived in Washington DC, New York, and now you're in Chicago. With barely a thousand residents, Wissota Falls is a far cry from the big city."

Roy's knowledge set him on edge. If the sheriff knew about where he'd lived, he likely knew that he was former FBI, about his reasons for leaving the Bureau and joining CORE. "Been doing your homework or did Ian tell you all of this?"

The sheriff shrugged. "Does it matter?"

"Consider me inquisitive?"

"That's what Ian said about you, and what makes you one of the best out there. Blow it off, John. We're just bullshitting here."

Blowing off bullshit had never been his strong suit. Considering they'd likely caught their killer, he supposed it didn't matter what Roy knew about him, or what the sheriff's connection was to Ian. He'd likely be back in Chicago within a day or two, and on to another case. "Okay, bullshit aside, so you and Bev are a couple that no one in town is supposed to know about, but everyone does?" So strange, yet he understood. His family was just like that. Telling one person the latest gossip, that no one was supposed to know, but they all somehow did.

Roy sighed. "To be honest, I wanted to make our relationship public—officially. I've asked her to marry me, to move in with me, but she's turned me down." He shook his head. "We've been together for about six years now, and I love her dearly. She had a rough go of it with her ex-husband and is a little gun shy. I'm a patient man, though. I'd wait forever for her. Yep, she'll come around. Just wait and see."

John didn't think he could be so patient. If he'd found himself in the same situation he'd...Celeste came to mind. Her bright blue eyes, beautiful smile, God, the way she tangled up his insides with crazy emotions. Needing to change the subject he said, "Tell me about the suspect."

The sheriff smiled. "What, my love life's not interesting enough? Okay, here's what we've got. The guy's name in Garrett Winston. Like you thought, he's a trucker. Owner/operator, has his own rig, no home address, just a post office box in Illinois."

"So he probably lives in his cab. Was he driving his truck when they arrested him?"

"Yep, no trailer though."

"We'll have to find out who contracted his last job."

"I'll have one of my men take care of it in the morning."

John nodded. "Good, we need that trailer. We want as much evidence as we can find to ensure a solid case against Winston. It'll also give the prosecutor a premeditation angle."

"He's a sick son of a bitch keeping dead girls on ice while going off to find his next victim. Damn I wish Wisconsin still had the death penalty."

"Eye for an eye." John took a sip of coffee, then after setting it back in the cup holder, he asked, "What time was he picked up?"

"Midnight. I guess he was swerving all over the road. The arresting officer thought the driver might've been falling asleep at the wheel. He wasn't expecting Winston to be drunk, but boy was he ever. Blew a two point four seven. He's sleeping it off in his cell and has no idea the shit that's about to hit the fan." Roy twisted his mouth into a sneer. "Yeah, that SOB's days are numbered."

"His rig's a potential crime scene. Please tell me no one went inside. We don't want to screw this up on some stupid technicality."

"Those guys aren't a bunch of backwater asses. I know their commander. Trust me, nothing's been touched. Winston's truck is in the impound lot waiting for us. The forensics unit will meet us there and comb the cab." Roy blew out a deep breath. "God, I hope they find something. I wouldn't be surprised if Boysen runs the story, that little prick."

"They will. I guarantee his truck is loaded with incriminating evidence, hopefully enough to lock him away for four lifetimes."

Roy glanced at him. "So the profiler's become the psychic now?"

He shook his head and laughed. "Yeah, I don't think so." The mention of the word psychic turned his thoughts back to Celeste. Was she sleeping peacefully tonight? Hopefully, curled in a ball, snuggled into her warm blankets, soft, blond curls spread out on her pillow, a few loose tendrils caressing her face.

"You know." Roy interrupted his thoughts. "I never had the chance to talk with you about Celeste's notes. Did you read them?"

Shit, the sheriff was right, Wissota Falls was a small town. With Dan's unexpected visit, not to mention her brother's, word could be out by morning.

"I read through some of them, then," he sighed, "I went to see her."

"Yeah, I heard about that."

He looked out the window. "Small town?"

Loud laughter filled the squad car. "Boy, don't I know it. Yeah, Dan filled me in, and called right after you left. She's a special gal and we're all concerned about her."

"I understand, but she's no longer needed now. We have Winston, and hopefully the evidence will take over from here."

"I'm not as convinced."

"Why's that?"

"You heard what she'd said in Carl's office. There are *two* killers." He shrugged a shoulder and looked back to the road. "We just haven't found the bodies."

He'd been so wrapped up in protecting her after the reading in the ME's office, he'd almost forgotten about that enigmatic prophesy. Okay, honestly he'd blown it off. As much as he wanted to believe in her, he still couldn't wrap his logical brain around her prediction of more than one killer. It simply made no sense. What were they going to do, start combing the woods for more bodies based on a psychic's hunch? Besides, what were the odds that two killers were stalking the same town?

"You seriously believe that?"

The sheriff toyed with his mustache and bobbed his head. "It's like I told you, she's got a gift. Yes, I believe her and already have Jesse and Lloyd doing a little checking."

"Checking what? Do they carry crystal balls, too?" He didn't like this. Not at all. If Winston was the killer they were looking for, it would give her what he knew she needed...closure. If they continued on this ridiculous assumption, the only thing they would accomplish was to feed into Celeste's belief that there was another killer out there. That theory would only add to her fears, something he wanted put to rest. He liked her. A part of him was starting to care about her, and he wanted her to be able to sleep through the night, not worry about dead bodies and killers. That was his job.

"Look John, I get that you're the type of guy who needs to see the hard, concrete evidence. But like I said, Celeste is special and I trust in her, something I'd think you would reconsider after yesterday."

He gave him a sidelong glance. "What the hell does that mean?"

"I saw how you were with her. You were ready to rip any of our heads off if we tried to get near her."

"I was concerned about her state of mind."

"Bullshit. You're just too stubborn to let yourself see her for what she is and you know it." Before he could argue, Roy waved him off. "It doesn't matter what you think, I'm having Jesse and Lloyd running checks throughout the county and state. I want them looking for any female missing persons and runaways which may have occurred when Celeste's visions started."

"You're on a wild goose chase. Besides, half the victims we have are known prostitutes, and from out of state." John tried rolling the tension from his neck, but it was useless. If Celeste was right, if she'd found their killer through her vision, then that meant...he didn't want to think about it. There were no other bodies to back up her prediction.

"She told me otherwise when I took her home. She sensed the girls in her dreams were local. Young, vulnerable, not quite living the life of a prostitute, but edging close."

"That's news to me. So you're going to waste the minimal manpower you have based on psychic intuition?"

"Back off, John."

"That's right, I'm the hired help."

Roy grinned, but the smile didn't reach his eyes. "That you are. So I guess you have no choice but to go along with me here."

"Suppose not," he said, and didn't bother to hide his bitterness. He didn't like being involved in an investigation without full disclosure, and both Roy and Ian were hiding something from him. What, he had no idea. But when the investigation was finished, he'd find out, or resign. He was nobody's fucking patsy, not anymore. If he didn't have Ian's trust, he no longer wanted to work for him or CORE.

***

Garrett Alan Winston sat in the interrogation room shackled to a worn, metal table. The short chain of one handcuff pulled taut as he held a pen over a stack of papers.

His confession.

The sheriff leaned toward the two-way mirror. "I don't get it. He has no record, not even a traffic violation. We've got jack shit, except for small amounts of blood spatter, a few hairs and fingerprints which haven't even been processed, yet he's signing a confession without an attorney?"

John nodded and folded his arms across his chest. Not only stunned by Winston's quick confession, but how eerily he resembled the sketch created based off Celeste's vision. Comb his hair, trim his beard, give him some Visine, and that sketch could have been a photograph. "I don't get it, either."

The door opened. A trooper ducked his head inside to tell Roy he had a call. While John had come to like the sheriff, despite whatever game he was playing with Ian, he was pleased to have a moment alone. He needed to weigh the options, consider other recourses should Winston find a sharp-tongued attorney willing to take his case.

Winston, even in his disheveled state, appeared arrogant, confident as he signed the confession that would convict him of killing four women. Once he finished, the paperwork was quickly removed, and he leaned back in his chair. Bound to the steel table, he stared at the mirror, his eyes, wild, alert. Then he sneered.

The man should be on edge, worried, rather than arrogant. Odd. Why was that? Even though the lab results would take time, John was hopeful the evidence would convict and condemn him. So why the look of triumph? Like he held the winning lottery number?

Winston continued to stare at the mirror. His feral eyes held a ferocious glint that bore into him through the glass. They said he wasn't done. Not by a long shot.

As his skin crawled, his mind raced. He tried to quickly

assess the man cuffed in the opposite room, but couldn't shake the dread lodging deep in his chest enough to concentrate.

The door bounced against the wall, making him jump. "Jesus, Roy, don't do that shit to me."

"We've got to get back to Wissota Falls," he panted as if he'd just run a hundred yard dash. His face ashen, his eyes filled with horror, he gave Winston a quick glance. "Now."

His earlier dread turned to a fear so intense he fought to catch his breath. "Celeste?"

"No," Roy said, already moving for the door. "Bev just called, they found another body."

"Where?" He hoped Roy would tell him Winston's dumping grounds. Maybe this was his last victim. Maybe CSU missed the body.

"Cranberry bogs," Roy said over his shoulder as he left the room muttering that he'd meet him at the car.

Cranberry bogs? Then it hit him.

Little red balls, floating in my nose and mouth...

Celeste's trance, her vision. No amount of antacids would cure the burn running through his chest and gut. She'd been right all along, and he'd been too stubborn to believe her.

He glanced back at Winston who still wore a cocky, mocking sneer. As if he knew.

Impossible. They were in a sound proof booth, in front of a two-way mirror. Paranoia had him thinking irrationally, because he'd allowed himself to become too close to what appeared to be their only witness. Celeste.

As he exited the room, a deep wicked laugh rolled through the intercom. Stopping, he turned and stared at the mirror.

"I know something you don't know," Winston sang off key in a scratchy voice. He sprung from the chair, knocking it to the floor. "Do you hear me?" His face turned purple, blue veins stuck out of his wide neck as he screamed and pulled on his bindings.

"I know," he shouted, spittle oozing down his scruffy beard. "You'll come back. You hear me? You fuckers need me. You'll come back."

115

The officer guarding the interrogation room pinned Winston, as two others entered to help. John gaped at the scene. An eerie sense of foreboding consumed him, ate at his gut and sensible mind. All the while, Winston's disturbing eyes pierced into his through the mirrored glass. They looked at him, into him and he had this niggling feeling Winston might be right.

"Hey Celeste, sorry again for just poppin' over last night, but the wife isn't. She loves your cookies. I swear she devoured half the box before kissin' me hello."

She poured Dan a cup of coffee and smiled. "I told you it wasn't a big deal. I'm glad to know I've got you looking out for me, even if it was a lame excuse to raid my stock of kalachkis." She winked then turned to Lloyd. "How you doing today?"

"I'll be better after I have one of your Western omelets."

"You got it. What about you, Dan? The usual or are you going to take a walk on the wild side and try something new?"

He grinned, his red mustache stretching across his thin lips. "You know me. I'll stick with the usual."

"Okay, I'll have it for you in a jiffy."

"Oh and Celeste?" Lloyd grabbed her arm before she walked away. "Is your brother around? I wanted to talk with him about hanging those kitchen cabinets I ordered."

"He's in the back doing inventory."

"You mean avoiding the customers."

She laughed. "Yeah, that too. You can head on back and talk with him if you like. You know the way."

He shifted his big body off the stool, then nodded to Dan. "I'll be right back. I want to pin Will down to a date he can come by and help finish this pain-in-the-ass kitchen remodeling."

Dan grinned. "I hear that. Hell, you've only been working on it for the past six months."

She walked away from the counter, then went about her

business, taking orders, filling coffee, smiling and making small talk with her customers. Although dead tired, she hoped it didn't show. It was her fault. No, it was John's.

He had been the reason she'd tossed and turned all night. Thank God she hadn't had any dreams though. Maybe a little loving and a couple glasses of wine had done the trick. Maybe the killer took the night off. Or maybe she'd been just having good old fashioned nightmares after all.

As she dropped an order off at a table, Lloyd rushed from the back room. She immediately tensed. Wiping her hands on her apron, she followed him, hoping that he and Will weren't arguing again. Over the last few weeks, they'd been bickering like an old married couple, and she didn't like it, or how it had been affecting her already brooding brother.

"Lloyd, are you okay?" she asked, when she caught up with him at the end of the counter where Dan sat.

His silvery eyes were alert and darting between her and Dan. A sense of foreboding had her knees weakening and her hands gripping the counter for support.

"Cancel our breakfast." Lloyd turned to Dan. "We have to leave. *Now.*"

Dan nodded as if he understood Lloyd's cryptic command, scooted off the stool and shot out the door. Lloyd turned back to her, his eyes flat, bleak, his face pale. "I've got to go. Hell, I...Celeste." He leaned over the counter. "Honey, don't say anything. Bev just called. They found another body." He gave her upper arm an affectionate squeeze, then left.

Another body. Her head spun. The room tilted and closed in on her. She tried to steady herself against the counter then searched the restaurant for a lifeline.

Will stood in the hallway leading to the back rooms. He darted over to her and clasped her hand in his. "Keep it together," he whispered. "Just hold on until I can get you away from the crowd."

She tried to nod, but violent images blurred her mind. When they reached the stock room, she fell into his arms and sobbed. "Oh God, I hoped I was wrong, that they were bad dreams, that they'd stop." She hiccupped and wiped at her tears, then looked into her brother's comforting green eyes, a part of her wishing they were John's chocolate brown. "But the nightmares are real...they're so real."

"Shhh, you don't know that. It's probably the same guy John came here to look for."

She froze in his arms. "Lloyd told you?"

"Hell yeah he did. I go to my sister's house and see a strange guy there, and you won't give me an explanation? Why didn't you tell me about all of this?"

She pulled away and rested her hand on a shelf. "I didn't want you to worry."

"Is that all? Or are you lumping me in with Eden?"

Sending him a wry smile, she shrugged. "Since Mom died, you've made it clear you didn't want to hear about—"

"No, since mom died you've been coddling me. Making sure I'm okay, Dad's okay, and running yourself ragged over the diner. You've been keeping yourself too busy, worrying about everyone else, you've forgotten about you."

"Not true, and this isn't—"

"Celeste, I'm not like Eden or Dad. I've always believed in you and your gift. Dad believed in Mom's, too, but didn't want you to have it." He shrugged. "For whatever reason. You could have come to me about this. I would have stayed at the house, looked after you. The fact I had to hear about your visions from Lloyd pisses me off. I thought we were closer than that."

"We are, but you don't understand. I don't understand." She shook her head. "God, I wish Mom was around to help guide me on this."

He touched her shoulder. "I do, too. But she's not. Lloyd filled me in on everything, and it sounds like it's the same guy who killed those other women. Don't jump to conclusions. And quit shutting me out," he finished, giving her shoulder a squeeze.

Wishing they'd had this conversation before, because he was dead right, she hugged him, then nodded into his shoulder. "I won't." She held onto her brother for a few more moments, then pulled away. "Thanks for believing in me."

"I always have, just like you've been there for me. Now let's get you cleaned up. We've got a full house out there. I'll even throw on an apron and pour coffee."

She rolled her eyes. "My hero."

His smile wavered. "No matter what happens, I'll be here for you."

She nodded and squeezed his hand. "Thanks, I needed to hear that." Wiping her eyes she started for the door, then stopped. "Did Lloyd mention where they'd found the body?"

Will was already tying an apron around his waist when he turned to her. "Yeah, Bev said Stu and Glen found the body when they were harvesting their cranberry bog."

Air whooshed from her lungs, and her knees gave way.

Little red balls floating in her nose and mouth...she couldn't breathe, she couldn't...

"Celeste?" Will grabbed her before she hit the floor. "What is it?"

She couldn't see her brother's face, her vision distorted by tiny, red orbs of light.

CHAPTER 10

AS JOHN CLIMBED out of the sheriff's cruiser a warm breeze drifted over him, carrying the tainted smell of death. Drawing deep breaths in through his mouth, which didn't lessen the odor, he glanced at Roy. The sheriff wore a frown, and winced when the wind blew again, likely from not only the putrid odor, but the knowledge that he'd soon face its source.

The girl in the bog.

Plunking his state-issued hat on his head, Roy met him at the front of the cruiser. "That's Glen and Stu over there." He nodded to two men sitting in the grass approximately fifty feet from a gentle slope that John assumed led to the bog.

One of the men stared off into the clear sky, the sun reflecting off his bald head ringed with gray hair. His lips moved, but John doubted anything coherent was uttered as he wrung his hands and rocked with the mild breeze. The other man, stocky, maybe a few years younger, held a faded red bandana to his forehead, while keeping a hand on the older man's shoulder.

Looking away from the two men, John focused on the landscape. He could only view the opposite shore, lined thickly with trees, pines mostly. A gentle ripple, caused by the westerly wind, moved along the water, but no cranberries were visible. "Where are the berries?" he asked.

"They're along the edge here," Roy said, and pointed. "You just can't see them from where we're standing."

"I assumed the entire bog would be filled with them."

"No, this lake runs into a few other smaller ones and they all connect to the Chippewa River. The cranberry vines grow along the shore. When it's time to harvest them, Glen and Stu flood the area with the lake water using an irrigation system."

"How deep?"

"That's a question for Glen and Stu."

John pushed off the cruiser. "Along with a few others. How well do you know these two?" he asked, as they walked toward the cranberry farmers.

"Pretty well. They're good men. Both happily married with kids. About eight or nine years ago, the owner of this cranberry farm…" He motioned to the bog. "David Leland passed on. Glen and Stu had been working for him for years. They pooled their money together and bought it off Leland's widow and have been running it since."

When they were a few feet from the men, the one with the bandana rose, then moved toward them. "Roy, I…" He covered his mouth with the bandana, then looked away, a tear trickling down his tanned cheek.

The sheriff laid a hand on the man's shoulder. "Glen, this is John Kain. He's here to help us sort this out."

Tucking the bandana in his back pocket, he offered his hand. "Glen Anderson, and this is Stu Clemens," he said, and jerked his head toward the man still sitting on the grass.

John shook his hand. "Tell me how you found the body?"

"Well, I was running Denise—"

"Denise?"

"Sounds dumb, but that's what we call our harvester. Anyway, as Denise churned through the bog, I caught something…you know, in my peripheral vision, and that's when I saw the girl. I radioed Stu, and he called Bev." He blew out a deep breath, withdrew the bandana from his back pocket and wiped it across his face again. "I never saw anything like this in all my years." Tears welled in his eyes. "And I hope to God I never do again."

Car doors slammed behind them. John turned as Dan and the Viking approached from their vehicles. Two other cruisers pulled in, skidding to a halt on the gravel. Jesse stepped out of one and Ed out of the other.

CSU would be arriving any minute, and while they'd done a decent job at the last dump site, he worried about the investigation aspect. Roy's deputies weren't homicide detectives, and as each man neared, all pale, all wearing an acute sense of dread on their faces, he wondered if he shouldn't call Ian for help.

Roy turned to him. "If it's okay with you, I'm going to have one of my men take their official statements, and let the others wait for CSU."

John nodded. Maybe Roy was psychic, too, because he'd been about to suggest the same thing. That thought trigged another. "Do you get much traffic along this road here?" he asked Glen, pointing to the narrow two lane road. "Big rigs in particular".

"No big rigs," Glen said. "We use our own flatbed trucks to deliver our product. Besides, this road doesn't lead to much. Mostly, we get kids heading out to the lake for some necking or whatever they do these days."

Stu remained silent. He continued to sit on the grass, his focus on the woods surrounding the clearing that led to the bog.

John looked to the woods then, and couldn't help but think of Celeste's trance. How she'd spoken of the trees, a clearing, hitting something metal before the killer had ended the life of the woman she'd become during the trance. He swiveled and leveled his gaze on Denise. Could the harvester have been what she'd referred to?

"The sheriff would know better," Glen continued, nodding in Roy's direction. "He sends his men out here to make sure no one is gettin' into trouble."

"This is usually Jesse and Lloyd's territory, sometimes Dan, or even Gary who I don't think you've met," Roy said. "Kids like to come down here. Drink a six pack or two, smoke weed, have sex."

John removed his sunglasses, and tucked them in his pocket, then looked toward the water. From this angle, red berries coated the surface along the shore. "Glen, how deep do you flood the area?"

"Twenty inches, give or take. Which made it easy to spot..." Glen cleared his throat. "To spot the woman. But the lake itself is about fifteen to twenty feet at its deepest point, depending on rainfall."

The deputies who'd been dragging their feet finally approached. Roy ordered Dan to take the cranberry farmers back toward the cruisers to make their official statements, then told the others to hang tight until CSU arrived. He didn't miss the relief on the men's faces before pulling two pairs of shoe covers out of his back pocket. He handed Roy one pair, then used the other to cover his shoes.

"Is there another highway close enough where Winston could have parked his rig, then walked over here?" John asked, while waiting for the sheriff to cover his boots.

"The next main highway's miles from here. Plus, he'd have to have walked through those woods." He pointed west. "And that wouldn't have been easy. That's a rough patch, no trails. If he works during the night, it would have taken him hours to make it here, then back to his rig."

"Maybe Winston isn't our guy," he said, as they approached the shore.

"Then why the quick confession?" Roy asked, then gasped. "Oh my God." Turning away, he bent and rested his hands on his knees.

You'll come back. You hear me? You fuckers need me. You'll come back.

Winston's parting words taunted him as John stared at their latest victim lying in the shallow water. Flies swarmed on and around her nude body. Her pale skin appeared stark white against the dark, red cranberries floating around her. Inky, long black hair drifted around her bruised face which had been sliced at least a half dozen times with either a razor or a knife.

The water slightly undulated. Cranberries moved over and around the torso which had been deeply cut from the pubic bone to the ribcage. The flesh surrounding that wound, along with those on her face, had shriveled and puckered. The ragged skin seemed to have been nibbled, likely from the fish in the bog. Even several feet away, insects he couldn't name festered in her wounds.

He'd seen drowning victims in the past. Most had been bloated two to three times their normal weight, trapped gases causing the body to blow up like a balloon. This woman lacked that bloat, he assumed, due to the open wound on her torso.

Swallowing the bile rising in his throat, he finally turned away only to catch the sheer horror in Roy's eyes. "This girl wasn't killed like the others," the sheriff said, his voice cracking.

He looked back to the victim, zeroing in on her neck. With the way her black hair and the cranberries shadowed her throat, he had a hard time finding any indication she'd been strangled with a thin cord like the other victims. "No, but we'll know more once her body is removed and Carl takes a look at her."

"Celeste was right then. There's more than one killer, and now we've found one of his victims."

"Roy, we don't know—"

"She had four visions," the sheriff continued as if he hadn't said anything. "I'll have to reread her notes, but I'm betting this one matches the first, which means there are three other bodies out there."

"We won't know anything until—"

Fury darkened Roy's eyes. "Quit being so damned pigheaded."

Before John could reply, more car doors slammed. Banking his own irritation, he looked away from Roy, and watched as Mitchell and his crime scene techs descended the area.

Then another van pulled up and came to an abrupt halt, the tires kicking gravel. Matt Boysen. "We have an uninvited guest." He jerked his head toward the reporter.

"Shit," Roy muttered. "That prick just won't quit."

John agreed. Boysen wasn't going to back down until he had a story. If they had another killer on the loose, Celeste could be in danger if Boysen leaked her name. Heartburn kicked in again as he turned to the sheriff. "Give him something then, but only if he gives his word that Celeste's name stays out of whatever story he runs."

"Boysen doesn't know Celeste's involved."

Releasing an exasperated sigh, John shook his head. "Does he know Celeste, that she's a psychic?"

"Sure, everyone does."

"Then don't you think he might put two and two together? He might be a small time reporter, but I guarantee he didn't miss her car parked outside of the Sheriff's Department yesterday, *after* those four women were discovered. If he goes on a hunch and hints we're using a psychic..."

"Damn it, Celeste could become a possible threat to the killer." Roy wiped a shaky hand down his face. "That girl's like a daughter to me. I couldn't live with myself if something happened to her."

Neither could he. In less than a day, she'd somehow managed to crawl under his skin, and weasel her way into his tarnished heart. He'd thought the unexplained emotions he'd been dealing with since meeting her had everything to do with lust, but knew himself better than that.

While he wanted her, every which way physically and sexually possible, he wanted her laughter, quick wit, even her sarcastic barbs more. So unlike any woman he'd ever encountered, she made him restless, made him want a life outside of the career and reputation he'd fought for. She had him longing for companionship, making love on rainy afternoons, or snuggling on the couch watching TV. While those thoughts scared the hell out of him because he'd never truly had a real relationship, the thought of Celeste being hurt or worse scared him even more. He might have no right to want what he did from her considering he didn't have much to offer but a bunch of emotional, bullshit baggage. Still, he needed her safe.

"Then let's make sure Boysen keeps her name out," John said. "Dangle our suspect in his face. Tell him we've potentially apprehended the man responsible for the other murders. No name, just that the suspect is being detained and investigated. But only tell him that much if he promises to keep *this* murder and Celeste's name out of his story. Then ensure him another exclusive later."

"And the mayor? I didn't tell him anything about Celeste, but he's not a stupid man. He knows about her, hell he's had her do a reading for him a few times. He'll wonder—"

"Let him. Celeste name stays out of this, and make sure your deputies and even Bev keeps a lid on it. No one is to know about her. *Period.*"

As Mitchell and his team drew closer, Roy stomped off to deal with Boysen. Instead of focusing on the dead woman in the bog, John's thoughts remained on Celeste. He'd never, in his life, his career, had thought that he would believe in a psychic, but he believed in *her*. She might hold the key to unlocking this murder, and help them find the other victims yet to be discovered. She might also be in danger.

That thought didn't settle well. The heartburn intensified and had him patting his pockets for antacids that weren't there but left in his motel room. Clenching his jaw, he knew the slow burn in his chest wouldn't have been eased by any medication. Making sure Celeste was safe, that she was in one piece—he glanced at the victim and zeroed in on the gaping wound running along her torso—in every sense of the word.

Celeste grabbed the remote and turned off the show she'd recorded earlier on her DVR, then paced her living room. Not even Rachel Ray could keep her attention. The only thing she could think about was the way John had sounded when he'd called a few hours ago.

She'd left the diner early. When the lunch rush had settled, Will insisted she should go home and rest. But after John had called, she couldn't relax. His somber tone had worried her. He'd assured her he was okay, but she hadn't believed him. How could anyone be okay after watching a body being dredged from a bog?

Her visions had displayed the torture women had been put through at the hands of a sadistic murderer. They'd created everlasting images which would not fade over time. *Ever.* Today, John had witnessed the end result of her nightmares and she wondered if it would be the same for him, a memory which would not fade.

The doorbell rang. Her heart skipped a beat. She drew in a deep breath and headed for the foyer. When she opened the front door, the aroma of spicy, Italian sausage wafted through the air.

Her mouth watered, nothing to do with the pizza John held in his hands, but the man himself. Not only was he heart stopping sexy as hell, beneath his rugged exterior she sensed so much more. A good man, strong, honest, dedicated, he'd never lied about his opinion regarding psychics, and while he hadn't wanted her involved in the investigation, he'd included her anyway. He'd offered her comfort when she'd needed it. In his arms she'd known what it was like to truly feel protected, wanted, desired.

She leaned against the door jamb. "Hi. Thanks for bringing dinner."

He responded with a noncommittal grunt. His body rigid, his eyes unreadable, and a frown furrowing his brows, he moved passed her toward the kitchen. She shut the door, then leaned against it.

He was worse than she'd thought. Today had to have been pure hell for him. First, Garrett Winston, then the body in the bog. She desperately wanted to offer him the same comfort he'd given her yesterday. To ease him, let him know he wasn't alone in this.

With a deep sigh she followed him and the zesty scent of

pizza, to the kitchen. "John, I know—"

He dropped the pizza on the table. His files, which had been tucked under his arm, fell and scattered across the smooth surface.

Instead of straightening the mess, he moved to her, cupped her cheeks, then crushed his mouth to hers. Desire replaced the worry and fear that had been tormenting her since she'd learned about Winston and the latest murder victim, especially when John's firm lips parted.

Cradling her face, he deepened the kiss. His tongue dominated and possessed. With each demanding stroke of his tongue, she swore she sensed his fear and his relief. Almost as if touching her, kissing her assured him she was safe.

Breathing hard, he tore his mouth away, and grazed her lips with his thumb. "Celeste, I'm sorry," he whispered, and met her gaze. "I shouldn't have..."

Running her fingers through his hair, she pulled his head down and silenced him with her mouth. She wrapped her arms around his neck and pulled him closer. She didn't want to talk, not right this second. His eyes had told her what she'd needed to know. He'd faced a killer today only to discover there was another one out there. He'd seen what she'd seen, only worse.

Moving her hands along his biceps, she gave him a soft, lingering kiss, then leaned back in his arms. "Are you okay?"

He pressed his forehead to hers. "I am now."

A deep rumbling exploded from his stomach. Grinning, she ran her hand along his cheek, loving the rough, end-of-the-day beard stubble tickling her palm. "You'll be even better once you've had something to eat."

His smile filled her hand.

With reluctance, she stepped away. While she'd desperately wanted to offer him the same comfort his mere presence seemed to have given her, now wasn't the time. He needed to eat. She was just as hungry considering she hadn't had a bite since breakfast and it almost seven o'clock. Plus there were the files scattered on the table. Case files on yesterday's murder victims, she assumed.

Neither spoke as she rummaged through her utensil drawer, and he poked around her cabinets, bringing plates and glasses to the table. As they worked in tandem, she couldn't help but enjoy the simple domesticity of the moment. Their shoulders brushed as they moved around the kitchen, their fingers touched as they reached for the same things. Small smiles, hints of desire were shared. As much as she'd love to see this man in her kitchen every day, explore the heated desire and comforting emotions she'd found whenever she was with him, she had to caution herself. After the investigation ended, he would leave.

Just like everyone else.

Once they were both seated, John pulled a piece of pizza from the box. The mozzarella cheese stretched taut then snapped. Before placing the greasy slice on her plate, he raised a dark brow. "Gnome plates?"

"Don't make fun, they're cute. My sister gave them to me for my birthday last year. They're
 supposed to be one of a kind."

He smiled as he placed a slice on his own plate. "Really, you don't say?"

She ignored the teasing sarcasm and eyed the pizza. "Sausage, my favorite." As she was about to take a bite, she caught sight of the scattered papers lying next to the pizza box. Her stomach tightened when she saw her handwriting and realized he'd brought copies of her visions. The pizza fell from her hands and dropped on the plate.

He looked to her, his concerned gaze searched hers. "I thought we could talk about a few things over dinner." He frowned, his eyes penetrating. "Unless it will ruin your appetite."

"I'm fine." She started to lie, but couldn't under his scrutinizing gaze. "Okay." She blew out a deep breath. "Not really, but it's important we get through this."

"A lot has happened today." He stacked her notes, and shoved them on the other side of the table. "This can wait." He reached across the table and placed his hand on hers, then gave her fingers a light squeeze. His touch inspired and stimulated, gave her strength and renewed her confidence.

You can do this, she told herself. You have to, for John, for those women, for yourself.

She twisted her wrist then twined her fingers through his. "Thanks, but I'm okay." Releasing his hold, she picked up the pizza, which now seemed as appetizing as ketchup covered cardboard. "How did things go in Eau Claire?"

He paused, the gooey pizza inches from his mouth. "How did you know...never mind, I get it. Small town," he said, then took a bite.

"Pretty much. You can't empty the trash without everybody knowing what's in it."

"That was much more eloquently put compared to how Roy described small town life."

Knowing Roy, and his way with words, she laughed. "Regardless of how either of us describes it, it's true. For the record, though, Lloyd told me. He was at the diner with Dan for breakfast when he got the call from Bev."

He frowned. "Lloyd told you?"

"Sure, he knows I'm involved, and we're tight. I've known him forever." She shrugged. "Besides, if he hadn't told me what had been going on, I might still be wondering if we were ever going to finish our *discussion*," she said, hoping to ease the sudden tension emanating from him.

The corner of John's mouth kicked up in a slow grin, his dark eyes sparkled and teased. "If you weren't so popular, we would have finished last night."

She playfully batted her lashes. "What can I say?"

"That you have no regrets."

Did she? Yes. No. She wanted him, no doubt about it. But to get involved with a man who was basically passing through?

"Nope." She wiped the grease from her hands on a napkin. "And you?"

"Nope," he answered back, a smile tugging at his lips.

"Good, so tell me about today."

He pulled another slice from the box. As they ate, he told

her about Garrett Winston, the little evidence they'd found and how the sick bastard had signed a confession.

Using her fork to shove the pizza around her plate, she rested her chin in her hand then met his gaze. "What about the girl today?"

"Between your notes on the first vision and what you told me yesterday in the car..." He puffed his cheeks and blew out a deep breath.

"You believe me now?" She studied him and held her breath, waiting for an answer she wasn't quite sure her heart wanted to hear.

John reached for his glass, then drained the soda in a couple of quick gulps. After he'd witnessed firsthand the results of her nightmares, he couldn't dismiss her predictions as merely a state of psychosis or some sort of strange need for attention. Besides, in the short time he'd known her, she'd shown no signs of mental imbalance, and her character spoke of nothing disreputable.

She was an ordinary woman. Honest, decent and respectable. Well, not *exactly* ordinary. She was a beautiful woman full of surprises. Like the fact she was an accountant turned talented baker. Or that she had a houseful of creepy gnomes and liked it. Then there was her passion.

He hadn't been lying last night when he'd told her she'd made him feel alive. Her arousing caresses had brought out a desire he'd never experienced before. They were making it difficult for him to remain detached, to keep his feelings for her filed away in their rational, logical place.

There had been nothing rational or logical going through his mind when he'd kissed her today, or even last night. Unfortunately, he wanted to kiss her again. Fortunately, she seemed to like kissing him as well. Or was that unfortunately? He'd leave after the investigation, then move on to the next case. Where would that leave them?

Alone.

He stared into her expectant eyes, which didn't hold an "I told you so" triumph, but instead, understanding. Then she offered him a small smile, and shook her head.

"I shouldn't have put you on the spot," she said, "I'm sorry, you don't have to—"

"Yeah, I do." He reached for her hand. "I believe in you, Celeste. I can't discount what you've already done for this case. Without your help, Winston might have been released on a DUI, then likely disappeared without a trace."

"Thank you." Relief flashed in her eyes as she gave his hand a squeeze. "Now that we have that out of the way, how should we start?"

"What do you mean?"

"You said you'd read some of my notes, you'd also witnessed my trance. The one I don't remember and that you were *supposed* to tell me about." She cocked a brow. "Now you've seen the results, how should we start?" she repeated.

He hesitated. "I haven't had a lot of time to correlate between your visions and your trance. But as I reread your notes, I think we might have a few leads to follow."

"Really? Okay, lay it on me."

This was what he admired about Celeste. She seemed game for anything, open and honest, blunt to a fault. He liked that. Hell, he liked her and the last thing he wanted to do was recreate her nightmares and put her through any kind of trauma. He wanted to protect her, not use her to track down a killer.

He had little choice in the matter, though. If she was right, there were three more bodies waiting to be discovered. Leaning into his chair, he scratched the back of his head. "Let's start with the car ride. You'd said that had never happened before, the trance I mean."

"Not that I'm aware of, but how would I know if I didn't remember," she said, her brow creasing.

He nodded and tossed his napkin over his plate. "Okay, in the car, sometimes you'd described the scene as you saw it, while at other moments you'd become the victim. You'd started talking about your long hair, how you should have listened to Judy when she'd suggested you cut it. You'd also talked about how you should have listened to your parents and how you wished you could smell your mother's prized gardenias and the Old Spice cologne your father wore."

"Really?" She frowned. "I didn't get any of that in the original vision. Did the girl you found today have long hair?"

He nodded as the memory of the dead woman surfaced. Ink black hair floating in a bed of red cranberries. Ebbing and flowing against a sliced, bruised and ghostly pale face.

"Were you able to identify her?" she asked, and although she appeared nonchalant, fear and anxiety showed in her eyes. Her angst caused a trickle of worry to run through him. Were the murders going to take a toll on her vivacious personality? Change her? He hoped not, but he'd seen it happen before. Witnesses, victims, spiraling into deep depression or worse. The question was how to protect her from the repulsive details of this case. Better yet, how to protect her from her own mind.

"No, not yet."

She shoved her plate away and stared to the window at his back.

"You okay?"

"Mm-hmm. I was just thinking that if Roy checks all the surrounding counties for missing young women..."

"He has Lloyd and Jesse already on it, and I gave them the leads on the hairdresser and the gardenias. Any bit of information, as insignificant as it seems, may give us a break in the case. Could be she knew the attacker or someone saw him with her before she died."

"During the trance, did I say anything about what the killer looked like? Because I honestly never felt as if the victim knew her attacker."

"I asked you to describe him, but you said he wore a ski mask. The only other thing you said as a way to describe him was that he smelled."

She wrinkled her nose. "Did Winston stink?"

"Like alcohol, from what I understand. I never actually interviewed him. He'd confessed to Highway Patrol before Roy and I had arrived."

"Don't you think that's strange? I mean, why confess without even knowing the kind of evidence you have on him."

"Roy and I have been wondering the same thing."

"Is it possible Winston killed the woman in the bog?"

"We're not ruling him out, but I don't think so. The girl wasn't killed in the same fashion. Besides, the road to the bogs isn't well traveled, and it has a weight limit, one Winston's truck, even without a trailer, wouldn't meet." He held up his hands. "It just doesn't make sense. Considering the other victims were prostitutes, I believe Winston killed when the opportunity rose and would stick with his original dumping grounds or at least something similar. He needed a clean getaway. This one was different."

"Yeah, but in my vision, I remember running through woods. Isn't it possible he was going to dispose of her like the rest of the other women, and she found a chance to escape? She may have run off, he chased her and..."

He shook his head. "We'll know more results when the lab has them, but I'm guessing Winston raped and killed those women *in* his cab. Besides, like I said, this victim's cause of death was different."

"How so?"

He looked away. While he'd known he'd eventually have to tell her in order to jog her memory, he still didn't want her to face the same image he'd witnessed today. An image he knew he'd carry for a lifetime.

"John," she prompted.

"The other victims' had been asphyxiated, likely with a thin cord. The woman from the bog was...stabbed."

"Stabbed," she echoed. "You mean repeatedly?"

"No, I mean..." He rose from the chair, paced for a moment, then leaned against the kitchen counter trying to figure out a way to sugarcoat the murder, but came up blank. "He cut her...deep, from the pelvis up to the breast bone."

She gasped. "Oh my God, that's...that's, oh my God."

Moving quickly, he knelt next to her. "Listen to me. I didn't get any of that from your notes, but in the car, you'd..." He closed his eyes as the memory emerged.

"Gone through her final moments," she whispered, her eyes widening with alarm and astonishment. "I had no idea I was capable of that sort of power."

She stood and took their plates to the sink, then turned. Wiping her palms on her jeans, she drew in a deep breath. "I want to go under another trance."

"No," he stated firmly. Standing quickly, he nearly knocked the chair to the tile floor. "There is no way I want you doing *that*." Reining in the fear of witnessing her become another victim, he moved to the counter and reached for her.

She flinched, and her eyes immediately sought his. "You're worried about me."

He looked away. "It's not that."

She laid her palm along his hand. "Don't lie to me."

Worry didn't cover even an iota of what had his stomach coiling. He couldn't shake the girl from the bog's image, or the trance Celeste had undergone in his car. The two mingled and meshed. There had been times today when he'd broken into a sweat picturing Celeste, her body jerking, tensing as if a knife were slicing through her. He'd seen the final result of that trance, and he didn't want to witness the death of another victim through another one. Hell, he just wanted Celeste to be Celeste, not some sort of vessel to victims.

"You have to understand." He cupped her face and searched her eyes. "What if you do remember the trance this time? These images could be worse than the ones you already have locked in your mind."

Smiling into his palms, she lightly grasped his wrists. "Let's worry about that if it happens, and considering I have no recollection of the first trance, I doubt I'll remember the next."

"How can you be sure?"

"Hunch?"

He narrowed his eyes.

"Okay, so I don't know. But we have to try. I need this, John. Please. I need to make the visions still swirling in my mind go away. I'll do whatever it takes. Besides, since we've been through one trance, you'll now know what to expect, and maybe know the right questions to ask me."

He knew she was right, even if every part of him wanted to deny it. He believed in her abilities, but selfishly didn't want to subject her to anything more that had to do with the case. He liked her, cared for her, and wanted to protect her from not only the atrocities she'd witness during her visions, but from what could come from another trance. She could also shed additional light on the investigation. Firm up their case against Winston, and possibly lead them to the second killer.

Nodding, he moved his hands to her shoulders. "You're relentless."

"Does this mean..."

"Yes, I'll go along with another trance. But this time we do it right. We'll have a doctor present, along with Roy. I'll want it recorded and—"

She pulled away and started heading for the living room. "Nope," she called over her shoulder. "We do this here and now."

With reluctance, he followed her, adding stubbornness to her list of traits he'd been cataloguing in his mind, along with brave. While he admired her courage, he was still concerned about her safety, about her mind remembering what it might witness during the trance.

As she glanced back at him with a small sexy smile curving her lips, he started to worry more about his heart. If he wasn't careful, she just might end up owning it.

CHAPTER 11

DR. ALEX TRUMANE leaned into the leather sofa cushion and pushed a hand through his hair still damp from a recent shower. He'd run track in both high school and college, and after taking the plunge into sobriety, he'd reacquainted himself with running again. And tonight, he'd run hard and long.

Staying sober had meant changing his lifestyle. During the first few days of sobriety, rather than stopping off at one of his favorite watering holes after work for a drink, he'd gone home to pace his spacious condo. Sleep had eluded him. The night sweats had been beyond terrible. The shakes, the hallucinations, so unbearable, he'd had to cancel appointments for nearly a week until the alcohol had worked itself out of his system.

He'd warred with the need to drink, to alleviate the symptoms of delirium tremens with benzodiazepines, which, as a doctor, he had easy access to. But as a medical practitioner, he'd understood the disease, and knew the DTs would wan with time. And they did. The moment he'd finally broken free of them, alone, soaked in his own sweat and tears, he'd donned his running shoes and pulled a Forest Gump.

Although weak and tired, he had run out his front door, out of the posh condo community he lived in just outside of Jackson, Mississippi. For hours, he had run aimlessly until he collapsed at a school playground thirteen miles from his condo. The next night he'd attended his first AA meeting, and hours later, had met Kira.

Like a beacon, he'd been immediately drawn to her. She had been the light he hadn't realized he'd sought. During the two months he'd visited her at the diner after his AA meetings, she'd managed to worm her way into his broken, beat-up heart and blackened soul. She had given him hope. When the need to fall off the wagon had pulled at him, she had been there. She had given him encouragement with a simple smile when he'd been ready to say "fuck it" and have a drink. He'd fallen in love with her. Whether she knew it or not, she'd never let on. Despite the fact most of his relationships were short lived and blurred from booze, he knew women. And he knew she liked him. But could she love him?

Leaning forward, he grabbed the paper place mat bearing Dudley's Diner along the front, along with its simplistic menu, then flipped it over. He stared at the names he'd written last night. The names of every person he'd harmed while a full-blown alcoholic. Every person he'd needed to make amends with...number eight according to AA's Twelve Step program.

Today he'd spent his day off on step number nine, making those amends. From the moment he'd woken this morning, he'd made painful, humiliating calls to people he'd loved and had ultimately disappointed. His mother had cried, and had forgiven him for everything, even his drunken debacle during his father's funeral. His older sister had done the same, and he'd cried along with her. The tears had cleansed him, and had washed away so many years of guilt.

Carla, his ex-wife, who he'd at one time loved fiercely, and had wronged on so many inconceivable levels, had been the toughest call to make. She, too, had cried. But not out of pain, or the humiliation he'd caused her with his numerous infidelities or cruel words when he'd been intoxicated, but out of joy. She'd been happy for him, supportive, and had offered whatever help she could to rekindle his relationship with their two children. His kids, though, had not been quite as receptive.

Brendon was an eighteen-year-old who'd just started his

freshman year at college. He didn't mind that his drunk of a father paid for his ghastly tuition, but had made it clear he'd had no time to talk with him. Carla had said to take "baby steps" with Brendon because he'd witnessed the worst of his drunken tirades. That once he'd proven himself to his son, he'd eventually be able to reestablish a relationship with him.

He hoped so. He had loved the bond he'd shared with his father, even when he'd been drunk. He'd always been able to go to his dad, talk about anything, and wanted the same for his own son.

His daughter had given him a small sliver of hope. At sixteen, Tanya seemed somewhat willing to reestablish a relationship with him. Then again, he had given her a brand new Honda Accord for her sixteenth birthday. Maybe she looked at him as a cash cow, her personal Daddy Warbucks, he thought cynically. Or maybe she wanted her daddy back.

With a deep sigh, he reached for the bottle of water resting next to the place mat, his list of atonement. He stared at that list, all twenty-two names checked off, but one. That last one was what had made him run harder, farther tonight. Everyone on that list had been someone he'd known well, had loved in some way, shape or form.

Everyone except number twenty-two.

She'd merely been a pawn. He'd used her, had gone against his Hippocratic Oath to maintain his medical practice and stay out of prison. What would his peers think of him if they knew? What would Kira think? She respected him now, but would she after he'd made his final amends?

More importantly, what about the woman? Number twenty-two. He could handle her hatred. He could live with her disgust in him. He just hoped to God she was still alive, that she could still scream and shout. Accuse him of being the bastard he'd been those many years ago. If she had died because of him...

He shook his head. There was only one way to find out, and if he discovered that she had died, he'd go to the authorities. He might not have facilitated her death, but he'd played a part in it, and he knew her true killer's name.

His stomach cramped. A shiver ran through him that had nothing to do with the cranked up AC.

After placing his laptop onto the coffee table, he powered it up and waited. Her last known residence was in his files. He'd call her, tell her what she would need to know, then he'd finally find atonement.

If she was still alive.

"I'm not comfortable with this," John said as he followed Celeste into the living room. After what had happened in his car during the first trance, he worried about her safety. While he did want her to go under another, he'd rather they were in a contained environment. He wanted a doctor present, Roy available to ask additional questions, and a camera rolling to catch every nuance of the trance. Believing in her abilities was one thing, but understanding them would take time, time he didn't have considering they might have a second killer on the loose.

"C'mon John, we've been through this before. I have faith that you can do it again," Celeste countered as she sat on the couch and folded her legs under her.

"Can you, though?" he asked. "You said you've never lapsed into a trance until yesterday. How can you be sure it will work today?"

Smiling, she tucked a curl behind her ear. "I'm not, which is why I'd rather do this now, instead of in front of a bunch of people. I'd hate to look like a fool if this doesn't work. Do you understand what I mean?"

He did. Not everyone believed in psychics, and if they'd gone through the effort to film a trance and nothing happened, she'd be humiliated. While she came off as a confident woman, she had obvious insecurities when it came to her gift. He couldn't blame her. After all, he hadn't showed any faith in her, and had been the proverbial Doubting Thomas until he'd seen the proof of her visions.

Before the image of the girl in the bog could resurface, he tamped it down and focused on Celeste. "I do, but what if we wait and just have Carl—you seemed comfortable with him— and Roy in the room with us. I'd feel better if we—"

"No." She leaned forward onto her knees and took his hands. "Please," she said softly. "I want to help, but I can't bear to do this in front of anyone but you. While Roy and Carl might believe in me, you...soothe me."

He sucked in a deep breath as her trust filled parts of him he'd thought were long dead after Renee. In that moment something blossomed in his chest. Not the heartburn that had periodically tormented him for two years and had him addicted to antacids. The sensation was completely different and unlike anything he'd ever experienced. He welcomed it, loved it. For the first time, *he* mattered. Not the criminalist, but the man inside.

Staring into her eyes, which held so much trust, had him clearing his throat and kneeling on the carpet next to her. "I understand, baby," he murmured, and caressed her cheek. "Just you and me."

"I like the sound of that."

So did he. He'd love to spend quality time alone with her, away from the prying eyes of her small town and without the murder investigation hanging over them. He'd considered them complete opposites at first. He'd needed facts to survive, and he'd needed those facts to fit securely into their logical places.

Celeste's open mindedness, her belief in fate and otherworldly possibilities had not only changed his logical approach, but gave him a whole new approach on life. His heart burned, not with acid reflux, but with possibility. Was it possible he and Celeste could have something more than a few stolen kisses? More than the lust that he knew they both shared?

But how could they have more? Once the investigation ended, he'd leave. He had a life in Chicago. A job to do. And she was tied to Wissota Falls.

With that thought in mind, he eased her back to the couch. "We'll do this together, but I'm going to record your trance. Are you okay with that?"

"Absolutely. Only you have to promise to let me listen to it afterward. I'd like to *finally* hear one of my trances," she said, the teasing sarcasm not lost on him.

He nodded, but made no promises. If this trance ended up being like the first, there was no way in hell he'd allow her to listen to the recording. He wanted to protect her, not only from these violent murders, but from herself.

After setting the recording feature on his cell phone, he placed it on the coffee table. "Before we start though, I'd skimmed through your second vision, which was vague. Actually, it seemed as if you were being pulled in different directions."

She frowned. "I had the same feeling. I'd woken up that morning in the basement. At first I'd felt safe, then I remembered."

"You woke up in the basement?"

"Yeah. With the first vision, I'd woken up in the bathtub—no water—thankfully. The second, the basement. The third? That was weird. I was under the kitchen table, my legs and arms tangled in the legs of the table and chairs." She drew in a deep breath. "Fortunately, I'd woken up in my bed after the fourth vision. I'd been starting to worry that I might get into my car or walk aimlessly into town."

"Have you ever been prone to sleepwalking?"

"Just once. The night I realized I was psychic. A boy had gone missing that day. He was a couple of years younger than me, and I'd been so scared for him. He was on my mind as I drifted off to sleep. Apparently I walked into my parents' bedroom and started rambling on about being cold and wet along with a bunch of other gibberish." She drew in a deep breath and leaned back against the cushions.

"My mom woke me up with a hard shake. I remember being confused, wondering why I was in my parents' bedroom, but just that quick, the memory of my dream hit me. I knew where the boy was because my dad liked to fly fish there. My mom called Roy, who had just been elected sheriff. They'd found the boy, unharmed, but with a bad case of hypothermia."

She relaxed, stretched her legs along the couch, and curled her bare toes, painted pink. "You know what's funny?" she asked, her voice sleepy as she closed her eyes. "Lloyd was the boy."

The Viking?

"He's a big badass now. Back then he was nothing but skin and bones. Some kids that used to pick on him had dared him to meet them at the river that night and he'd gotten lost." She shrugged. "But I found him."

That prick of jealousy was there again, but he tamped it down. He had no claims to Celeste. "Okay, so no other episodes of sleep walking until the first vision. Got it." He blew out a deep breath. "Now, when the trance in my car happened, you started telling me about the first vision, how the night of the dream you felt groggy and tired, then bingo, you were under. Do you think you could go under a trance the same way?"

She covered her mouth as she yawned. "Don't know, but I'll try. Just let me get more comfortable." She moved a bit until her body was deep into the cushions, then rested her forearm along her head. "That night I'd come home from the diner and had the same odd feeling as the night before. Deep exhaustion, as if I'd just worked back-to-back double shifts days in a row." She closed her eyes and stayed silent for a few moments before curling on her side. "After a hot shower, I crawled into bed," she said, her voice thick. "I felt so tired...sleep, I needed sleep."

She grew quiet. Her breathing regulated, and her eyes remained closed.

He stayed on the carpet, kneeling next to the couch, and waited. Minutes passed, and he began to wonder if she'd gone under a trance or simply fell asleep.

"Celeste," he whispered. "Are you with me, honey?"

She didn't respond. He smiled and brushed a curl from cheek. Nope, not a trance, more like a much-needed cat nap. He started to rise when she suddenly grasped his wrist.

"Celeste?" he asked, and tried to calm his racing heart.

Her eyes flew open, but she stared past him. They'd turned that same eerie midnight gray just like during the first trance. Staring wide-eyed at the brick fireplace, she lifted her shoulders and whispered, "He's over there. Shhh, don't move. He thinks he knocked me out, but doesn't know what I'm capable of handling. My mom has hit me worse, but at least I knew she'd eventually stop. Not him. Oh, man, not him. He's not going to stop. Shh. He's turning around...I...close your eyes. Close your eyes. Pretend. Just pretend."

He looked to his cell phone recording every word she said, wishing they were in an environment with a doctor or a forensic psychologist. But he'd stupidly allowed his emotions, his feelings for Celeste to rule his sensible mind. Now he was stuck, treading in unfamiliar territory.

Sweat began to coat his forehead and upper lip. His stomach soured. The case wasn't worth putting Celeste through another trance. Even if she wouldn't remember her own words and visions, he would. Ready to shake her out of it, he moved forward. She recoiled, then scooted against the couch cushions.

"He knows I'm awake. Oh God. Not again." Tears hung, unshed around her blue gray eyes. Her mouth gaped open, puffs of air coming in quick succession. She blinked once and an odd look of relief crossed her pale face.

"What is it?" he asked tentatively. Not sure if he wanted to know.

"I...I don't know, I think I'm safe for now. He raped me, you know." Tears streamed down her cheeks. "Raped and punched me so many times. I tried to fight him. My mom used to beat me, say I was nothing, just a little slut, but I was a virgin." She bit her trembling lip. "I was a virgin," she whispered again. "And he knew. I know he did." She raised her voice.

John swallowed back grief for the woman using Celeste's body to tell her story. While he desperately wanted to end the trance, end the pain crossing Celeste's beautiful face, he couldn't. Not yet. They'd come this far and if she had been willing to risk herself to undergo the trance, he hoped they could walk away with some answers and leads. "What's he doing now?" he asked.

"Staring at me," she said, her tone devoid of emotion.

"Honey," he coaxed. "Can you see him?"

She nodded. "I'd thought he was so hot. How stupid. Why would a good-looking guy want anything to do with me?"

"Can you describe him?"

A wan smile touched her lips. "The ideal, only the ideal fucking sucks. I was better off sticking with those skinny, dorky guys."

"He's big then?"

Tears slid down her cheeks. "Too big. He...he hurt me so bad. I ache." She reached between her thighs. "I was a virgin," she whispered again.

Hating himself, hating putting her through this, he asked, "Please, honey, can you tell me what he looks like? If I know, I can help you."

"Dark hair, trimmed beard, oh God, I was so stupid to think he'd like a girl like me."

Winston? Was it possible? "Shh, you're beautiful," he said, hoping to soothe her.

"No, I'm fat, but he said he liked my curves, and he smelled so good, and I thought he was sexy. If only I'd known," she said, then gasped.

Panic clawed at him. "What's happening?"

"Shut up and listen. Someone's coming, can't you hear it? The leaves are crunching. Closer...closer." Breath whooshed from her lungs. "Oh my God, there's another one. He's wearing a mask," she said in a rush. "His eyes are beady, like a little rat. I can't see anything else."

"His build, scent?"

"No, I can't," she sobbed, hiccupped then calmed herself. "Wait, okay, I can do this. He's tall, but skinny. And he stinks. Like bleach."

She suddenly shoved at her breasts and stomach. "Stop touching me. It hurts, he's so rough. I need to get away...wait."

She gulped as a deep frown creased her forehead. "They're talking about me and laughing. It's not funny you pricks," she shouted. "It's not funny. Oh no, the guy with the mask is coming for me." She scooted her legs under her and edged into the corner of the couch.

Watching, witnessing, taking part in her horror, he didn't know what to do. Even though he knew Celeste wasn't the one being tortured, his heart raced and instinct kicked in. "Run, honey. Run."

"I can't. He's—" She screamed, and flipped onto her stomach, then released another muffled cry into the cushions. Her body began to rock in deep forceful jerks as if an invisible force slammed into her backside. Gasping and wailing, she strained her neck back away from the cushions and flailed her arm behind her reaching for her hair.

"It hurts so bad." She began to cry. "He's pulling my hair, grunting like a fucking pig and laughing. Laughing because they both took my virginity." Her head slammed against the cushions, her body jerking violently. "Make it stop, make it stop," she pleaded into the cushions, tears streaming down her face.

Disgust ran through his already soured stomach. The urge to hurt, to maim, to kill settled deep in his soul. The powerful force spread through him, along with helplessness. The victim Celeste had become was not only raped, but now was being sodomized. Right in front of his fucking eyes.

For the first time in years, tears burned and swelled. He couldn't stand watching Celeste undergo this horror, whether she was reenacting another person's nightmare or not. As he was about to shake her from the trance, she flipped onto her back, reached out, scratching, clawing. He ducked and missed a swing.

Her breathing grew heavy, she panted and gasped. Blond curls stuck to the sweat coating her face. "Get away from me you sick fucks. Get away," she yelled and kicked at the air. "How'd you like that?"

Tears stained her cheeks and her breathing calmed. A slow, chilling smile shaped her lips. "I hurt the masked one, got him right in the balls. Now's my chance, I've got to run. I've got to...he's on me. My neck...I...I..." As she kicked her legs, she gasped and clawed at the loose collar of her sweater. "I can't breathe. I can't..."

She suddenly stopped moving. Her breath came in short, shallow puffs as she dropped her arms away from her neck and closed her eyes.

"Honey, are you with me?"

"It's so dark," she whispered. "No moon tonight. The blackness is good, though. I'm not scared anymore."

Gulping, he stared down at her. "Why do you say that?" he asked, even though he already suspected the answer. Celeste was the vessel of a dying woman. As the thought ran through his mind, so did another. Could she go into cardiac arrest? Damn it, he should never have allowed this to happen without a doctor present. Stupid, so stupid.

"Celeste, wake up. You have to wake up," he shouted.

She furrowed her brows, then a serene smile crossed her lips. "So dark. No sound but the mill. It always did help put me to sleep. The humming and drumming...it's relaxing. I'm going to sleep now."

Fear had him grabbing Celeste by her upper arms and shaking her like a rag doll. "Wake up, baby. Please." He cradled her to his chest. "Wake up, wake up," he begged over and over, as he tried to jar her from the trance. As he rocked her body against his, a tear escaped and rolled down his cheek.

She drew in a deep, gasping breath, and wrapped her arms around his neck. Embracing her tight to his chest, he held her and swore he never wanted to let her go. Ever. He wanted to cherish her, love her, keep her safe and secure. Always. They might have only known each other for a short time, but he knew in his gut, in his heart, in his soul, that she was his. He'd tried to deny their connection, tried to deny the chemistry that had confused his logical mind and set his body on fire, but he couldn't any longer. Watching, witnessing Celeste suffering the death of another woman made him realize how short life truly was, and that life without her would be meaningless.

He held her tighter. Until Celeste, he'd been running on autopilot. Punishing himself for Renee's crimes. Tired of living like an unemotional robot, he wanted the warmth, the trust Celeste offered. He also wanted her off the investigation.

"You're crushing me," she half-giggled.

"Sorry," he said, and with reluctance, eased back. She'd scared the hell out of him tonight, and he didn't want to let her go.

Her smile faltered as she lay her hand against his cheek, wiping the single tear away. "John?" Her eyes had returned to their normal bright blue. She looked confused, disoriented and blessedly alive.

"What happened? Did I...?" She let her hand fall away and winced. "Was it that bad?"

He cupped her face then kissed the corner of her mouth. "Worse. You won't be doing this again. *Ever.*"

She stiffened. "*Ever?*"

"That's what I said. It's for your own good." There was no way in hell he'd allow her to go through another trance. She might not remember it, but what if in the dark recesses of her mind, the vision showed itself? He didn't want to take that chance. He didn't want to risk her remembering the beatings, the rape and sodomy, the death.

"For my own good," she echoed.

"Exactly."

"So you're not going to tell me about the trance."

Not in this lifetime. "Now's not the time. I need...to listen to the recording." Remembering his cell phone, he quickly shut off the recording device then slipped the phone in his pocket.

"You promised to let me listen," she said, her tone firm and laced with accusation.

"Not tonight," he spoke louder than he'd meant, the fear, the terror of what he'd witnessed ran strong. He'd break every damned promise to protect her. If she heard herself being...

She crossed her arms over her chest. "Then when?"

Never. He shoved a hand through his hair. "I don't know. Just let me listen to it again and then maybe—"

"Forget it." Her eyes hardened into blue shards of ice. "It's time for you to go."

"Celeste, no." He laid his hands on her shoulders to keep her from storming away from him. He hadn't meant to hurt her or betray her. He only wanted to protect her.

"Then at least tell me what I said."

He looked to the ceiling before meeting her gaze. "I can't. Not tonight. I need—"

"To go," she said, knocking his hands from her shoulders.

Panicking, he snagged her hand before she stalked off, then turned her to face him. "I can't leave you alone."

"I'm a big girl. Besides, I'm used to being alone."

"You don't have to be," he said softly. "After what you said during the trance, I can't leave you here by yourself."

She frowned and shook her head. "What are you talking about?"

"You know how you'd said that during the second vision you'd felt as if you were being pulled in two different directions? That's because there were two men attacking the victim in your vision."

Her eyes widened and she sucked in a breath. "Was one of them Winston?"

"Could be, but I'm not sure."

"And the other? Did I describe him?"

"I'm not going into details until I've listened to the recording again. Please believe me. It's for your own good."

Shaking her hand free of his, she stomped toward the foyer. "Stop saying that. I'm not a child."

"Then quit acting like one," he countered.

"Really?" She laid the sarcasm on thick.

"Okay, I didn't mean that, but you have to trust me on this.

149

Look, in all likelihood, there's another killer out there. If he knows about you, you could be a threat to him."

"Give me a break." She rolled her eyes. "Do you really think a killer is going to look at me as a *threat*? Hell, half of this town thinks I'm a crackpot. I highly doubt—"

"Why are you being so stubborn about this? Damn it, Celeste, you didn't see the woman from the bog. He sliced her face, cut her stomach wide open. I'm not about to discount anything where you're concerned. But if you don't want me here, then I'm calling Roy. He can find someone else to babysit you then until this investigation is over."

As he reached for his cell phone, she gripped his arm. "I do *not* need a babysitter."

"The hell you don't."

A knock at the door had them both pausing. She quickly released his arm, then moved to the door. After peering through the peep hole, she released a sigh. "Hey, Will," she said as she let her brother into the foyer.

Will glanced between the two of them, then settled his gaze on Celeste. "Everything okay?"

"Just fine," she said, "John was just leaving."

"Celeste," he began, then stopped when she raised a hand.

"Will you stay here tonight?" she asked her brother.

"Sure. Mind if I do some laundry?"

"Not at all," she said, and kept her gaze on his rather than Will's.

"Cool, I'll just run to the apartment and get my things. I'll be back in a few minutes."

After Will left, John moved toward her. "Look, I know you're upset, but before you kick me out, let me just say this." He cupped her cheeks, then sifted a hand through her soft curls and held her head. "I believe in you. Can you give me the same? Can you just hang tight for tonight and let me sort out what happened during the trace? I want to talk to Roy about it, and see what Carl finds during the autopsy on the girl from the bog."

The kitchen door banged shut. "It's just me," her brother

shouted, but thankfully didn't enter the living room.

"Please, Celeste." He stroked her cheek. "Can we talk tomorrow?"

"You know where I work," she said, and looked away.

He resisted rubbing his thumb along her pouting lips. "I was hoping for something more private."

She met his gaze then, and stared at him as if he were a stranger. As if they'd never met or shared a deep, unexplainable intimacy.

"Let me sleep on it."

"I think you need to understand something." He held his ground, not wanting to leave things the way they were. She had no clue what she'd put him through and she had to understand his motives. He wasn't trying to boss her around or throw her off the investigation. He was trying to protect her.

"Good night, John." She ushered him to the door, then closed it in his face without an ounce of hesitation.

As he stalked to his car, he tried to figure out where he'd gone wrong. He looked around the yard and caught a few accusing glances.

"Goddamn gnomes," he muttered to himself. What the hell did they know?

More loose ends.

Rage settled deep in his gut as he watched John Kain leave the psychic's house. Had they been discussing his little Deb from the bog? He'd been so careful with his sweet Deb, gutting her enough so that her body would sink into the lake, rather than bloat and float.

Fucking cranberry farmers. They'd harvested two weeks earlier than last year. If they hadn't, her body would have likely moved with the gentle current. It would have either ended up at one of the adjoining lakes, or traveled down to the river. If that had happened and she'd washed up on shore in another county, no one would have tried to connect the Deb to the women Garrett had dumped. And he knew they were trying to make a connection.

He crouched low, the evergreen he'd been hiding behind giving him cover as Kain backed out of the driveway, then sped down the street. Five dead bodies discovered in less than twenty-four hours. That kind of shit didn't happen in this county, which hadn't seen a murder in decades. The odds against two killers could likely have them furthering their investigation against Garrett.

Another loose end.

He closed his eyes and shook his head. The rage remained, but now mingled with painful shards of regret. He couldn't, wouldn't dispose of Garrett.

So far, Garrett had done as they'd planned if he was ever caught—he'd confessed—but his brother was arrogant, impatient, and vengeful. It would be days before he could free Garrett. Days he couldn't afford. The risk of the sheriff and that know-it-all prick, Kain, furthering their investigation scared the shit out of him. What if they discovered what Garrett had done in Florida or Alabama before they'd made their first kill together? Wisconsin no longer carried the death penalty, but those states did. What if Garrett talked? What if he spilled what he knew about him for a lesser sentence?

Garrett had seen his safe house and the alternate identities he'd stashed there. Passports, driver's licenses, credit cards. Garrett also knew where he planned to run once he'd tied up all of his loose ends.

With his stomach twisting, and the thought of killing Garrett leaving him hollow, he brushed the ground with his gloved hands. Once he'd made sure he hadn't left any evidence behind, he edged away from the evergreen, then stopped short when a dog barked. Crouching low once again, he waited and listened, but his thoughts drifted.

Could he survive without seeing Garrett's face again? Hearing his voice? The sexual release when they shared the bitches they'd killed together?

They'd raped and killed dozens of filthy whores over the

past twelve years. As those memories flashed through his mind, each whore, each kill, each sexual gratification...none of them had compared to his Deb. She'd been different. Soft and demure. Sweet and sexy. Unlike the prostitutes they'd taken in the past, his Deb had been special. Clean, pretty, and so unlike the filth Garrett had brought to him. Although his Deb was the daughter of a minister, she wasn't a virgin, which hadn't bothered him. Her ass had been virginal enough. If only he'd had the time to fulfill his ultimate fantasy with her, she would have been the absolute perfect kill.

The more he thought about his Deb, the more he realized he could find the satisfaction he needed *without* Garrett. He'd taken his Deb alone, and the pleasure of the act had been more fulfilling than he'd ever imagined. For the first time, he had been able to walk away from a kill without remorse. While he hadn't felt an ounce of guilt over the junkie whores they'd murdered together, he'd hated himself for the immoral, impure thoughts he'd had while fucking those pieces of trash. He'd always hated the need to look into his brother's eyes and imagine...

He blocked the depraved thought as bile rose in his throat. He wouldn't go there. He wouldn't allow himself to fantasize about something that could and would never, ever happen again. Stumbling back, he landed on his rear and ran a shaky hand through his hair.

Our time was about to become a thing of the past. He no longer wanted another of Garrett's pieces of shit, used up whores to fuck and kill. He wanted another like his Deb. He wanted them clean, pretty. Not used, abused, hard and diseased. Damn it, he wanted to cleanse his soul of the immorality he'd been living with since that night when he'd realized his love for his brother wasn't brotherly.

The fucking dog finally stopped its yapping. As he rose from his hiding place again, he caught the psychic drawing the blinds in her front window. Too bad her brother had shown. He needed a way to release the violence coursing through him. While he'd always known that eventually his own depravity

153

would lead to Garrett's death, he hadn't been prepared for it to happen this soon. They were forcing him to take action, to react and retaliate. Garrett had become a liability that now must be dealt with, and so did Celeste.

While he didn't necessarily believe in her psychic bullshit, a smart man always kept his bases covered. And he was smarter than the sheriff, Kain, and hell, even Garrett, combined.

He knew she'd been having visions, but he hadn't had a chance or opportunity to read the notes she'd made for Roy. Was that why Kain was with her tonight? To discuss the murders? Or maybe he was banging the little hottie. Nope, he decided. He'd known her for years. Celeste rarely dated, and he doubted she'd spread her legs for some guy passing through on a murder investigation.

Once her blinds were closed, and the street had grown quiet, he checked his hiding spot for evidence again, then made his move. He'd parked his pick-up three streets north behind an abandoned mechanic's garage. As he jogged, he couldn't stop thinking about Celeste. What if her psychic shit was for real? What if she knew about the others he and Garrett had killed?

He relaxed into a slow, steady jog. If those women were discovered, they'd pin those victims on Garrett. The MO had been the same. Raped and strangled. Still, what if she gave them information that could somehow lead to him?

Another loose end.

A loose end he would enjoy killing.

He cracked a smile. Killing Celeste would not only fuck up everyone who loved her, but everyone who had taken Garrett, his forbidden love, away from him.

Fuck. So many loose ends.

Killing Garrett would hurt. He was his brother, his partner. Although with his death came resurrection. A purification of a sort from the immorality Garrett had driven him to with his husky voice and sensual smile. But Celeste?

His pulse raced. On many levels she reminded him of his Deb. Sweet and innocent, Celeste was a pretty woman. He'd enjoy silencing her and taking her out of the investigation. Hell, maybe he'd use *her* to fulfill the fantasy he hadn't been able to complete with his Deb. Ramming his hunting knife into her gut, slicing the blade up to those perky tits she was always showing off in her tight t-shirts, while he fucked her curvy ass.

By the time he reached his truck, his dick had grown painfully hard just thinking about what he could do to Celeste. Yet as much as he'd love to fulfill that fantasy, he had a few other things to take care of first.

Garrett ranked at the top of that list.

CHAPTER 12

"GOOD MORNING," JOHN said to Bev as he entered the Sheriff's Department. He'd tried for a chipper tone, but with his current mood, the words fell flat.

"Mornin'. Roy's expecting you if you want to head back."

After thanking her, he moved out of the reception area, then into the corridor that would lead to the sheriff's office. As he approached, he slowed his steps. Male voices, spiked with anger drifted down the hallway. Realizing Roy wasn't alone, he hovered just outside the opened office door. Lloyd, Jesse, and Dan all had their backs to the door. The deputies surrounded the sheriff like a pack of wolves.

"C'mon, Roy. This is a bunch of bullshit," the Viking bitched, and slammed his hand on the desk. "We don't need outside help, at least not from him."

"I agree with Lloyd," Jesse said. "Five dead bodies? We need DCI or FBI, not some private investigator from...where's he from anyway?"

"Does he even have experience?" Dan asked.

John leaned against the door frame, wondering why he'd bothered to leave his lumpy motel bed. Last night had sucked. His argument with Celeste, after her god-awful trance, had kept him up most of the night.

This morning hadn't been any better. He'd tried contacting Ian again, but his call had rolled straight into voice mail. After leaving a message that had bordered on insubordinate, he'd huffed out of his room in search of caffeine. Unfortunately, all he'd found waiting for him at the Chippewa Inn's front foyer was a Styrofoam cup filled with coffee grounds and thick sludge.

Now, he had to deal with the sheriff's deputies and their bullshit. Considering he already had a pissed off psychic, five dead bodies, and not just one, but probably two serial killers to contend with, they were the least of his concerns. Still, if he was going to make any headway with this investigation, he'd need Roy's men on his side.

The sheriff chose that moment to make eye contact with him. His mustache twitched above a sly smile as he shrugged. "Why don't you ask him yourself?"

All three men turned and stared at him. Lloyd snarled, then turned his back and moved to the window, while Jesse and Dan looked away and hung their heads.

"Morning, Roy," John said. "Apparently I'm a hot topic today."

"Apparently," the sheriff said, amusement lacing his tone.

He rubbed his jaw. "Okay, you three want to know a little about me? Fire away."

Silence.

With a shrug, he dropped into one of the office chairs. "CORE, the company I work for, isn't just your average private investigative agency. Our resources are immeasurable, and our agents are fully trained with backgrounds that would blow you away." Sighing, he shifted in his chair wishing for a decent cup of coffee to help him deal with the overwhelmingly negative testosterone emanating in the room.

"To answer your questions, CORE is based in Chicago, and I'm former FBI." He leaned forward now that each deputy had their eyes on him. "And yes, I've dealt with these types of crimes. Actually, this isn't the worst I've seen."

Dan shook his head. "Really? Former FBI?"

Jesse released a low whistle. "What was your specialty?"

"My specialty?" He raised his shoulder. "Finding the bad

guys."

"Finding the bad guys," the Viking echoed, sarcasm dripping with each word. "I worked with a few FBI agents out of the field office in Minneapolis." He turned to Roy. "Remember that meth case?"

The sheriff nodded, but said nothing.

"You don't talk like FBI," Lloyd continued, "don't use their terms, don't—"

"Because I'm not FBI anymore," he interrupted, then looked to the sheriff. "Are we done here? There's some things I'd like to discuss...privately."

"Personally I'm done with this bullshit conversation. How 'bout it, boys? Did John answer your questions?" When no one responded, Roy leaned back in his chair. "Good. You have your assignments for today. Head on out."

"Wait," Lloyd blurted. "What about Celeste?"

"What about her?" Roy asked.

With an exasperated sigh, the Viking rounded the desk. "She could be in danger. I doubt Winston killed the woman in the bog. The MO doesn't fit and everyone in town knows she's a psychic. Have you thought about that? About the fact that the guy who sliced up that girl could go after Celeste thinking she knows something?" Lloyd asked, his steely gaze now focused on him.

"Yeah, we've considered that," John responded, reluctantly impressed with Lloyd's take on the crimes.

"Really? And what do you plan to do about it?" He turned to Roy. "Look, I know we don't have the manpower to give her round the clock protection, but I talked the situation over with Will and—"

"I'll worry about Celeste," John said, trying to keep the growl out of his tone. There was no way in hell he'd let that fucking Neanderthal stay at Celeste's house. As far as he was concerned, she was his to protect. After some groveling, he'd make her understand why he'd reacted the way he had last night, then make her his in every way possible.

Logic be damned. He wanted her. And every crazy, scary

and warm emotion she'd evoked.

"I heard about how well you were worrying about her." Thumbing toward him, Lloyd turned to the sheriff. "Celeste kicked Kain's ass to the curb last night, then ran to the basement crying."

Crying? Shit. Once again he wished he'd handled last night differently.

He met Roy's gaze. Instead of anger, the sheriff's eyes revealed a combination of curiosity and understanding.

"I think that's about enough, Lloyd. Like I said, you boys have your assignments for the day, get on out of here. And keep in mind, John's here to help. If I find out any of you are interfering with this investigation hoping to get rid of him, I'll come down on your asses. Are we clear?"

All three deputies nodded as they left. Of course the Viking had his final say by slamming the office door shut hard enough the walls rattled, skewing a few of the paintings and county maps.

"That was *exactly* what I needed this morning." John leaned into the chair. "So, I guess you'll want to know why Celeste was crying last night."

Roy raised a bushy eyebrow. "You guessed right."

John shoved out of the chair, then moved to the wall and straightened one of the pictures. "After I left the bog, I went to see her." He'd needed to after witnessing her vision come to life. He'd wanted news of the girl's death to come from him. To not only offer her comfort if she'd needed it, but to prove that he trusted her as a partner. "I...there's something I haven't told you. Celeste has graduated from her nightly visions to...trances."

"Trances? What the hell are you talking about?"

He finished straightening another painting, then lean against the wall. "When you found us parked on the side of the road, on the way to the original dump site, I'd pulled off because she'd gone into a trance. I should have told you about this right after it had happened, but Celeste had asked me not to. She's worried about putting more stress on you, and quite frankly, I...hell." He crossed his arms and rested the back of his head against the wall.

"You didn't believe her."

"Bingo," he said, with a rueful half-smile and shrugged.

"What was the trance about?"

Taking a seat, he explained what had happened in the car, how her trance had correlated with not only her notes, but the girl they'd found in the bog. Roy stayed silent, thoughtfully stroking his mustache.

"I've never known her to go into a trance before," the sheriff said. "Her mom? Well, never mind, that's not important. What happened last night?"

"Wait, her mom used to have trances, too? This is good." He nodded. "Did her mom remember anything after she woke? Was she able to control when the trances occurred? Better yet, if she were asked the right questions—"

"John, I'm sorry, but I don't have any answers for you."

"But from what I understand, you were close with Celeste's family."

"Her mom is gone, along with any knowledge about how the trances affected her. Now, let's move on, tell me about last night."

"What about her husband? Wouldn't he know?"

"Let it go," Roy said quietly, while his face reddened with irritation.

Not needing another enemy this morning, he decided to let it go—for now. "I filled her in on Winston and the girl from the bog. Then she insisted on trying to go into another trance."

Rubbing his temple, Roy asked, "For the second victim from her visions?"

He nodded. "I tried talking her out of it. I wanted you and a doctor present, but—"

"She's not only hard-headed, but she's insecure about her psychic stuff, I get it." Roy sighed. "What happened?"

He pulled his cell phone out of his pocket and set it on the desk. "Hear for yourself."

Ten minutes later, and Roy a few shades whiter, John

pocketed his phone. "Celeste doesn't remember anything from either trance, and I refused to not only let her listen to the recording, but even tell her what she'd said or done. I wanted time to think, to talk to you. But she, as Lloyd put it, kicked my ass to the curb before I could explain."

After scrubbing a hand over his face, Roy looked away. "That's some pretty powerful stuff. Hearing it's one thing, but seeing it? I'd have done the same thing. But you also have to understand Celeste. She's not only a fixer, but likes to be in control. She can't necessarily control her visions, but she can at least remember them. You said she has no memory from the trances? Well, that's going to bring the control freak right out of her."

"It probably didn't help that I'd basically ordered her off the investigation."

With a chuckle, the sheriff shook his head. "No, that's a woman you don't tell what to do."

"No shit."

"No shit," he echoed, then smacked his hand on the desk. "Can you replay her trance for me?"

Reluctantly, he set the phone back on the desk and replayed her trance. He'd listened to it several times last night, and again this morning, after he'd tossed the cup of shitty coffee down the bathroom sink. Each time he heard Celeste's tormented voice, something broke inside of him.

When the recording ended, Roy rose from his chair and went to the county map hanging on the wall. "Do you realize the leads she's given us?"

"If the man with the beard is Winston, she's confirmed that he wasn't working alone," John said. "I also believe this victim was not only raped, but sodomized. I'm anxious for the autopsy report from Carl. If the girl from the bog was anally raped..." He let his words trail. Celeste's visions and trances might not hold up in court, but they would give them leads, along with a deeper insight into the second killer.

Still squinting at the map, Roy said, "Carl had finished the final Jane Doe from the first dump site last night and is currently working on the girl from the bog. He said he should have a full report by early afternoon."

"What do you make of the mill Celeste mentioned?"

"That's what I'm looking for and...here." He jabbed his finger to a city on the map and smiled. "Tilden."

He rose and moved next to the sheriff. "Tilden?"

"There's a sheet metal factory there, the only one of its kind around these parts. I'm betting she was describing it. Lloyd's going to be heading that way, so I'll have him stop and check around the mill."

Although he hated the idea of using the Viking for anything considering he was becoming a pain in his ass, he had to admit that Lloyd seemed like a decent cop. "Sounds good, but this is even better." He skimmed a finger along highway fifty three, which ran through Tilden. "This is one of the routes Winston took when he worked for Booker Foods."

Roy pulled on his mustache. "Booker Foods?"

"Sorry, I just found out about it this morning. After I left the bog yesterday, I called one of our people at CORE, Rachel, on my way to Celeste's."

Rachel Davis, a former Army Intelligence Officer, and forensic computer scientist, had become an asset to CORE since she'd joined four years ago. She had a knack for finding things no one wanted found and had been a tremendous help on many investigations.

"I wanted Rachel to dig around and look into the companies Winston had been contracted with, starting with the most recent. If he hadn't been picked up on the DUI, he'd be heading for the West Coast as we speak."

John went back to the map. "Winston's last contract was with Booker Foods. They were gracious enough to give us his route and said your CSU team could examine the trailer. Unfortunately, that trailer is currently heading to Minnesota. CORE, with the cooperation of Booker Foods, is going to have it detained once it reaches St. Cloud and their local CSU will examine it."

"Ian's connections will never cease to amaze me," Roy said,

his tone filled with amusement and admiration. "But we have an issue I don't like. Booker Foods is a vendor Celeste uses for the diner."

He moved his finger along Winston's route, then stopped when he reached Wissota Falls. The hairs at the back of his neck rose. "Then Winston had been in contact with Celeste. He and whoever he could be working with would know about her. Maybe her schedule, her—"

"No, she doesn't deal with the drivers or the deliveries. Either Will or one of her cooks handles that. Still, with Winston working for Booker Foods…what if his partner is a local?"

Utter dread ripped a hole inside of him. He'd figured Winston had pegged the perfect place to dump the bodies because he knew the route, and when and where the deputies would patrol. But what if the second killer *was* local? What if he knew of other obscure places to leave a body? The bigger question nagging him, why would two men kill together?

"Tell me more about this mill."

"Tilden's a small town, much like Wissota Falls. The mill is its biggest business. They get big rigs through there all the time. Winston could have parked his rig there. For some reason, the owner never put up gates. There's no third shift. I think the place closes up around midnight, so no one would have noticed if he parked for a few hours during the night."

John moved away from the map and slumped into the office chair, then rubbed his chin with the back of his hand. "Okay, let's say Winston takes the victim, rapes and beats her, then waits for second guy to finish the job."

"But Winston didn't mention an accomplice in his confession."

"Maybe because he killed those women alone?" Damn, the whole situation made zero sense. Was it possible they had two killers, who sometimes worked together, and at other times killed alone?

The sheriff moved to his chair. "I'm not so sure about that. Mitchell faxed this over this morning." He waved a paper in the air. "The lighter they'd found at the dumpsite had Winston's prints on it, the coat button revealed nothing, but the footprint they'd found was two sizes too small to be his."

"Shit." There had been no footprints near the bog to even match what had been found at the original dumpsite.

"Right."

He blew out a breath. "None of this makes sense. Let's say, hypothetically, that the coat button and boot print found at the dumpsite belongs to the other killer. Why would they be working together? Did this unknown killer somehow catch Winston in the act, wanted a piece of it and then blackmailed him into playing a role in the murder?"

"And for his silence Winston helps him kill the other girls? I'm not following. How does this help Winston? He's sitting in county lock-up while the other guy is roaming free."

"I'm not sure, but yesterday, Winston shouted that he knows something I don't and that I'll be back. That I needed him." The hairs on his arms raised under his shirt sleeves as Winston's eerie words ran through his mind. "Maybe it was just the ranting of a guilty man, but what if...?"

"Yeah, what if," Roy echoed as the phone rang. He picked up the receiver. "Hey, honey. Uh-huh, you did what?" The sheriff glanced at him, then covered the receiver. "Mind giving me a minute? Bev has fresh coffee up front. I could use a cup, too."

He masked his irritation as he rose from the chair. As he made his way to the reception area and poured coffee into Styrofoam cups, his irritation turned to anger. Tired of being dismissed, not only by Roy, but it seemed by Ian considering he wasn't answering his calls, he decided it was time for answers. Starting with why Roy couldn't talk to Celeste while he was in the office. And he knew she'd been the caller based on the way the sheriff had softened his tone along with his use of the term of endearment, one he'd heard him call Celeste several times.

By the time he'd returned to the office, the sheriff was off the phone, and leaning back in the chair. His hands were folded behind his head, as he kept a thoughtful gaze trained on the ceiling.

"Here you go." He placed the coffee cup on Roy's desk, then took a seat. "You want to tell me what Celeste had to say?"

The sheriff didn't change his position, but he did release a deep sigh. "I do and I don't."

"Why's that?" he asked, then blew on the coffee before taking a drink.

"Because I know you care about her."

He froze. "Roy, I—"

The sheriff leaned forward. Resting his forearms on the desk, he shook his head. "I know it's none of my business, but Celeste is. I made a promise to her mother, her father and to...well, the point is, she needs closure. She needs to be part of this investigation in order to gain some comfort from the nightmares she's had, especially now that one of them has become a reality."

"I'm well aware of that, Roy. Why do you think I let her talk me into doing the trance last night?"

The sheriff smiled. "You're a good man, logical, perceptive."

"And you're buttering me up. What gives?"

"Celeste did a little of her own detective work this morning and found our hairstylist, Judy."

He swore he could literally feel the blood drain from his face. Fear came with a cold sweat along his forehead. "She's supposed to be at the diner," he said through clenched teeth as anger and anxiety tensed his body. "And according to Lloyd, Will was keeping an eye on her. What the fuck happened?"

The sheriff raised his hands. "It's not that big of a deal. She's fine and besides, she gave us a helluva lead."

Shoving out of his chair, he leaned into the desk. "I don't give a shit," he shouted. "I don't want her involved anymore than she already is. You heard the recording. She could be in danger." Hell, even the Viking understood that point. He shoved off the desk, then stomped to the wall and stared at one of Will's paintings. When he'd first seen the painting, the colors had soothed him, calmed him, but they didn't now. All he could picture was the girl from the bog. Her face and torso sliced. Her lifeless eyes staring back at him.

"Look," Roy began as he rose and moved next to him. "I love Celeste like a daughter, but I can't control her, and I wouldn't even try. I don't know if she's told you this, but she moved back to Wissota Falls to take of her sick mother. When her mom passed, she'd been ready to move back to Madison. To her job, and the life she'd had there. Her dad talked her into running the diner while he went off to deal with his own grief instead, despite her own dreams. Like I said though, she's a fixer. She wants everyone happy and hunky-dory, and puts others before herself."

His chest burned. Not with the chronic heartburn, but with sympathy for Celeste. She'd given up her dreams—dreams he had yet to learn about—to take care of her mom. Then, she remained in this small town, shoving her own agenda aside to help her dad.

As pissed as he was considering she'd potentially placed herself in danger, he couldn't help admiring her. She'd stepped up to the plate when her sister hadn't, keeping her career in Chicago her main focus. Will was around, but from what he understood, the brunt of the family business rested on Celeste's shoulders. Now she had the nightmares, the trances and the accumulating dead bodies to contend with, but not alone. He wanted to be there for her, but after yesterday he wasn't sure if she wanted him around, period.

"Did she mention last night?"

"No. She didn't. Celeste's not like that."

Relief and hope slipped passed the edge of fear coursing though him. She might be mad at him, but she'd kept their personal business, personal. "How'd she find the hairstylist?"

Roy grabbed the keys to his cruiser. "I'll explain along the way."

Five hours later, the sheriff dropped him off at his car. Although bone weary, mentally and emotionally drained, he started the ignition and headed for The Sugar Shack. While it was only three in the afternoon, he swore it seemed more like three in the morning.

Thanks again to Celeste they'd tracked down the hairstylist, Judy Frank, at the Slinging Scissors Salon located in Altoona. From a photo, Judy had ID'd the girl from the bog as Courtney Harrison. From there everything went to shit. They'd contacted Harrison's parents, who had just returned from an all-inclusive trip to Mexico this morning, only to inform them that their daughter was likely in the morgue.

Having parents ID their child's body was never easy. The Chicago case he'd been assigned to before coming to Wissota Falls had been tough, but still not enough to prepare him for any of this. Courtney Harrison was an only child. A seventeen-year-old beauty queen, with a potential full ride to Harvard, she had more opportunity than most. But now she was dead, and the grief he'd witnessed from her parents had left him hollow and aching.

Carl had confirmed that Courtney had been sodomized. Cause of death, a sharp object, likely a long, serrated knife, had damaged major organs as it ripped through her torso causing her to bleed out. She'd been dead before she'd hit the water.

With this knowledge, coupled with Celeste's trance, he tried to come up with a profile for Courtney's killer. Winston had been easy. He appeared to be a true sociopath. He'd charmed the women he'd killed and had felt no remorse. The man who'd killed Courtney? Something didn't settle well with him as he tried to dissect him on the drive over to The Sugar Shack.

There was something diabolical in the way he'd cut Courtney's face and torso. Something John couldn't quite grasp. Normally, he'd peg a killer for what he was, but this time he couldn't put his finger on it. Because he'd allowed his emotions for Celeste to cloud his judgment? Or maybe because this was just one fucked up case?

He had hoped Harrison's autopsy would have revealed more, but it hadn't. He'd also hoped Lloyd would discover something in Tilden that could help their case. That end came up empty as well. Not that he wanted another dead body on their hands, but another lead would have been nice.

He parked the sedan in the street outside of The Sugar Shack. While apprehensive about how Celeste might react to seeing him, he also couldn't suppress the anticipation. Being in the same room with her gave him a calming effect. He just hoped to God she'd at least talk to him, give him a chance to explain why he'd reacted the way he had yesterday.

As he entered the diner, he immediately searched for Celeste. When he didn't see her, he settled into the same stool he'd sat in just two days before. How things had changed in a matter of forty-eight hours. She'd turned his world upside down, and had made him think long and hard about his life, his career. She'd made him realize he didn't *have* a life outside of his career. She made him want more. Did she?

"What can I get for you?" a forty-something woman, with a pinched expression asked as she walked toward him.

"Is Celeste around?"

She eyed him with skepticism. "No, she's left for the day."

"What about Will?"

"Will's out back dealing with inventory, but if you're a salesman, you could talk to me. I'm Karen, the assistant manager," she finished with a raise of a haughty, penciled eyebrow.

He drew some cash from his wallet, then laid a five dollar bill on the counter. "Thanks for your time," he said, then left before he searched out Will and rearranged his face. Why the hell wasn't he watching Celeste? According to that fucking Viking, they'd had her covered. Bullshit. And from here on out, the only one covering her would be him. He'd prefer naked, but at this point fully clothed would work so long as she was protected.

He sped down Main Street, ignoring every traffic law until he reached Celeste's driveway. With Courtney Harrison's autopsy came the confirmation that they were dealing with another killer. Celeste could be in danger, especially if the killer was local, as Roy had suggested. He might know about her gift and suspect she'd been working with them on the investigation.

With the ignition off, he sat in Celeste's driveway gripping the door handle tight enough his palms started to sweat. During the drive over to The Sugar Shack, and again to her house, he'd done a mental play of how things could go down when he confronted her. Although he'd appreciated the leads she'd given them, he was still pissed at her total disregard for her own safety.

Maybe you should have given her a reason to worry last night.

Shit. He hadn't. He'd channeled his fear into anger, and laid down an almighty decree. She couldn't, wouldn't play a part in the investigation. Regret punched a hole in his stomach as Roy's words filtered through his memory. Celeste liked control, but held little over her life thanks to her mother's death, her dad's grief, and her siblings' lack of involvement. She'd lost control of her visions, the trances, and he'd done what everyone else around her had done—he'd tried to take more control away from her.

He hadn't meant to. Protecting her had been his first priority. But she deserved more than just his protection. She deserved to know what happened during her trances. She deserved to be his partner in every sense.

Determined to set things right between them, he climbed out of the sedan, then walked up the brick pathway leading to her front door. A dozen wide-eyed gnomes grinned at him with menace, reminding him of her vindictive streak. The story she'd told him about her neighbor, coupled with the temper he'd encountered last night, had his gut clenching as he knocked on the door.

Would she see him? Probably. Would the sparkle of desire heat her eyes? Or would she kick his ass straight to the curb again?

The door opened.

Time to find out.

***

Running a hand through his hair, Dr. Alex Trumane paced his living room. Every few seconds, he stupidly glared at his silent phone, waiting for the call that might lead to his final atonement.

Number Twenty-two. Miranda Gates.

He'd called her last night, but the number had been given to someone else. Some young punk who'd told him to fuck off, that the woman he'd been looking for didn't live with him and to not call again. He dug deeper.

In the files he had on his computer was the phone number to her next of kin, her grandmother. Unfortunately, that proved to be another dead end. The phone had been disconnected. He dug even deeper.

After hours of searching, he'd discovered the grandmother, Anna Gates, had been a patient of one of his former colleagues, Doug Broen. He'd done his residency with Broen, and had more shit on him than the man knew. Broen wasn't a lush like him, but had issues with prescription drugs. He'd witnessed his drug abuse, and hadn't been afraid to threaten him to obtain the information he'd needed. Information that would hopefully lead to his final atonement.

He'd called Doug at home, late last night, and had been waiting for him to call back since early this morning. With a glare at his cell phone again, he slumped on the couch. Broen was pulling utter bullshit on him. He knew how doctor's offices worked, hell, he'd had his own practice for nearly fifteen years. All Doug had to do was look into her files and give him Gates' new address and phone number. If that prick...

The phone rang. His heart jumped.

Not recognizing the number, he answered, "Trumane."

"Alex, it's Doug."

His heart rate kicked up a notch, along with hope. "What did you find?"

"You do realize this goes against policy, right?"

Broen's fear made sense, along with why he'd used a different phone to call him. Doug wanted nothing traced back to him. "So does taking prescription drugs illegally," he shot back.

"God, I hate former abusers who think that now that they're clean, they're holier than thou."

"Cut the shit, what do you have for me?"

"She's dead," Doug said with a heavy sigh.

He gripped the phone, wishing, not for the first time today, for a cold beer or a shot of whisky. "When?"

"Five years ago."

He'd given Miranda Gates her diagnosis around the same time. Anxiety had him clutching the phone tighter. "Cause of death?"

"Hell, Alex, she was eighty-eight. She'd been found dead, in her bed. You know the drill, at that age, no autopsy was done, and cause of death was listed as natural."

"Natural," he echoed. How convenient. "Sorry for bothering you, but thanks for your time." He hung up the phone, then rebooted his laptop. He found the number he was looking for and placed the call.

"Hi," he began, then decided to thicken his southern accent and pour on the charm. "I'd like to order a copy of a will. Do you think you can help me? I sure would appreciate it."

The woman on the other end assured him she could, but only in a hard copy. Mississippi didn't offer archived wills to be viewed online. Although disappointed, because he wanted the information now, he gave his credit card information to pay for the copy. Afterward, she'd promised him that the Last Will and Testament of Anna Lynn Gates would be in his mailbox within the next two days.

Two days. He'd have to sit and bide his time. Wait.

God, he wanted a drink.

CHAPTER 13

CELESTE SHOULDN'T HAVE opened the door knowing John was on the other side. Last night's argument had given her the perfect way to sever whatever it was between them and keep her heart intact. But she couldn't help herself. Devastatingly gorgeous, with thick black hair, dark eyes and broad shoulders a woman could hang on to, physically, he was everything she craved. Yet that craving ran deeper. She couldn't deny the connection they shared, the unexplainable need and deep emotional attraction. Or the way he'd already wormed his way into her heart.

"Ever hear of calling first?" she asked, going for ticked off nonchalant even as her pulse raced. "I know you own a cell phone. If I recall, you used it last night."

"Do you think we could leave the sarcasm at the door and talk inside? Please. It's important. To me, to us."

She raised her gaze to his, caught the regret and longing in his eyes and caved. "Sure, but I don't have much time though. I have paperwork to do and—"

"Why aren't you at work?" he asked, an edge to his tone.

"Will's there, and besides, as of today, I have a new assistant manager." Something she should have done several years ago rather than completely burden herself with the business. Maybe now she'd finally find the time to have a life outside of the diner.

"Karen? I met her when I stopped by the diner looking for you."

"Yeah, she's great. She's been working at The Sugar Shack for years, and knows everything about it. I should have given her the promotion a long time ago."

"But you didn't want to lose control." He moved into the foyer, glancing between the living room and dining room. "You're alone?"

"Duh," she muttered with exasperation, and took a seat on the couch.

"I thought you were leaving the sarcasm at the door."

"I'm not being sarcastic, I'm pissed. Would you like me to show you another example to help clarify the difference?"

He raised his hands and dropped to the other end of the couch. "Please, don't indulge me." With a weary sigh, and an even wearier frown crossing his face, he pulled his cell phone from his pants pocket, then set it on the coffee table.

She eyed the phone. "What are you doing? And why shouldn't I be alone?"

"Your last trance will give you the answers. You did want to hear it, right?"

Panic rose to the surface and had her scooting her legs beneath her. "I did, I mean, I do. Why the turnaround?"

He reached for her hand. "Last night, I didn't mean to come off all hard-assed. I'm sorry for that. But I was only trying protect you, not control you."

Rolling her eyes, she released a heavy sigh. "There's a novelty," she said, then cringed. "Sorry, no more sarcasm."

His eyes darkened with anguish and regret. "No, actually, I think sarcasm fits. When was the last time you did something just for you?"

She looked down at the new acrylic nails, applied this morning and painted cherry red. The manicure had been done on a whim, but she knew he wasn't talking about trivial vanity. He was talking about every aspect of her life.

Apparently Roy had filled John in on the other details she hadn't divulged. Although she'd prefer him to have kept his big mouth shut, she understood. Roy wanted nothing but the best for her. If he'd shared personal information about her to John, he'd done it to protect her.

Just like John had last night.

"I know where you're going with this."

His brows rose as he edged closer. "You do? Is this some sort of psychic thing?"

"No," she half-laughed. "I meant that I understand you were looking out for me, not trying to control me."

"Good."

"But I'd still like to hear the recording."

A flash of disappointment crossed his face. "Fine, before you do though, that lead you gave us on the hairdresser paid off big time. Great job."

"Really?" She hadn't expected that. After he'd left last night, she'd practically run to her basement where she'd put her anger, frustration, and hurt into some serious baking.

While she'd placed the croissants that were needed for this morning's breakfast rush at the diner into the double oven, she'd had a Nancy Drew moment. She'd been unable to shake the lead on the hairdresser out of her head. She'd also been determined to show John she deserved to remain a part of the investigation, so she'd called the hair salon she used and made an appointment.

At the time, the idea had seemed brilliant, but this morning as she'd stood in Eau Claire's only posh salon, she'd thought it plain stupid. How many hairstylists by the name of Judy worked in Wisconsin? Yet her stylist, Tish, knew her, and had not only given her a well needed trim, but a lead. She'd also been the one to talk her into the manicure.

"Yeah, thanks to you, we were able to ID the girl from the bog. Her parents had been out of town, which was why there hadn't been a missing persons report on her." He sighed, and she caught the sadness in his eyes before he spoke again. "They saw her body earlier this afternoon and confirmed that she's their daughter."

"What was her name?"

"Courtney."

"Courtney," she echoed, and with her stomach churning, she hugged a throw pillow to her chest and nodded to the cell phone. "Let me hear."

"You're sure? You don't have to. I could just tell you what you'd said."

"Like you did with the trance I had in your car *about* Courtney?"

"Welcome back Miss Sarcasm."

"Sorry," she said with a sheepish shrug. "Were you able to gain any leads off this last trance?"

With a gusty sigh, he nodded. "Yes."

"Good, tell me about them afterward. Could you please play it for me now?" she asked before losing her nerve. She'd never had a trance until two days ago. Her mother never mentioned having them, either. While she needed to know what she'd said, what she'd physically gone through, a part of her would rather bury her head in the sand. She feared the trance might be way worse than any vision she'd ever endured.

"Fine." He hit a button on his cell.

The living room filled with her recorded voice, rambling on about how she'd saved Lloyd. She smiled at the memory, and the man he'd become, then again as John's soothing and affectionate voice mingled with hers. She looked at him then, and realized this was only the calm before the storm.

His eyes had grown wild with anger and fear. She'd seen the same look last night, but it hadn't registered. Dread gripped her, especially when the recording went dead silent.

She waited, her heart pounding with anticipation. Then a low whisper drifted from the cell phone. She barely recognized her own voice, the sheer terror it held as it ebbed, then faded. Cold fear wrapped around her, sending chills through her body.

Suddenly a shocking, horrifying scream sliced through the room. She jumped, then cowered into the sofa cushions. The cold fear that had cocooned her with icy fingers became a frightening maelstrom of panic and dread.

She rocked back and forth as her living room filled with her voice, so desperate and scared. Gripping the pillow tighter while tears streamed down her cheeks, she wished the stupid cell phone would somehow malfunction. All she'd have to do was tell John to put an end to it and she knew he would. She couldn't bring herself tell him, though. Somehow the second victim from her visions had channeled herself though her body last night, and as much as she didn't want to hear anymore, she forced herself to listen. The woman deserved to be heard. She deserved justice.

Silently crying, her stomach knotting, then twisting with horror and anxiety, she sat through it all. The brutal sodomy and the eventual death of the woman who had been beaten by her mother, been called fat and useless, then murdered by two sick bastards without a care.

As her tinny voice faded, she honed in on the alarm that edged John's voice as he'd tried to rouse her from the trance. Regret, sharp and painful, sliced her to the core. She'd been selfish and childish, and now wished to God she hadn't forced him to relive the trance once again.

Wiping her eyes, she met his gaze. "I think I've heard enough...wait," she said, as the almighty decree he'd laid on her after the trance filtered from the cell phone. As she listened, she couldn't stop the guilt resonating through her mind. She'd remembered that moment, when she'd first woken, disoriented and discombobulated. He'd only wanted to protect her from herself and she'd lashed out at him.

The recording ended. Deafening silence followed.

Yet her head swirled with her voice and his. The rape and murder of the unknown woman mingled with his compassion and his panic. At that moment, the cold fear which had been clutching her tightly diminished, warmth spread throughout her body and straight into her heart and soul. She'd abruptly stumbled into the impossible. A man worth risking her heart, despite the consequences.

"Are you okay?" he asked, his eyes trained on her, his fists clenched as if he was holding back from touching her.

She needed his touch right now, his comfort and strength. "The leads from this," she said, waving a hand at the cell phone. "God, John, there's so many."

He pocketed the phone. "I know."

"Winston had to be the man with the beard. If he's in jail that means..." She tossed the pillow to the floor and ran a shaky hand across her forehead. Fear greater than she'd ever experienced rippled through her. "That means the other killer could be anywhere. Even here, in Wissota Falls."

Now she understood why he didn't think she should be alone. Why he'd been angry, afraid and determined to protect her. If the killer knew she was involved with the investigation, she could become one of his victims. She shuddered, swiping the tears from her face. "I'm so sorry, John. I didn't know."

In an instant he was beside her, cradling her in his arms. "I know, baby. I'm sorry you had to listen to it."

"My fault. I'm the one who insisted. You tried to stop me, tried to protect me."

He drew back, then cupped her face with his large, warm palms. "I promise you'll be protected. Even if it means I have to sleep on your couch every night until we catch him. I swear. I won't let anything happen to you."

The vehemence and determination in his voice, along with the prospect of having him at her house every night, made her heart clench. Only...while he'd said he cared about her, she'd rather have him staying the night because he wanted to, not as a watchdog. "Thank you. But you don't have to do that. I could have Will or Lloyd—"

"No." He dropped his hands to her shoulders and gave her a gentle squeeze. "I mean, that's fine if I have to be away for some reason, but I'd rather..." He sighed and rested his forehead against hers.

Slipping one hand into his hair, she asked, "Stay with me?"

"Yeah," he whispered, his breath fanning across her lips as he nudged his nose against hers. "How do you feel about that?" He brushed his mouth against the corner of hers. "How do you feel about complicated?"

She raised her head and stared into his eyes. The need and passion in their dark depths nearly took her breath away. Yet her stomach tightened with a combination of hopefulness and despair. Complicated could break her heart. But she'd endure the hurt, the pain of losing him once he left Wissota Falls. He'd come to mean so much to her in such a short time. She'd rather give herself to him, take what he offered now, however much he was capable of, and worry about the consequences later. She'd been so lonely, and cared for him too deeply.

She slipped her hand to his cheek. "Complicated? I think I can handle that."

He sifted his hands through her hair and held her head, her lips inches from his. "You're sure?"

"Yes," she whispered, then with their eyes locked she leaned into him.

His firm lips crushed against hers. She met his searing kiss, savored his taste, his hot caress as he moved his hand down her back forcing her chest against his. As he deepened the kiss, thrusting and twining his tongue against hers, she knew what was about to happen went way beyond complicated. The complexity of their relationship, their situation could be dealt with later, though. Right now, she wanted to feel. His passion, his lust, his hands and mouth on every inch of her body.

The clouds shifted, and afternoon sunlight spilled into the living room through the large bay windows. With reluctance, she drew away from his burning kiss afraid her nosy neighbor might pass down the sidewalk and catch her and John on the couch having sex. She hadn't been with a man in years, and there was no way in hell she'd allow the wicked witch next door, or the afternoon paperboy, or anyone else to interfere with her pleasure.

She caught his frown and smiled. "I like a little kink, but I'm not an exhibitionist," she said, and nodded to the windows.

Grinning, he took her hand, and he helped her from the couch. "I'm intrigued. Define a little kink for me."

Rising to her tiptoes, she leaned in then gave his lower lip a playful tug with her teeth. "Would you really rather stand here and talk the afternoon away?"

His eyes grew impossibly darker and swirled with heat. "No way," he said against her lips before he kissed her. His tongue, teeth and lips seduced hers as they made their way from the living room. When they reached the foyer, anxious to have his hands on her, she jerked her t-shirt over her head and dropped it on the floor.

He cupped her breasts as they moved toward the steps leading to the second floor, to her bedroom. Teasing her nipples through the lace of her bra with his fingers, he dragged his lips and tongue along her neck. When the first step hit the back of her calf, she clung to his broad shoulders for support. With a rough chuckle, he lifted her in his arms.

"What are you doing?" She hadn't been carried like this since she'd been a child.

He kissed the tip of her nose. "Getting us to your bedroom before we wind up making love on the steps."

Making love.

That wasn't what they were about to do, but it did have a nice ring to it.

Sex.

That's all this afternoon would amount to. Hot, raw, passionate sex.

And she'd take what she could, even if she knew deep down, to the darkest depths of her soul, that she wanted more. That she wanted to take things beyond complicated.

When he finally reached her bedroom, his lips still locked on hers, he set her down on the bed. Breathing hard, he broke away, then kissed a path from her neck to her stomach. "You have too many clothes on." He unfastened her jeans, then dragged them down her legs.

Heat flooded between her thighs. "Same goes for you." Prepared to try to play the part of a seductress, loosen his belt, unbutton his shirt, she moved toward him. Her hands shook, along with her entire body. The need to have him over her, under her, inside her was too overwhelming. The heat and lust in his eyes made it difficult to navigate the buttons on his shirt.

He brushed her hands away. "Let me."

With amazing speed, he unbuttoned his shirt. As soon as he'd stripped down to his boxer briefs, he covered her with his hard body. She wished he would have waited a second or two. Unsure if this was a one time thing, she wanted to memorize each and every detail of the contours of his body. The moment his lips met hers he twisted and positioned her on top of him. She lost all sense of thought.

Releasing her lips, he peppered the column of her throat with firm, open-mouthed kisses, then followed the trail with his velvety tongue. Nibbling and nipping at her sensitive skin, he skimmed his hands along her spine.

He sighed into her ear before giving her lobe a gentle nip. "Take your bra off for me. Let me see you."

The wannabe seductress inside her took advantage. She straddled his erection, wishing he would have removed his boxers when he'd stripped. She wanted him naked and inside of her. But they had time for that.

With her hands balanced on his chest, she stared down at him. His eyes gleamed with passion. His heart drummed under her palms. With a shamelessness she'd never experienced before, she teased her fingers through the hair lining the slabs of muscle across his chest. She loved the feel of his hardness under her hands and moved lower to explore, trailing her fingertips to where the hair disappeared beneath his boxers.

She scooted down a bit, then rubbed her hand along the length of him, and lifted her lips in a small smile when he caught his breath. When he dropped his head against the mattress, she stroked him. Rubbing, gripping...

John sucked in a deep breath and covered her hand with his. "Stop." Christ, he hadn't had sex in two years, if she kept touching him, he'd come in a matter of seconds. And he wasn't ready for that yet. He wanted to enjoy her body, make her his in every way possible. "The bra," he reminded her.

She cocked her head to the side as if she were considering, then flashed him a seductive smile. Damn, she was something else. Her head fell back, blond curls brushed her shoulders as she reached her arms behind her. He held his breath while he watched her take her sweet time, toying and teasing, tormenting and inflaming his lust.

Finally, she slipped her lacy bra down her toned arms. Her breasts danced with the movement and his mouth watered for a taste of her nipples.

"You're absolutely beautiful." He leaned forward, then grabbed her rear. Grinding her against his cock, he latched onto one of those rosy peaks. She tasted as sweet as she smelled. Sugar and spice. He feasted, sucked and tugged on one stiff peak before moving to the other. Heaven. Pure bliss. He wanted...needed more.

He moved her beneath him, gave one wet nipple a final kiss, then stood between her outstretched legs. She was an erotic picture. Creamy skin flushed and heated. Loose blond curls spilling across the bed, pink nipples begging for attention.

He leaned over her, ran his hand along the column of her throat. Caressed her full breasts then trailed his fingers across her flat stomach. When he reached her panties, he grabbed the waistband and practically tore them from her body.

No more teasing. Not now. He'd lusted after her since the moment they'd met, that initial erotic, sensual touch never far from his mind. But what he'd felt for her had become more than that. He cared. Deeper than he'd ever cared about a woman before. He'd joked about making love on the stairs, but in reality, it wasn't a joke. He wasn't about to make that leap between lust and love, or caring and love, or sex and love.

Fuck. Talk about complicated.

He pushed his thoughts aside and focused on her, on now. Skimming his fingers up her legs, he spread her thighs, then bent his head and took her the way he'd hungered and craved.

She jerked as he covered her with his lips. Moaning, she rocked her pelvis to meet each and every stroke of his tongue. Her taste filled his senses and flared his hunger. He nipped and licked, lashed his tongue.

Her little pants and gasps drove him crazy, spurred him.

Catching her clit between his lips he sucked, long and hard, then plunged two fingers between her thighs. She came. Her orgasm shook her body, clenched around his fingers, and the taste of it on his tongue had him harder than he'd ever been in his life.

Needing to bury himself inside her, feel every erotic, sensual sensation, he stood and stripped off his boxers. She'd pushed herself onto her elbows and stared at his stiff cock. Her eyes grew adorably wide. He nearly came on the spot when she licked her lips and gave him a seductive, sexy grin.

"Is it my turn?"

He stroked his cock. "Not today, baby, I need you now."

"Next time?"

The uncertainty in her tone made him pause. Not a plea. Not a need of promise. A simple question that he couldn't believe she'd even ask. He hadn't been with a woman in two years. Before that, his relationships had been casual.

How would she know?

She wouldn't, and now wasn't the time to explain his past.

He didn't want casual with Celeste, and knew once he was inside her, he'd never want to be anywhere else. She'd become important to him on so many levels he couldn't comprehend, not with the taste of her still lingering on his tongue and her gorgeous thighs spread wide for him.

"I asked you if you liked complicated." He kissed the entrance of her wet, swollen sex with his cock, and locked his eyes on hers. "And I want complicated. Next time can't come too soon."

He thrust inside her.

They both groaned.

The feel of her gripping his cock magnified the untried emotions ripping through his body. Straight to the darkest parts of his soul. Buried between her thighs, her sex convulsing around him magnified the emotions he'd tried to deny, emotions he now welcomed. Blatant trust, true devotion, from him, from her...

"John," she moaned. "I swear...I've never felt anything like this..." The rest of her words were lost on another husky moan when he pumped deeper.

"I know, baby, I feel it too." Making love to Celeste had become the most intimate moment of his life. He'd never felt this connected to someone. And he never wanted the connection to end.

But he wanted to feel her release wrapped around his cock. To feel every emotion she wouldn't share with words race through his body. She'd tried to hide so much from him, but couldn't now. Not when they were joined, skin to skin, flesh to flesh.

He quickened his rhythm. Like a piston, he worked his slick cock between her outstretched legs. Needing to make her come, needing to feel the ripples of her release, he drove deeper.

She wrapped her legs around his rear and arched her back. She surged her body, met each hard thrust. As he pressed his body into hers, her hot breath caressed his throat. She reached around and hung onto his ass, stroked and massaged, pushed him deeper. Possessed him as he possessed her.

He released a low groan and raised himself above her. Cool air seeped between their damp bodies and he already missed the feel of her breasts against his chest.

He looked down at her and caught his breath. She had to be the most beautiful woman he'd ever known. Her cheeks glowed. Her eyes were heavy lidded. Her swollen lips parted. Golden hair spread across the pillow.

He wrapped her ankles around his shoulders and moved his hips.

Once. So hot. Twice. So tight.

"Oh, John...that's it, right...there," she gasped and with her elbows propped under her, she thrust her hips to meet him. "Yes. Harder. Please...harder."

Her muscles tightened around his cock. Her nipples jutted forward. Unable to resist them, he bent his head for another taste. She gasped and his balls tightened in response. He popped the nipple from his mouth and drove deep. Hard, fast, he pressed himself into her, felt her release nearing and knew he wouldn't be far behind.

"That's it, baby, let me hear you."

He plunged himself over and over, as if he were a battering ram knocking down the doors of sexual ecstasy. She arched her body, then dropped her head against the mattress. Tiny gasps escaped her parted lips. "John, I..." she said, then cried out.

As her orgasm shot through her body, somewhere, in the deep recesses of his brain, he realized he wasn't wearing a condom. He had to pull out, but not just yet. Her muscles stimulated him, sucked him deep into her womb. He didn't want to miss a minute, yet couldn't take the chance. So close, so...

He quickly pulled out and released himself across her flat stomach. His breath came in harsh pants as he emitted a deep growl.

It took him a moment to gather his wits. Celeste's sexy legs were still propped over his shoulders and she wore a naughty, little smile which made his spent cock pulse and his blood hum.

"I...uh." He tucked his head toward his shoulder and kissed her ankle before drawing her feet back to the mattress.

She reached up, ran a hand through his hair, then arched her body to give him a slow sensual kiss. "Shhh, thank God one of us had sense enough. I'm not on the pill and the thought of condoms never entered my mind." She nipped at his lower lip. "Next time," she whispered, her smile curving against his mouth.

He brushed his lips against hers. "I can't wait for next time." Kissing her forehead, he rose from the bed, then returned with a towel from the master bathroom. "I'm sorry," he said as he wiped away his passion. "I should have been better prepared."

She placed her hand on his cheek. "If you were, then I might wonder if this is how you usually operate."

Gripping her hand, he kissed her palm. "Celeste, I haven't..."

Her eyes widened. "I'm sorry, I didn't mean to imply...God, I really need to think before I speak," she finished with an adorably rueful smile.

"No, you're fine. It's just...I've never—"

His cell phone's muffled ring stopped him midsentence. Damn it. He wanted to talk. Tell her this wasn't his MO. That he'd never been involved with a woman during a case, and for some reason, tell her all about Renee.

As he rose from the bed, searching for his pants and ringing phone, that last thought stunned him. With the exception of the grueling queries from his FBI supervisors and psychologists, he'd never talked about Renee. Yet, he'd wanted to spill every detail. He wanted to make her understand. Why she was special to him. Why he was a bastard.

Jerking his ringing cell from his pant pocket, he immediately recognized the number. "Sorry, it's Roy," he said to her.

She stretched, arching her back as she stifled a yawn. "Take your time," she said, her voice drowsy, as she curled to her side.

He couldn't take his eyes off her nipples, or the curve of her hips. If the sheriff hadn't called...

"Kain," he answered, terse, pissed. He wanted to snuggle with Celeste, sleep the afternoon away, then make love to her all over again.

"We've got a problem," the sheriff said, his tone filled with dread.

He gripped the phone. "What is it?"

"John," he said with a heavy sigh. "We found another body."

CHAPTER 14

AFTER DROPPING CELESTE off at The Sugar Shack, John plugged the address Roy had given him into the portable GPS, then hit the gas. As he drove, he contemplated calling Ian, then decided against it. Rather than piss himself off again when he'd likely end up with Ian's voice mail, he called Rachel Davis instead. He needed her help more than Ian's.

She answered on the first ring, the steady tapping of her computer keys apparent in the background. "Hey, John. Things getting any better in Wisconsin?" she asked, exaggerating her own Midwestern accent.

He smiled despite the severity of the situation. "Not good. We have another victim. I'm heading to the crime scene now."

The tapping stopped. "That makes six, right?" she asked with a lisp, meaning she was likely chomping on a pencil. A bad habit she'd picked up before joining CORE, and one she always did when her mind was spinning with angles and ideas.

"Pop the pencil out of your mouth before you get a splinter, or chip another tooth. Keep it up and Ian might revoke your dental coverage."

"Don't nag me," she said. "I'm not in the mood. Owen had me on a wild goose chase earlier today and ended up putting me behind on my own stuff, which Ian's been bitching about." She released a frustrated sigh, and he pictured her fisting her short, auburn hair, and narrowing her large green eyes.

"Sorry you're having a bad day," John said. "I think I'd

rather deal with Owen and Ian's bullshit than look at another dead woman."

"Always one upping me, aren't you? Okay, you got me beat. What do you need?"

"Is Owen finished with his current case? I could use him here." Owen Malcolm was former Secret Service, an excellent investigator, interrogator and negotiator. He had a way with words, a way of fitting in where he didn't belong. The running joke was that he could probably steal the church collection basket while seducing a nun, and still charm a priest into forgiveness.

"Nope. He probably won't be back until sometime next week. If Ian didn't have me chained to this desk, I'd come help."

Rachel had yet to go into the field, and had been chomping at the bit for some out-of-office action for months. "You're our eyes and ears, along with the best researcher any of us could have ever asked for. You're needed at base."

"While much appreciated, the sweet talk isn't necessary. Now tell me what you need."

"You tracked the last contract Garrett Winston had, would you be able to do it again, only this time dig deeper?"

"Sure, how deep?"

While he suspected he was going to end up on the top of her shit list, he had a hunch that needed to be followed. "As far back as you can go. Rachel, I know it's a pain in the ass, but I think he's a serial rapist and murderer. I want to—"

"Take a look at all of his former routes, compare them to cold cases with the same MO that you're dealing with in Wissota Falls. Got it. And you're right, it'll be a pain in my ass, but it beats the hell out of what I've been working on today. I'll call you later when I have something."

Damn she was good. "Thanks, Rachel."

"No problem. And John? Um...oh geez," she muttered, her Upper Midwestern accent rising to the surface again. "I never know what to say when one of you are heading out to look at a crime scene."

Celeste's face, while she'd been under the second trance, flashed in his mind. Reddening as she fought to breathe, hands clawing at the phantom cord around her neck. "Not a whole lot. Just call me when you have something. And keep that pencil out of your mouth." He disconnected the call and eased off highway fifty-three, turning into Tilden.

Minutes later, he drove his rental through the gates of Hess Steel and Fabricating. The mill was not only Tilden's largest manufacturer, but employed more than half of the town.

Slowing down, he realized they weren't going to be able to keep this murder from the media. Mill workers flooded the parking lot, some nodding toward the CSU vans and deputy cruisers, while others were either on their cell phones or using them to film the scene. News of the murder would spread fast. The Internet and small town gossip would see to it, and Matt Boysen, who'd been true to his word so far, would probably spill every detail he had on the other five murder victims before someone else did.

He parked his car next to one of the police cruisers, then went to the trunk to retrieve a couple of pairs of shoe covers and Latex gloves. As he slammed the trunk shut, a muffler backfired and the crowd ducked. He swung his head and caught sight of a rusted-out minivan.

Speak of the devil.

As Matt Boysen parked his van, John headed toward where Roy stood.

"Matt makes a hell of an entrance," Roy said with a shake of his head.

"You're going to have to give him something. With the amount of people hanging around here, it's going to leak anyway."

"What about Celeste?"

"Her name stays out."

"I'd already made that crystal clear to him yesterday. What I want to know is where she is now and who's looking out for her?"

"I dropped her off at the diner. Will said he'd bring her

home and stay at the house."

Relief crossed the sheriff's face before he narrowed his eyes. "You ready for this?"

"Not really. Tell me how the hell Lloyd came out here today, found nothing, then a few hours later—"

"I know you've got a hard-on for Lloyd, and I don't blame you after the way he's been acting. But he was out here. I talked with the owner of the mill and he confirmed it. A couple of kids were playing in the woods that butt up against the mill's property. There's a drainage pipe that filters to a little creek. Kids like to look for crayfish there."

The heartburn returned. "Kids found her?"

"Unfortunately. Dan's with them over there," he said, and nodded toward the deputy's cruiser.

Two boys, both appearing to be around ten or eleven years old, slumped against the cruiser, their faces pale, their eyes hollow with fear. "Where are their parents?"

"They've been notified and are on their way. The kids have been questioned. They said they didn't touch anything, just ran as fast as they could to the mill when they saw the girl. The good news? They've already ID'd her as Lauren Sundahl."

A quick ID was a great start. If they could pinpoint her last known whereabouts, who she'd associated with, those leads might help them. "Excellent. How did they know her?"

"She works at the Mini-Mart—a convenient store and gas station at the center of town. The kids said she was cool because she used to give them a break on candy and gum when they didn't have enough money."

He glanced back at the boys again, wondering how this would affect them. "Have you seen the body?"

"No, I was waiting on you. Lloyd was first to the scene. I arrived the same time as Mitchell and his team. They're already working the area."

John pulled an extra pair of boot covers from his pocket and handed them to the sheriff, who shook his head. "I'm prepared this time." He pointed to his boots, which were already covered.

"Good, then I guess we're ready."

"Hardly," Roy muttered as they made their way up a small slope. When they reached the top, he pointed to a well-used path.

Nodding, John followed him. As they moved deeper into the woods, the trees thickened, darkening the area, making it appear more like dusk than late afternoon. When bright yellow tape caught his attention, he reached in his pocket and drew out a few antacids. Like the sheriff, he'd come prepared this time. While the heartburn hadn't completely set in yet, he had a feeling it would in a matter of minutes.

While working for both the FBI and CORE, he'd viewed many dead bodies. But this one in particular had him on edge. Through Celeste, he'd felt *this* victim's pain and fear.

He had watched her die.

No, he had watched Celeste die in her place.

Mitchell approached as they neared the police tape. "John, Sheriff," he said with a curt nod. "Been seein' way too much of each other lately."

"No shit," Roy grumbled. "What have you got for us?"

"Come see for yourself."

As they followed Mitchell, John couldn't help the sick anticipation twisting his stomach. Since the second trance, he hadn't been able to push the image of Celeste being raped and murdered by two men from his mind. Although irrational and illogical, considering Celeste had simply worked as the woman's conduit, he hadn't been able to stop the memory. Still, he needed to erase Celeste's image from his mind and replace it with the victim's.

"There she is," Mitchell said, pointing to the drainage pipe.

Conscious of his steps, he moved toward the victim. When the stench of her decomposing flesh hit him, he stopped. His eyes burned and watered, nausea tumbled through his stomach. Blinking, he turned away and coughed into his shoulder, fighting the bile burning the back of his throat.

"This area clean?" he asked Mitchell.

"Yeah, I had my team work the victim first. They're

combing the surrounding area as we speak. Once we move her, we'll take another look inside the drainage pipe. For now, go ahead and look all you want."

"Roy?"

"I'm good, I can see enough from where I'm standing."

"Wussing out on me?" John asked as he slipped a small flashlight from his pocket, and began moving toward the victim.

"You betcha."

He couldn't blame the sheriff from keeping his distance. And as he moved closer, flicking the beam of light into the drainage pipe, he suddenly wanted to wuss out, too.

A slow steady stream of murky water trickled passed the young woman's nude body, and led into a small creek. Her head, partially coated in mud, and fully coated in bruises, dangled from the edge of the cement pipe.

He crouched closer, and gagged.

"Flies might be disgusting, but in this case, they're a beautiful thing." Mitchell crouched next to him. "The girl in the bog—"

"Courtney," John snapped, tired of the bog tag line. Hell, he was tired of this entire fucked up case.

"Right, Courtney had insect larva on her, several kinds in fact. Because she'd likely been submersed in water for a while before she'd surfaced, the timeline wouldn't be as concise as what you see here." He pointed to the cuts on Lauren Sundahl's face. "Based on the insect activity, my guess is that she's been dead for at least four or five days. The majority of the maggots appear to be molting to the pre-pupa stage. I just dabble in entomology, though, so I made sure we took samples to be certain. I'll have them sent to the same lab we used for the girl in the...I mean, Courtney."

"Good." John moved the flashlight over the victim's neck. With the way her head dangled, he had to shift and crouch closer.

The stench had his gag reflex going into action. Again, he fought it, tried not to let her become personal, and viewed her body as an investigator.

She'd become more than personal.

This victim, this young woman who had so much life to live, had spoken through Celeste. She'd used the woman who had snared his heart to tell her story, to explain how she'd died.

"Did you check her neck?" he asked, and handed the flashlight to Mitchell.

"Not yet."

"Keep the flashlight on it," he said as he whipped the Latex gloves from his pocket, then shoved his hands into them. Knocking the fly larva away, he shifted her throat, then sucked in a breath.

"She's been strangled." Mitchell leaned closer. "Just like the four women from the dump site."

John stepped away from the body, needing distance, fresh air and a moment to think.

"We've canvassed a fifty foot radius and found nothing," one of Mitchell's crime scene techs said as he approached. "No footprints, and no fibers so far, but we're still searching."

"Thanks Tom," Mitchell said, then pinched the bridge of his nose, and looked to the ground. "This doesn't make sense, John. Are we looking at two different killers? The evidence points—"

Roy's cell phone stopped Mitchell short. The sheriff stepped away to take the call.

"The evidence points in that direction," Mitchell continued. "From what we found at the first dump site compared to the girl from the...I mean Courtney, and now this victim?"

John peeled the gloves from his hands, the same questions banging through his mind in time with the drumming from the mill not more than a hundred yards away. "Hopefully the autopsy will—"

"John," Roy shouted, as he shoved his cell phone back into his pocket. "We've got to go. Now." He looked to Mitchell and raised a hand. "I don't have time for the particulars, but I'll need one of your techs."

"You've got me," Mitchell said without hesitation, then

shouted a couple of quick orders to his men.

With a nod, Roy ran faster than John had anticipated. He caught up with him, and gripped his arm. "What the hell, Roy?"

"Keep moving," he panted, as he jogged down the path leading to the parking lot. "We've got a dead prison guard and Winston in the ER."

John stood inside Winston's small jail cell, eyeing the dead guard, Curtis Hoyt. An empty syringe, the alleged murder weapon, rested a few feet away from the body. Near the entrance of the cell, a pool of blood coagulated. Winston's blood.

"What do you think?" Roy asked from behind him.

"Are you finished taking pictures?" he asked Mitchell.

"Yep, you're free to snoop."

During the drive to Eau Claire County Jail, he'd called Rachel and already had her snooping into Hoyt's background. "Thanks," he replied, then looked to the sheriff. "You told me Hoyt served as an Eau Claire traffic cop, right?"

"Twenty-two years before he had a massive heart attack. He came to work at the county jail afterward, less stress."

He snapped a pair of Latex gloves on his hands, then crouched next to the syringe. "More like less pay," he commented under his breath.

Roy narrowed his eyes and knelt next to him. "What are you saying?" he whispered, his eyes moving to the hallway where the Jail Captain and the three guards who'd sent Winston to the ER stood.

"I had a search done on Hoyt during the drive here." As much as he hated Rachel's habit, he'd send her a couple boxes of number two pencils to gnaw on for her quick response. "Hoyt was up to his ass in debt, over thirty thousand with credit cards, several loans against his house, not to mention the college tuition he'd been paying for his three kids."

He picked up the syringe and held it into the light. Less than a CC of blue liquid remained. He sniffed it, then shook his head. "Smells like window cleaner."

"Window cleaner? How the hell would Winston get a hold of not only a syringe, but window cleaner?"

"Exactly," John said. He set the syringe next to the yellow marker Mitchell had placed earlier, then moved to Hoyt's body. "Look here." He pointed to a spot on the pants pocket of the prison guard's tan uniform.

Roy knelt beside him. "It's dried, but stained the material."

"Mitchell," John said, "Can you make sure you find out what this is?"

"I saw it earlier. If you look close enough, you can see a hint of blue. It might match the liquid in the syringe."

"So you think Hoyt carried the syringe in his pocket with the intent to use it on Winston?" Roy asked, disbelief in his tone.

"People do strange things for money," he said as he viewed the dead guard.

"No doubt. Okay," Roy said on a sigh, and stood, "We should have enough evidence. I'm going to see if we can get a search warrant for Hoyt's house while you finish here."

Jail Captain Fredrick Ambrose, mid-forties, big, beefy and slightly balding, narrowed his eyes as he stepped over Winston's blood and into the cell. "You aren't suggesting one of my men decided to go vigilante, are you?"

Not yet. "We won't have our answers until the ME and CSU file their reports." John looked passed Ambrose, zeroing in on the security camera across the hall. "Have you looked at the video surveillance?"

"Yes, but unfortunately, the camera is aimed at the hallway, not directly into the cell."

"Why should it be *that* easy," Mitchell said. "Thank God for a little thing called *evidence.*"

John half-smiled, with a "no shit" on the tip of his tongue, then stood. "What's Winston's condition?" he asked Ambrose as they moved into the hallway.

"I haven't heard." He narrowed his eyes on the three guards. "But a full investigation into what happened here today will be launched."

"What did you see when you walked into the cell?" John asked, turning his attention to the three guards.

A lanky, twenty-something, with an enormous Adam's Apple and an even bigger nose, spoke first. "We heard Curtis screaming and by the time we entered Winston's cell, it was too late. That bastard had already shoved the syringe in Curtis' throat, and still had his thumb on the plunger."

"And you...?"

The guard's Adam's Apple shifted. "Detained the prisoner with necessary force."

"Brantner," Ambrose shouted at the guard. "What you three did went *beyond* necessary force, and—"

"Sir," John interrupted, "Please, let him finish."

"Well," the guard continued, shifting his eyes between the Jail Captain and him. "We went at Winston with our batons. He's a big dude, and it took all of us to contain him."

"Your idea of *containment* has just landed all three of you a suspension," Ambrose yelled. "Don't leave the building without an official statement. Now get out of my sight." Running a hand over his shiny head, he looked to the ceiling. "This has never happened before. And by God, I'll make certain it never happens again. Even if Winston was a piece of shit."

More than a cop, Ambrose was a wannabe politician. According to Roy, he'd been biding his time, hoping to be promoted to Undersheriff, then eventually elected Sheriff of Eau Claire County. With this blemish on his record, he might be screwed.

What Ambrose didn't understand was that the *piece of shit* his guards had sent to the ER had been their only link to the second killer. Based on Celeste's last trance, the evidence from Courtney, and what happened here today, he firmly believed Winston had been working with someone.

Before he could remind the Jail Captain that it wasn't all

about him and his career, Roy approached. "Let's go."

John thanked Ambrose, then caught up with the sheriff. "Will we get our warrant?"

He waved an envelope. "The ADA just dropped it off."

"Quick work."

"Six dead women, a dead guard and an attempt on an inmate's life greased the wheels," Roy said after they signed out of the jail and headed through the door.

"Have you heard back from Carl yet?"

"I called while I was waiting on the ADA. Carl was busy prepping Lauren Sundahl, but Dean said they have all the toxicology reports on the first five victims. All were clean except one Jane Doe. She had traces of cocaine in her system along with alcohol."

Once they were in the parking lot, John stopped him. "I'm surprised Courtney didn't have anything in her system. The prostitutes I could understand. They'd likely gone willingly with Winston. But Courtney? I'd think the killer would have used something to sedate her, unless..."

"She knew the guy."

"Who somehow knows and worked with Winston."

Roy nodded. "Right. And now his partner wants him dead. But what about the evidence? It points back to Winston. You heard Mitchell. Sundahl had been dead for four or five days. And Carl believes Courtney was likely killed last Friday, six days ago. Winston was on the move then."

"We have an extra set of foot prints at the original dumpsite."

"Which could have been there before Winston dumped the bodies," Roy countered.

"Then why change his MO with Courtney? Why gut and sodomize her?"

Roy grimaced. "Maybe he just changed things up that time."

"Guys like Winston don't *change things up*, they stick with what works. And based on Celeste's trance—"

"Stop. You know as well as I do, that I believe in Celeste,

but her trance proves shit without concrete evidence. Today's victim was strangled, just like all of Winston's victims. You saw it. Mitchell confirmed it."

"But if she was sodomized?"

"Who's to say Winston didn't rape her both ways?"

John winced, and turned away toward his car. Logically, he knew the sheriff was right.

Three days ago, he would have assumed Winston had killed all the women alone, except for Courtney. She had been different, and he stood by his theory that someone other than Winston had ended her life. But Celeste had changed his perception. He believed her, in her...and his gut. Right now his gut was overriding that side of his brain that insisted on a purely rational approach and depended on hard evidence.

He stopped in front of his car, then turned to the sheriff. "Then explain today. Actually, explain why you're fighting me on this? *You* were the one who bought into Celeste's psychic stuff when she'd said there was another killer and more bodies. Not me. Now I'm the one defending her?"

The sheriff looked to the ground and leaned against the rental car.

"Roy, I firmly believe Winston has a partner. A partner who wants him dead. Hoyt was up to his ass in debt. Maybe Winston's partner knew this, or knew something else he could blackmail Hoyt with to coerce him into killing Winston."

"C'mon, Kain," the sheriff snapped. "A guy doesn't just wake up one day, meet a guy on the street and decide the two of them should start raping and killing together."

"Right, trust is the key here. What Winston and our second killer have done requires a heavy amount of trust."

Roy shook his head. "Look, in the beginning, based on Celeste's vision, I thought maybe we were looking for a second killer—separate from Winston. But you truly believe we're looking for Winston's partner?"

"I do, and I guarantee he wants Winston dead, because he doesn't trust him to keep his mouth shut."

"Then why would Winston confess without an attorney

present?" Roy threw his arms in the air. "Hell, why confess at all?"

"Maybe he and his partner had a backup plan."

"Backup plan?" the sheriff scoffed. "Like he'd been prepared for this to happen? Had an escape already planned out?" He shook his head. "Sounds too Hollywood to me."

Boysen pulled into the parking lot.

"Here we go," Roy said with disgust.

"It's time to give him something, and I'd rather have him run his article the way *we* want."

The sheriff narrowed his eyes. "How's that?"

"Without Celeste's name being mentioned."

Roy's eyes softened. "We've already been over this."

The sheriff was right. He was repeating himself, making his feelings for Celeste clear. Too clear. "Roy, I..."

He raised his hand and took a step back. "I get it, and I'm going to make my conversation with Boysen quick. I want to get home to Bev on good time. I need..." He drew in a deep breath. "John, I knew Curtis Hoyt for over twenty years. I'm sorry if I've been a kind of a prick, but the thought of telling his wife her husband is dead, then waving a search warrant in her face isn't settling well with me."

Shoving a hand in his pant pocket, John touched the roll of antacids he'd remembered to carry today.

Roy's mustache tilted as he gave him a sympathetic smile. "Don't bother asking. Not to sound all sappy, but because of Bev, there's no room for heartburn. She owns my heart, and wouldn't allow it." He started toward Boysen, then stopped. "A good woman could cure what ails you," he said over his shoulder. "And when you find that woman, no matter the odds, the end result is well worth it."

"What's that?" he asked without thinking, a rarity for him, and he could have kicked himself in the ass. He'd opened himself up too much, left himself too vulnerable. To Roy...to Celeste.

A slow smile spread across the sheriff's face. "A woman you'd die for, or die without. Take your pick."

Before he had a chance to digest Roy's words, his cell phone rang. "Kain," he answered.

"It's Celeste." *A woman you'd die for, or die without.* "Are you okay?"

"It's been a long day." Just hearing her voice almost evaporated what he'd seen today. Almost.

"Bad?"

"Yeah, bad."

"John," she said with sympathy, as a gruff, male voice shouted in the background. "I'm sorry, I've got to go. We're in the middle of the dinner rush, but you've been on my mind. I wanted to check in and see if...if you wanted to stop by later."

Hell yes. "Will's still taking you home?"

"Right after things slow down, probably around seven or so. Having an assistant manager is a beautiful thing."

He swore he felt her smile through the phone. "It's nice to give up a little control, isn't it?"

"Exhilarating."

He wanted to share that exhilaration. Hell, he was starting to go beyond want to pure need. He'd tasted her this afternoon, felt every delicious inch of her body and it still wasn't enough. He needed more, except... "I have a few things to take care of yet, and paperwork to do." Rachel had sent him a text while he'd been in Winston's jail cell, stating that she had a bunch of stuff waiting in his email inbox.

"Bring it with you. Maybe I can help. I'll even hook you up with tonight's dinner special. I'm sure you haven't eaten all day."

"I haven't. But if it's liver and onions..."

"Nope," she chuckled. "Try chicken marsala, and I'll even snag a piece of cheesecake for you."

His stomach grumbled. "I'm game."

"So I'll see you around..."

"Seven or so."

Dishes clanked in the background. "Gotta go. See you soon."

As he slipped his cell phone back into his pocket, Roy

walked toward him. "Finished with Boysen already?"

"Guy's not a dumbass," he said as he opened his car door. "He pretty much had most of the story figured out. I just filled in a few, *very* selective details." He looked over his shoulder. "Where to?"

"First Hoyt's, then Sundahl's, then a check on Winston."

With his shoulders slumped, Roy climbed into his cruiser. "After that, I'm going home to Bev."

As the sheriff shut his car door and started the ignition, John sighed and did the same. While anxious for any information that might help lead them to the second killer, he couldn't help the punch of disappointment. It would be hours before he saw Celeste.

He needed to see Celeste.

A woman you'd die for, or die without.

CHAPTER 15

CELESTE SHOVED THE dusty box from the guest bedroom closet across the hardwood floor. Kneeling on the area rug, she traced the letters she'd printed on the side of the box three years ago.

Mom.

Overwhelming sorrow squeezed her heart. She missed seeing her mother's face. She missed hearing her voice, her laughter.

"What are you doing?"

She jumped. "Will, you scared the crap out me."

"Sorry." He leaned against the door jamb. "I was just in the basement figuring you'd be baking."

She should be in the basement kitchen or experimenting with her recipes, but she needed answers. "Not tonight. I'll get up early tomorrow."

He walked into the room, a frown lining his face. "What's in the box?"

"Some of mom's things she'd saved over the years. Old high school yearbooks, pictures, cards...journals."

"Does dad know about this stuff?" he asked, and touched the lid, but didn't remove it.

"I'd told him about the box when I'd found it the day I'd cleaned out mom's closet for him. He'd said to do whatever I wanted with it. I swear I'd mentioned it to both you and

Eden."

He winced. "Now that I think about it, you did. Why are you going through it now?"

"The trances. I was hoping mom had something in her journals that might help me understand why I'm having them or maybe even learn how to control them."

"Why didn't you read her journals before?"

"Why didn't you?"

Sighing, he sat on the bed. "It hurt too much, it still does."

"For me, too," she whispered, and grabbed his hand. "Wanna help me go through them now?"

"I thought John was coming over."

"He called and said he'd be late."

"Oh."

She caught his disappointment as he stared at the box, along with the grief that still lingered in all of them. "Go work in your studio. John will be here in about an hour. You don't need to babysit me."

"Celeste," he started to protest.

"You're thirty yards from the house. All of the windows and doors are locked. Nothing is going to happen to me. Actually, I think John and Roy are being way too overprotective."

"Lloyd doesn't think so."

She rolled her eyes. "He's as bad as they are. Now either help me read through mom's journals, or go to your studio. The gallery opening is coming up and I know you still have a few things to finish."

"I do, but..."

She pulled her cell phone from her pocket. "I'll call if I need you."

"No, I'll just wait downstairs."

"And pace a hole in my rug? Uh-uh, go home."

"Okay, but, um, considering this is the room I'm going to be sleeping in tonight, could you at least move the box back in the closet when you're finished. I don't want to look at it."

Bleak sadness filled his eyes. Her throat clenched and she

nodded. "I understand, but don't worry. You might not need to sleep here anyway."

"Why?" he asked, then he widened his eyes. "You and John are..." He shoved off the bed, a red blush creeping up his neck and staining his cheeks. "I don't want to know." He stopped and turned. "Actually I do. What are his intentions?"

"Intentions? Seriously, Will, you sound like dad. It's not a big deal, just a sorta fling."

"Seriously, Celeste, you sound like Eden," he mocked. "And she's had way too many *sorta* flings, where you...you..."

Her temper flared. First Roy, now her brother? "Where I live like a fricking spinster, collecting creepy gnomes and wasting my life in this small town."

He frowned. "What the hell are you talking about? You're not wasting your life here."

"Bullshit. Eden's in Chicago living the life she'd always wanted. She has a successful career, friends, *flings*. Dad's down in Florida golfing, fishing, and according to Roy, has had more dates in the past six months than I've had in three years. And you." She stood, and pointed a finger at him as a tear slipped down her cheek. "You'll be gone soon, while I..."

He hugged her, awkwardly patting her back. Will was a great guy, but clumsy when it came to expressing emotions. Just like their dad and Eden. She knew this, knew how sensitive he could be, and regretted her outburst.

"I shouldn't have blown up at you like that. I'm sorry. I've been stressed out lately," she said, trying to soothe him. Will tended to brood. He'd likely go into his studio and dwell on everything she'd said, rather than work on his painting.

He stepped back and held her at arms length. "I can't believe I didn't see any of this before."

"What do you mean?"

"I always thought you liked running the diner. Living here. Why didn't you say anything? Why didn't you just tell dad?"

She pulled away, and leaned against the wall. "I couldn't. He needed me to stay, so I stayed."

He slumped on the bed and ran a hand through his hair.

"When mom's cancer became bad, Eden refused to move back to help, and I was totally useless. I couldn't stand watching mom die, and I couldn't stand watching dad deal with it. But you gave up your career, your dreams to come home to help. God, Celeste, I feel like such an ass because I don't even *know* what those dreams are."

She sat next to him, and nudged him with her shoulder. "Don't worry about it. They weren't all that great anyway."

He nudged her back. "Tell me and I'll decide."

She thought about the stack of recipes she'd perfected over the years. "Not today."

"Then will you at least promise me that you'll talk to dad? He would never have asked you to take over the diner if he knew how much you hated it."

"I don't exactly hate it and I've made my choice with dad, just as I did with John, who's going to be here in an hour. So go. I want to look through some of mom's journals before he gets here."

He moved for the door, then hesitated. "You're a great person, and I, um..."

"Go," she said, saving him from having to express himself any further. She knew he loved her, the words weren't necessary. "And if I find out you're worrying about me, rather than working, I'll give you a noogie."

"You haven't been able to do that since I outgrew you."

"Wanna test it?" she asked with a grin.

He acted as if he were considering it, then smiled. "Some other time. Call if you need me."

After she heard the front door slam shut, she released a deep sigh. What happened between her and Will might come back and bite her on the ass. She knew he wouldn't call Eden, but he might call their dad. She didn't want her dad to know how she truly felt. It would break his heart.

She stared at the box.

He'd had his heart broken enough.

Pushing that thought aside, she lifted the lid off the box. The scent of her mom's perfume, delicate, and slightly stale from age, whispered through the air. Tears stung her eyes. She fought them back, along with so many memories, and sifted through the box. She didn't want to reminisce tonight. Reminiscing would lead to the grief she hadn't dealt with, nor wanted to. After three years, her mother's death was still like an open wound that hadn't healed yet.

When she found the journals, she placed them on the bed. There were only five. Five black and white composition notebooks held her mother's thoughts, her secrets. She grabbed the oldest, then sat on the rug and began to read.

Forty minutes later, she closed the journal, her mind spinning. She hadn't known her mother as well as she'd thought.

Before moving to Wissota Falls, her mom had lived in Baltimore. That hadn't surprised her. Both her mom and dad were born and raised there, and still had plenty of family in the area. The big surprise? Her mom had worked as a psychic consultant, to both the local police and the FBI. Even more surprising, her mom had been in love with another man before she'd met her father.

Why hadn't she told her about him? She'd joked about past boyfriends, but never mentioned this man. And why hadn't she told her she'd used to be a psychic consultant? Better yet, why had she stopped?

She returned the box to the closet, then made her way to the kitchen for a much needed glass of wine. There was one person, other than her father, who might have the answers to her questions.

Roy.

She picked up the phone and called him. He answered on the first ring.

"Are you okay?"

"I'm fine. Got a sec?"

"Who's watching out for you?"

"Will," she lied, "And John will be here soon."

"Good," he said, and released a deep sigh. "After today..."

"I didn't mean to worry you, and John filled me in on what

happened. I'm sorry about Curtis."

"Me too. So what's up?"

Now this didn't seem like a good time to bring up her mom, or her journals. Roy and John had been through enough, she didn't need to dredge up the past. Her curiosity could wait until later.

"Nothing. Just checking in to see how you are."

"Celeste, don't bullshit a bullshitter."

She smiled as she took a sip of her wine. "You know me too well. Okay, I was looking through my mom's journals, hoping I'd find something in them to help with the trances I've been having."

"Go on."

"You knew my mom before she met my dad."

"I did."

"Well, there's a name that keeps popping up and I was wondering if you could tell me anything you know about him."

"Sure, hopefully I can help you out. What's the name?"

"Ian."

When his private line rang, Ian Scott stilled his fingers above the keyboard of his laptop. He stared at the phone, his stomach clenching with dread, and answered on the second ring.

"It's Roy."

He would have relaxed, except he'd talked to Roy less than twenty minutes ago. "What's wrong?"

"I just got a call from Celeste, and *you've* got a serious problem."

"Me?" he asked not missing Roy's emphasis, then it hit him. Roy had told him that he'd suspected John's interest in Celeste had gone beyond the investigation. He'd had a hard time believing him considering John's past, but in a small way, he'd been pleased. John deserved a good woman, a woman who could finally help put his demons to rest. And Celeste deserved a good man. She'd gone too long without a relationship. She was young, bright, beautiful, and had wasted too much of her life catering to everyone else. But if John hurt her...

"What did *he* do?"

"Who?"

"John."

"Oh, this isn't about him. It's about *you*."

"Me?"

"Yep, see, Celeste's trances had her rattled enough she finally decided to look through her mom's old journals hoping to find some answers."

"Janice kept journals?"

"Appears so."

"Did she tell you what was in them?"

"Your name."

He shut his laptop closed, then pulled a bottle of Scotch from his desk cabinet, along with a glass. "Explain."

Roy did, and when he finished, Ian asked, "Did Janice mention anything about the investigation she'd been working on with me...with the FBI?"

"No, not a word. More like how it had emotionally impacted her."

"That's good."

"Not really. I'd rather have that than Celeste asking me who Ian is and why her mom never mentioned she'd been in love with him before she'd met Hugh."

He swore under his breath, then downed the Scotch he'd poured. Wincing from the burn—Scotch should be sipped and savored, not pounded like a shot—he set the glass aside. "What did you say?"

"I told her Bev and I were about to sit down for dinner, that it had been a long day, and we'd meet in the morning to talk. Look, with everything we've been dealing with here, she caught me off guard." He sighed. "I didn't know what else to say. Hell, I don't even know what to say to her tomorrow."

"Where's Hugh?" Ian knew Celeste's father would flat out

tell her what she wanted to know. He'd always wanted to but Janice had been adamant about keeping the truth from Celeste, a condition Ian had hated but endured out of respect.

"Fishing in the Florida Keys. I spoke with him before he left for the trip."

"Good. Meet me at the Eau Claire airstrip tomorrow morning. I'll be there at seven."

"Hold on a sec, what are you doing?"

"What I should have done years ago," he said, ignoring the protective edge in Roy's voice before he changed his mind.

"You promised Janice."

"She's dead." He grimaced at the thought. He'd loved her once, and hadn't loved another woman since. And this might be his last chance of finally having something other than the legacy of his agency.

"I don't like it," Roy said. "You could end up tearing their family apart. I think you should talk to Hugh first."

"I respect Hugh. I always have. He's a better man than I am, and gave Janice more than I could," he finished, the words so damned bitter on his tongue, he poured another Scotch, and took a hard swallow. "Besides, you know as well as I do that Hugh thought Janice was wrong, that Celeste deserved to know the truth."

"Still," Roy said. "Well, whatever. You'll do what you want anyway. You always have."

He smiled wryly at that, while years of regret ate at his soul. Because he had—and still did—what he wanted, he'd led a very lonely life. "I also think I might be able to give Celeste some insight on her gift."

"If you say so."

"I do."

"Fine," Roy snapped. "I'll pick you up at seven. But I'll be there when you meet with her. Understand?"

"I do, and Roy, for whatever it's worth, thank you for taking care of her."

"It wasn't a job, it was a privilege."

The line disconnected. Roy had hung up on him for the

first time in thirty years.

A knock at the door had him straightening. "Yes?"

Rachel Davis poked her head inside his office. "Do you have a sec?"

"Of course." He poured himself another drink. "Scotch?"

She wrinkled her lightly freckled nose and sat in the chair across from him. Even after sitting behind a desk for more than ten hours, she still looked crisp and professional. Except for the pencil, pitted with teeth marks and tucked behind her ear. "No thanks. The only cocktails I like are sweet, one of the colors of the rainbow and usually garnished with a tiny umbrella."

"Do you gnaw on those, too?" he asked with a smile, even though his heart tripped at a rapid pace. He'd finally meet Celeste. Tomorrow.

"First John, now you? I'm starting to get a complex," she said, and removed the pencil from behind her ear.

He raised his glass. "We all have our vices. Now what can I do for you?" he asked and glanced at the clock. He had a lot of things to take care of before he left for Wisconsin, but he'd make time for Rachel. She was one of his favorite finds. Brilliant but quirky, temperamental but reliable, she was concise and direct and helped keep his agency running smoothly.

"I'm leaving for the night," she said as she leaned forward and placed a folder on his desk. Like every evening, she consolidated a quick recap of what each of his agents were working on, and where they were with their investigations.

"Any progress on Garrett Winston?" Ian hadn't been surprised that John went straight to Rachel, bypassing him. After all, he hadn't bothered to return one of John's calls, not that he hadn't wanted to talk with him. He'd just been worried his feelings for Celeste would become too obvious, and John was a very perceptive individual. His quick mind would suspect, and he'd begin asking too many questions, questions he was finally willing to answer...but only to Celeste. While he'd made it a goal to know everyone else's business, his was non-negotiable. He was the boss, the rock of CORE's foundation, and planned to remain in that position.

"Not much, I spent an hour creating a program to speed the tracking process, and so far it's working. I checked it about fifteen minutes ago and the codes I'd written have already tracked Winston's truck routes back five years, along with any unsolved murders bearing Winston's MO. Unfortunately, the program has matched over two dozen unsolved murders."

"Unfortunately?"

"Uh-huh, because Winston started driving *fourteen years* ago." She twined the pencil between her fingers. "While I'm sure not all of these murders will be linked back to him, I have a gut feeling this guy killed a lot of women during his career."

Based on Roy's reports, the dozens of unknown female DNA Eau Claire's CSU had found in Winston's cab, he did, too. "Did you hear back from St. Cloud?"

"Yes, what their CSU faxed me is in the file." She nodded to the folder on his desk. "And I've already emailed the report to John. To recap, St. Cloud's CSU examined the refrigerated trailer Winston hauled for Booker Foods and discovered small traces of blood. They're sending the samples to Eau Claire for comparison on the four women found at the original dump site."

"Excellent. Anything else?"

"Nope."

"Head home and keep me posted on your tracking progress. I won't be in the office for a few days, so call me on my cell phone."

She pursed her lips as she rose from the chair. "I know it's none of my business, but you weren't scheduled to go out of town. Is everything okay?"

"Everything's fine. Go get some rest. I'll call you tomorrow."

"Okay. Have a safe trip," she said, then closed the door behind her.

The room grew silent again. Contemplating another Scotch, he stared at the empty glass.

Not tonight, he decided. For thirty years he'd been waiting for the moment to come face to face with Celeste. Janice might not have approved, but she was gone. And while so many secrets had died with her, it was time to reveal a few. He only hoped Celeste would accept them...accept him. For who he'd been thirty years ago, and the man he was today.

With a shake of his head, he stowed the Scotch and glass away as the past surfaced with a sucker punch. He was screwed, especially if John discovered he'd been to Wissota Falls. He could lose a good agent, but having this chance with Celeste would be well worth it. He hoped.

And for the first time in years...he prayed.

CHAPTER 16

JOHN WALKED PAST the ugly gnomes lining the flowerbeds, and rang the door bell. As he waited, feeling as if someone was watching him, he glanced over his shoulder. A gnome being carried off by a pair of metallic aliens caught his attention. He hadn't noticed this particular one before, and couldn't help but smile.

Life with Celeste would be interesting, if he was given that chance. After the investigation ended, he'd try. He wasn't stupid. Maybe skeptical about relationships considering what had happened with Renee, but not stupid.

Celeste had breathed life into parts of him he hadn't realized had been dead. He envied how deeply she cared for her family and Roy. He wanted her to care about him just the same if not more. Hell, he wanted her all to himself. Especially after today.

Since dropping her off at the diner, his day had gone to shit and now he needed to talk...to her and her alone. For a reason he couldn't explain, she soothed him, brought peace to his soul. Tonight, he needed her comfort.

The door opened. In an instant, the victims, Winston, the entire fucked up case, disappeared from his mind.

She stood in the doorway wearing low-cut jeans, and a long-sleeved t-shirt that hugged her breasts and brought the blue out in her eyes. Her curly, blond hair framed her pretty face. The memory of twining his fingers through her hair as he'd made love to her that afternoon had his fingers tingling. Her vanilla and cinnamon scent had his mouth watering for a taste of her smooth skin. He stared at her lush lips, and a hunger that had nothing to do with his empty stomach made him move fast.

Needing to touch her, to erase away everything bad, he dropped his briefcase, kicked the door closed and pinned her against the wall. Unable to stop himself, he cupped her cheeks and kissed her. Kissed her the way he'd been aching to do since he'd left her bedroom this afternoon.

She released a throaty moan and parted her lips. The arousing vibration hummed through his body and straight to his cock. Hard, ready, and aching to bury himself between her thighs, he tangled his tongue with hers, and made love to her mouth.

Gripping the back of his head, she held onto him, surged her body against his. Her response fueled his need. He raised one of her legs around his back, then gripped her rear and ground his dick between her thighs. Dragging his lips along her neck, he pressed a lingering kiss where her pulse beat hard at the hollow of her throat, then snared her gaze.

Her eyes were bright, glittering with both desire and shock. The desire he welcomed, but the shock? He looked to the wall. God, he was a presumptuous ass. While she'd responded the way he'd hoped, the way he'd needed, he might have moved a little too fast. He was sure there had to be some sort of rule out there about when it was appropriate to kiss someone hello, and he was also sure he'd just broken it. Besides, her brother could be in the next room. Distracted by her warm curves and inviting scent, he hadn't bothered to check.

She placed two fingers on his cheek and forced him to meet her eyes. "What?" she asked.

"I'm sorry, I shouldn't have done that."

"Kiss me hello?"

"Yeah, with Will in the house—"

"I sent him to his apartment a little while ago. I knew you'd be here soon." She rubbed her fingers along his jaw, the light, feathery touch arousing. "Why did you really stop?"

"I didn't just kiss you hello, I was ready to..."

"Fuck me against the wall."

Her bluntness had him impossibly harder. "You betcha," he mimicked the accent the locals used with a grin.

Smiling, she brushed her lips against his. "Did I look like I was complaining?"

"No, but—"

"Celeste? I saw headlights," Will called from the kitchen.

She disentangled their bodies. "John's here, we're in the foyer."

He quickly grabbed his briefcase and hid his arousal as Will approached. Her brother eyed him for a second, then nodded. "Glad you're here. I didn't like leaving Celeste alone."

"Quit worrying." She took her brother by the elbow and led him back to the kitchen. When she reached the sliding door that led to a pathway to Will's studio apartment, she stopped. "Get back to work. I'll see you in the morning."

Will hesitated and stared him down for a moment. "Call if you need me," her brother said, then walked toward the garage.

She closed the door, locked the deadbolt, then met his gaze in the reflection of the glass. "Were you planning on going back to the Chippewa Inn tonight?"

"I thought I'd leave that up to you." His heart raced. He wanted to spend the night with her, needed to. In a matter of days, he swore she'd become the best thing about him. And even if whatever they had ended after the investigation, he wanted to soak up every chance he could with her. Making love, holding her throughout the night...

She swiveled, a big, saucy grin on her face. "Good, let's get you fed. After this afternoon, and your hello kiss, I've got plans for you tonight." She waggled her brows, walked toward him, then planted a quick kiss on his lips. "Have a seat. How was your day?"

He did, his mind busy, his body still hard and wanting. With Renee, he'd have sex to ease the tension. Afterward, pillow talk involved whatever case they'd been working. Celeste had become his pseudo partner. But the kind of pillow talk he'd have with her would *not* involve the investigation. While he liked the idea of spilling details and bouncing ideas off her, once in the bedroom, whatever happened would only have to do with them.

"Other than making love to you and kissing you in the foyer, terrible."

She blushed. "It's nice to be the highlight of someone's day." She placed a Styrofoam container on the counter, then dished the chicken marsala onto one of her gnome plates before popping it into the microwave. While his dinner cooked, she went back to the fridge and grabbed a bottle of wine. "Want some?"

"A beer would be better."

She gave him one, and when the microwave dinged, pulled the plate out, then set it in front of him. His mouth immediately watered and his stomach grumbled. "If this tastes half as good as it smells...where's yours?"

"I already ate." She took a sip of her wine. "Dig in and enjoy."

He did, and as he ate, he told her about Lauren Sundahl first. "Roy and I went to see her mom, but she wasn't home. One of Roy's deputies, Ed Young..."

"I know Ed, he's a good guy. His wife's an ER nurse at Eau Claire Hospital."

"Ed mentioned that. He also said that he'd remembered seeing Lauren—when she was a few years younger—in the ER when he'd stopped by to pick up his wife. Apparently Lauren was a frequent visitor. Either she was exceptionally clumsy or..."

"Her mom beat her," she finished, rubbing her finger around the rim of the wine glass. "What about...how she was killed. Were you able to tell if two men..." She shivered and looked away.

He pushed his plate aside, then her wine, and reached for her hand. "Carl has made her his first priority. We'll know something in the morning."

"And Curtis Hoyt?"

Releasing a deep sigh, he looked to the ceiling. "Carl and Dean are pulling an all-nighter for us. After they're finished with Lauren Sundahl, they'll take care of Hoyt. CSU did conclude that there were two sets of fingerprints found on the syringe Winston used against Hoyt, and that it was likely some type of ammonia-based cleaning supply. They also found traces of this same substance in Hoyt's front pants pocket. They'll know exactly what was intended to kill Winston once they get the tests back, hopefully tomorrow."

"You honestly think Curtis tried to kill Winston?" she asked, her eyes wide with disbelief. "I knew him, and his wife. Everybody loved the guy. He was a former cop. I just can't imagine..."

"It gets worse. Roy and I went to see Mrs. Hoyt after we'd left Lauren Sundahl's home. CSU met us there, and we searched the house." Rachel had already run through bank accounts in not only Hoyt's name, but his wife and children, too. She'd found nothing that would prove someone had bribed him to kill Winston, but they had. "Underneath a floorboard in his bedroom, we discovered an old tackle box, containing ten thousand dollars in small, unmarked bills. Along with the money, we found pictures of Hoyt gambling at a casino, as well as cheating on his wife."

Her eyes grew even wider. "What are you saying? That he was being blackmailed?" She shook her head. "That doesn't make sense. Why would a blackmailer *pay* Curtis? Wouldn't the pictures be enough of an incentive?"

"You'd think," he said with a shrug. "There was also a typed note in the box stating that once 'the job' was done, Hoyt would receive another ten grand. Between the money and the note, Roy and I think Winston definitely had a partner." He leaned back in the chair. "A partner who wants him dead."

"Based on my last trance, that makes sense."

"It does, but, no offense, your trances aren't considered hard evidence."

"True, but what about Winston's confession?"

I know something you don't know.

Winston's parting words from the night he'd been arrested still taunted him. He'd been coked up that night, based on the urinalysis they'd forced on him. Arrogant and self-assured. Why?

"I'm still not sure, and we might never know. Thanks to the beating he took, Winston's in a coma."

"A coma? Oh my God. What did the doctor say? Is there any chance he'll recover? Not that he deserves to live. I'd rather see him suffer in prison." She picked up her wine glass. "Actually, I wish Wisconsin still had the death penalty."

"Eye for an eye?"

"Oh yeah. Especially when it comes to a monster like him."

"After what I've witnessed over the years, I wholeheartedly agree with you. As for his doctor, he said these next few days will be crucial as to whether or not Winston will survive. He sustained a subdural hematoma."

"Which is?"

"Bleeding around the brain is the gist of it. Once they drilled a hole in Winston's head to drain the blood, the doctor said the swelling around the brain should dissipate, but that the coma could linger for days or weeks. And, if Winston does wake up, he might not be...normal."

"Like he was normal to begin with," she said, and reached for her wine.

He lifted his beer in a mock toast. "No kidding. I just hope to God he does wake up. If Winston does have a partner, and they've been killing women for years, he'll know everything about the other man. Roy and I never had a chance to interrogate him. Every time we tried, he'd refuse to speak to us."

"Let's get back to his partner. Do you think Winston confessed as quick as he did—and I know it sounds like something out of movie—because he and his partner had an escape plan?"

Damn if they weren't sharing the same thought patterns. "I thought that, too. Only Roy thought it was too Hollywood."

She rose and picked up his empty plate. "Roy would know. He and Bev watch more movies in a month than I do in an entire year."

"You don't like hanging out and watching movies?"

"I do, but there never seems to be any time. But now that I have an assistant manager, I might be able to catch up on the stuff that I've recorded on my DVR."

"They have that kind of technology in this small town?" he teased.

She stuck her tongue out at him, which he knew was meant to be playful. Only he imagined the things she could do with that tongue, those full lips...

"Have you looked into Winston's past?" she asked as she shut the dishwasher door. "I mean, if he's been killing women for some time, maybe along his truck routes—"

His chuckle stopped her mid-sentence.

"What?"

"You'd seriously make a good investigator. I'm already on it, which was why I brought my laptop with me." He explained that Rachel had created a program to match all of Winston's truck routes to any unsolved murders matching his MO.

"Impressive." She a raised brow. "How many years back are we talking?"

"Fourteen."

"Scary."

"Tell me about it. Rachel has already sent me data spanning the past five years. I need to look at each unsolved murder. Hopefully she'll have more for me tomorrow. When Winston wakes up, if he wakes up," he amended. "I want to hit him with everything and anything we've got against him to coerce him into giving up his partner."

She wiped the counter clean. "I told you I'd help. What do you say we get at it?"

Work was the last thing on his mind as he drifted his eyes to her kissable lips. "You don't have to help, just keep me company."

"Nope, the sooner we can get this done, the sooner..." She

cocked a brow and her mouth curved in a sexy grin.

"You're sure?"

"I wouldn't have offered. So where do you want to work? Living room or kitchen?"

He loved her cozy living room, all of the family pictures, the fireplace, the comfy couch. He grabbed his beer and briefcase. "Living room."

Ninety minutes later, between the two of them, they'd reviewed the two dozen unsolved murders Rachel's program had matched with Winston's MO and his truck routes. Fifteen of those murders looked more promising than the rest, which meant he'd be on the phone in the morning calling the homicide detectives who had worked those cases. While time consuming to investigate, those crimes might give him more insight into Winston, and his partner. And if they were lucky, maybe even more evidence, too.

"This is depressing," she said. "And hell on my back." She stretched her arms behind her, the tight shirt tugged against her breasts.

He didn't bother to pretend he didn't notice. Despite what they'd been researching, his mind had been focused on the promises their kiss in the foyer held. "Need a break?"

"Definitely." She leaned back into the couch. "I forgot what it was like to sit, hunched over a computer."

"It doesn't help that two of us are sharing my laptop, or that we're not exactly in sturdy office chairs." They'd been sitting on her couch, legs brushing, heads together, her scent bombarding his senses and putting him in a constant state of arousal.

"True." She placed her bare feet on the coffee table, wiggled her toes, and rested her head against the couch cushion. "What do you do for fun, John? You know, when you're not looking for bad guys."

"Where'd that come from?"

"I dunno, maybe because this is *more* than depressing." She pointed to the laptop. "You've got to have some way to blow off steam."

Thinking of a few ways he could blow off steam, he glanced at her breasts.

"Besides sex," she added with a raised brow.

He laughed and leaned back into the couch, his gaze on hers, their faces inches apart. "I watch some TV, news and sports mostly."

"Movies?"

"Not really."

"Do you go to baseball or football games, or meet friends at a bar?"

His face heated. "Not in a...long time."

Not since Renee.

"So when was the last time you had any *real* fun?"

"This afternoon," he said honestly.

His confession earned him a shy smile. "Seriously?" she asked, moving closer.

"Seriously. Your turn. What do you do for fun?"

"Um, bake."

"Bake. Boy do you know how to live on the wild side."

With a sexy smile, she lightly slapped his chest, then surprised him by straddling his thighs. "Crazy wild." She rotated her hips along his arousal.

Gripping her rear, he pulled her closer. "Feeling a little crazy wild now?"

Her breath hitched as he nibbled her neck. "What I feel is an impressive erection between my thighs." She scooted down his lap, dragging her fingers along his chest and stomach until she reached his belt buckle. "Work can wait." She loosened his belt buckle. "Let's have some fun for a while."

The door bell rang. Her hand stilled over the erection beneath his jeans.

Frowning, she rose. "I can't imagine who it could be."

Tense, alert, he stopped her. "Wait, I'll check." When he looked through the front door's peep hole, he swore under his breath, and unlocked the deadbolt. "It's Lloyd," he said as he opened the door.

The fucking Viking barreled into the foyer, sweeping his

gaze between him and Celeste. "I need to talk to you," he said ignoring him, his eyes on Celeste. "Alone."

"About?"

"I said *alone*, Celeste. Now."

She crossed her arms over her chest. "*Now?*" she repeated, her cheeks flushing.

"Yeah, *now*."

"Does this have anything to do with my brother?"

Lloyd slid his gaze to him. "No."

"John, then?"

"Most definitely."

"Then say whatever you have to say in front of him."

He slammed the door, and crowded the foyer. "Fine. Maybe it's better this way. I'll throw all the cards on the table and watch him squirm."

She dropped her arms, and wrinkled her forehead. "What's wrong with you?"

"It's not me, it's *him*." The Viking stared at him with self-assured satisfaction. "Yeah, I'm onto you, Kain. Remember my contacts with the FBI field office in Minneapolis? Well, I did some checking. While you've been trying to put the moves on Celeste, did you tell her about your *last* partner?"

John looked to Celeste to gauge her reaction. Her blue eyes had become shards of ice as she stared at Lloyd. "No, I haven't."

But maybe I should have.

"It's none of my business," she said. "Leave. Now. Whatever happened with John's partner is none of my business."

"It should be. She's dead."

Her eyes widened a fraction. "Get out," she demanded, her jaw clenched tight.

"No way, you need to know. He'd been sleeping with his partner, and was dirty. Filtering money into his own bank accounts, using the system, his *badge*, to get what he wanted. His partner ended up dead, with *his* gun. And I'm not about to allow you to—"

"Leave now or I'm calling Roy," she shouted.

The fucking Viking gripped the door handle. "Will's out back?"

"As always. Now leave."

"Fine. But I don't like this."

"I'm sure you don't."

She shoved him. With Celeste being no more than five foot four, on any other occasion, he might have laughed at the way she made Lloyd cower. But he couldn't. Lloyd had opened a can of worms. Celeste would have questions. He would have answers. But would she believe him?

"Celeste," Lloyd pleaded.

"Stay out of my business. And I had better not hear anything from Will, either. If you go see him tonight, don't you dare mention a word of this."

Lloyd's cheeks developed red splotches. "Yeah, I got it." Then he looked to him. "Do anything to hurt her, and I'm coming for you. Understand?"

He didn't like Lloyd's possessiveness, and as he was about to counter the threat, Celeste rolled her eyes. "Quit with the BS and leave."

"Fine, but—"

She slammed the door in his face. She stood for a moment and he had no idea what the hell to say.

Tell her or wait until she asks?

"Okay," she began, resting her forehead against the door. "*That* ruined the mood."

Tell her.

"Celeste, what Lloyd said—"

She held up a hand behind her. "Were you planning on telling me?"

"Eventually," he answered honestly, and wished she'd face him. He wanted to read her eyes to know where he stood.

"Good." With a curt nod, she pushed off the door. "Now or later?"

"Now."

She faced him then. There was no accusation, no wariness

in her eyes.

He knew then and there that while he'd been over what had happened with Renee a million times, tonight was different. What he'd tell her wasn't about saving his career or his reputation, but about saving his relationship with Celeste.

Instead of flooring the gas pedal like he wanted, he slammed his hand against the steering wheel and stuck to the speed limit. How the hell was he going to find a way to catch Celeste alone when her fucking house had a revolving door?

After he'd learned Hoyt—that stupid prick—fucked up and got himself killed rather than taking care of Garrett, he'd needed a release. And he couldn't think of a better release than gutting Celeste while he fulfilled his wildest fantasy. And she would fulfill his wildest fantasy.

Not tonight.

He considered the bitch at his home. Worthless. Pathetic. In no way, shape or form, could she satisfy him. Well, he thought with a small smile, not anymore. He'd seen to that, and he'd eventually put her out of her misery when he was good and ready to tie up *that* loose end.

As for Garrett. He scrubbed a hand along his jaw. Images of him, of what they'd shared crept through his mind. He loved Garrett, more than a brother should, but he needed him dead. A coma was nice, but when Garrett woke—if Garrett woke, he amended—he could be screwed.

Garrett might be arrogant, self-serving, and blasé at times, but he wasn't stupid. He'd know who had signed his death warrant. And he'd tell. Everything. He knew first hand Garrett was the most vindictive son of a bitch he'd ever met. Knew it the moment...he didn't want to think about the past. Those memories weren't worth dick, and were better left where they belonged.

In the past.

As he drove through town, he smiled despite the situation.

He'd find a way to take care of Garrett. This time, it wouldn't cost him ten grand. An ICU nurse, with a penchant for drugs, would do the trick. And he knew just the one.

Grinning now, he headed for home. Yes, he'd take care of Garrett, and in the meantime, he'd find a way to take care of Celeste. She hadn't been part of his plan until that jackass, hotshot, Kain showed his GQ face in town, and he'd learned she was working with him.

Damn, he couldn't wait to see the look on Kain's face when he discovered what he'd done to his pretty little girlfriend. He'd at least stick around for *that*, then he'd tie up his last loose end, and he'd be off to...maybe Brazil, or Canada. No, Canada was too cold. The Philippines? Bangkok? Hell, it didn't matter. He had plenty of passports, IDs, money. The world was his. He could go anywhere. Be anyone.

And the women? After what he had planned for Celeste, he'd have to become more...creative. After all, how do you top the ultimate fantasy?

His smile widened. With the ultimate kill, of course.

CHAPTER 17

AS CELESTE PLOPPED on the couch next to him, John's stomach balled into a knot and made him want to reach for his antacids. He was about to reveal one of the darkest moments of his life. A betrayal that, even two years later, made it difficult to trust.

But there wasn't any heartburn, now that he thought about it. Maybe Roy was right. There wasn't any room for heartburn, not with Celeste sitting by his side, willing to hear his story, and filling his heart with emotions he still had a hard time defining.

"So…" She twirled a curl around her finger. "Your last partner ended up dead and you were left to blame."

He released a nervous chuckle. "Sarcastic and blunt. What else could I ask for in a woman?"

Her smile didn't reach her eyes. "You don't have to tell me anything you don't want to. We could…stop whatever is going on between us and—"

He tensed. "That's not what I want. At all."

"What do you want?"

You. Every day, every night. "Right now I want to clear up what Lloyd accused me of, because the last thing I want is for you to even think that I could be *that* kind of man."

"If I thought you were, I would have already kicked you out of my house," she said with a deep sigh. "I mean, come on, John, I *trust* you. More than I've trusted anyone in a long time. To help make this crystal clear, I don't have sex with just anyone. Until you, I haven't been with a man in over three years. That relationship soured when I found out he was cheating on me. I don't trust easy, but with you, I felt it immediately."

"Me too," he said and meant it. Maybe it was the instant connection they'd shared, or maybe it was as simple as her openness and honesty. Whatever the reason, he did trust her and wanted to set the record straight.

Leaning back into the sofa cushions, he ran a hand through his hair. "My partner's name was Renee Toth. I was paired up with her when I was transferred to the FBI field office in New York City. We spent a lot of time together. Neither of us had a spouse or lover, but we had each other."

"She became your lover?" she asked, without a flicker of jealousy.

"Yes, eventually. Some cases...sometimes there was a need to just release the stress and I found that release with Renee."

"Did you love her?"

"No. Not to sound callous or cold, but Renee and I had an understanding. We came together when it was...necessary, if that makes sense. Afterward, we'd talk about whatever case we were working on."

She nodded her head. "I get it. You were blowing off steam."

"Pretty much. But it was more than that. I trusted her with my life. We were agents first. She had my back, and I had hers, only..."

"Only..." she prompted.

"She set me up." He fisted his hands. Even two years later the bitterness, the regret still clawed at him. "She'd played me for over a year and I had no idea."

"What did she do?"

"About a month before things went bad, she told me an

FBI agent out of the Newark, New Jersey field office had asked for assistance on a case they'd been working. Renee knew the agent, Wes Foster, from her academy days. She briefed me on the case and asked if I was interested."

"Newark, Wissota Falls, your job takes you to some pretty glamorous places," she said, her tone light, teasing and not matching the concern in her eyes.

He gave her a reassuring smile, appreciative of the way she was trying to make what he had to say a little easier. "Yeah, all part of the perks. Anyway, Foster was trying to find the man suspected of murdering eight prominent figures in the Newark community. They'd been linked to one man, Vito Pappeli, a wannabe mobster who'd probably watched the Godfather way too many times. Pappeli was trying to run a bunch of neighborhoods, extort businesses into paying him and in return give them protection."

"Really? Why wouldn't those people just go to the police?"

"They did, then they ended up dead. And while Foster knew Pappeli was behind those deaths, they couldn't pin anything on him. He was squeaky clean. But the word on the street was that he had a thug working for him who took care of his dirty work, only Foster and his people couldn't figure out who. I thought the case sounded interesting, and a day later, after our superiors cleared our involvement, Renee and I were in Newark trying to get a fix on this guy."

He released a deep sigh, hating this part of the story, hating his stupidity. Why did everything have to be so clear in hindsight? Maybe if he'd consulted a psychic before heading to Newark, he could have saved himself a world of shit. He stared at Celeste, her patient, concerned eyes. No, it was a good thing he hadn't known Celeste then. He'd been full of himself. Renee had taken his ego down more than a couple of pegs, though. While he still regretted what had happened, what he hadn't paid closer attention to, he knew he was a better man today than he was two years ago.

"A couple days in," he began, "after reviewing all of the evidence I suggested the man we were looking for was well trained...former military or a former cop. Renee argued with me about my assessment, which never had happened in the past, and changed the profile. At the time, I'd shrugged it off. After all, she'd been in the field longer than I had, but as the days passed, I'd realized something wasn't right. Renee started blowing off any suggestions I'd make, and would closet herself inside Foster's office leaving me twiddling my thumbs."

A wry smile shaped her lips. "I can't imagine you twiddling your thumbs. Let me guess, you started doing your *own* investigating without her."

He tried to smile back, but couldn't, not with the guilt still weighing on him. He shoved off the couch and moved to the fireplace. "I did. And about ten days later, I ended up finding the one guy that could take Pappeli down. Tony D'Angelo had worked for him for years. They'd grown up together and at one time, had been as tight as brothers. Tony was a screw-up though, and Pappeli had grown tired of bailing him out of his problems, not only financially, but with the Newark police. I happened to catch him after Pappeli balled him out, and threatened not only him, but his wife and kids. Tony was scared. He wanted out of Pappeli's organization, and he wanted protection. He'd told me he had evidence that would lead us to not only Pappeli's assassin, but prove Pappeli wasn't as squeaky clean as he appeared on paper."

In the reflection of one of her framed pictures, he saw her rise. He wanted to turn and take her in his arms, wash away the memories, but he couldn't. Not yet. Not until he finished the painful story he'd started.

"Tony died that night, and it was my fault. I'd gone to Renee and Foster, told them what he'd told me, and the next morning they found him dead. A bullet to the head, and his tongue cut off."

He turned to her then, and didn't bother to mask his emotions. Not after the way she'd defended him to Lloyd. And not with the way she stared at him now. Her eyes filling with tears, her beautiful face tight with pain...for him.

"I'd gotten him killed, because I'd trusted the wrong

people. The next day, Blake Thatcher, a friend of mine from my academy days who also worked out of Newark, called me. He said my DNA was found on Tony's body."

"*Yours?*"

"Forensics found my hair. But it gets better. The bullet that had killed Tony had come from a gun similar to the one I'd carried. Blake warned me that I was about to be detained for questioning, especially because they'd just discovered that the day Tony was killed, a deposit of one hundred thousand dollars was placed in my bank account."

She moved toward him. "Oh my God, John."

The smothering, claustrophobia that had swamped him that day didn't consume him like it had each time he'd told this story. Instead, he felt...liberated. The woman that had captured his attention, his heart, looked at him with raw, utter faith. With her, there was no room for regret, for the pain he'd endured. Just being near her, close to her, made him feel whole. She barely knew him, but was ready to defend him, to deny what his fellow agents had prepared to accuse him of...murder.

"I went to my hotel and discovered my weapon was missing, I also found out that Renee had checked out of her room. As the pieces began to fall into place, I drove back to New York. At that point, I didn't know what to do. I knew I was being framed, and didn't know who to trust. But I suspected who'd set me up."

"Renee."

He nodded. "I went to her apartment. Late. Two in the morning. When she opened the door she held *my* gun in *my* face and told me to walk inside. As I stepped into her apartment I asked why. And she smiled." He grimaced at the memory. "I'd trusted her. She'd been my partner, my lover, and she laughed in my face. I'd been a pawn, she said. Then she went on to tell me that she and Foster were lovers, that they'd been working with Pappeli for a year, that she had a plane ticket to Argentina and a shitload of money in some off-shore account. She'd killed Tony, and Foster had been

Pappeli's assassin. But what she didn't know was that I'd been recording everything on my cell phone. What I didn't know? Before Tony died, he had sent his lawyer enough evidence to bury her, Foster and Pappeli."

He ran a hand through his hair, then pulled at the ends. "She'd taken hair from my brush and planted it on Tony after she'd killed him and severed his tongue." He dropped his hands to his sides. "At that point, I'd never felt more betrayed in my life."

"H-how did she die?" A tear slipped down Celeste's cheek and he wanted to capture it. Own it. No one had ever cried for him before.

"Tony's attorney contacted Blake, thankfully. If he'd gone to Foster, I'd probably be in prison right now. Blake called it in to our superiors and as Renee waved my gun at me, sirens were screaming up and down her neighborhood. She knew she was finished. And I...I told her she had two options." He gulped around the knot in his throat, petrified of what Celeste would think of him once he told her what he'd never told another soul.

She took another step closer. "And they were?"

He caught her vanilla and cinnamon scent, and wanted to wrap his arms around her and lose himself in her body. Forget everything that had happened. But not yet. He'd started this, and would finish it, and he hoped to God she still respected him when he was through.

"Either she faced prison—not a great place to be as a former FBI agent—or kill herself." He choked back the memory of those words and gripped Celeste's shoulders. "She...she looked out her window, then back at me." He squeezed Celeste tighter. "She shoved my gun into her mouth, then pulled the trigger."

She jerked beneath his hands, tears spilling down her face. "John, I..."

"I went through hell after that. The questioning from my superiors, the hours with their psychologists, even after the evidence pointed in my favor. And when all was said and done, and I was exonerated from having anything to do with Renee and Tony's deaths, there was still that stigma."

"Which was why you left the FBI."

"Yeah, my boss might be a bit manipulative, but he saved me the day he asked me to join CORE. He gave me a second chance. And I owe him, which was why I came to Wissota Falls, and why I ended up working with a psychic even if it wasn't what I'd wanted."

Her breath caught. "And now?" she asked, her eyes glistening with tears.

"I wish we'd met under different circumstances, but I'm glad to have been given the opportunity to know you. And if you asked me to leave, it would hurt like hell." He cupped her cheeks and grazed his thumb along her lower lip. "You've shown me what I've been missing in my life."

"What's that?" she asked, breathless, as another tear slipped down her cheek.

"You. But I don't deserve someone as special as you, Celeste. Because of me, Tony died. And I can't help, but feel guilt over Renee, even with her betrayal. Damn it, I told her to kill herself."

She gripped his wrists tight. "You didn't kill Tony or Renee. She did it. She pulled the trigger both times. Stop punishing yourself for something you didn't do. Stop letting your guilt control your life, and don't you dare let it interfere with what we have."

"And what do we have? I have a life in Chicago, and you have one here. It will hurt when I walk away from you once this case ends, but I *will* walk away. I won't drag you into my life and watch the sparkle in your eyes dim once you realize I'm not the man you thought." God, he hated himself. Hated that he couldn't man up and admit that he didn't want to walk away, that he wanted to drag her back home with him and cherish her the way she deserved. With her, he'd become a better man, a different man. She'd become the best part of him. But he worried he couldn't live up to her expectations, that if he gave his heart and soul to her she might eventually reject it once she realized how hardened and tainted those parts of him had become.

A half-smile tilted her lips. "You're so full of it. I have a feeling you've been using Renee and Tony's death as a crutch. As a way to shut people out and keep the real John Kain locked in his own personal prison. Don't shut me out, too. I'm a big girl, and I've walked into this relationship with my eyes wide open. You want to walk away, then walk." Breathing hard, she looked away and released his wrists, then moved toward the foyer. "There's the door. You know how to use it. Keep in mind, though, I don't want you to leave. You're the one who's already making up excuses and reasons why what we have shouldn't work. Make it easier on yourself and go now."

She'd given him an ultimatum. Man up or walk. He didn't want to do either. He wanted to time travel back to the moment she was straddling his thighs before Lloyd dropped by and forced him to face his past. At that point, he hadn't fully opened himself up to her. At that point...hell, even then he knew he'd have to face the reality, the fact that he'd either have to cut bait or own his feelings for Celeste. Then, though, he'd still had time to figure out what to do. Now, she wasn't giving him any time at all.

She gripped the door knob. "Well, what are you waiting for?"

Before she could turn the brass handle, he was on her, pinning her to the wall, and her hands to her hips. His heart pounding hard, he stared into her wide eyes. "I can't."

"You can't what? Leave? Or take a chance?"

The challenge in her eyes, in her husky voice had him hard, ready, and aching to confess more than he'd already done tonight. He couldn't walk away from her. He couldn't risk losing the one woman, the only woman, who'd captured his trust, his heart, and his soul.

"I can't leave you."

She leaned into him, brushed her breasts against his chest, and tipped her pelvis against his erection. "What can you do?"

He nipped her lower lip. He knew this was about more than sex. But sex was on the forefront of his mind. Touching her, caressing her, showing her his emotions was easier than explaining what the loss of her, what they had, would do to him. Not being able to see Celeste, touch her, talk to her, hear her laughter and share her life would kill him. He'd die a slow, lonely death. He also didn't want to drag her down into his private hell. Into the depths of guilt that still weighed on his conscience and haunted him more than he'd admit to anyone.

"Is that the best you've got?" she taunted, when he soothed the nip with a flick of his tongue.

Framing her face with his hands, he stared into her eyes. "Are you sure you want this?"

"Meaning?"

"Me. The man I am. I told you about Renee, about Tony, but do you have any idea what I've become since that day?"

She ran a hand along his jaw. Her caress so soothing, so filled with deep tender affection, had him swallowing around the lump in his throat.

"John, the man I know is hard, but not cruel. Everything about you has to fit into a nice little slot of logic, and yet you've opened yourself up to me. Not just with your personal baggage. You believed in me, and you have no idea what that means to me. And I believe in you. Whether or not there is an us when all is said and done...I don't know. I'd like there to be, because you've touched a part of me I didn't know existed."

He rested his head against hers, his mouth mere inches from hers. "Celeste, being with you has been the best days of my life. I don't want it to end, I don't want to walk away, but I also don't want to hurt you."

"Then don't."

He raised his head, their gazes collided. Simple as that, he realized he didn't have to. He could have her. Now. And later, when the case was over, suggest she join him in Chicago. Hell, he had the money. He'd buy out her dad, and sell the diner. He'd take her away from a life she was living for someone else. He'd take care of her, cherish her, give her anything she wanted to have her with him.

Couples joked about their better half, but in all honestly, he believed she *was* the better half of him. She'd filled him with hope for the future, a future that before setting foot into Wissota Falls had seemed bleak.

"I won't," he promised, and captured her lips. Sealed that promise with a searing kiss that left them both breathless. She owned a part of him now. Now he wanted to own a part of her. He needed that part of her heart, her soul. Without it, he'd survive, but his existence would be lonelier than it had been before he'd met her. He'd tasted affection, the promise of more with Celeste. To lose that? He kissed her harder, with more determination. He refused to lose what he had with her when she was willing to give, to receive. When he was willing to give right back and open to whatever she had to offer him.

Breaking the kiss, he took her hand and kissed her knuckles.

She ran a hand through his hair as he gazed up at her, a teasing smile playing on her lips. "Come to bed with me."

"To sleep?" he asked as he inched his lips up her wrists.

Fisting his hair, she halted his ascent. "I'm not sleepy." She reached down, ran her palm along his erection, then snagged his belt buckle. "Actually, I want to get back to where we were." She stripped the belt away. "Before we were so *rudely* interrupted."

She pushed him back, then headed up the stairs, a sexy sway to her hips as she dangled his belt behind her. "Are you coming?" she asked over her shoulder.

They both would be soon. Very soon.

He pulled his shirt over his head as he followed her. By the time he reached the bedroom door, he had his jeans undone.

"No fair," she said with a slight pout. "I wanted to do the honors." She dropped to the floor, hooked her fingers into the waistband of his jeans and tugged.

He gripped her wrist. "Stop."

"No. You said next time it would be my turn. And it's next time. So..." She nipped at the cotton of his boxer briefs, her hot breath warming the material and searing his dick. "My turn."

After everything that had just happened, he wanted to be the one giving the pleasure, not taking. Before he could utter another word, she slipped his boxers over his hips, and ran her hand along his cock. He clenched his teeth, and looked down at her.

Her face was flushed, her eyes glittered with need, desire and so much tenderness, it humbled him. Holding his gaze, she took him into her mouth.

Exquisite, he thought through the sexual haze now consuming him, as he ran his hand through her soft curls. He'd never met another woman like her, and doubted another would ever compare. He'd be a fool to walk away from her. She accepted him. His faults, his baggage. Without question, without hesitation. And at this point, he didn't care if he'd only known her for a few days, or that the circumstances that they'd met under were not exactly ones that they could share with their children.

He gripped her hair as the thought of seeing Celeste, her belly round with his child, pierced his heart. She looked up at him, her mouth poised at the head of his cock. The words were there, at the tip of his tongue, but he couldn't say them out loud. The fear of voicing any more than he already had tonight stopped him. Now wasn't the time. He wasn't sure if he could fulfill the promises he wanted to make, or whether or not she wanted to hear them.

She kissed his arousal, his stomach, then inched up his torso until she stood toe to toe with him. The uncertainty on her face, in her eyes, had him cupping her cheeks. "Don't."

"I...I'm not all that experienced. If I didn't—"

"Don't," he repeated, and unsnapped her jeans. "I love the way your mouth feels on me." He tugged at the material, drawing her closer to him, then leveled his lips to hers. "I need to be here." He cupped the apex of her thighs. "Now."

A smile curved her lips. "Then what are you waiting for?" she asked, her voice breathless as she reached for the hem of her shirt.

While she tossed her shirt and bra off, he shucked her jeans over her hips, then knelt and placed his mouth between her thighs. Though her lacy panties, he nipped and suckled. She drove her hands through his hair, rocked her hips against his mouth and released a harsh moan.

The scent of her, the heat radiating from her, had him hard and ready. He shoved the panties around her ankles and kissed her sex, licked and teased until she flew apart screaming his name.

Something primal swelled inside him. Something he'd never experienced before. He wanted to hear his name on her lips again as he made her come. Hell, he wanted the whole fucking world to know who she belonged to.

He stroked himself as he stood. "On the bed."

Celeste couldn't tear her eyes off his hand, the way he moved it over his thick erection. Poised at the brink of orgasm, just from the sight of him, she somehow obeyed, somehow moved her body.

"Spread your legs."

She snapped her gaze to his and had to bite back a moan. His brown eyes had grown darker. They glimmered with something more than lust, and had her head spinning. He didn't just want her. He needed her. And she needed him. Every day. Always.

The realization slammed into her. She'd fallen for him. Hard. He'd opened up to her. Let his defenses down, and allowed her to see the man he truly was, the man she truly...loved. Was that possible? To love someone she'd only met a few days ago? Yes, her inner voice screamed and told her not to overanalyze. To show him how she felt, even if she was too afraid to voice the words.

Scooting to the center of the mattress, she did as he'd demanded. She spread her legs. Let him look his fill, and shuddered at the way he devoured her with his eyes.

"I want to hear my name coming from those beautiful lips." The bed dipped and he centered himself above her. "I...need you, Celeste." He pressed his arousal between her thighs.

She arched her back as he impaled her with one long thrust of his hips. "So good," she whispered against his throat, then nipped at his skin.

"*Very* good," he groaned as he began to move above her. Rotating his hips, thrusting slowly, deliberately.

Not enough. She grabbed his ass, loving the way his muscles bunched under her palms. "Harder."

"Is this what you want?" he asked against her ear, then began pounding into her and taking her so close to the edge.

"Yes," she hissed, meeting each thrust. "Oh, yes."

Sweat beaded along his brow as he held her gaze and gave her what she wanted. Him. All of him. He filled her body with his hard arousal. He filled her mind, her heart with his unspoken emotions. She swore they coursed through her body with each sensual rock of his hips, searing her soul with unspoken, veiled promises.

She wrapped her legs around him, locking him to her body, to her heart, and flew. The orgasm ripped through her, took her to a plain she'd never been in her life. Crying out his name, she let the intense pleasure shatter her, and hoped to God that in the end, he didn't shatter her heart.

As she rode out the ecstasy, the sheer erotic moment that sealed her love for him, he let himself go. With her name on his lips, he shuddered above her, staring into her eyes.

Dazed, dumbstruck with so many tremulous emotions, she held his gaze, then worried about giving too much of her feelings away, held him to her breasts. Tears stung her eyes. She loved him. She needed and wanted him in her life. Yet John thought he wasn't good enough for her.

Stupid man, she thought as she held him tighter. He was everything she'd ever wanted, everything she'd ever needed. Now she had to convince him that she belonged with him, that they belonged to each other.

CHAPTER 18

WITH HEAVY-DUTY oven mitts covering her hands, Celeste pulled the baking sheet filled with chocolate chip cookies out of the oven, then placed it on the stovetop. The scent of melted chocolate suddenly overrode the smell of the buttery croissants and apple pie she'd baked earlier.

Normally, her mouth would water. Chocolate was her biggest vice. Well, it was until she'd met John. The taste of him could become more addictive than chocolate, and that was a *huge* problem.

Last night, okay more like today, considering it was six in the morning and they'd made love again sometime around the wee hours of two, was incredible. The sex...she'd never experienced anything more intimate in her life. Again, a *huge* problem.

Not that she was complaining about how John had literally rocked her freaking world, but she did have issues with the way he'd still held back. She understood that he'd been through a bad time. Her heart nearly broke when he'd told her what he'd gone through during his final months with the FBI. But sometimes you had to cut bait and move on, which was something John had done by joining CORE. Yet he'd never really moved on like he seemed to think.

She was a psychic, not a mind reader. But she sensed guilt still ate at him. She had no regrets in telling him he'd used what had happened as a crutch, and obviously he had no hard feelings, either. Considering he'd been hard and ready for her, not once, but twice.

Still. Where would they go from here? Where *could* they go from here? She had too much pride to up and move for him, and it wasn't as if he'd asked her to in the first place. Plus, she had her dad's diner to run. Without her, where would that leave The Sugar Shack? Without John in her life, where would that leave her?

Alone.

Again.

The timer dinged and she quickly pulled the pie crusts from the other oven. As they cooled she began mixing the ingredients to fill them. While whipping the chocolate concoction that she'd use for two of the four pie crusts, her thoughts drifted to Roy. What information would he reveal about her mother? She still couldn't believe her mom had been in love with another man. Did her dad know?

"Now I know why you smell so delicious."

She whipped her head toward the bottom of the staircase. John's sleepy, sexy voice made her instantly regret not taking care of all her baking yesterday. She could still be in her bed waking up to his warm body and a few more orgasms.

He came around the corner, dressed in the jeans and shirt he'd worn last night, and released a low whistle. "Hell of a set up you've got here. Two double ovens?"

"I do all the baking for the diner at home. I'd rather do it out of the house than be stuck at the diner at all hours of the night trying to prep for the next day."

As he approached, her heart thudded with anticipation.

He kissed the curve of her neck. "I was disappointed you weren't next to me when I woke up."

"I was hoping to finish before you woke," she said, and her breath hitched as he trailed his lips lower. "I would have slipped back into bed, then woke you up...properly."

"Properly?" he murmured against her collar bone.

"Decadently."

He cupped her bottom, swiveled her around, and raised her on the big island she used for kneading dough and mixing ingredients. "I don't know." He dragging open-mouthed kisses along her jaw line. "Watching you bake turns me on," he said, grinding his erection between her thighs.

"Does it now?" She practically purred.

"Mmm, I'm picturing you in nothing but that apron, and my cock between—"

"Celeste? You down there?" Will called from the top of the stairs.

Damn. "Yeah, Will," she shouted back, then gave John a quick kiss. "Sorry."

"Don't be. I'll be back later. I mean, if that's okay."

"Are you serious? Of course it is."

"Good." He kissed the tip of her nose, then pulled away before Will reached the bottom of the staircase.

"Morning." He eyed the two of them with both curiosity and disgust. She got it. No one wants to walk in on one of their siblings fooling around, it was just...gross.

"Morning," they both said at the same time, then laughed.

Will shook his head and smiled. "How long before you're ready to leave?"

"I'm going to head into the diner later. Roy's stopping by for coffee. But I'd appreciate if you hauled what I've baked. Just give me a half hour to finish up and box the stuff."

"Will do." He kept his eyes trained on John. "Holler at me when you're ready."

After Will headed upstairs, John moved back toward her. He rubbed his palms along her hips and kissed her cheek. "Can I help with anything?" he asked as he slid his hand under her apron, then moved lower, cupping the apex of her thighs.

She moaned at the friction, and let her head drop to his chest. "As much as I'd love to fulfill your 'banging the baker' fantasy, I've got to finish this up, so..."

"All work and no play." He nipped her earlobe. "Okay,

what do you need me to do?"

After John washed his hands, she had him boxing the croissants, cookies and apple pies, while she finished making the chocolate and banana cream pies. Normally she hated having anyone intruding in her basement kitchen, but she loved the way John's big body was always in her way. The accidental touches, the way he brushed against her, the easy intimacy between them. She'd miss him when he left, and once again wondered how the hell they could make what they had between them work.

After the last batch of cookies was boxed, she gave him a quick kiss. "Thanks for helping. But next time, if it doesn't fit in the box, you don't just eat it, you find a new box."

"Huh, so that's how it works," he said with a big grin.

"I'm heading out," Will called down the steps.

"Me too." John gave her another kiss, this one a lingering, sultry kiss that had her toes curling and once again wishing they were back in her bed. "I'll take some of these boxes on my way out." He kissed her again. "I'll call you later."

With a smile on her lips, she watched John's tight butt as he ascended the stairs. She couldn't wait for later, but right now, she had a heck of a mess to clean up before her coffee date with Roy.

An hour later, showered and jacked up on caffeine, she paced the living room and wondered if maybe she should grab her mom's journal. A part of her didn't want Roy reading her mother's words. They'd been her private thoughts, and as it was, she'd felt like a bit of a voyeur after reading them last night.

Before she could decide, the doorbell rang. Her stomach somersaulted. She didn't know why. After all Roy might not even know anything about Ian. But what if he did? How would it make her feel to learn about the man her mother had loved before marrying her father?

Drawing in a deep breath, she opened the door and smiled. "Morning, Roy."

"Morning, honey," he greeted her, and entered the foyer.

As she was about to shut the door, he stopped her, then craned his head back outside. "Are you coming or not?"

She frowned. "Who's with you?"

His green eyes held wariness and concern. "A friend I want you to meet."

Just then, a man who she figured to be somewhere in his early fifties approached. She studied him from his salt and pepper hair, to his bright blue eyes, to the tailored suit he wore down to his shiny shoes. "Sorry about that, I got caught up checking out all those little men you have surrounding your house like an army of soldiers. Hope you don't mind that I tagged along with Roy."

"No," she said, unable to tear her gaze from his as a weird sense of déjà vu tore through her. He seemed so familiar, yet she'd never met him before in her life. At least she didn't think so. "I've got a full pot of coffee and plenty of fresh baked croissants in the kitchen. You're more than welcome to join us. I'm Celeste Risinski." She offered her hand.

He took her hand, and she swore his eyes misted before he blinked. "It's a pleasure to finally meet you, Celeste. I'm Ian Scott."

Pulling her hand from his, she looked to Roy, her temper flaring with betrayal. "What the hell, Roy?"

"Now don't get mad at me about this."

"Really? I called you last night hoping you could shed some light on my mom's past. I didn't expect this." She waved her hand at the man she assumed was her mom's former lover.

"I see you've inherited not only you're mom's temper, but her beauty as well. Come on." Ian took her arm. "Let's talk this out. I think you'll find what I have to tell you very interesting."

She eyed Roy, and the amusement in his eyes calmed her. Surprisingly, so did Ian's charming disposition. Deciding she actually wanted to hear what Ian had to say, she led him into the kitchen.

After he and Roy took a seat at the kitchen table, she drew in a deep breath, pulled her gnome coffee mugs and plates from the cabinet, then set them on the table along with the croissants. "So..." She filled the coffee mugs.

Ian thanked her, then gave her a broad smile. "Gnome plates and mugs, too." He smiled as he took a croissant. "Did you bake these?"

"Just this morning," she said, then grabbed a water bottle from the fridge. She'd already had enough caffeine, between that and Ian's unexpected visit, her stomach was an absolute mess.

After she took a seat, Ian stared at her. "What?" she asked, unnerved by the way he perused her. Not sexually, but as if she were a science experiment.

"Sorry." He shrugged. "I didn't mean to stare, it's just...your resemblance to your mom is truly uncanny."

She didn't know what to say, even though a million questions buzzed through her head. So she blurted the first one that came to her mind. "How did you meet my mom?"

"Roy told me about her journal. Didn't she say?"

"No, just that she'd worked as a psychic advisor for both the Baltimore police and the FBI."

His lips jerked into a quick, wry grin. "Well, I used to be FBI."

"Used to be?"

"I'll get to that. Back to your mom, I'm sorry for your loss. She was a wonderful woman."

"Thank you. And while I appreciate—"

"You'd rather I skip the formalities and get to why I'm here, right?"

She shrugged as her cheeks heated. "I don't mean to be rude."

"You're not. I've sprung a hell of a surprise on you this morning. So let's get at it." He gave her an easy smile. "I learned about Janice after she helped the Baltimore police solve a high profile case. At the time, I was working an investigation involving a serial killer. A detective with the Baltimore PD recommended that I contact your mom. So I did."

"You weren't skeptical?" she asked, considering how most

people had treated her over the years, and how John had first reacted to her gift.

"A little. But at that point in my investigation, I was willing to do anything to solve it. Taking down that serial killer meant everything to me. It would seal my career with the FBI, and while it eventually did…I hold many regrets about it now."

She shot her gaze to Roy, who had his eyes narrowed on Ian. "How so?"

"Did you know your mother was a medium?" he asked instead as he dropped a teaspoon of sugar into his mug.

She froze, the details of her trances rushing through her mind. "No. I didn't."

"Janice and her secrets." He shook his head. "She should have told you, especially when she realized you shared her gift. But that was her way. Controlling. Secretive."

"My mother wasn't controlling. We had a very open relationship. She was my best friend," she said defensively. This man obviously had had a brief affair with her mom. He didn't know her. At all.

She looked to Roy for support, but he only offered her a sheepish shrug. "It's true. With your mom, everything was on a need-to-know basis. Hell, she was worse than Ian, or anybody else I'd worked with during my stint with the FBI."

"*You* worked for the FBI?" Her head was spinning with even more questions. She'd never known what Roy did before becoming sheriff, and until now, had never thought to ask.

"I did and so did your dad."

Wow. Her dad was former FBI, too. Her stomach did a double somersault this time. She knew her dad had been in the Navy, then afterward, she'd assumed he'd worked at her grandparents' diner in Baltimore until he and her mom decided to move to Wissota Falls and open up The Sugar Shack. Now that she thought about it, she'd never asked why her parents had moved all the way to Wisconsin. Had they been running from something? Had they been running from Ian?

"I can understand why my mom wouldn't have told me about being a consultant to the FBI. She always downplayed her gift in public. But why wouldn't my dad have told me about being in the FBI?" She thought about John. "Did he do something wrong?"

"God, no," Ian said. "Your dad was a huge loss to us."

"Then..." She shook her head. "Maybe you should start at the beginning. As it is, I'm having a hard time digesting all of this."

"Rightfully so," Ian said. Stirring the teaspoon in his mug, he looked out the window. "Does Will still live above your garage?"

"How do you know about Will?" she asked, and looked to Roy, who kept his eyes focused on the plate of croissants. Why were they both stalling?

"I know everything about you, Celeste. I've made it my business."

"Why?"

"Did you like growing up in Wissota Falls?"

"Yes."

"Do you still like living here? You had a wonderful job in Madison after you'd graduated from college."

"Stop answering me with more questions," she demanded, crinkling the water bottle in her hand. "How do you know so much about me?"

"I told you, I've made it my business."

"Again. Why?"

He looked at her then, and the regret, the guilt in his eyes made her downright angry. "You've come into my house with more questions than answers. It's time for you to either leave or say whatever it is you have to say."

A wistful smile crossed his lips. "So much like your mother," he said, then with a deep sigh he leaned back in the chair. "That case I'd asked your mother to help me with wouldn't have been solved without her. She was good. Very good. As a medium, your mom was able to slip into these trances and connect with the victims. Something Roy told me you've been doing with his current investigation."

"I've been *doing* that, but I didn't *do* it on purpose."

"Neither did your mom at first, from what she explained to me. Somehow she'd learned to control the trances. Her ability to connect with the dead helped lead me to the killer I'd spent over two years tracking. During the time we spent together, your mom and I grew close. Actually, from the moment I met her, I knew I was a goner. She was a beautiful woman. Smart. Strong. I loved her dearly. I still do." He cleared his throat. "Because of her, I was able to catch my killer, and secure my career."

"Why do I feel like there's a big 'but' coming?"

"Because there is." He leaned forward, resting his arms on the table. "What I didn't know was that Seth Ryker, a psychiatrist who had also worked with me a time or two, had learned about Janice. See, we're going back thirty years, before we had a profilers unit. So I would consult with Ryker, hoping to gain some insight on who I'd been looking for. Only...only when he learned about your mom..."

"He what?" she prompted.

"He'd been running experiments on people who claimed to have psychic powers. I didn't know this, and while I had been chasing after my killer, he kidnapped Janice." A visible shudder tore through him. "When I found out, I was deep undercover, getting ready to make the biggest bust of my career."

Her heart rate shot up as she stared at him. Her mom had been kidnapped? Why would she have hidden any of this from her?

"I made the biggest mistake of my life that day." Guilt lined his face as he ran the tip of his finger along the gnome etched on his coffee mug. "Instead of going after the woman I loved, I called Roy and your dad, and told them to handle it. To do whatever was necessary to get your mom back."

She looked to Roy then, who gave her a sharp nod. "Hugh and I, along with a couple of other agents, stormed that bastard's house. He not only had your mom, but five other people. Those victims he'd kidnapped didn't fare as well as Janice. He'd given two of them lobotomies, and the rest electric shock treatment. Fortunately he hadn't had a chance to run any of his experiments on your mom. Especially because…" He looked to Ian.

Silence filled the room.

"Especially what?" she asked, glancing between Roy and Ian.

Ian sighed and gripped her hand. "Especially because she was pregnant with you."

She pulled her hand free of Ian's. "That doesn't make any sense." The man was slime. He'd left her mom helpless while he'd gotten his shot at a serial killer her mom had helped him find. He'd had her dad and Roy rescue her while…a thought occurred to her.

A dreadful thought.

Her stomach did a triple somersault, and her head grew dizzy. She dropped the water bottle on the table, and glared at Ian. "If you were having an affair with my mom when all of this happened, when did my dad come into the picture?"

Ian held her gaze, his eyes didn't shift, but the emotions raging through them were enough to make her gasp. "No." She shook her head, and rose.

He stopped her. "Celeste, I am your father."

A hysterical bubble of laughter welled in her throat. She suddenly pictured the scene in *Star Wars* between Luke Skywalker and Darth Vader. Composing herself she looked at the slimy trash who'd been sipping coffee, her coffee, and narrowed her gaze.

"Get out."

His eyes flashed with disappointment. "What?"

"You heard me. Get out. Now."

Roy laid a hand on her shoulder. "Celeste, honey, it's all true."

She stared at the man who'd been like an uncle to her. Tears welled in her eyes, distorting the room. "Roy…I…"

"I know it's hard to accept. Sit down, and let's sort this out."

"Sort what out?" she shouted, and wanted to shout some more. Her fucking life had been a lie. She turned to Ian. "And you. So you know all about me. Know about my brother. Do you know about my sister, too?"

"Of course I keep tabs on Eden. After all, we live in the same city."

"You live in Chicago?" She couldn't hide the hurt in her voice. This man, her supposed biological father, had only been hours away and he'd never once contacted her?

"I would have come to you sooner, but your mom made it clear she wanted nothing to do with me. The only time I ever laid eyes on you was right after you were born. By that time, your mom was head over heels in love with your dad. She made me promise that I'd never contact you, that I'd never interfere with your life."

"Why?" God, she was going to fall apart. This was all too much. She needed John. In a bad way. He had such a logical spin on things and just being near him gave her a calming effect.

"I chose my career over your mom, Celeste. I was selfish and self-centered. I was young and stupid. If only you knew the regret that has tormented me for thirty years. I hated not being part of your life, to have to watch you grow from a distance." He grabbed her hand, his grip gentle, yet his eyes fierce. "Janice denied me the right to be her husband. That I could accept. But she denied me *you*. That was unacceptable. And that's also why Roy has been here, in Wissota Falls all these years. I needed to know how you were, what you were up to, every scraped knee, lost tooth, all of it."

She gasped and shifted her gaze toward Roy. Disappointment and betrayal rolling through her, as the tears spilled down her cheeks. "You pretended to care so he could keep *tabs* on me?"

"I never *pretended* anything when it came to you," Roy said with vehemence. "And don't you *ever* think otherwise. I love you, Celeste, like the daughter I've never been blessed to have." He squeezed her other hand. "What Ian gave me, this job as sheriff, and a chance to be a part of you and your family's life, has been the best thing that could have ever happened for me. I wasn't cut out for the FBI. Janice, your dad, and Ian, they all knew that. I've never once regretted what I've been doing the last thirty years, until now." He caught one of her tears. "Seeing you cry, and the way you're looking at me like I just smashed one of your gnomes, is making my heart break."

She hiccupped and released a shaky laugh. "You'd never smash one of my gnomes. I think you bought half of them."

Seconds passed. "You mad at me?" he asked.

Squeezing his hand back, she looked away. "Yes, no. I don't know what to feel right now." She shifted her gaze to Ian. "Does my dad know the truth?"

"Yes. He'd always thought you should know, but your mom was a stubborn woman."

She looked to Roy for assurance. "He's not kidding. I tried to convince her, too. But Janice wouldn't hear of it. The arguments Hugh and I had over you...well, they don't matter now. The bottom line, your mom was afraid that if you knew the truth, she might lose you to Ian. She knew how much you'd been itching to leave Wissota Falls. When your sister went off to Chicago, she worried you might follow. She worried you'd run into Ian considering he knows Eden."

"You said you'd kept tabs on her, but do you actually *know* her?" she asked Ian.

"We're well acquainted, but she doesn't know how well. I made a promise to your mom, after all."

This was all way too much to handle. She wanted to hate Ian. She wanted to rant at Roy. Everything she'd believed about her family had been a lie. She couldn't do either, though. Her mom *was* a stubborn woman, with a vindictive streak than ran bone-deep. Ian had wronged her mom. She'd been pregnant with his child and he'd left her to tackle a career-building case. As her thoughts raced through her mind, a big one came front and center.

"How did my dad end up marrying my mom over you?"

Ian released a slow breath. "Hugh and I had entered the academy together. We were great friends, and after I met your mom, we'd argued constantly. We'd both fallen for Janice. I'd see the way he looked at her, at the way she looked at him. I'm a competitive, shallow man, Celeste."

"No shit," Roy mumbled.

Ian glared at him for a second, then looked back to her. "I wanted her, but not the white picket fence, and two point five kids she had been looking for. Your dad wanted those same things. Even when I knew they'd be better together, I pulled out the charm. I didn't know she was pregnant with you when she'd been kidnapped. If I did, I'll be honest, I'm not sure if I'd have done anything differently. Like I said, I was dumb and full of myself. My career meant more to me than anything else, until I lost your mom to Hugh."

A deep scowl lined his face as he slipped his hand from hers and leaned back in the chair. "After that, my career did rise, but with nobody to share the success with, it didn't seem to matter. I kept at it, though. For years I did my job, lost the passion, then finally quit and created CORE."

"CORE? Oh my..." She looked to Roy, who stared at Ian as if he wanted to smash *him* into pieces. "*You* sent John here?"

"When Roy told me about your visions, then the bodies, I needed to make sure you were well taken care of."

John took care of her all right. In more ways than one. Her stomach twisted, as her head grew dizzy with the deceit. John had been Ian's babysitter. Not her lover. He'd used her. God, he'd *used* her. "You have to leave," she said, fighting back the fresh tears, the pain. She'd fallen in love with John, and he'd—

Ian stopped her. "No. And don't you believe for one second what you have with John is because he works for me. He doesn't know about any of this. But Roy has been keeping me posted on your relationship with him. Not that I have any say, but I approve. He's a good man. He deserves a good woman."

The relief that slammed into her had her sitting back down in the chair. John didn't know. Which meant what was between them was just that. Between them.

"I still think you should leave. No offense, but you've

turned my entire life upside down. I need time to...accept this. God, I need to talk to my dad."

Ian didn't appear to be offended. Instead, he offered her a smile. "I understand. But I also understand you've been having issues with your trances. Like your mom, you're obviously a medium, too. I can help you with that, Celeste. I worked with your mom. Watched and witnessed her trances and visions. I can help you."

She looked to Roy, who nodded. "It's true. He knows more about your mom's psychic stuff than your dad and I put together."

As much as she wanted time alone to deal with what she'd learned this morning, she couldn't help but take the bait. She did want to know how to deal with her trances. Her mom wasn't here. And Ian—as much as she didn't want to deal with him right now—might be her only source. "Then tell me."

"I will. But on a few conditions."

She shook her head. "Dropping all of this on me isn't good enough?"

"This isn't how I wanted to introduce myself to you. And trust me, I've dreamed of this moment since you were born. Still, you want something and so do I."

"What's that?"

"A chance to know my daughter."

The pain in his eyes was unbearable. The whole situation made her want to crawl into bed, pull the covers over her head and forget she'd ever read her mom's journal. In a matter of minutes, Ian had changed her life. She realized she didn't know her mother—at all—and that her dad wasn't her biological father. Not that it mattered, he'd been her father in every sense and she loved him dearly.

"I think I should to talk to my dad about all of this first."

"And you should. But he's not here right now. I am. And if you're game, I can help shed some light on your trances."

She wanted to know her mother's secrets. Yet a part of her hesitated. Was she really a medium like her mom? Did she really want to have the capability to talk to the dead? The memory of her nightmares rolled through her mind. Yes. She did. Anything to have this investigation closed, the murders solved and Winston's partner behind bars.

"Fine," she said, not liking the way he was insinuating himself into her life. "I'm game."

"Good. The other condition? I don't want John to know you're my daughter or that I'm here in Wissota Falls."

She tensed. Defensive where John was concerned, where *they* were concerned. The impact of Ian's admission placed a whole new spin on her relationship with John, and he needed to know. "Why?"

"I don't want him distracted."

She rolled her eyes. "Try again."

Ian blew out a deep breath. "Okay, I don't want this to bite me on the ass. John's one of my best agents and I don't want to lose him. He'd walk away from CORE if he knew I'd sent him here with ulterior motives."

"Which are?" she prompted.

"To protect my daughter." He gripped her hand again. "John's a tough guy to understand. He's been through...a lot."

"I know, he told me."

His brows rose. "He did?"

"Yes."

"Good. Very good," he said with a cryptic smile. "So, are you up to a few psychic lessons, or do you still want to kick me out of your home?"

She swung her gaze to Roy, who shrugged. "Up to you, honey. But I've got to leave. John and I have work to do."

Staring out the window to the back deck, trying desperately to rein in the caustic emotions bombarding her, she sighed. "Why do I feel like I'm being manipulated?"

Roy's bark of laughter made her jump. He stood, then kissed the crown of her head. "'Cause that what Ian's known for best. I've got to run. But I'll drag his sorry ass out of here if that's what you want."

Sliding her gaze to Ian, she tried to weigh her options, but came up empty. Damn, she wished she could talk to John about this. Right now she needed his rational brain to set things straight for her. Her emotions were distorting everything inside of her and making it difficult to think straight.

But she really wanted to solve this case and make the nightmares go away, and never happen again. If Ian could help her with this...

"Go do what you need to, Roy," she finally said. "Apparently, Ian and I have some catching up to do."

Hours later, still grinning stupidly, Ian drove his rental back to the Eau Claire Holiday Inn. He finally had what he'd dreamed. A cup of coffee with his daughter. His smile widened. And possibly a future with her in his life.

After her initial shock had worn off, and Roy had left, she'd proved her resilience. An eager pupil, she'd soaked in everything he'd learned from Janice and passed the information along to his daughter. He'd been tempted to talk her into going into a trance, but figured she'd be reluctant. Performing a trance required trust, something he'd have to earn, something that would take time to develop between them.

Instead, he'd offered her a job at CORE and a way out of Wissota Falls. She'd been right when she'd asked why she'd felt as if she were being manipulated. He wanted the chance to know his daughter, and having her in Chicago with him would give him that opportunity. Plus, after having worked with Janice all of those years ago, he'd love to put Celeste's skills to use at CORE as a psychic consultant.

The moment he'd proposed his plan, he could tell she'd been interested. And he knew why.

John.

Considering John had actually told Celeste about his past, something he never discussed, not even with the other CORE agents, Ian suspected the criminalist had fallen for her. And with the way her eyes lit with relief when he'd made it clear John knew nothing about Ian's connection to Celeste, he wouldn't be surprised if she'd fallen for him as well.

Yes. Everything would fall into place nicely. He'd give his daughter financially stability, a career, and the perfect excuse to move to Chicago to be with John. In the process, this gave him the perfect excuse to finally have the chance to know and love his daughter.

CHAPTER 19

JOHN RUBBED THE tension from the back of his neck. After spending the past three hours staring at the data from the program Rachel had created, and making phone calls to various police departments, he needed a break.

As he leaned into his chair, his thoughts lingered on Celeste. He wished he could head back to her house and crawl into her bed—with her in it, of course.

After spilling his guts, his past, his emotions, he knew in his heart he couldn't walk away from her. He'd decided last night that he'd somehow find a way to make what they had together work. He couldn't imagine his life without her. In less than a week he'd fallen—hard—for a woman that was his polar opposite. Yet they were so in tune with each other it was scary, overwhelming, and just what he needed. She'd given him a swift kick in the ass. She'd called him out and had told him to stop using his past as a crutch. She'd set him straight, made him think. About the future, about the life they could share.

Roy released a deep sigh. He glanced at the sheriff, then at Bev. The two of them had been working alongside him since Roy had returned to the Sheriff's Department after his coffee date with Celeste. They both looked as if they could use a break, too.

He closed his laptop, then stood and stretched. "How about we head to The Sugar Shack for lunch? My treat."

Bev stacked the papers she'd been working on, then shoved them aside. "We have pizza on the way."

Roy nodded his head. "Yeah, I thought the sooner we could get this done, the sooner we could have more evidence against Winston. I gotta hand it to that gal of yours over at CORE." He pointed to his pile of data. "Without this we'd probably never have been able to uncover all the murders Winston committed."

"Alleged murders," John reminded him.

"Whatever," Roy mumbled. "There's no doubt in my mind that Winston did at least the majority of the prostitutes we've been looking at all morning. The MO fits."

"It does, and once Rachel has a copy of the DNA from these unsolved murders, she'll send it to our genetic specialist who will compare them to Winston's."

"How long will that take?" Bev asked as she stood and yawned.

"With CORE's resources, maybe a day, hopefully sooner. As it stands, between what Celeste and I found last night, and what the three of us have researched this morning, we have over thirty murders matching Winston's MO in five different states."

Bev furrowed her red brows. "God, and we've only researched the past ten years. Hasn't he been on the road longer than that?"

"Fourteen to be exact," he answered. "Keep in mind, the DNA from these unsolved murder cases might not match Winston's."

"But," she prompted.

"I wouldn't be surprised if the majority will, and there might be more that we've missed. The way Winston made sure the bodies were clean of any evidence with the four women he'd dumped here shows he's conscious of leaving DNA behind. But I've noticed there's been gaps between murders, which makes me wonder if Winston's partner might be the brains of their operation."

"Alleged partner," Roy said with a smirk.

"Alleged," he repeated, smiling back at the sheriff.

"Because this *alleged* partner made sure Winston didn't get sloppy with the women they killed together?" Bev asked.

"That's what I'm thinking. Again, we'll know more once a DNA comparison has been done. Hopefully we'll find additional DNA that doesn't match Winston's."

"Then all we'll need to do is find his partner."

The front doors to the Sheriff's Department chimed.

"Must be the pizza," Bev said, rising from her chair, just as Roy's phone rang.

As Roy took the call, John wished for something other than pizza. He'd wanted a sandwich from The Sugar Shack. Actually, he wanted to see Celeste. The sandwich, the offer to buy Bev and Roy lunch, were excuses. He'd missed waking up to her this morning, although helping her in her basement kitchen wasn't half bad. He'd made sure she knew he was there, and had touched her whenever the chance arose. While doing so, he'd conjured all sorts of ways they could utilize that big island in the middle of the kitchen. He'd pictured spreading her body on the counter and feasting on her, or bending her over it and—

The slam of the phone jarred him from his fantasy. He whipped his gaze to Roy who rose from his chair.

"What's going on?" he asked.

"Yeah," Bev said as she walked into the room carrying a couple of pizza boxes.

"That was Winston's doctor. Our boy is finally awake."

By the time John and Roy reached Eau Claire Memorial's ICU, John's thoughts were focused solely on Garrett Winston and the case. On the unknown partner.

"Sheriff, Mr. Kain," Winston's doctor greeted them, his expression somber, distressed. "I know you're anxious to talk with my patient, but there's something you should understand."

"That is?" John asked, ready to interrogate the hell out of Winston.

The doctor pulled them aside. "Look," he began. "I told you that the subdural hematoma could cause a coma, which it did. I also told you that once he woke, the effects of his injury could change him."

John looked to Roy, who shrugged.

"What are you getting at, Doc?" Roy asked.

The doctor sighed. "I don't know what he was like before, but he's pretty much a basket case right now."

John scratched the back of his head and glanced toward Winston's hospital room. "A basket case, meaning?"

"Meaning, he's a bit, um, emotional right now. And rightfully so," he quickly added. "He's been through a lot and I recommend you keep your tone gentle."

Gentle? The image of the six dead bodies, along with Celeste's horrifying trances raced through his mind. "He doesn't deserve *gentle*," John snapped, his temper flaring. "He deserves the death penalty. The only reason I'm glad you saved him is because he has answers to questions we haven't been able to ascertain. He might be your patient, but he's also killed a lot of women. In ways you don't even want to know."

Winston's doctor leaned against the wall. "I read the article from the local paper this morning. As a doctor, trust me when I say it was hard to deal with the fact that I'd saved a killer's life." Shoving off the wall, he added, "Have at him, but I'm warning you to be prepared."

"Prepared for what? Come clean, dammit," Roy snarled. "I'd just spent the past three hours looking at the women he'd killed."

The doctor gave them a solemn nod. "From the moment Garrett woke up he's been crying."

"As in yelling kinda cry?" Roy asked.

"No. As in sniffling like a baby crying." The doctor glanced at his watch, then opened the door to Winston's room. "See for yourselves. And if you distress him, you'll be dismissed. He might be a murderer, but he's still my patient."

John gave him a curt nod. "Understood," he said. He and Roy entered the room, just as Winston released a gut-wrenching sob.

"What did I tell you?" the doctor asked as he glanced at the curtain drawn around Winston's hospital bed. "I have to check on another patient. I'll see you later."

"Ho-*lee* shit," Roy muttered under his breath after the doctor left the room. "What do you think? Is he playing us, or is what the doc said for real?"

John shook his head. "I've seen plenty of shit over the years," he whispered. "Criminals having their coming to Jesus moment and all that BS. But I'm not sure what to make of this right now with the way he's blubbering like a baby."

"Okay. So, how do you want to handle this?" Roy asked. "Like we're talking to a four-year-old, or do we go balls out?"

John grinned. "Considering he's murdered four women, and *allegedly* even more, I say we skip the good cop/bad cop routine and hit him straight on."

"I knew there was a reason I liked you." Roy grinned. "You gonna go first?"

"With pleasure." Metal scraped against metal as John tugged open the curtain. "Ma'am," he said, greeting the nurse.

She widened her eyes in exasperation when Winston eyed them and began bawling with renewed vigor. "Shh," she soothed him, as she checked the IV. "Can I get you anything before I leave?"

"You're leaving?" he asked, childlike.

"Mmm-hmm, but I'll be back in a bit to check on you," she said as she peered at the bandage wrapped around his head.

"Okay, but can you grab me another box of tissues?" Winston's eyes leaked fresh tears. "I can't stop crying. I can't stop..." He broke into another hysterical sob, hiccups and all.

After the nurse dropped a box of tissues next to Winston and left the room, John moved to the edge of the hospital bed. The bastard sported a couple of black eyes, stitches on his cheek, and a swollen lip. Tears streamed down his pale face as he darted his eyes between him and Roy.

"It's true, isn't it?" Winston sniveled and reached for a tissue, then blew his raw nose.

"What's true?" John asked.

Winston tugged on the handcuff secured to the bedrail. "I woke up and...and...oh God, I—" More crying, moaning, and nose blowing.

John glanced at Roy, who gave him an encouraging nod. Not that he'd need any encouragement. He'd take advantage of Winston's vulnerable state to obtain what he wanted. Answers.

"Do you know where you are?" he asked, then placed a mini tape recorder on the night stand next to the bed and hit record.

"The hospital," Winston groaned as he wadded the tissue in his hand.

"What's your full name?" he asked.

"Garrett Alan Winston."

He then asked Winston if he knew who was president, the current year and all that bullshit. He wanted to be certain Winston was cognitive enough for interrogation.

He answered everything perfectly.

"Good," John said with an encouraging smile. "You refused an attorney when you were arrested. Would you like one now?"

Please say no. He didn't want to have to wait any longer than they already had to question Winston.

"No attorney can save me now. Only...God," he mumbled, while tears streamed down his face, catching in his beard.

John doubted that. For what Winston had done, he'd likely burn in hell for an eternity—at least he hoped so. On the bright side, Winston's coming to Jesus moment could help speed up the process. He'd questioned prisoners who've gone through this before, and they'd always been eager to confess all of their dirty secrets in their search for redemption.

"Do you remember how you ended up in the hospital?"

Winston's chin trembled, his lips quivered as new tears

sprung from his eyes. "Hoyt, one of the guards at the county jail, was bringing me food. The next thing I knew he was trying to stick a needle in me."

"What happened next?"

"I don't know," Winston howled, as he swiped his face with the back of his hand. "I...reacted. Him or me, that's all I thought, and then...is he okay?"

"No, he's dead."

Winston became a slobbering mess.

"Get it together," Roy shouted, surprising both him and Winston. "Tell us what happened. Otherwise we're adding cop killer to your résumé."

"No, you don't understand," he yelled as he grabbed at the box of tissues. "I didn't mean..."

"Garrett, you reacted in self-defense." John kept his tone calm, hoping to keep Winston from becoming hysterical again. "But we need to know what happened."

Drawing in a big breath, Winston leaned against the pillows, and nodded. "Like I said, Hoyt brought me food. He told me to wait on my bunk, so I did. After he dropped the tray on the table, he gave me a funny look and told me to remain seated. Then he moved, quick. Pulled something out of his pocket and came at me." His chin trembled, but he kept his composure. "I grabbed his wrist and fought him. When I realized what he was holding, I just got plain pissed."

"It came down to you or him."

"That's right. So I did what I had to do and shoved the needle in his neck. Next thing I know, I've got three guards on me, hitting me with their clubs." He closed his eyes. "Now here I am, wishing I'd let Hoyt put me out of my misery."

At this point, John thought about bringing up the four women they were certain Winston had killed. But they already had enough evidence on those murders to put him away for four lifetimes. He couldn't bring up the unsolved murders they'd been working on until all of the law enforcement agencies submitted their DNA reports to Rachel, who would then send them out for comparison. That left him with

Courtney and Lauren's murders and Winston's partner.

"Why do you think Hoyt tried to kill you?" John asked.

"I have no idea."

"Really? You don't have any enemies? Anyone that would like to see you dead? Anyone that might be worried you know something you're not supposed to?"

Winston hesitated, then shook his head.

"Don't pussyfoot around, tell him," Roy said.

Winston whipped his gaze to Roy. "Tell me what?"

John looked to the sheriff, knowing he was right. Enough time had been wasted. "Garrett, Hoyt was blackmailed into killing you."

Winston's red-rimmed eyes flickered with pain and betrayal before fresh tears spilled from them. "That don't make no sense."

"That's what we thought at first, until we found two more victims."

"One of them had been sodomized before being gutted and tossed in a lake," Roy said, his tone dripping with disgust. "The other had been found near the mill in Tilden. You know the place don't you? 'Cause according to Booker Foods, Tilden was part of your truck route."

"The thing about that victim," John added. "She wasn't stabbed, but strangled, just like the women you'd dumped in Wissota Falls."

Winston closed his eyes and actually whimpered like a dog. "Please, I don't want to hear any more."

"But we're just getting to the good part," Roy said with sarcasm.

"That's right, Garrett. See, that second girl, she'd been raped by *two* different men."

Winston opened his eyes wide, and stared at him in shock.

"Evidence, Garrett," John began. "DNA, fibers, hair samples, one set was yours." He shrugged as he lied. Other than a hunch and Celeste's trances, they had zero evidence against Winston, or even a second killer. "And I'm betting the other belongs to your *partner.*"

"I...I work alone," Winston sputtered.

"Then explain the evidence. Explain why you're here." John slammed his hand on the bedrail. "We know you were working with someone, why would you protect him? Why would you confess and spend life in prison while he roams free? And why would you continue to keep your mouth shut when *he's* the one that blackmailed Hoyt into trying to kill you?"

Winston's face crumpled as a sob tore through him.

"Damn it, Garrett. Do you want God's forgiveness? Do you want deliverance and salvation for what you've done?"

"Yes," he hissed.

"Then start here. Start now."

"I...I can't," he cried, bawling like a baby.

"He wants you dead. What do you know about him?"

Covering his face with his hands, Winston sniveled and blubbered, rocking his body as far as the IV and handcuff would allow. "How could he?" he muttered over and over beneath his hands.

"*Who?*" John demanded. "Garrett, who did this to you?"

Winston tore his hands away and fisted the sheets. Veins bulged in his neck as his pale, bruised face became crimson with anger. "My fucking brother," he screamed, then in a frenzied fit of rage, he ripped the IV from his arm. Blood trickled from his wrist and splattered onto the white sheet as he tore at the sensors stuck to his chest.

John and Roy both jumped back as Winston lunged. "I've got to get out of here," he shouted.

Three nurses raced into the room, followed by Winston's doctor who ordered, "Strap him down, we need to sedate him."

"No," Winston growled as he tried to untangle his legs from the sheets. "I'll kill him for this! I'll kill that bastard so he can't kill again."

The doctor helped two of the nurses pin him down as the other nurse took a syringe to Winston's arm. Within seconds, Winton slumped against the bed, his eyes rolling back, his breathing harsh and ragged. Then he was out cold.

Wiping sweat from his brow and drawing in deep breaths, the doctor turned to them. "Leave. He'll be out for hours. Besides, I need to make sure he didn't damage any of his sutures, and probably give him a few stitches."

As he pocketed the tape recorder, John looked to the small gash on Winston's arm where the IV had once been. "We'll be back tomorrow."

"I expected as much." He ushered them into the hallway. "Call me before you come in," he said, and handed Roy his card. "I don't know if whatever happened today will affect him tomorrow. No sense on you wasting a trip if he's not lucid."

"Thanks, Doc," Roy said.

As they walked through the hospital corridors, the sheriff kept shifting his gaze toward him, a smirk beneath his mustache. Once they'd reached the parking garage, John stopped him.

"What?"

"I can picture the headlines if the media catches wind of this," Roy began chuckling. "The Crybaby Killer."

"God, you have a sick sense of humor," John said with a grin. "Is that what you were coming up with while I was interrogating Winston?"

"You call that an interrogation? 'Do you want God's forgiveness? Do you want deliverance and salvation?'" Roy's bark of laughter echoed throughout the parking garage. "Hell, you'd have made a mighty fine preacher. I was waiting for you to get all fire and brimstone on his ass."

Laughing with him, grateful for a release from the tension he'd endured during their time with Winston, John climbed into the cruiser. As he slammed the car door shut, he sobered and looked at the sheriff, who gave him a solemn nod.

"You did good, kid. We might not have gotten the name of his partner, but we've got ourselves a lead."

"His brother," he said, as he retrieved his cell phone. He needed Rachel and her research skills.

"How can two men decide to rape and kill together?" Roy

asked as he drove out of the parking garage. "I've got a couple of brothers, and couldn't even imagine it."

"That's because you're not a sociopath, and I'm assuming, neither are your brothers." He punched in Rachel's number, but didn't place the call as a thought occurred to him. "I think our answers to why they committed the murders are buried in their past. I already had Rachel perform a background check on Winston, and there wasn't any mention of siblings."

"What about a fraternity brother or brother at arms?"

John shook his head. "Winston never went to college or joined the military." He hit send and waited for Rachel to answer.

"Hi, John. How's things hanging in Wisconsin? Did you receive the rest of the data I sent?"

"Hey, Rachel, no I didn't. The sheriff and I just left the hospital after interrogating Winston."

"Holy crap, he's awake? He better not have rolled over and confessed everything after all the work I've done for you."

"You're a real riot. I love how it always comes back to you. And no, unfortunately your efforts weren't undermined by a quick confession."

"Damn, that's too bad," she said, with genuine disappointment. "Did he give you anything?"

"That's why I'm calling. Winston claims his partner is his brother."

"I found no siblings when I did his background check. Could he have meant 'brother' figuratively?"

"The sheriff suggested that, and it's possible, but I'd still like you to dig deeper. Maybe you can look into—"

"His parents' past, see if there are any half-brothers lurking around, maybe with a different last name, gotcha."

"When did you become a mind reader?"

She half-laughed. "It's a side-effect from pencil lead. I'll see what I can dig up for you. Be safe."

Smiling, he shoved his phone back into his pocket.

"Look at you, friendly with a psychic and now a mind reader," Roy said as he glanced at him.

"Rachel's a real piece of work. But if anybody can find out what we need, she can."

"So...how *friendly* are you with this Rachel?"

"Not like how I think you're implying."

"And Celeste?"

Damn. He knew this was coming, but he'd hoped to avoid the overprotective, surrogate dad routine with Roy. "Since you're sheriff in these here parts," he drawled. "I already know you own a gun. If you want to know something, why don't you ask me straight?"

With a chuckle, Roy turned toward Wissota Falls. "Okay."

A minute passed, then another. "Okay what?"

Roy shrugged. "You know I own a gun, you're involved with Celeste, so the way I figure, at this point asking anything else seems redundant. Don't you think?" He parked in front of the Sheriff's Department, and cut the ignition. "C'mon, let's eat some cold pizza and finish researching all that stuff your gal Rachel keeps sending us. I want to cut out early. Bev and I have a hot date tonight. How 'bout you?" he asked as they walked into the building.

John frowned. What about him? Maybe he should be asking Celeste to go out with him on an actual date. She deserved to be wined and dined. Romanced. Maybe a quiet, candlelit dinner for two at a cozy restaurant. A place where they could talk about their future, and definitely *not* about the investigation. Sure, he'd tell her about today. He loved hearing her take on things and including her in his job. But he also wanted to learn more about her, about her thoughts, of them...of their future.

And he did want a future with Celeste. Some way, somehow. He'd never been in love, but whatever he was feeling for her was the real deal. Of that he was certain because there was no way in hell he'd walk away, then spend the rest of his life lonely and wondering. He stopped Roy before they entered his office. "Where's a good place to eat *besides* The Sugar Shack?"

Roy gave him a big grin and clapped him on the shoulder. "Thought you'd never ask."

CHAPTER 20

AFTER A HOT shower, Celeste threw on a t-shirt and a pair of panties, glanced at the clock, then her bed. She had an hour and a half before John would arrive for their first, official date, and after a little indecision, she crawled under the covers for a quick catnap.

Unfortunately, even though exhausted, she couldn't keep her eyes closed. Staring at the ceiling fan as it spun in lazy circles, her mind raced. She never would have imagined today turning out the way it had when she'd woken at the crack of dawn to do her baking.

Ian Scott had more than shocked her. He'd pulverized everything she'd known about her life and family. Her mom had been kidnapped. She'd been pregnant with her but not by the man she'd called dad her whole life. Her dad had been former FBI, as had Roy, who'd been placed in Wissota Falls to keep watch over her. So many secrets, so many deceptions.

She'd wanted to toss Ian out on his ass when he'd first dropped the bomb that he was her biological father. She'd wanted to hate him for ruining everything she'd ever believed about her family. But after Roy left and she talked with Ian, she began to realize none of this had been Ian's fault. He hadn't been just a sperm donor, he'd actually tried to insinuate himself in her life.

The blame had lain with her mom.

She couldn't be mad at her, either. While she hadn't known about her mom's secret past, she knew in her heart that whatever decisions her mom had made—right or wrong—had been with her daughter's, and the rest of her family's, best interests in mind.

A few good things had come from meeting Ian, though, that both excited and worried her. He'd not only given her a better insight into how her mother had dealt with her trances and her role as a medium, but he'd offered her an opportunity at CORE as a psychic advisor. He'd pay her a generous salary, plus benefits, and had even offered to find her a place to live. He'd also said that if working for CORE didn't interest her, he'd still love to have her come to Chicago.

While she hadn't commented one way or the other about the potential job, she couldn't help considering his offer. How many times had she'd dreamed of leaving Wissota Falls again, going to a bigger city, living her dreams? But what about her dad and The Sugar Shack? And did she really want to be involved in criminal investigations, witnessing and viewing the horrors investigators like John saw on a regular basis? What about John, for that matter? How would he feel if she moved to Chicago? He'd said he couldn't walk away from her, but he'd never said how they could make what they'd started work, either.

The whole situation had exhausted and confused her. She'd spent the lunch rush on autopilot. Around two, she'd headed home to bake. There was no way she'd wake up at five in the morning again to take care of the diner's needs if John planned on spending the night. There was no way she'd miss the opportunity to wake up in his arms...properly, decadently.

She smiled as she remembered saying those same words to him in her basement kitchen as he'd pressed his erection against her and nibbled her neck. Her smile grew bigger at the thought of him taking her out on a date. She hadn't been on a date in over a year. And to think, he planned to take her to Eau

Claire's finest restaurant. She hadn't tasted anything but her own cooking or that of The Sugar Shack's for months. And half the recipes used at the diner were her dad's, which she'd doctored up a bit, while the rest were hers, so it had been like eating her own cooking anyway.

Dad.

Her smile fell as she imagined his strong face, and twinkling, playful green eyes—eyes so much like Eden's and Will's. What would they say when they learned about Ian? How much would change between them? Nothing, she decided. She was still the same person. She just had a different father.

A car door slammed. Unable to fall asleep, she rose and looked out the opened window.

Lloyd stood next to his truck, parked in the apron of the driveway. He glanced toward her house and sent her a tentative wave. Although she'd been angry with him last night, with the way the big lug now slumped his shoulders in defeat and offered her an apologetic smile, she knew she couldn't stay mad long. They had too much history together, and he'd always been a stable and important part of her life.

She waved back, then yelled, "Will's in his studio."

"Why isn't he with you?"

"Because I'm a big girl. Besides, the house is locked up and John's coming by in an hour or so."

He set his mouth in a grim line, then nodded and headed for the steps leading to Will's apartment above the garage. "You'll call if you need anything," he shouted over his shoulder.

"Duh," she said with a roll of her eyes that earned her a small grin from Lloyd.

After he disappeared into the apartment, she drew the blinds, then crawled back into bed.

Twenty minutes, that's all she needed. Just enough of a little catnap to help her rejuvenate before she finished preparing for her date with John. Her clothes were already laid out, all she had to do was apply her make-up and touch up her hair. She had plenty of time.

She glanced at the clock, and realized she now only had nineteen minutes, then stared back at the rotating ceiling fan. The wooden blades began to blur as she pushed the day's events from her mind and finally began to doze.

Dr. Alex Trumane arrived home after a late appointment at the office, and for the first time in months, he had no desire to go to his AA meeting. Tired from the past two sleepless nights and exhausted after playing catch-up with his patients, he wanted to lie in bed and zone out watching Sports Center. But if he didn't go, Kira would know. He'd always gone to the diner for coffee and pie after a meeting. And as a long-time AA member, she knew when his meetings were, or if for whatever reason, they'd been cancelled.

He parked his Lexus, then walked toward his mailbox. He absently sifted through the mail as he moved to his front door, then came to an abrupt halt.

His heart hammered with hope as he studied the return address on one of the envelopes. Mississippi State Department of Health. Anna Lynn Gates's will and the only lead he had to Number Twenty-two on his list of atonement.

After quickly unlocking the door to his condo, then slamming it behind him, he tore open the envelope. As he scanned through the contents of the will a punch of hope jabbed him in the stomach. Anna had left everything she owned to her granddaughter, Miranda. Yet what good did that knowledge do for him when he'd tried every route to find the granddaughter and had come up empty?

His hope deflated. He tossed the document on the coffee table, then slumped onto the sofa. Running a hand through his hair, he leaned back with a deep sigh.

Number Twenty-two's delicate features, her pale face, equally pale blond hair, and soft, hazel eyes formed in his memory. She'd been so slight, so pretty, and so damned scared. And he'd allowed the bastard she'd been with to manipulate her.

No, you manipulated her to save your ass.

Shoving off the couch, he grabbed the will again, this time reading every detail. A spark of optimism flickered in his pessimistic heart.

Wissota Falls, Wisconsin.

Anna Lynn Gates had left a house, along with several acres of property in this community to her granddaughter. Could Miranda be there? And if so, was *he* still with her?

At this point, it didn't matter if that bastard was with her or not. There had to be some statute of limitations that would keep him from losing his practice, his livelihood, and what little self-respect he owned. If not, at this point, he didn't care. What he'd done to her had been abysmal, and had gone against every oath he'd sworn to uphold. Because he'd been scared, drunk, drugged up, and a fucking coward.

He'd rectify what he'd done. He'd atone for his sins, even if it meant losing Kira, his family, and his practice. Even if it meant...going to prison. He could live sober. He could live behind bars. He couldn't live if he knew his cowardly actions had cost the life of a young, vibrant woman.

Checking his watch, he frowned in disappointment. He wouldn't be able to research this new information and make his meeting or see Kira.

Tomorrow.

Tomorrow he'd do some serious digging, and now he knew exactly where he'd start.

Wissota Falls, Wisconsin.

John climbed into his rental, freshly showered, and wearing what he'd hoped would suit the restaurant Roy had recommended, then headed for Celeste's house. The nervousness fluttering through his stomach was something strange, new, and a little exhilarating. He hadn't been on a date in years, and while he'd already been intimate with Celeste, this was their first *official* date. He wanted it to be special. He wanted something that the two of them could look back on fifty years from now and reminisce with smiles lining their wrinkled faces.

God, he was in deep. He half-laughed as he drove the car down Main Street. Already he was looking ahead, looking to the future, which was something he'd never done before unless it had dealt with his career. And with his line of work, he'd spent most days looking into hell—gruesome murders, sadistic and sociopathic killers, rapists, arsonists.

He'd chosen his career, though, and couldn't imagine doing anything else with his life. Someone needed to help the victims. Besides, he liked the rush, the investigative aspect, and the high when a murderer was brought to justice.

Unfortunately, he'd been too career-oriented to look outside the box, to realize that there was more to life than dead bodies and killers. Being with Celeste helped soften the rough edges of a bad day. She'd brought him hope with her pretty smile and intelligent, knowing blue eyes that sparkled every time she looked at him. With her, he didn't have to suffer the day-to-day routine alone. But did she want to be with him? Better yet, would she want to share a life with him?

His stomach fluttered again. He reached for his antacids, but tossed them into the center console. This wasn't acid reflux or the onslaught of heartburn. Nope, this was plain old nerves kicking in and giving him a wakeup call.

He couldn't let her go, at least not without laying all the cards on the table. Tonight, after dinner, he wouldn't just suggest she come to Chicago for a visit. Nope, he'd man up and tell her how he felt about her, then ask her to move in with him.

Releasing a deep sigh, the nervousness dissipated now that he'd made his decision. Yet as he turned down her street, it kicked back up a few notches. What if she said no? What if she didn't feel the same? What if this was just an affair to her?

The questions rolled through his head, but as he pulled into her driveway, they came to a screeching halt. The headlights from his sedan beamed against the tail end of the Viking's truck. Fucking Lloyd. He hoped like hell the jackass was here to see Will and not Celeste. After what he'd attempted last night, John still wanted to kick his ass.

Before he climbed out of the car, he grabbed the bouquet of flowers he'd bought for Celeste, then slammed the door shut. As he moved along the walkway, he ignored the gnomes and considered every worst case scenario, should he have to confront Lloyd, until he reached the front stoop.

Panic, fear and adrenaline moved through him. Celeste's front door stood wide open, the foyer rug, bunched and skewed. In an instant, he had his gun drawn from his shoulder holster and held low to his thigh. With cautious steps he moved into the foyer, then paused and frowned as he stared at the mirror above her fireplace.

A wave of anger and jealousy suddenly replaced his fear. He glared at the mirror, at the reflection of Lloyd's naked back as he leaned over Celeste who lay half against the wall. The fucking Viking's overlong hair hid their faces. But with the way her body jerked, her blond head sliding slightly up and down the wall, along with her low groans and his heavy breathing, it didn't take a rocket scientist to figure out what they were doing. Had she wanted him to walk in on them during the act? She knew what time he'd planned to pick her up for their date.

He crushed the stems of the bouquet in his hand. How could he have been so stupid? How could he have allowed himself to be duped again? He'd believed in her, in the idea of them, and he'd obviously been a simple fuck to her, nothing more. And now she was rubbing it in his face.

Damn, what a fool he'd been. He'd confessed things to her he'd never told anyone else. He'd planned to tell her how he felt about her tonight and ask her to move in with him. Thank God that never happened. Witnessing this, the betrayal, especially after he'd told her about Renee, was bad enough. To have opened himself to further humiliation would have left his ego, hell, his heart, in shambles.

Damn it, he *loved* her.

Defeated, depressed and downright pissed as hell, he holstered his weapon, then tossed the bouquet on the floor. As he was about to walk out the door, and out of her life, he caught a quick glimpse of Will in the mirror's reflection.

Racing from the kitchen, wearing nothing but a pair of jeans and holding a cordless phone, Will shouted, "I'm calling him now."

Celeste released a harsh scream the same moment John's cell phone rang. In that split second, his entire body tensed, and his scalp tingled as dread slipped down his spine.

Lloyd and Celeste weren't having sex on the living room floor. She was deep in another trance.

Before he could berate himself for his lack of trust in Celeste, he ran into the living room. His thoughts focused on her. On making sure she made it through another trance unscathed.

When he reached her, he held back a gasp. He'd witnessed two of her trances, but what he saw now scared the hell out of him. With her bare legs splayed open, her hands pinned to her sides, and her head and body jerking hard against the wall, it appeared as if an invisible force was...raping her.

He loved Celeste so much he wanted to shake her awake from whatever horrors this victim was putting her through. But the investigator overruled the lover. If there was another victim, they needed whatever help they could to find her. And he knew this was what Celeste would want him to do.

"Move," he ordered Lloyd as he turned on his cell phone's recording device.

"Thank God you're here," Will said, his voice filled with anxiety, his eyes bloodshot and brimming with tears. "We tried to wake her up, but—"

"How long has she been like this?"

"I...I'm not sure," Lloyd said, his tone matching Will's. "We heard her scream about five minutes ago, but she'd dropped a wooden pole into the back sliding glass door, so we couldn't get in the house that way. We had to run around the front and when we finally got the door open, we found her like this."

John focused on Celeste, her pale cheeks, the sheen of sweat coating her face and mingling with her tears. "Honey," he said. "Can you hear me?"

Her body seized up, then arched. She opened her eyes, and stared at him. He hated when they changed from blue to murky gray, hated the helplessness he felt every time he endured these trances.

"You're here," she whispered on a sob.

"Celeste?"

Frowning, she shook her head.

"Can you tell me your name?"

"Lisa."

"Okay, Lisa, where you are? What's happening to you?"

"I'm so tired," she said, thickly, as if she'd been drugged. "I just want to sleep forever. I just want them to get it over with and kill me."

"Don't talk like that," he said, wanting to touch her, but worried any physical contact would draw her from the trance. "Can you find a way to escape?"

She let her head loll back and forth against the wall. "They tied me to a tree after the man with the ski mask beat me and...I can't talk about it." She released a quiet sob. "What he did was so vile and degrading."

A good start, she'd given him her name, and confirmed there were two men. "You said they. Who's with the man in the ski mask? Do you know him?"

Her face screwed into a grimace. "Yes," she hissed. "I know him. Gary's been a regular at the coffee shop for months. When he'd asked me out, I couldn't believe my luck. I'd had a crush on him, thought he was good looking with those silver eyes, dark hair, beard, and sexy southern drawl. I guess my luck ran out, huh?" She shrugged and closed her eyes.

This victim was so unlike the others who had used Celeste to tell their story. Rather than ranting and raving, flying off into hysterics, she remained eerily calm. Unsure if that was a good or bad thing, he said, "Let me help you. Tell me where you are so I can find you."

"I have no idea. Gary and I went for a drink, but I think he slipped something in it." Her chin trembled. "I passed out and when I woke up, the guy with the mask was...raping me."

He wanted to kill both Winston and his partner with his bare hands for what they'd put their victims through. Shoving his anger aside in order to keep his tone calm, he said, "Look around you. Can you describe where you are?"

"I can't," she said in defeat. "They beat me so bad, my eyes are swollen shut. I actually choked on my front tooth when Gary punched me for screaming too much. He didn't care, though. He just kept grunting over me while he...How could I have ever thought he'd like a girl like me? How could I have been so stupid? How could I have—"

"Shh, please," he begged as the image she'd described nauseated him. "Help me so I can help you. What do you hear?"

"Them," she snarled, and for the first time showed spirit. "Arguing."

"What about?"

"I don't know, and I don't care," she said, her voice rising. "I just want them to end this. I can't bear to have them touch me again. I can't take another blow, I can't—"

"I know, but you have to be strong. Please, Lisa, tell me what else you can hear. I just want to be able to find you."

She rolled her head to the side and squeezed her eyes. "Water. It's rushing all around us." Her frown intensified. "Like...like it's coming in three different directions."

"You're in the woods?"

She nodded, then froze, her eyes widening in horror.

"What is it?"

"They're coming toward me. I can't see them, but I can *hear* them. The leaves crunching, twigs snapping. Oh God, one of them has something on my stomach." She twisted the lower half of her body and kicked her legs. "It's metal, cold, flat, long and...sharp."

He moved to stay clear of her legs, and noticed Lloyd and

Will had done the same. "Stay calm," he ordered, and somehow managed to keep his voice from rising.

"I can't," she screamed. "It's a knife, he has a knife and he's swiping it along my stomach like he's buttering a piece of bread. Stop. Please stop. Please don't...no, no, no."

The terrifying image caused goose bumps to race along his skin. He wanted to drag her in his arms, and put an end to this fucking nightmare. "What is it?" he asked instead, driven by the need to know the details behind this woman's death, even as he watched the woman he loved suffer through it.

"The other one is behind me. Has to be Gary, his beard is tickling my neck." She cocked her head to her shoulder and cringed. "His hot breath is surrounding me. He's—wait, they're talking."

John looked between Lloyd and Will, the pain and horror in their eyes reflecting his own. Then he stared back at Celeste. "What are they saying?"

"The one with the knife just said, 'Here's to a new beginning.' I don't know what that means," she wailed as tears streamed down her face. "I don't understand, I don't—"

Her neck arched the same time her spine bowed. She released a hoarse scream as her face grew red.

"Make it stop," Will shouted, then moved for Celeste.

John shoved him out of the way. He knelt on the floor, pulled her into his arms, stroking her hair, her back, and murmuring into her ear. "Wake up, baby. Wake up. I've got you now. Wake up."

Cradled in his embrace, her body relaxed, then grew tense again as she drew in a deep gasping breath. Before he could explain, or hold her tighter like he wanted, she shoved her hands against his chest and pushed her body against the wall. She stared at him, surprise in her bright blue eyes.

"John?" she asked, then as if realizing where she was and who was in the room, she glanced between Will and Lloyd. "Oh my God." She snared his gaze. "Did I just have...?"

He nodded and wiped the tears from her cheeks. "Yeah, honey, you had another trance."

"I'm so sorry. I never wanted you to see this," she said, as she scrambled up the wall and reached for Will.

John moved and allowed her brother access to Celeste. He didn't want to. He needed time to decompress, to hold her and assure himself she hadn't been affected by the trance. But Will was her brother. Her very emotionally overwrought brother, who also needed time to accept what had just happened. As for Lloyd, while he could give a shit about him, he had been there for Celeste, and he supposed that counted for something.

"Celeste," Will said with relief as he hugged her. "Are you okay?"

She nodded against her brother's shoulder. "Yeah, just a little tired." She rubbed the back of her head and grimaced. "And sore. Did I bang my head?"

"Yeah, a bunch of times." Will sifted his fingers through her hair, and winced. "You've already got a lump. Let's get you some ice."

As Will headed toward the kitchen, his bare back tense, his hands trembling, she said, "Better grab a few ibuprofen, too. There's a bottle next to the gnome glasses above the sink."

"On it," he called over his shoulder without looking back.

"Come on, let's warm you up, and get you somewhere more comfortable," John murmured as scooped her in his arms, then carried her to the sofa.

"I can walk, you know."

"I know. Just let me pamper you." He gently set her on the couch. "That was the worst of the three," he said as he covered her with an afghan.

She grimaced and looked to Lloyd. "Thanks for being here for me. I'm so sorry you and Will had to see that."

He moved toward her, then took her hand. "You know I'd do anything for you."

"I know."

"And I'm sorry for last night. I shouldn't have interfered. It's just—"

Will approached with an ice pack, ibuprofen and bottled water. "Here you go."

While she chased the ibuprofen down with water, John turned off the recording device on his cell phone, then shoved it in his pocket. He wished they were alone, as he sat next to her on the sofa and wrapped an arm around her shoulders. After watching her relive the brutal last moments of another victim, all he wanted to do was hold her.

"So," she began, then pursed her lips. "Anybody interested in telling me what happened?"

He squeezed her to his chest and kissed her temple. "I recorded everything. Keep the ice on your head, and let the ibuprofen kick in, okay? You can listen later. Right now isn't the time."

"Much later." She sent her brother and Lloyd a worried look. "Are you guys okay? I mean, this is the third time John's seen me this way, and I know it still bothers him."

"No, I'm not okay," Will said. "I just watched my sister..." He shook his head, drew in a deep breath and looked to the ceiling. Will was fighting back the tears, and John understood. Watching someone you love go through something that traumatic didn't settle well on the soul. At all.

"Hey." She dropped the ice pack, stood and kept the afghan wrapped around her as she moved to him. "I'm okay. Seriously," she added when he refused to look at her. "I still have all my pinkies and toes, and—"

"It doesn't matter, Celeste," Lloyd interrupted. "When we finally unlocked the front door and saw you…" He shook his head. "Well, it's an image I won't ever forget."

"I'm sorry," she repeated again. "I honestly don't even know how it happened. After I talked with you through my bedroom window right when you got here, I laid down for a quick nap. The last thing I remember was staring at my ceiling fan..." She frowned, then shook her head. "Whatever. It doesn't matter how it happened, as you can see I'm okay. So why don't you two steal some bakery from the basement, and head back to the apartment."

"I take it you don't need me to stay in the guest room?" Will asked.

She looked over her shoulder at him. "I plan on staying the night," John said. When he'd left his motel room earlier, he'd planned on the evening going in a completely different direction, too. Either way, it would end the same...with Celeste in his arms.

"See." She moved back to the sofa. "John will be here if I need anything. So grab what you want from the basement. You can even take a few bottles of wine if you want to."

"None for me, thanks." Lloyd pushed off the fireplace and unfolded his arms. "Kain, I just need to grab my things from Will's place, then I'll need you to move your car."

Will stared at the Viking as if he'd lost his mind. "You're leaving? Why?"

Lloyd darted his gaze between him and Will. "I think it's best, don't you?"

"No." Will ran a hand through his hair. "I think it sucks," he muttered. "And typical."

"Sorry, Will, I'm not taking the bait," Lloyd said, as he moved toward the foyer.

"Fine. If what I'm dangling doesn't interest you, don't bother coming back."

"Will," Celeste gasped. "You don't mean that."

"The hell I don't. I'm so sick of his bullshit attitude."

"Mine?" Lloyd shouted as he swiveled on Will.

"Yeah, *yours*. For years I've kept quiet. For years I've suffered to protect you. I'm so fucking tired of living a lie because you're worried about your reputation. I'm so tired of *you* being ashamed of *me*." Will turned to him. "John, go ahead and move your car. Lloyd's leaving."

"I never said I was ashamed of you," Lloyd said through clenched teeth.

"Actions speak louder than words. Now just go."

Lloyd turned his back on them, but when he reached the door, instead of walking out, he slammed it shut. "Fuck it," he said, then stomped back into the living room. Every muscle in his arms and chest flexed as he moved toward Will.

Cheeks flushed, eyes wild and heated with anger, John

thought for sure Lloyd was going to knock Will flat on his ass. Ready to defend Celeste's brother, he stood.

"Actions speak louder than words, huh?" Lloyd snarled. "How's this for action?"

Instead of clocking Will in the jaw as John had expected, Lloyd cupped the other man's head and...

Oh. My. God.

...kissed him.

CHAPTER 21

CELESTE LOCKED THE deadbolt on the front door, then rested her forehead against the wood. Even though Will and Lloyd had left, the tension within the house remained.

"That was interesting," she said, trying to lighten the mood as she turned to face John.

He leaned against the banister, arms folded across his chest. With his face impassive, he nodded. "That's putting it mildly."

Was he mad? At her? She hadn't exactly planned on going under tonight. As for Lloyd and Will, she thought John had handled that shock quite well.

Other than turning beet red when Lloyd lip locked her brother, he'd showed no reaction. Even when Lloyd threatened to kick John's ass if he breathed a word about them being gay, he hadn't flinched. Instead, he'd told Lloyd he didn't care about his and Will's relationship, and that the only one John did care about was the one he had with her.

At that point, she'd been anxious for Will and Lloyd to leave. She'd wanted to be alone with John. The trance had left her more exhausted than she'd been when she'd lain down earlier for a nap. And after the day she'd had, all she wanted was to curl up against him and absorb his warmth and strength.

She glanced at the clock. "I guess dinner's out," she said, still trying to keep her tone light, and hoping she was misreading him. That he wasn't angry with her, but maybe the situation.

Another nod.

"Look, I'm sorry about tonight," she blurted and tossed the afghan she'd had wrapped around her, on the floor. "I need to get dressed." She needed to distance herself from his probing gaze. "If you still plan on sticking around, I'll make us some sandwiches."

In two strides, he had her pinned to the door. "You better believe I plan on sticking around. And quit apologizing. Nothing that happened here tonight was your fault."

"Really? Lloyd would never have outed himself and Will if it wasn't for me."

He ran a finger along her cheek. "It seems to me like it was a long time coming. Maybe tonight was just what they needed. A little push in the right direction."

His soothing voice, the trail of heat his finger left on her cheek, and the assurance in his eyes made her smile.

"Besides," he said. "Now I know Lloyd doesn't have a thing for you."

"What?" she half-laughed. "You thought Lloyd had the hots for me? That's just gross. He's like a brother to me."

"I see that now. But you're so gorgeous, fun, and smart, I couldn't help being jealous every time he was around you."

"So you're not mad about tonight? Because you were kinda giving off that vibe."

"Is reading my aura part of your talents, too?" he asked with a wry grin, then tilted her chin with his finger. "I'm not mad, at least not at you, more like at myself."

"What are you talking about? You didn't do anything wrong. Actually, I'd say you were in the right place at the right time."

"It's more than that. Honey, I...need to be honest about something."

Her breath hitched at the regret in his dark eyes, and the guilt lining his face. Confused, she asked, "Was it something I did during the trance?"

"No, it was something I did, or rather assumed." He released a deep breath, the warmth of it brushing against her lips like a caress. "When I got here tonight, with the way the door had been left open, at first I thought you were in trouble. Then, when I caught your and Lloyd's reflection in the mirror, with the way you were on the floor, and the way Lloyd was over you, I instantly thought..." He looked over her shoulder.

"You thought Lloyd and I were having sex."

He moved his gaze to hers. "I'm sorry I didn't trust you, and that I assumed the worst."

She settled her hands around his neck. "You're human, John. I don't blame you for how you reacted. You've been betrayed in the past, and trust is new to you. If the situation were turned around, I might have assumed the same thing."

He ran his palms along her arms. "How is it you know me better than I know myself."

She shrugged. "Didn't I tell you I was a mind reader, too?" She gave him a quick kiss on the lips. "Now let me go change, and then I'll make us something to eat."

"Nope. You've had a rough night, even if you don't remember half of it." He gently sifted his fingers through her hair until he found the small lump at the back of her scalp. "How does your head feel?"

"Better."

"Good, but I still want you to take it easy, not wait on me. Why don't you go upstairs?" He turned her toward the steps. "And relax in the tub. I'll bring you up a glass of wine and then *I'll* make us something to eat."

Not willing to fight such a tempting offer, she headed upstairs, then paused and looked over her shoulder as a thought occurred to her. "You know I don't remember my trances or anything that's happening around me during them. Why did you tell me about how you'd assumed Lloyd and I were...ya know?"

"Because I don't want any lies, half-truths or misunderstandings between us. Ever."

Her heart melted. "Thank you," she managed as she

wondered if he could be any more perfect. She'd never met a man like him, and doubted any others would compare.

When he slid his gaze to her bare legs, the heat in his eyes sent a wave of desire straight between her thighs. He cleared his throat, and quickly looked away. "Head upstairs," he said, his tone now rough and husky. "I'll be up in bit with your wine."

She took a few steps, the sexual tension thick between them, even as she began distancing herself. Swearing she could feel his hot gaze still on her, she looked over her shoulder again and caught him staring at her ass. "I thought you were heading to the kitchen."

"It's pretty tough to move with a view like this."

"How about now?" she asked, and shimmied out of her panties.

With a groan, he said, "You're killing me." Then he disappeared around the corner.

Smiling at the promise of what was to come, and pleased the night would be salvaged after all, she turned on the faucet and finished undressing. After several minutes, she added a couple drops of scented oil to the bath water, then stepped into the tub. She sloshed the few inches that had accumulated over the cold porcelain, then relaxed into the tub, lying back and letting her toes receive a massage from the forceful spray gushing from the faucet.

As the water rose, the fragrance of vanilla and hazelnut mingled with the steam filling the small bathroom. The heat from the lapping water, the scent from the bath oil, and the memory of John's hot gaze had her primed and ready to explode with sexual need. Yet she couldn't stop her mind from wandering. She couldn't stop the guilt from interfering with what her body and heart wanted.

John had admitted to assuming the worst when he'd arrived tonight. He'd apologized for believing she'd cheat on him, and for not trusting her.

Because I don't want any lies, half-truths or misunderstandings between us. Ever.

His words echoed in her mind. She wanted to dunk her head in the water and drown them out. While she hadn't lied or told any half-truths, Ian's secret, make that her secret, might fall somewhere in between.

From the moment Ian had revealed the truth, she'd wanted to talk to John. He had a logical spin on everything, and she valued his opinion. But she'd promised Ian she wouldn't confide in John, and while she owed the man nothing, he could hold a valuable key to her future. Not necessarily the job offer at CORE, but more importantly, information about her mother that only he knew.

Although he'd given her better insight into her gift today, he'd told her there was so much more for her to learn. So much more he could teach her about the trances, the visions, and how to handle being a medium. She needed to know these things, especially after what had happened tonight.

As the bath water lapped against her breasts, she thought back to when she'd lain down for a nap. She suspected she'd slipped into the trance when she'd cleared her mind and had stared at the ceiling fan as it made hypnotic, lazy circles.

She frowned. She'd stared at that ceiling fan before, and had never had a trance because of it. Maybe it had been her state of exhaustion. Or maybe something else had been the trigger. Either way, she needed to know how to control her gift. She needed to know the true capacity of its power.

In order to obtain this knowledge from Ian, she had to keep the secret of her parentage from John. A condition she didn't like, but would endure, even if she suspected Ian's reasons for keeping John in the dark were more than he'd described. Sure, she understood, Ian didn't want John distracted from the investigation, or worried about the boss's daughter's involvement. Still, after how upfront and honest John had been, not only tonight, but last night when he'd told her about Renee, she wished she could be just as honest.

Ian said he'd stick around Wissota Falls for a couple of days. She'd keep his secret from John until he left. Then she'd tell him the truth. John would understand. He had an easy way of rationalizing things without allowing his emotions to be involved. And he worked for Ian, so he likely understood his boss better than she did.

With a deep sigh, she let the heat in the room and the aromatic fragrances relax her. Thoughts of Ian fled and were replaced with John. The way his hungry gaze had traveled along her bare legs, the way his eyes nearly devoured her when she'd slipped off her panties.

A small rap at the door made her jump. Water overflowed onto the floor and she quickly shut off the faucet.

"You're supposed to bathe, not swim in the tub," John said with a chuckle as he closed the door behind him.

"It's not *that* high."

He set the wine glass on the counter, then placed a towel in front of the tub. It instantly soaked up the water.

"Okay, so I guess I wasn't paying attention."

As he handed her the wine glass, he arched a brow. "Why's that? What were you thinking about?"

Heat that had nothing to do with the temperature of the room raced across her cheeks. "You," she answered honestly.

His gaze traveled over her breasts as she scooted up a bit to take a sip of the wine. "Care to share the details?"

"Care to join me and find out?"

Smiling he let his eyes move over her body. "I'd love to, but if I hop into your tiny tub, you might end up with water stains on your downstairs ceiling."

"We don't want that," she said, and took a sip of the wine.

"No, we don't." He kissed her forehead. "I checked the fridge. What'll it be? A turkey or ham sandwich?"

"Don't worry about fixing us something to eat now. Stay. Keep me company."

He acted as if he weighed the decision, then a crooked grin slid across his lips. "I suppose I can suffer the torture of watching you bathe."

She laughed and set her wine glass on the ledge in the corner of the tub. "Such a martyr."

After replacing the wet towel with a dry one, he knelt on

the floor in front of the tub. "Aren't I, though? I guess if you're going to make me sit here with you, I might as well put myself to use." He dipped a washcloth into the water.

"An excellent idea," she said as he began at her toes, then dragged the soaked cotton to her calf.

He moved the washcloth up her legs. "I thought so."

Unfortunately, he bypassed the apex of her thighs, and drew circles on her stomach. Lying naked in the tub, with him fully clothed, had her more turned on than she'd imagined. The idea of having him wash her body, concentrating on every erogenous zone made her nipples harden, and caused a dull ache between her thighs. As much as she loved taking a long soak in the tub, a rare treat with her schedule, she wanted to forget the bath. She needed him on top of her, in her.

"So tell me about your day?" he asked, as he massaged her torso, her rib cage.

Was he kidding?

She didn't want to talk about her day. She wanted him. Obviously he meant to torture her, though. Some martyr. "Seeing as how you know how it started, how it ended, and I'd already told you the in-between stuff when you'd called. Why don't you tell me about your day?"

Shifting the washcloth, he edged closer to her breasts. Close, but still not touching.

"There's not much to tell. Nothing earth shattering happened after we talked this afternoon."

"Until you walked in on another one of my trances. And then there was that whole Lloyd kissing Will thing."

He chuckled. "True."

"Does it bother you that my brother and Lloyd are gay?"

"I could care less," he said, still stroking her.

Considering John's proclivity for honesty, she believed him. His opinion of Will mattered to her. She loved her brother, and couldn't imagine being with a man who would be prejudiced against him.

She rested her wet hand over his, stilling his movements along her torso. "Thank you."

"For what?" He met her gaze. "It's like I told your brother and Lloyd, I don't care about their relationship, I only care about ours."

Her heart pounded hard enough she wouldn't be surprised if he felt it beneath the washcloth. She wanted them to be in a relationship. She wanted to know what his *idea* of a relationship actually meant. While she'd fallen in love with him, he might not feel the same. Yes, he obviously enjoyed being with her, but what if she told him about Ian? That she had an offer to move to Chicago?

She was about to ask him to define their relationship, but chickened out and forced him to drag the washcloth to her breast, instead. Did she really want to know? She'd walked into this knowing he'd eventually leave. Was there any need to define what they had together?

He cupped her breast, and dragged the terrycloth along her nipple eliciting a strong tug, a deep throb between her thighs. "Uh-uh." He leaned over the tub until they were nose to nose. "This," he said, and thumbed her nipple, "isn't the only thing I want from you."

Feathering his other hand through her hair until he gently cupped her head, he brushed his lips against hers. "Sex is sex," he said against her lips. "But when I'm with you, all I can think about is your pleasure, your release, and showing you how special you are to me."

He moved the washcloth between her thighs. She gasped and arched. "I love the way you respond to me." He held her gaze as he rubbed the wet material against her clit. "God, the scent of you drives me crazy." He nipped at her lower lip, then nuzzled his nose against her ear.

"I love the way you laugh, the way your quick mind works." He tickled her earlobe with his teeth, his hot breath sending goose bumps along her skin despite the warmth of the bath water. "I love that you accept my faults, the way you've brought peace and fulfillment to my life. I love everything about you, and I can't imagine living in Chicago without you."

She froze. A split second ago, she'd been lost in his words, his praises, his touch. Now her heart swelled with relief, and burst with love.

He hadn't exactly said he loved her, or even asked her to move to Chicago with him, though.

As much as what he had said meant the world to her, she needed crystal clear clarity before she'd allow her hopes and dreams to rise, only to have them plummet because she'd misunderstood. "Maybe my mind isn't as quick as you think, because I'm not sure what you're saying," she said.

He dropped the washcloth and cupped her cheeks. His dark eyes swirled with a multitude of emotions, as he brushed the pad of his thumb along her lips. "I want you to move to Chicago with me. After being with you, and the way you've filled the other half of my soul, I can't imagine living in my condo alone, waking up without you, falling asleep without holding you. I love you, Celeste. I realize this must seem sudden, and if you need time to think about it we could—"

She grabbed his head with her wet hands and kissed him with all of the love she'd been bottling inside. He met her kiss, his lips melting against hers, his tongue demanding, intoxicating as he ran his hands along her back and cradled her to his chest.

Water sloshed around her, splashing him and soaking his shirt as she tried to lessen the inches between them. The air in the small bathroom became humid, steamier. The bathwater lukewarm compared to the heat radiating from his body and the hot need that scorched her with each press of his lips, each dip and stroke of his tongue.

Yet, in the dark recesses of her mind, she sensed he held back. She needed him to let go. She needed his love, his heart, his soul—because he already had hers.

Breaking the kiss, she held his strong jaw and stared into his eyes. They were hooded with desire, love and uncertainty. At that moment, she realized he needed more than her simply showing him how she felt. He needed to hear the words, too.

During the last two days, she'd been so uncertain of his feelings for her, she hadn't wanted to risk the humiliation of rejection or appear as if she were angling for him to sweep her away from Wissota Falls to live with him in Chicago. But now that she knew he loved her, she could tell him the same, without risk, without shame, without the worry of him breaking her heart.

She couldn't stop her eyes from misting, or the tear that slipped down her cheek. "I love you, too." She dug her fingers into his hair. "I can't imagine my life without you."

He tightened his arms around her. "You'll come to Chicago? I know it might not be the city you would have chosen on your own, but my job..."

Ian's own job offer hung on the tip of her tongue. Now didn't seem like the appropriate time to bring that information to light. There would be too many questions from his end, and quite frankly, she didn't want to dredge up the roller coaster of emotions Ian had sent her on today. The only emotions she wanted deal with now were the ones between John and her.

"I'd go anywhere with you, as long as it means we'll be together." She reached the waistband of his khakis and tugged his shirt free. "And that I can bring my gnomes with me," she added with a small smile as she slid her hands beneath his shirt.

Cupping her bottom, he lifted her from the tub, then draped a towel around her. "*All* of them?"

"Of course. Each one has sentimental value."

With a sexy grin, he scooped her in his arms, then carried her to the bed. He rubbed the towel over her damp body, giving her breasts more attention than necessary. "The plates and glasses, too?" he asked, moving the towel lower and spreading her thighs.

She released a moan as the soft, fluffy material rasped against her clit. "They're collector's items," she managed to say despite the burning need racing through her.

With a light chuckle, he tossed the towel on the floor. Cool air from the ceiling fan rushed over her, puckering her nipples and sending another series of goose bumps along her skin.

"You drive a hard bargain," he said, with mock admonishment as he pulled his shirt over his head.

She shifted up, and attacked his belt. "Is it one you think you can live with?" she asked as she shoved his pants and boxers over his hips.

His erection bobbed as he toed off his shoes and removed his socks. Then using his elbows to keep from crushing her, he settled his hard, naked body over hers. "On one condition," he murmured as his arousal kissed her sex.

"What's that?" she asked, breathless, her insides coiling with sensual anticipation.

"No gnomes in the bedroom."

She ran her palms over the valleys and groves along his biceps, loving the feel of him. "Performance anxiety?" she teased, then groaned as he impaled her with a quick thrust of his lean hips.

"I just want you all to myself," he said, punctuating each word with long, deep thrusts.

What had started out as playful suddenly turned carnal. Without teasing foreplay, he drove himself hard between her thighs. This was what she wanted. This was what he hadn't allowed her to see before. While tenderness and love still shown in the dark depths of his eyes, he'd finally let himself go.

He held nothing back. With each touch, stroke and rock of his hips, she sensed more from him than words could ever convey.

His love poured though her, in her, and settled so deeply in her heart and soul, she knew she'd never be the same. They shared a bond that could never be broken. A trust, an understanding, and a love strong enough to combat any obstacle that might come their way.

He'd said he loved her. She'd declared her love, as well. But to feel that love coursing through her body, took her to a higher, more intensely sensual and emotional level. She never wanted it to end. She wanted to keep that steady connection sizzling through her, but he was driving her closer to the edge of release.

His hard length penetrated, his coarse hair rasped against her clit. The friction became too much. Her over-sensitized body sought release. Moaning, groaning, wanting the orgasm each swift thrust of his hips promised, she still held back. She wanted the moment to last longer, to last forever.

"Come for me, baby." He dropped to his elbows again as he drove impossibly deeper. Skin to skin, her nipples rasping against the dusting of hair along his chest, he pressed open-mouthed kisses along the arch of her neck. "Let me hear you," he demanded, his hot breath fanning across her lips.

Digging her heels into his tight rear, gripping his back with her fingers, she sought his mouth. His kiss.

He delivered. Catching her moans with his lips and tongue, he mimicked each sensual drive of his hips, each potent penetration of his hard arousal, until her world began to slant and spiral.

Sensations she'd never known existed tore through her, radiated through her soul and set her body on fire. Whimpering, groaning, panting hard, she let go.

Crying out his name, she came in a rush. As the orgasm ripped through her, her muscles contracted around his thick arousal. He locked his eyes on hers and groaned her name over and over again, his love pouring into her until his entire body grew rigid with his own climax.

Breathless, she held him to her, and for the first time in her life, she realized she'd found her place in the world.

And that place was with John.

CHAPTER 22

THE ICU NURSE with a penchant for little girls was unfortunately on vacation at the moment. With the shit he had on him, the man would have made an ideal Grim Reaper. He would have flashed the few pictures he'd had on the nurse, drooling as he'd hiked up his neighbor's eight-year-old daughter's skirt, and bingo. Garrett would no longer be a loose string.

Too bad, he thought as he sat in the far corner of the dimly lit parking lot of Eau Claire Memorial Hospital, tapping his fingers on the steering wheel. He could have reaped double justice of his own with that sick bastard. The nurse would have killed Garrett to save his reputation, and in turn he'd kill the nurse because he preyed on innocent little girls.

Who the hell does that?

The second on his list as Garrett's personal Grim Reaper had broken both her collar bone and wrist with a supposed fall. Bullshit. He knew all about her, too. She was one of those dominatrix types. Into the kinky side of things with her gal pals, and apparently *things* had gone further than planned.

Which left him his third and last choice. Evie Lumbford.

Twenty-something with a fetish for drugs—he still didn't understand how she'd ended up employed in a hospital—she'd do anything for a fix. Even if she *did* refuse to do what he'd demand, he'd make sure a day in his workshop would change her mind.

His dick throbbed as anticipation built. The nurse who liked little girls would have been gutted, and buried deep in the woods. The other one, well, he would have enjoyed showing the dominatrix who was boss before killing her.

Evie?

She was hard on the eyes, her IQ bordered on retardation, and the drugs she took had likely fried what little smarts she had left. But she would serve his purpose. In more ways than one. Once she took care of Garrett, he'd use her as his...rehearsal.

He pictured Celeste and all of the things he wanted to do to her. She was so much prettier than his Deb. When he would finally have the opportunity to slice Celeste while fucking her at the same time...he wanted to make sure he did it right. He wanted the extreme pleasure. After all, once he shoved his hunting knife into her stomach, there would be no turning back, no second chances for a do over.

Dead is dead.

He came alert and sat straighter as Evie exited the door the hospital employees used when taking a smoke break. She lit a cigarette, the flame from the lighter casting a glow over her features. With eyes too far apart, a nose upturned like a pig's snout, and teeth that hung over her bottom lip, the woman gave a new meaning to the definition of ugly. No matter her face, she'd do.

He had no other choice at this point. He was out of options and time.

Thinking about time had him glancing at the clock on the center console of his truck. Half past ten. He had to leave, but he'd be back in the morning after Evie finished her twelve hour shift. She usually worked six to six as one of the hospital's custodial skeleton crew, and moved under the radar of suspicion. No one would consider dumb, ugly, little Evie Lumbford a threat. With Garrett heavily sedated after his freak show, crybaby shit, he doubted the Eau Claire prison guard that had been placed in front of his hospital door was on full alert. Hopefully Garrett would remain incapacitated.

He'd heard that Garrett had accused his "brother" of being his partner. No name, though. Still, he'd almost panicked. Almost. But when he'd learned that his doctor doped him up, to the point Garrett didn't even know his own name, he'd relaxed and devised plan C. Evie Lumbford.

He knew he was taking a risk, but again, he didn't have a choice. He most certainly couldn't waltz into Garrett's room and kill him. While he would have preferred to have him dead sooner rather than later, the timing hadn't been right. By the time Garrett had woken from his coma, little, ugly Evie had already started her shift. So now he had to hope that Garrett remained a virtual vegetable until Evie made her rounds tomorrow. He'd have her go to ICU to perform her regular rounds cleaning rooms, and when she entered Garrett's, she'd finish off the bastard.

A simple plan.

And if she were caught or went to the cops? His only disappointment would be that he'd lost a lab rat. He would never allow her to see his face, or his home and workshop. She'd have no knowledge of who he was, but by the time he was finished with her tomorrow afternoon before her shift began, she would know what he was capable of doing.

And if Garrett woke and told them about him? He had a plan for that, as well. One that he'd already set in motion. His hidey-hole in the woods was well stocked. He could disappear there, and with the food and water he'd stored over the weeks, live there for months undetected. When the search for him grew cold, he'd use the money, fake IDs and passports he'd accumulated and put Wisconsin behind him.

As he drove out of the parking lot, an inner peace settled within him. Garrett would hopefully be dead by this time tomorrow, leaving him two last loose strings.

Guilt no longer entered the equation when he thought about Garrett lying dead and rotting in a pine box. They'd had their fun, but he'd become too much of a liability. Besides, when it came to them killing together, the old adage, three's a crowd, rang true.

Garrett had crowded him, had suffocated the raw need to dominate the means and facilitation of how the women they'd taken suffered and died. A cord around the neck had become boring and anticlimactic. He needed more to regain the rush he'd felt when they'd started killing twelve years ago. He needed a replacement for the incredible orgasm that shot through him when he'd stared into Garrett's eyes as he gave the whores they'd killed what they deserved. After the time he'd spent with his Deb, his fifteen-inch hunting knife had given him what he needed. A release as powerful and potent as any drug. A powerful and potent replacement for Garrett.

As he drove home, to *her*, dark talons of lust sank their claws inside him, hardened his dick to the point of pain, and caused him to break into a sweat. The stress brought on by Garrett's original arrest, Hoyt's failure to kill him, and now the uncertainty of whether Garrett would reveal his identity had him on the verge of running before even placing plan C into motion.

He sought the peace that had settled over him as he'd left the hospital parking lot before a full-blown panic attack overtook him. Gripping the steering wheel with sweaty palms, and clenching his jaw tight, he fought back the anxiety, the haze of fear. He thought about Evie Lumbford.

Ugly Evie.

She would be his eyes and ears. He would make her tell him what gossip traveled around the hospital regarding Garrett. He'd even have her place a few phone calls while he held her in his workshop. Monitored of course. Gossip traveled fast in the hospital, and if Garrett did wake and tell the Sheriff and Kain about him, he'd know, and he'd run.

The peace returned. His heart rate slowed, and now the sweat cooled his feverish skin. Everything would go according to plan. Garrett would die, thanks to Ugly Evie, and while Roy and Kain tripped over themselves trying to figure out who Garrett's partner was, he'd have fun experimenting on Evie.

After that, he'd take care of the noose around his neck.

He'd finally be able to free himself of the necessary mirage and burden. She'd served her purpose, but at this moment, with the lust and need for release—any release—still burning his brain cells, a part of him wished he hadn't broken her. Not out of love, there was only one being on the planet that he loved, and he would be dead this time tomorrow. Right now, he needed a body, willing or not, to ease him until he took what he needed from Evie.

Impossible. He shook his head in the dark cab of his truck as he eased into his driveway. He couldn't use the bitch in his bed tonight. He'd have to wait. For Evie. The appetizer to his main course. Celeste.

Dr. Alex Trumane sat at the counter of the diner, stunned and staring at Kira's sugary sweet smile.

"Well?" she asked, her hazel eyes sensual, wanting, yet holding a hint of nervousness.

She had asked him out on a date. To be precise, she'd asked him over to her apartment for dinner. While elated at the prospect of actually spending quality time with her outside of the diner, he also panicked at the thought.

He hadn't had a date since he'd been sober, and before that, he wouldn't call meeting a woman in a hotel, doing drugs, drinking and a night of sexual debauchery a date. He hadn't taken a woman to a restaurant or to a movie since he'd been married, and even then, those evenings had been a rarity. Because he hadn't been able to stay sober, he hadn't been able to remain faithful.

While he'd changed for the better, he knew in the depths of his soul that given the chance, he'd never betray Kira's trust by falling off the wagon and womanizing again. He wanted to hold her, kiss her, make love to her. He wanted to wake in the morning to her bright smile, and fall asleep at night with her lying next to him.

He'd love nothing more than to take her from this crappy

diner, give her financial security, pretty clothes, a new car, and exotic vacations. How could he, though? Once he found Number Twenty-Two, his life could change for the worse. He could face the loss of his medical license. Hell, he could face a prison sentence.

"I'm sorry I put you on the spot." Kira absently wiped the counter, the disappointment evident on her pretty face. "Forget I asked."

He grabbed her hand before she could walk away. "You didn't put me on the spot. You just surprised me. Honestly, I've wanted to ask you out since the first moment I laid eyes on you."

She cocked her head. "Really," she said with a hint of sarcasm.

Grinning, he rubbed his thumb across her rough knuckles. She had nice hands, but working at the diner had left them raw and chapped. He'd add weekly manicures and pedicures to all the things he wanted to give to her. "It's true."

"Uh-huh, so then what have you been waiting for?"

The million dollar question and one he'd answer honestly. He'd learned from his mistakes and refused to begin a relationship with Kira based on lies. "I, uh, needed to make sure I came to you a whole man."

She dropped the rag on the counter and gripped his hand with both of hers. "What are you talking about, Alex?"

"AA's twelve steps, I haven't completed them yet. I think the only way I can feel...worthy enough to be with you, is to complete the program."

"Admirable," she said with a twinkle in her eyes. "And I respect you for wanting to succeed. But don't let those twelve steps be your only guidance. Let your heart guide you, too. I've been where you are. I know what you've gone through, what you'll continue to go through."

"And you still want to get involved with me?"

"Why wouldn't I? You're funny, when you're not being so serious. You're smart, thoughtful, and ah..." She wet her bottom lip before glancing around the diner. "Quite a hunk of man," she added, lowering her voice to a sexy, husky drawl.

He laughed even as his cheeks heated. He didn't think he'd ever been called a hunk in his life. "You're something else," he said. "Something very special."

"So, does this mean you'll come over for dinner?"

"As much as I'd love a home-cooked meal, for our first date, I want to take you somewhere nice."

"You don't have to do that."

"I want to. I'm tired of watching you wait on everybody else. You deserve to be waited on and treated like a princess."

A blush stole across her cheeks. "My best dress is from a thrift shop. I'm more pauper than princess."

"Do you think I care?"

"You're a doctor. I don't want to embarrass you."

"Embarrass me? Kira, before I became clean and sober, I was a despicable, selfish man. I would drive around in my flashy car, drunk, high, with even flashier women while my wife and kids sat at home. I'm embarrassed by my past. Embarrassed and ashamed for everything I've done." Number Twenty-Two flashed in his mind. "If anything, you should be embarrassed to be seen with *me*."

"You're a good man, Alex. Don't let anyone tell you otherwise, least of all yourself. I'd be honored to go to dinner with you."

"Kira," the short order cook shouted. "The food's not gonna walk itself to the table."

"I've got to run."

"I do, too." The diner would start to fill with the bar crowd, and he wanted a chance to research Wissota Falls for any link to Number Twenty-Two. Miranda Gates. "When is your next night off?"

"Sunday."

"Sunday it is, then. Can I call you tomorrow?"

She quickly scribbled her number on her note pad, then handed it to him. "I'm looking forward to Sunday." She gave him a shy smile, then quickly turned and retrieved the plates of food waiting under the heat lamps.

"Me, too," he murmured to himself, then after leaving her a hefty tip, he sauntered into the balmy night. As he walked toward his car, he passed numerous bars along the way without an ounce of temptation.

He didn't need to complete the whole twelve steps to come to Kira as a whole man. But he did need to find Miranda before he could offer Kira the love and life she deserved. His past embarrassments, the shame and disgrace he'd placed upon his family, would pale in comparison if he lost his medical license, or even worse, ended up in prison.

AA's twelve steps had forced this journey to atonement. He could quit his search and simply cross Number Twenty-Two from his list and leave Miranda in the past. He'd made headway with his family and friends. Why dredge up something that could ruin the life he'd struggled to put back together?

Because the only thing he'd ever quit in his life had *been* alcohol. He wasn't a quitter, and quitting his search was not an option. Not because of the twelve steps, they were there for guidance as Kira had said. No, his heart and conscience had been guiding him on this search. Now he prayed Anna Gates's will would help guide him the rest of the way.

CHAPTER 23

UGLY EVIE LUMBFORD sat strapped to a wooden chair. Duct tape kept her hands and feet immobile. An old rag shoved into her mouth would keep her screams muffled once she woke. *If* she woke, he thought and scratched an itch through the ski mask that had begun to grow suffocating.

Shortly after six this morning, with dark, gray clouds hiding the early morning light, he'd attacked her as she'd walked home from her night shift at the hospital. Wearing the ski mask, along with a mechanic's jumpsuit he'd soak in bleach later—as he'd always done after a kill—he'd slapped a rag doused with chloroform over her mouth until she'd grown limp and passed out cold. Petite and weighing next to nothing, he'd easily stashed her in his waiting truck, then he'd brought her to his workshop.

He glanced at the digital clock on the workbench. He'd knocked her out over an hour ago, and now he worried he'd underestimated the amount of chloroform she'd inhaled. Usually his victims, or even Garrett's, were awake within twenty minutes. He knew she was alive, though. Her pulse thudded at the base of her throat. Bits of the rag sticking out of her mouth moved from the air exhaling from her nose.

He glanced at the clock again. Time wasn't on his side. He needed her awake, he needed her to understand what he expected from her. He needed to do it now. Normalcy and his rigid routine would keep him from any suspicion. Showing up late for work was not an option, even if he could fabricate a legitimate excuse.

With a gloved hand and no room for patience, he slapped her face. Not hard, he didn't want to leave her bruised yet. She did have to show up to work later.

When she didn't respond, he gave her shoulders a hard shake. Over and over, her head whipped back and forth like a bobble-head doll. Finally, she moaned and her lashes began to flutter.

"Wake up, Evie. I have a job for you."

She snapped her eyes open, darted her gaze around her surroundings, until landing it on the hunting knife next to him. Screaming beneath the rag, she twisted against the duct tape and thrashed her head.

Worried she'd cause a noticeable injury to herself, he waved the knife in her face. "Don't move. Don't scream. Don't do anything unless I say. Do you understand?"

Wide-eyed, staring at the knife, tears streaming down her face, she nodded and whimpered.

"Good." He stroked the flat of the blade along her cheek careful to not leave a mark. "Have you heard of Garrett Winston?"

She nodded again, her eyes nearly crossing as she followed the movement of the blade.

"Have you cleaned his hospital room?"

Another nod.

"Excellent," he said as set the knife on the workbench. He pulled a stool from the corner and sat in front of her. The fear in her eyes made his dick hard. He loved the fear, the power, but knew he had to caution himself.

He didn't want to kill her yet. Well, he really did want to. He eyed the hunting knife, the way the blade shined beneath the lone bulb hanging from the ceiling. But she was Plan C. She was all he had left.

"I will let you live," he began with his first of what would likely become many lies before he was finished with Ugly Evie.

"I will not harm anyone you love. But you have to do one thing for me. And after you've done it, I'll never ask you for another thing again." Because she'd be dead, he smiled beneath the ski mask.

"If you don't do this for me, or if you go to the cops, I will kill you. Slowly, painfully. Do you understand?"

More tears streamed down her face as she bobbed her head.

"Good girl," he crooned as if talking to a dog. "Now, I need you to sleep some more." He withdrew a syringe from the pocket of his mechanic's suit. "You've used these on yourself, haven't you?"

She shook her head vehemently.

"Don't lie to me, Evie. I know you like your drugs. Maybe you don't shoot up, or maybe you like to snort it or smoke it. Either way, I don't care. Get used to the syringe." He pressed the needle into her arm. "Because you're going to use one like this tonight when you kill Garrett Winston."

After Celeste had woken him...properly, John lay in bed while she showered. He would have joined her, but he was so relaxed and satisfied curling against her pillow, smelling her scent on the sheets, he couldn't bring himself to move.

His cell phone rang. With a frustrated sigh, he rolled to his side and grabbed it off the nightstand. Rachel's name lit up the caller ID and he tensed.

"Hey, John. Hope I'm not disturbing your beauty sleep."

"I've been up for hours."

"Liar. If that were true you would have already called me after the emails I sent you."

Busted. "Okay, okay," he grumbled and climbed out of the warm bed. "So I had a late night. What do you have for me?"

"How about a stack of pictures of Winston's known victims sitting at the Sheriff's Department? Or even better, how about the scoop on Winston?"

A rush of adrenaline pushed through his veins as he headed for Celeste's home office at the end of the hallway. "DNA comparisons?" he asked as he searched for paper and a pen.

"Oh yeah, he's cooked."

"Excellent. Let's hear."

"Okay, so, Winston was born in Pensacola, Florida. His mother, Susan Haney, was only seventeen at the time. Apparently, her folks were fanatical Christians, and when they found out their daughter was pregnant, they kicked her out of their trailer park."

"There's some good Christians," he said, and let the sarcasm roll. "What about the father?"

"Patrick Winston was eighteen. His parents wanted to take Haney in, but she refused, then disappeared. Right after, Winston's dad took off, too. He'd gotten into some trouble with the law and has been in and out of prison since. He's currently doing a short stint in Georgia right now for B & E and won't be released for another two years."

"Where's the mom, now?"

"Dead, but don't rush me. I'm going for the big dun, dun, dun moment."

He smiled. "Right. Sorry."

"Anyway, mom was a piece of work. Involved in drugs and prostitution, she was arrested a few times, but never served any time. After Pensacola, she bounced around Alabama for a while, had another son, then ended up in Mississippi...Biloxi, then Gulfport. Eventually she landed in Jackson where she died from an overdose years later."

He stopped taking notes. "Please tell me your dun, dun, dun moment has to do with the name of Winston's brother."

"It does. Thanks for ruining my big moment." She let out a dramatic sigh. "Winston's half-brother is Tobias Haney. Only I have no record of him once he turned eighteen."

"Did you check—?"

"Everything. Trust me. I was able to get a sample of Haney's fingerprints, though."

"Really? How'd...never mind. I don't want to know."

"Probably not."

"What about a photo ID, or driver's license?"

"No driver's license. The only picture that I've found was taken when Haney was first placed in the foster care system. It's black and white, grainy and basically useless for performing an age progression. I tried, though."

"What else?"

"Okay, so when I found out that Susan Haney died in Jackson, on a hunch, I made some calls. After I'd gotten the whole, 'you need to go through the proper channels' crap from some bozo with his PD, I did some...um, hacking and found the home phone number for the homicide detective who'd worked Susan Haney's case. He's retired now, but—"

"Homicide? I thought you said she'd died of an overdose."

She blew out a deep breath. "She did. Only who overdoses on heroin and window cleaner? By the way, she'd apparently broken her neck, too."

He hovered the pen over the paper as a chill ran through him. "And this retired detective..."

"Jack Conahan."

"What does Conahan think?"

"That her kids murdered her. But because he had other ongoing investigations, he'd been told to let this one lie. Haney was a known junky and there was no evidence of foul play. It looked as if she'd OD'd on some bad crank."

"But?" John prompted.

"Conahan said he'd done as he was told, and let the case drop, but only to a degree. He was so convinced the kids had killed their mom, that on his own time, he'd looked into her background. He talked to neighbors, Haney's friends, and discovered good ol' mom was trading sexual favors for drugs."

"So, she was a prostitute."

"She didn't only trade herself, she traded her sons. She'd let her dealer use the boys, or bring in a john to use them. Sometimes she made them use each other, and other times she joined in."

John sat sickened. What their mother had done went

beyond repulsive. She'd destroyed Winston and his half-brother, and in the process, likely distorted their view on women. "How old were they when Haney died?"

"Winston was thirteen and the brother eleven."

"Where'd they end up, foster care?"

"Haney did. Winston's paternal grandparents brought him back to Pensacola. He lived with them until they died when he was eighteen."

"What, did they die at the same time?"

"Yep, a house fire took them both while they were sleeping."

"Where was Winston?"

"Supposedly at a friend's. The fire was ruled an accident, faulty wiring. However, it seems rather convenient, especially because Winston walked away with seventy thousand dollars thanks to his grandparents' life and homeowners insurance."

"That explains how Winston could afford his rig," he said. "Where'd he go next?"

"Back to Mississippi."

"Let me guess...to find his brother."

"That's what I'm thinking."

"We need to find Haney."

What Susan Haney had done to her sons offered an answer to the question of why two men would rape and kill together. The fact that most of the women that had been murdered were prostitutes, like Susan Haney, coupled with Winston's accusation toward his brother, only backed that theory. And Tobias Haney, whoever he was now, was still roaming free.

"Could be a challenge. He didn't go through legal channels to change his name. He simply disappeared. But I'll keep working on it."

"Thanks, Rachel, anything else?"

"Check your inbox. The DNA comparisons came in late last night. Ian's going to have to cut a hefty check for the fast turnaround, but it was well worth it. The geneticist was able to match Winston's DNA to twenty-nine cold cases spanning five states and seventeen years, beginning in Pensacola, before his grandparents died."

"Were there any DNA comparisons linked to Winston that didn't match?"

"Yeah. Eight victims had two different types of trace DNA evidence found on them. The rest were all Winston."

"When did this start?"

"The additional DNA? Twelve years ago. A prostitute was found decomposing in a field about seventy miles outside of Jackson. She was severely beaten, raped, both vaginally and anally, and based on the ligature marks around her neck, the evidence suggested she'd been strangled with an electrical cord."

Celeste stepped into the office wearing another one of her Sugar Shack t-shirts. This one was red, with "Sweet Tooth" emblazoned across the front in a funky, bubbly seventies font. With her blond curls framing her face, cherry lip gloss accentuating her mouth, that tight t-shirt and faded, low-riding jeans, she looked good enough to eat.

After losing focus, he cleared his throat. "Come again?"

"I said," Rachel lisped, signifying she'd plopped a pencil in her mouth. "The dual sets of DNA stopped about ten years ago. So, if Winston's partner was Haney, he either didn't kill those other women, or he discovered a little something about forensic evidence."

"This is great stuff, Rachel."

"What's even better is that the cold case detectives in Florida, Alabama and Mississippi are already foaming at the mouth for extradition. So you know what that means."

"Oh yeah. An eye for an eye."

"Yep. Winston might think he's safe in Wisconsin, but our guys down south want the death penalty."

His mind raced in all sorts of directions. He wasn't interested in making a deal with Winston, but he wanted Haney. He wanted to ensure the bastard could never kill again. The Eau Claire DA would have to battle it out with the DAs down south, maybe even Indiana, where several murder victims had also been linked to Winston. But to promise

Winston a life in prison for the twenty-nine murders he'd committed? In his opinion, the man deserved the death penalty. Still, he wanted his brother. Maybe if they found him, *he* could be the one extradited.

He needed advice. With the evidence they had, and the possibility that there was another victim, and maybe more to follow, he needed to make sure he had all his ducks in a row before he contacted the DA or confronted Winston. "Is Ian around? I'd like to pick his brain on this."

"Ah, no. He had to go out of town for a few days. Don't know where, but I'll let him know you're looking for him when he calls."

Don't bother, sat on the tip of his tongue. Ian had been out of reach all week. He'd talk things over with Roy and go from there. "Sure, I'd appreciate it."

"I'll keep looking for Haney. Call if you have any questions about the stuff I sent you, or if you need anything else."

After he hung up, he glanced at Celeste. Her earlier smile had faded, and her eyes held concern. "Did Rachel find Winston's partner?" she asked, her voice hopeful.

"Yeah," he said, then gave her a quick recap of his conversation with Rachel.

"Wow. I mean...wow." She shook her head in disbelief. "What kind of mother does that to her own children?"

"I know, but it still doesn't excuse rape and murder."

She crossed the room, and sank onto his lap. "Will you see Winston today?" she asked as she wrapped her hands around his neck.

"That'll depend on what kind of shape he's in today. I hope so, though. I want his brother. I want to end this investigation and move on...with you." He brushed his lips across hers.

"Me too." She nipped his lower lip, then groaned. "I better go before one thing leads to another," she said, and hopped off his lap. "Are you planning on coming over later?"

He grinned as he followed her to the door, then caged her against the wall. "Let's see, you...?" He kissed her cheek. "Or the Chippewa Inn?" He kissed her lips. "Hmm, what do you think?"

"That I'll see you tonight." Taking a key from her back pocket, she slipped it into his hand. "Lock up when you're finished."

The warm metal dug into his palm as he made a fist. He'd never owned the key to a woman's home, nor had he ever given his out to anyone, not even Renee. The significance of the small gesture spoke volumes. Trust, love, commitment. "I love you," he said before kissing her again.

"Stop," she protested with a giggle, and gave him a little shove. "Will's waiting for me."

Outside, he greeted Will and the blushing Viking. After he gave Celeste another quick kiss, he moved his rental car out of the driveway. Once everyone had driven off, he gathered his laptop from the sedan, then headed back to the house and went to work.

After printing the files Rachel had sent, he reviewed all of the evidence they had against Winston. He then spent time returning phone calls to the cold case detectives involved.

Hours later, showered, and armed with a binder filled with two hundred plus pages containing everything they had on Winston, he walked through Roy's office door. "Sorry I'm so late." He took a seat opposite the sheriff.

"I was wondering when you were going to finally make it in," Roy greeted him, and shoved the sandwich he'd been eating aside. "I was going to wait and take you up on that offer of lunch at The Sugar Shack, but when the clock struck one, I gave in to my stomach."

"Sorry. Time got away from me. Celeste had another trance last night."

Roy wiped his mouth with a napkin, then straightened. "Is she okay?"

"She's fine, and I recorded what I could."

"Good, let's have a listen."

He dropped the binder on the desk. "Later. What I have here is more important right now."

As Roy leafed through the pages that would condemn

Winston and possibly Haney, John rose, then paced the office. The excitement running through his veins gave him a natural high, and had his mind buzzing.

He and Celeste were an official couple. They loved each other and after this investigation ended, she'd move to Chicago to live with him. He couldn't wait to share his condo, his life, his love with her. He wanted to celebrate his good fortune. Tell everyone he knew, even total strangers, how happy she'd made him. With the information sitting on Roy's desk, they were one step closer to solving the investigation, which only drew him one step closer to his new life with Celeste.

Roy smoothed his mustache as he turned page after page, then sat back in his chair with a gusty sigh. "My tired eyes can't process all this. Why don't you just explain it to me."

"I'd rather explain it to Winston and watch him squirm. Have you checked on him yet today?"

"Other than the prospect of a free lunch, that's why I was anxious for you to get here. The Doc says he's awake and lucid."

"Still crying?"

Roy laughed. "Yep, our crybaby killer is still living up to his name."

He tapped the binder as he leaned over the desk. "Well, what I've got here will have him crying a fucking river."

After John filled him in on what he'd learned about Winston and Haney, then explained his concern about cutting Winston a deal, the sheriff nodded. "I'm personally for the death penalty, but at this point, I think our main focus should be stopping Winston's brother. Let the DA deal with the extradition when the time comes. Although…"

"What?"

"You opposed to telling a few white lies to the crybaby?"

John grinned, suspecting Roy's train of thought. Winston hadn't bothered with an attorney up to this point. Chances were he didn't know the steps involved with extraditing a criminal to another state. "I don't think my conscience will suffer. Let's pay Winston a visit and bluff our way through our interrogation and hope for some answers."

"Maybe we should stop by the R & P and buy a couple boxes of tissues for the crybaby. You know, as a little get well gift," Roy chuckled as they left the Sheriff's Department.

"You really do have a sick sense of humor," John said with a smile. "What's sick, is that I like it."

With the lunch rush over, Celeste finally took a breather. After removing her stiff, greasy apron, she sat in the small, cramped office in the back of The Sugar Shack and rested her feet on a milk crate that served as a file box. As she closed her eyes, her cell phone rang.

Releasing a tired sigh, she looked at the caller ID, then jerked to attention, knocking over the milk crate. She hadn't expected a call from Ian, but why wouldn't he call her? He was her father, and would only be in town for a couple of days. Besides, she had wanted to talk to him about last night's trance, but hadn't had the nerve to call him first. So much had transpired last night, and as she'd worked through both the breakfast and lunch rush, she'd contemplated whether she should tell Ian about moving to Chicago with John.

Still not sure how to broach the subject, she decided to play it safe and let him lead the conversation. Drawing in a deep, fortifying breath, she answered the phone on the fourth ring.

"Hi, Celeste. It's Ian. Is this a bad time?"

"No, not at all. How are you?"

"Bored. What time does your shift end? I'd like to see you later."

"I'll be here until after dinner. Probably around seven or so."

"Can I pick you up then? Maybe we could go for a drive or get an ice cream cone."

Her dad used to take her for ice cream after work when she was a kid. The thought of doing something remotely similar with Ian seemed like a betrayal to her dad. Which was stupid, really. Ian simply wanted to spend time with her. And a part of her wanted to spend time with him. Considering they'd be living in the same city, and she might actually decide to work for him, maybe she should put aside her petty concerns and allow the man into her life.

"That sounds great. Will drove me here, so I could use a ride home."

"What about John? I know he'll be busy throughout the day."

She almost asked him how he knew, then figured he'd probably spoken with Roy. "He's meeting me at my house later. If you're worried about running into him there, we could just have Roy drop me off at home," she said, and couldn't hide the bitterness in her voice. She loved John, and hated lying to him, or in this case, completely avoiding a situation that would concern him both professionally and personally.

"You're making me feel childish," he said with a chuckle. "As much as I'd love to let John in on our secret, I still want to wait. He's close to solving this investigation. I don't want to derail him now. Not with how close you two have become."

How did she know that?

Roy. She was going to have to have a long talk with that man. His loyalties had become quite questionable.

Still not sure how much she wanted to reveal about her relationship, she ignored his last comment. "Then I guess I'll see you around seven."

"Seven it is," he said, then the call disconnected.

She set her phone on the desk and stared at a crack in the wall. How many times had she asked Will to fix that crack and repaint the drab walls? Dozens. Now that she thought about it, there were a number of things around the diner that were in need of repair. Of course nothing that interfered with the business or required a quick remedy should a health inspector pay a visit. The Sugar Shack needed a makeover.

She'd never bothered her dad with the suggestions she had to give the place a polish that would make it shine. She hadn't wanted to commit more time to the diner. Or maybe it was because she knew deep down that if she made the diner her own, it would become hers. A crutch, a way to keep herself buried in the past and her grief. A reason to not move forward and on with her life.

She supposed it didn't matter now. She'd made a decision, and would move to Chicago with John. The fate of the diner would rest on her dad. Her stomach knotted just thinking about the talk she'd have with him. She didn't want to disappoint or hurt him. She wanted to put The Sugar Shack and Wissota Falls behind her and enjoy a new beginning in Chicago.

The diner phone rang, saving her from dissecting how she'd handle the conversation with her dad. "Sugar Shack, Celeste."

"Hi, Celeste, this is Sal Riviera from Booker Foods. I wanted to take care of the order mishap with your account."

Pleased, she quickly fired off everything that they'd missed on their last shipment. After Sal had assured her next week's delivery would be as it should, he rattled off a few new items on their seafood line. She doodled on a piece of paper as he droned on about shrimp and lobster, her thoughts still on the diner, her dad, Ian and of course John...always John.

Until Sal mentioned trout.

The tip of the pencil snapped against the paper as an image flashed in her mind. "Thanks, Sal, but I'm going to pass."

"But the—"

"I've got to go." She hung up the phone. Her heart beat fast as she stared at the doodle she'd created. Not just squiggly lines but a rudimentary sketch that would make Will grimace in distaste.

She quickly dialed John's cell. As she waited for him to pick up, she stared at the crude drawing, wondering how she'd missed the clues when she'd listened to last night's trance. She couldn't believe—

"Hey, hon," John answered. A car door slammed in the background. "Roy and I are heading into the hospital. Can I call you back?"

"Yes, no," she blurted.

"Celeste, are you okay? What is it?"

She looked down to the sketch she'd made. "I know where you'll find the third victim."

CHAPTER 24

AFTER JOHN TOLD Roy he'd catch up with him inside the hospital, he leaned against the sheriff's cruiser. "Where do you think we'll find the third victim?" he asked Celeste, gripping his cell phone tight, and wondering how he would have handled this investigation without her. Because of Celeste, they had Winston, which had led to the insurmountable evidence that he'd killed over thirty people. Because of her, they'd found two other victims, which had led them to a second killer that needed to be stopped. Now she was giving him the third.

She simply amazed him.

"Do you remember when I told you about my first vision, the one that involved Lloyd?" she asked.

"Yeah, you said you knew where to find him because your dad liked to fly fish in that same spot. Is that where you think she is?"

"No, not there. A place about a half mile south...God, I can't believe I didn't think of this before. But I was talking to this salesman and he said something about trout, which my dad used to fish for and I was drawing without even realizing when—"

"A half mile south and...?" he prompted, trying to keep her focused.

"Sorry. A half mile south there's a waterfall. Two, actually, because of a jutting rock thingy at the center. Between the dual waterfalls and the river, it can *sound* like the water is rushing in three different directions."

"Could you point this place out on a map?"

"Sure, but so could Roy. Just tell him about the waterfalls. He'll know the spot."

"Will do, maybe we could gather a search party together and comb the area in the morning." He stared at the hospital door, anxious to interrogate Winston, but not wanting to blow off Celeste, either. She meant so much to the investigation. She meant so much to him.

"Wait, a search party?" she asked, with a frustrated groan. "I thought maybe you and Roy could just take a look. I mean, what if I'm wrong? I don't want you guys to stick your necks out and look like a couple of fools because I had a hunch."

He smiled and pictured her twirling a curl around her finger. She had nothing to be nervous about. If they didn't find the third victim, then they didn't find her. He'd rather take the chance and look, than miss an opportunity to nail Winston for another murder. "I believe in your hunches. You haven't been wrong yet."

"*Yet* being the operative word," she complained.

"Stop." He sighed and ran a hand though his hair as he glanced at the hospital door again. "I love you. I believe in you. But I'm sorry, I really have to go. With the way things are going today, and your hunch, I have a feeling I'll be late. I'll meet you at home after I pick up a few things from the inn. Okay?"

"I love you, too. Good luck with Winston."

Ten minutes later, John met Roy outside of Winston's hospital room. While they waited for Winston's doctor, John explained his conversation with Celeste.

Finally, Winston's doctor approached. He gave them the same line he'd given yesterday—if they upset the patient, they had to leave. John had a feeling they'd leave soon, because he had every intention of upsetting Winston.

Once the doctor walked away, he and Roy pushed open the door. Without preamble, John shoved the curtain surrounding the hospital bed aside. The scraping metal immediately drew Winston's attention, and opened the floodgates.

"Oh brother," Roy mumbled as he stared at Winston with both disgust and amusement. "Boy, you're gonna dehydrate with all that crying."

"I...I can't help it," Winston bawled, and reached for the box of tissues he had resting on his stomach. Wads of used tissues surrounded him, and littered the floor, along with an empty box.

Roy bent down and picked up the tissue box. "What brand are they using in this hospital? With the way you're blowing through these things, I should consider taking out stock in the company," he said, then tossed it in the trash.

"Please, Sheriff," John admonished him. The man really did have a sick sense of humor. "Garrett's been through enough." He moved toward the hospital bed. "How are you feeling today?"

"Better." Winston hiccupped. "I...I'm sorry for the way I acted yesterday. It really wasn't very Christian-like."

"It's okay, Garrett," John assured him as he set the mini tape recorder on the nightstand. "But there were a few things we didn't have a chance to discuss."

"Like what?"

John withdrew the pictures Rachel had sent and set them on the nightstand next to the recorder. The photographs had been arranged in chronological order. Winston's first known victim's bruised and bloodied body now sat on the top of the stack.

Winston darted his gaze to the picture, then quickly looked away and blew his nose. "What do you have there?"

"Consider it a slide show." John held up the first picture. "Do you know this woman?"

Winston's chin trembled.

"Her name is...was, Jessica Bonaham," John said. "I know it might be hard to recognize her with her eyes swollen shut and all the bruises."

Fresh tears streamed down Winston's cheeks and into his beard.

He brought out another picture. "How about this woman? Her name was Lidia Shoat. Know her?" He flashed him the next photo in line. "Or how about this one?"

When Winston looked away with a groan, John released a deep breath. "I've got twenty-nine eight-by-tens in this stack." He tapped his fingers on the rest of the photographs. "And every one of the dead women in these pictures had your DNA on them when they were found. Would you like to see a few more?"

"What do you want from me?" he wailed, and reached for another tissue. "I've already confessed."

Roy knocked the box of tissues to the floor. "We want Tobias Haney."

Winston paled as he gaped at them. "How...?"

"You told us yesterday that you wanted to kill him so he couldn't kill anymore," John said. "Let us bring Tobias in, let us stop him from hurting any more women. We know what happened to you and your brother when you were kids. We know what your mom did to you. And I can understand why you want to protect your brother, but—"

Winston fisted the tissue, then tossed it on the bed with the others. "You know nothing about my mother," he said with an ugly snarl that reminded him of the old Winston.

"Did she get what she deserved?" John asked, deciding to change tactics. To reveal the ugly secret no one was supposed to know. "Susan Haney was a prostitute and drug addict. She made you live in filth, and spent more money on her clothes than food. Am I close to brushing the surface?"

Winston's earlier snarl had been replaced with an expression of innocence, maybe that of the young boy he'd been before Susan Haney had poisoned his soul. "Not even," he whispered.

"Right. It got worse, didn't it? When she couldn't afford to pay for her pretty things or her drugs, she found a *new* commodity."

"Stop. Please, stop," Winston pleaded as tears streamed from his eyes.

He might appear childlike, almost harmless now, but John knew what this man was capable of doing. Glancing at the pictures resting on the nightstand, he pushed further.

"She used you and your brother for money, didn't she? She made you have sex with her dealer, with other men, with her, with each other so she could maintain her lifestyle. Is that why you killed her? Is that why you and Tobias killed prostitutes? To make them pay for your mother's sins?"

Winston shot up, the line from both his IV and handcuff pulling taut. "Shut up," he screamed over and over while covering his ears. Then he suddenly leaned back against the pillow, his lips moving as he whispered a prayer John didn't recognize.

"Garrett," he said, then repeated his name in a harsher voice until Winston finally looked at him. "You and your brother killed all of these women." He nodded to the photos. "Because your mom abused you. I get it." A total lie. He'd known people who had suffered worse, and they hadn't gone off on a killing spree. They saw a shrink and went on medication. But he had to find a way to break through to Winston. He had to coerce him into giving him the location of his brother.

"The thing is though," he continued, and glanced back at Roy with a shrug, "if you don't give us your brother, you'll be looking at the death penalty."

Mid prayer, Winston glared at him. "Wisconsin doesn't have the death penalty."

Roy nodded. "True. But Florida, Alabama, Mississippi, and Indiana still do. If you don't cooperate, you'll be extradited to those other states for murder. And I can guarantee you, based on the evidence, you *will* receive the death penalty."

Winston looked to him, tears clinging to his eyes, and John nodded. "It's true. We're willing to make you a deal, to keep you in Wisconsin if you give up your brother."

Chin trembling, eyes watering, the crybaby killer lived up to his name. He shook his head from side to side against the pillow, mumbling nonsensical words and absently reaching for the tissue box that now lay on the floor.

"Tell us, Garrett. Give us Tobias. Stop the killing. You'd said you found redemption, prove it."

"W...what will happen to Toby?" Winston sobbed.

"*He'll* be extradited," Roy said.

"No," Winston uttered through clenched teeth. "I'll go in his place. It's my fault. I created the monster he's become."

John frowned. "I thought you two blamed your mother. That's why you focused on prostitutes, as a way of, I dunno, personal justice?"

The eerie grin Winston flashed made him take a step back. Once again the old Winston was with them. "Personal justice," he echoed, and released a bitter laugh. "I never looked at it that way, but Toby did. I just enjoyed the control. There's nothing more powerful than deciding who will live and who will die. I showed Toby that power. *I* warped him." He made the sign of the cross, and then as if a switch had flipped in his brain, he became the crybaby killer again.

As the tears flowed, he wiped them away with the sleeve of his hospital gown. "I forgive Toby for what he tried to do to me back in the jail cell. Forgiveness is a step in the direction to God's salvation."

"And murder takes you a step back. Twenty-nine to be exact, not including your mother or your grandparents," John said.

Winston's eyes filled with shame. "They were good people. A little over-protective and set in their ways. I regret what I did to them. But I needed the money. I needed to go back to Mississippi to save Toby."

"Save him from who? His foster parents? You were thirteen at the time of your mother's death. Why didn't your grandparents take your brother, too?"

"They didn't want him. They didn't even allow me to talk with him on the phone or send letters."

"So how did you know he needed saving?" Roy asked.

"The old lady that lived across the street from my grandparents paid me five dollars a week to mow her lawn, take out her garbage, and bring her mail and newspapers to her. I gave him her address, and he wrote to me every few weeks. He was eleven when he moved into his first foster home. By the time he turned eighteen, he'd been through fourteen different homes. Some were okay, others...they weren't any better than livin' with *her*."

"Your mother you mean."

He nodded. "Toby had survived it all. When I finally moved back to Jackson, I guess I realized he didn't need me after all. He had a good job, a girlfriend."

John moved to the nightstand and flipped through a few photos until he came to the one he'd been looking for. The prostitute that had been found outside of Jackson and the first victim with two sets of DNA found on her beaten corpse. "Explain Tracy Lyles."

Winston closed his eyes, and screwed his face as if in pain. "She wasn't supposed to die. I'd brought her to my apartment for a little fun. That's all. Just for me and Toby. She wasn't supposed to end up like..." He waved his arm, the line from the IV dangled. "That. She was supposed to prove we were real men."

"You said your brother had a girlfriend. Sounds to me like he didn't need to prove anything. Maybe you needed to prove something to him?"

Winston looked at him then, his silver eyes holding a dawning realization. "I guess I did. But I...you have to understand what we went through. Being forced to have sex with a man ain't right, it ain't natural."

"Neither is having sex with your brother."

The old Winston resurfaced again as his eyes narrowed and his mouth curved into a sneer. "I hated him. Hated that every time I looked at him I was reminded of what we'd been forced to do. There were times I wanted to kill him. But he was my only family. He was all I had left, and the only person on the planet who got me. I brought that whore to my apartment to give us some new memories."

"What did Toby think about this?"

"The priss acted all pissed off about it. So I taunted him as I fucked her. Told him maybe he liked guys instead. That maybe mommy had been right in letting men fuck him stupid." He snapped his fingers. "Like that, he went bat shit."

Winston's leer sent a chill through him.

"He raped and beat that woman," Winston continued. "And encouraged me to do the same. Like I said, I hadn't planned on her dying, but the rush, the high...it became too much. Toby couldn't stop hurting her, and I couldn't stop watching or wanting to do the same. What did you say her name was again?"

"Tracy Lyles," he answered with disgust.

"Yeah, Tracy. She saved us, you know. She wiped the slate clean. Wiped away the memories. I'm sorry she died now, but maybe God put her in our path for a purpose."

How Winston could validate murder, using God as a crutch while claiming he sought redemption, both baffled and sickened him. "You honestly believe God wanted you and your brother to murder Tracy Lyles? Do you also believe God wanted you two to murder your mom, too?"

"I guess it doesn't matter now, but I do want to set the record straight."

John fought from rolling his eyes at the absurdity. "Please, by all means."

"*I* killed her, not Toby. She'd forced us to have sex for over a year so she could keep up her habit and buy her slutty clothes. The day she died, she'd shot herself up with some sorta shit that messed her up bad."

A slow grin spread across his face. "She stumbled into the hallway, screaming for me. I ran up the stairs and found her lying on the floor, flopping around like a fucking fish, blood oozing out of her nose, her eyes rolling back. And I thought to myself, she's gonna die from whatever she stuck in her veins. But then I worried she might not. What if she recovered? So I decided to help her along, and kicked her. To this day, the sound of cracking bone makes me smile. It's the best memory I have of *mommy*."

Although disturbed by Winston's confession, John kept himself composed. From beneath the stack of photographs, he pulled out the binder and flipped through it, stopping when he reached the autopsy report on Susan Haney. "You killed your mother to protect yourself and your brother. You claim you were the one who created the monster he's become, correct?"

"Yeah, that's right."

"Which is why you would sacrifice yourself, and take the death penalty so that your brother could live."

"Exactly. Just like Jesus did to save our souls."

"Amen," Roy said.

"Do you know what your mother overdosed on?" John asked.

"Nope and I really don't care. She's dead and burning in hell, that's all that matters to me."

"This will matter. The night your mother died, she did shoot up, but it wasn't just heroin she plunged into her veins, but ammonia."

"So," Winston grunted and frowned. "I've seen people take just about anything for a rush."

"True, but what I think is ironic is that Hoyt attempted to kill you with a similar substance."

Winston stared at him. "Are...are you saying Toby...No." He shook his head. "He would have told me. Maybe not back then, 'cause he was probably scared. But when he was older..."

"He didn't need you to take care of him then, and he doesn't need you now. You've become a liability to him. He wants you dead to keep you from spilling his secrets."

The new Winston was back, crying and praying.

"Enough of this crap," Roy shouted, and gripped the rail at the edge of the hospital bed. "Quit hiding behind God and Jesus and your salvation bullshit and give him to us."

Other than the fast beeps ringing from the monitor next to Winston's bed, the room remained eerily silent. John looked to Roy, who shrugged. When he focused on Winston, he knew they were screwed.

What began with tears streaming from his wide eyes, suddenly turned into a cacophony of wailing sobs. "He never needed me," he cried as he wiped snot from his nose with the back of his hand. "All this time, he never needed me. I brought him the women, I confessed just like he told me to and now he wants me—"

"Dead," Roy said. "You were an expendable tool to him. And the moment you were tossed in jail, you became a liability."

John gripped the bedrail. "Fight him back, Garrett. Give him to us. We know he hasn't used his real name since he turned eighteen. What name is he using now? Where is he hiding?"

The monitor connected to Winston beeped louder, faster. He clenched and unclenched his hands into fists as his eyes grew cold, dead. He slowly curled his lips into a mocking sneer. As the old Winston returned, the monitor went off with quick successions of beeps. "You want a name? An address? Check your local white pages for Go Fuck Yourself."

"I've heard enough." Roy threw his hands in the air. "How 'bout you?"

With a nod, John turned off the tape recorder and slipped it into his pocket. The entire interrogation had been a waste of valuable time. He'd been so sure that Winston would offer up his brother. Apparently, too much of the old Winston lurked beneath the crybaby killer.

He gathered together the photos and binder. "I'm done."

"Run, run, run," Winston said mockingly, and leveled them with an unreadable look. "But consider yourselves warned. I know how Toby works. I know how he operates. I know he thinks I'm just as stupid as y'all do. But I also know that he's got a thing for tying up loose ends. He knows about you, Kain, and that psychic...what's her name? Something kinda weird and hippy-like. Celeste, maybe?" He smiled. "Yeah, Celeste. She could definitely be a loose end. Heard she's a real looker, too. Better watch out for her. My brother's got a thing for knives."

Raw fury caused John's vision to blur. He didn't think, he didn't rationalize. The need to shove his fist into Winston's face and rip his throat for even breathing Celeste's name had him lunging across the room.

Roy grabbed him around the waist and threw him against the wall before he even reached the bed. "Don't." He gave him a hard shove. "He's not worth it. We'll keep her safe."

Breathing hard, as both fear and adrenaline pumped through his veins, John nodded. At the same time a nurse and Winston's doctor entered the room.

"We're leaving," John said to the doctor.

"You'll be back." Winston grinned. With the bandage on his head, his face and eyes bruised, his beard unkempt, he looked demented, devious, and just like the old Winston. "Remember, I know something you don't know," he sang, then laughed. "Oh yeah. You'll be back."

A chill ran through him as he turned from the door to stare at the doctor and nurse who were once again trying to hold Winston against the bed. Several nurses brushed passed him as they rushed into the room to help.

"I know," Winston continued to shout. "I know everything. Who he is. Where he lives. He'll kill that pretty psychic and disappear. Just wait and see. Just wait and..."

The rest of Winston's words were muffled as they stepped from the room and Roy closed the door. As they moved down the hallway, John's head spun, with the rage still coursing through him, along with fragments of what Winston had said.

He stopped dead as Winston's words pushed passed his outrage and anger.

"What?" Roy asked.

"Winston knew Celeste's name, which tells me Toby knew she was involved with the investigation from the start."

"How? The night Winston was arrested, the only people who knew about Celeste or you, for that matter, were..." Roy stopped dead and stared at him with sheer dread. "My deputies."

CHAPTER 25

JOHN HELD ONTO the door handle as trees whipped passed the speeding cruiser. "Roy, I know you're a sheriff and all, but even you shouldn't be doing thirty miles over the speed limit."

"I want to get back to my office." Roy tightened his hands around the steering wheel and clenched his jaw. "I...need to think."

"You need to slow down, in every sense." Since they'd left the hospital, they'd wracked their brains trying to come up with who would have known about not only his, but Celeste's involvement *before* Winston's arrest.

Mitchell and his CSU team had met him at the dumpsite, but Celeste had never been mentioned to any of them. The ME, Carl, and his assistant, Dean, had witnessed her performing the reading that had resulted in a sketch of Winston. They'd ruled out Carl and Dean immediately. Winston was thirty-four, which made his brother, Tobias Haney, thirty-two. Carl was in his sixties, and while Dean fit the right age bracket, he'd grown up in Wissota Falls. Roy had known Dean since he'd been in diapers.

The reporter, Matt Boysen, had known about John's involvement, and even Celeste's because he'd seen her car parked outside the Sheriff's Department the day they'd gone to the dumpsite together. Again, Boysen was a native to Wissota

Falls and also in his early forties. Which left Roy's deputies.

"Think about it." Roy tapped a finger on the steering wheel. "It all comes back to my men. It's the only thing that makes sense."

John agreed. Yet after witnessing the array of emotions drifting across the sheriff's face, the betrayal, the disbelief, the anger, the hurt, he tried to think beyond Roy's deputies. Unfortunately, he came up empty.

"See," Roy said when he didn't comment either way. "Even that logical brain of yours knows I'm right."

"Logically, it *does* make sense," he said, "But what's your gut telling you? You've worked side by side with your men. Do you honestly believe one of them could be a killer?"

The sheriff released a deep breath. "No. I've known Lloyd since he was a kid."

John had already dismissed the Viking, knowing he'd grown up in Wissota Falls. "Okay, what about the others? Are they from the area, too?"

"No. They've all been hired within the last three to ten years."

"Any of them from Mississippi or any of the other states we know Winston had been?"

"No, none of them. The closest one to the Mason Dixon line is Dan. He and his wife moved here from Tennessee. But you're right. I can't see him or any of my deputies being involved with something like this. They're good men."

Even good men *and* women do things for the wrong reason. John had learned this firsthand, but didn't say as much. He needed the sheriff calm. He needed him rational and thinking straight. During the past week, he'd witnessed the camaraderie between Roy and his deputies. These men weren't just employees, they were his friends.

Rather than feed into Roy's suspicions, even if he believed the sheriff might be right, he'd have him look elsewhere. In the meantime, he'd have Rachel take a look into the background of Roy's deputies.

"Look," he began as Roy parked the car in front of the

Sheriff's Department. "We both suspect Haney looked at Winston as a liability, otherwise he wouldn't have tried to have him killed. But what if Haney had been keeping an eye on Winston? He follows him, sees that he's dumped four women—"

"Then worried they'd be found, he goes to clean up Winston's mess only to find us there?" Roy cut the ignition, then clutched the keys in his hand.

The scenario made as much sense as the killer being one of Roy's deputies. It also meant they could be looking at any local male, in his early thirties, as a suspect. And how large of an area would they look? Eau Claire was only a half hour drive, depending on traffic, to the original dump site, and there were over sixty thousand people populating that city. Or what if their killer resided in Madison or Green Bay, and Haney and Winston only used Wissota Falls as a place to dump their victims? The killer could drive to Wissota Falls from Madison in two hours, Green Bay in three.

A needle in a haystack. A killer walking among John Q. Public, as maybe an accountant, or a salesman, with a wife and two-point-five kids.

"Anything's possible." John stepped out of the car, and met Roy at the front end of the cruiser. "I've got some calls to make. In the meantime, do you think you could get a search party together to look for the third victim?"

"Right." The sheriff nodded. "With everything that happened, I'd almost forgotten. I'll let my...men know." He cleared his throat and looked away. When Roy faced him again, he appeared to have aged ten years. The lines around his eyes and mouth were deeper, his face pale, gaunt, his eyes bleak and watery. "I'll see if I can get any extra bodies from Highway Patrol, too."

John lifted the keys to his rental from his pocket. "Good. Let me know what time."

"Before you leave, I'd like to hear Celeste's trance. I know this area. Any clues she might have missed will help when we set up a search perimeter."

He masked his disappointment and shoved the keys back in his pocket. He'd already heard the trance. Twice. And didn't want to relive the painful memories he'd witnessed last night.

What he wanted was to call Rachel and have her run background checks on Roy's deputies. Ruling them out as suspects would help keep the sheriff focused, and help them take their search in a different direction.

But what he really wanted was to see Celeste. Even if it was the start of the dinner rush and she'd be too busy to talk to him. Being near her was all he needed. *She* was all he needed.

He disconnected the call, then slipped his cell phone in his pocket. Removing the mechanic's suit he'd worn earlier from a hook on the wall, he dressed, then paced his garage.

In a good way, that call had changed everything, except he'd kidnapped Ugly Evie for nothing. Even though they knew his real name, Garrett still hadn't given him away, and was once again heavily sedated. While he still wanted him dead, sending Evie to do the job had now become an unnecessary risk. Especially because by this time tomorrow, he'd be gone, and all his loose ends neatly tied.

Still, what to do about Evie?

He shrugged and pulled the ski mask over his head.

Kill her, of course.

What to do with her body though, he wondered as he unlocked the door to his workshop. He wouldn't have time to dispose of her today. Then again no one would be by until tomorrow. Even if someone were to check inside his workshop, he'd already be long gone.

He couldn't have planned the entire situation any better himself, he thought, smiling beneath the ski mask. He'd been given time to rehearse his fantasy, and the opportunity for the real deal with Celeste. By the time they found Celeste, if they found her, he'd be drinking Coronas on a beach somewhere in Brazil.

Flipping the light switch, he closed the door behind him, then locked the deadbolt. Ugly Evie lay on the cement floor, still duct taped to the chair, eyes blinking rapidly as he stood beneath the lone bulb.

"Did you really think you were going to escape?" he asked as he righted the chair.

She shook her head, her eyes wide with fear. She should be afraid. Very afraid. He now had hours to play with her before he had to make last minute preparations for tomorrow. He had hours to practice, and he planned to use every single minute to draw out the pleasure.

Kicking her legs apart, he rubbed his dick and set his booted foot between her thighs. A scrawny little thing, he'd have to caution himself not lose control too fast on her in the beginning. He didn't want to break her yet, he wanted her kicking and screaming. Fighting him until she understood the absolute power he held over her.

"Today's your lucky day," he said, still stroking himself over the mechanic's suit. "I've changed my mind. You don't have to kill Garrett Winston for me."

The relief in her eyes would be short lived. Grinning, he removed his foot from the chair. Unsheathing the hunting knife, he slipped the serrated edge beneath the elastic waistband of her polyester uniform. "But there's something I still want from you."

He tore the knife into the polyester, splitting the pants in half, then ripped them from her legs. She screamed against the rag in her mouth.

"What's that?" he asked, mocking her cries, her tears. "Can't hear you, Evie. Something wrong?"

He swung the blade, slicing the air in front of her face, then laughed when her eyes bulged with shock and horror. "Oh yeah." He swiped the flat end of the knife along her skinny thigh, then up between her legs. "You and me are gonna have us a little fun."

Her breathing grew rapid, as she tried to inch away from the knife. The duct tape around her arms and legs gave her no leeway. The rag in her mouth kept her screams muffled as he used the serrated edge to cut the front of her shirt.

He stared at her naked torso, the quick rise and fall of her thin chest, then looked to her face when she let out a deep grunt. Her eyes were still wide, not with fear, but pain. He hadn't even touched her yet. Not so much as a nick to her pale flesh and still she screwed her face as if he'd already stabbed her in the heart.

"What the hell's wrong with you?" he asked, and gripped her face with his hand.

Her lips moved over the rag as she dragged in deep breaths and tried to speak. Rolling his eyes out of frustration, he tore the rag from her mouth.

"I..." she whispered, then grimaced, and sucked in a deep breath.

"You what?" He laughed at the pained expression on her ugly face. "Can't wait for me to fuck you? Ram my shiny toy into your bony body?"

His laughter died, when the corners of her mouth lifted into a slow, triumphant grin.

"Fuck you," she snapped, then her torso seized up, her arms and legs pulling against the duct tape as she cried out again.

He slapped his hand over her mouth as she released a hiss of air. "Shut up." He looked to the ground for where he'd dropped the rag. "Shut the fuck up."

She smiled against his palm.

He moved his gloved hand away, then reached for the rag. "What the hell are you grinning about? You like the idea of me killing you?"

"Can't...kill...me," she said, between short, gasping breaths. "Already dead."

"What are you—?"

Her body went taut again as her words sank in and penetrated his brain. *Already dead*. She was dying. Holy shit, she was dying right in front of him. Dying before he had a chance to kill her.

Dropping the rag and knife, he grabbed her purse. He ripped it open and spilled the contents on the cement. He quickly picked up two pill bottles and read the labels. Nitroglycerin and Coumadin. Both medications were used on people with heart conditions, and neither would do him any good now. The Coumadin was a blood thinner and the nitroglycerin worked to prevent heart attacks, not as treatment.

As her breathing grew shallow, he rushed to her and knocked the chair back. She thudded to the floor without a grunt. Worried he might be too late, he began pounding on her chest, over and over, hoping to jumpstart her heart. Sweat soaked his body. The ski mask grew damp from his exertions and made his face itchy. He stopped to check her pulse, then didn't bother.

Her head rested against the cement, her eyes wide, lifeless, her mouth gaping open without a sound or a single breath released. He sagged next to her in defeat and tried to calm his own racing heart.

The bitch had won. She'd died before he had a chance to kill her.

He caught the glimmer from the knife across the room and the anger inside of him swelled to the point he couldn't see straight. Without rising, he crawled toward the shiny blade, picked it up, then closed his eyes. Every fantasy that should have taken place flashed in his mind and only added to his outrage.

Tearing off the suffocating ski mask, he scrambled over to the scrawny, half-naked, lifeless body lying on the cement and still duct taped to the chair. He raised the knife high over his head. "This is what I should have done from the start," he shouted, and sent the blade straight through her dead heart.

The utter disappointment, the memory of Ugly Evie's mocking smile fragmented his mind into shards of raw fury. He stabbed her again, then again, and again. Rage consuming him, filling him and unleashing his hatred for her, for the bitch living under his roof. For Garrett. God, for Garrett.

As the image of his brother's lust-filled eyes permeated his brain, he sagged to the floor and wept. When he tasted a salty tear, he moved to wipe his face dry, but noticed the blood coating his gloves. He looked to Evie, to the knife sticking out of her chest, and laughed. Laughed and then cried some more. Over the irony of the situation, the loss of the only person he'd ever loved. While Garrett wouldn't die tonight, he was still dead to him. As dead as Ugly Evie. Figuratively, of course, he chuckled again as he peeled off his gloves and looked around the room.

He sighed, and realized that while Evie had robbed him of the prelude to the fantasy he'd play out with Celeste tomorrow, she gave him a different kind of release. With her death, he'd let loose his control. Something he'd done only once, twelve years ago when he and Garrett had first killed together. The memory of that whore still lingered. He might not remember the faces of the others that he'd killed, but he'd always remember hers.

She'd woken something inside of him, something he'd denied since the night he'd killed his mother. Something he'd sought to control ever since. Allowing emotions to play into any part of what he and Garrett had done led to loss of control, which led to sloppiness.

He shrugged out of the bloodied mechanic's suit, then dropped it into the steel barrel in the corner, along with the gloves — no amount of bleach would remove the stains. Sloppiness was what had led to Garrett's arrest. That and arrogance. Garrett had always considered himself the one who held the power. He'd considered himself unstoppable, uncatchable.

Dousing the suit and gloves with lighter fluid, he reached for a pack of matches. He lit the match, tossed it into the barrel, along with the entire matchbook. As flames swept over the clothing, he shook his head. Garrett used to laugh every time he wore the mechanic's suit, ski mask and gloves. How he'd spend hours washing the suit and gloves in bleach. He'd made fun of his numerous cell phones. The reminder of them had him moving to his tool chest, then dumping them into the burn barrel.

Garrett had been a stupid fool. Leaving evidence of what he'd done behind, because he was arrogant, because he thought he was unstoppable. Not him, though. He watched the flames lick at the clothes, the phones, let the heat from the small fire warm his naked body.

As he stood there, waiting for the fire to consume the evidence, he ran through what he had to do tonight to prepare for tomorrow. While making a short, mental list, his thoughts strayed to Celeste. To the fantasy that would become a reality. He began stroking himself, then stopped. He needed a release, but not here. Not where they might find traces of his semen. The shower would have to do. Again.

He used the fire extinguisher on the barrel. Once satisfied that the embers wouldn't reignite, he locked the room, without giving Ugly Evie's dead body a final glance.

Dead is dead.

In the closed garage he quickly dressed. As he buttoned his shirt, he grinned when he caught the scars on his fingertips. The pain he'd endured when he'd taken battery acid to his fingertips the day he'd decided to *kill* Tobias Haney, and resurrect himself as someone else, had been well worth it. They had none of his DNA, or a usable fingerprint.

They'd never catch him, he assured himself, not with arrogance, but with something Garrett had always lacked. Confidence.

And he was more than confident that by this time tomorrow, Celeste would be dead. By the time they found her, he'd be long gone.

Sipping a Corona and seducing senoritas.

Celeste finished filling the salt and pepper shakers, then placed them on the tray, while Rick and Karen wrapped up the rest of their closing duties. The rain that had been forecasted for Sunday had hit early, and had been more like a torrential downpour. Due to the weather they'd been slow for a Friday night, and since they hadn't had a customer in over an hour, she'd decided to close early.

Will had already left, Rick and Karen were looking forward to an early night, and she wasn't sure how to feel. Glancing at the clock, her stomach twisted into a knot.

Lack of customers had given her too much time to think. John had called earlier, briefed her about what had happened at the hospital, then went on to tell her Roy had managed to gather a search party for tomorrow morning. She still worried that she was sending them on a wild goose chase, but as John had assured her, they'd rather make the attempt to find the third victim than do nothing at all.

Shortly after she'd spoken with John, Dan had called. She'd figured he was looking for another order of kalachkis for his sick wife. Instead, he'd asked if she wouldn't mind staying at his house until the hospice nurse arrived around noon while he helped with the search.

She didn't mind, but the thought of sitting in Dan's home with his terminally ill wife didn't settle well. Although it had been three years since her mom had died, being near someone knocking on Death's door still hit too close to home. Will promised to open the diner in the morning after she'd let him leave early tonight, and if she couldn't be part of the search, at least she was still helping.

Thoughts of her mom had lingered after Dan's call, which had led her to spend the next few hours thinking about Ian and what they'd talk about tonight. Last night's trance? Most definitely. Maybe he could shed some light as to how it had happened, and better yet, give her suggestions on how to control them in the future. They'd likely spend no more than an hour together tonight. The trance would hopefully take up most of that time. But what if he wanted to discuss other things?

Ian had planned to leave tomorrow. The next time she'd see him would be when she moved to Chicago. Should she tell him that she'd decided to live with John? Or that she was actually considering working for CORE?

No. Not yet. She finished replacing all of the salt and pepper shakers, then dropped the tray to her side. Maybe instead of discussing the trance, she should use this short time to know the man her mom had once loved. Give him a chance at learning more about her.

She stacked the tray with the others and decided she was, once again, completely over-analyzing things. She'd go with the flow once Ian arrived and let him take the lead.

The bell above the front door rang, and her stomach did a somersault. So much for going with the flow. She glanced up, expecting Ian, then froze.

John stood in front of the door, wearing a sexy, crooked grin. Wet from the rain, his dark hair appeared even darker. His shirt stuck to his chest, revealing those perfect pecs she loved to hold onto when she rode him hard. The thought, the image made her hot, and brought heat to her cheeks as well as between her legs.

Then she noticed the time.

"What are you doing here?" she asked, rounding the counter while her skin prickled, her stomach flipped, and her head buzzed. Ian would be by any minute, any second, and John would realize she'd held back on him. After how honest he'd been with her, she'd owed him the same. Regret ate at her. She should have told him everything about Ian last night. Why the hell hadn't she?

Because Ian had asked her not to. Because she wanted to start her relationship with her biological father on the right foot. Because she figured she had more time. Ian would be gone tomorrow, and that's when she'd planned on spilling everything to John.

She should have gone with her first instinct and told John from the start. When, though? She'd learned about Ian being her father yesterday. Then there was the trance. The whole let's move in together and...damn. She should have just told him. In a matter of minutes Ian would waltz through the door and John would be completely sucker punched.

"I finished early and thought I'd swing by for some dinner, then give you a ride home. I see you've closed the place down though."

"Yeah." She glanced at the clock again. "But I saved you tonight's special."

"Great. How long before you're ready to leave?" he asked, brushing droplets of water from his shirt as he approached her.

"Soon, but—"

"Is Will still here?"

"No, he—"

John wrapped his arms around her waist and pulled her against him. He nuzzled his damp head against her neck, brushed his lips at the hollow of her throat. "Are we alone?" he asked as he kissed her chin, then her cheek. "I've fantasized about taking you against this counter. Bending you over, spreading you—"

"Stop," she said, even as the wicked image ran through her imagination and heated her body. "Just stop." She pressed a fist against his chest. "We're not alone, and I'm expecting...someone."

Still holding her, he leaned back and snared her gaze. "Someone?" he asked, his voice holding a hint a jealousy.

She laid a hand on his cheek. "John, there's something I should have told you about yesterday. I planned on telling you tomorrow when he left."

Releasing her, he took a step back, leaving her suddenly cold and insecure. "*He?* And who would that be?"

She crossed her arms over her chest to ward off the chill in his voice. "My—"

The bell chimed as the front door opened. Wind and a few dead leaves whipped into the diner.

Along with Ian.

CHAPTER 26

JOHN STARED AT Ian, who had the audacity to smile at him as he brushed rain from his coat. Ian had dumped him in Wissota Falls then had ignored his calls. After five days, now he was standing in the doorway of The Sugar Shack?

Confused as to why Ian was there, and whether or not this was the "he" Celeste had been referring to, he turned to her. Her cheeks bloomed scarlet, her wide eyes held shock and...familiarity.

When she met his gaze, a slow burn seeped into his chest making him wish he hadn't left the antacids in the car. She *had* been expecting Ian, but he'd guarantee she hadn't planned on him finding out that she actually knew Ian. The knowledge of it was clear on her face, with the way her pulse beat quickly at the base of her throat, and how she twisted a curl around a shaky finger. She knew *his* boss and hadn't bothered to tell him?

Ian had kept him in the dark for nearly a week, not returning his calls, and instead kept apprised of the investigation through the sheriff. Had he also been talking with Celeste? From the beginning?

He ran a hand through his damp hair as his stomach sank with a betrayal he hadn't felt since...Renee.

Two for two.

Twice now he'd allowed a woman to pull one over on him.

Only this time the betrayal hurt worse. He loved Celeste. Trusted her. He'd told her things he'd never told anyone else. He'd given her his heart, his soul. Hell, he'd asked her to move in with him with the thoughts of marriage and babies.

What had she done in return? Like Ian, she'd kept him in the dark, and now he wondered what other secrets she had hidden beneath that pretty smile and her bright blue eyes.

"I see this is rather awkward," Ian said as he approached, offering him his hand.

John didn't bother shaking the other man's hand. As far as he was concerned, his days with CORE were over. He'd rather flip burgers or bag groceries than have to deal with Ian and his bullshit.

Ian dropped his hand, then gave Celeste a kiss on the cheek. The affectionate gesture took him over the edge. "You'll have my resignation in the morning," he said to Ian, reached into his pocket, then set the key to Celeste's home on the counter.

She placed her hand over his, the warm metal from the key stuck to his sweaty palm. "What are you doing?"

He snatched his hand away. "Leaving. Tonight."

"What about the investigation?" Ian asked. "You've never quit anything in your life."

"Please don't," she said with exasperation, and narrowed her eyes at Ian. "This has nothing to do with the investigation. Does it?" She looked back to him, her eyes imploring, uncertain. "I should have told you about Ian."

He moved away from the counter. He couldn't stand being near her, catching her scent, the warmth radiating from her body, knowing that their relationship had all been a lie. Angry and upset, he didn't trust himself not to draw her into his embrace and pretend none of this was happening. But then Renee's image surfaced and the painful memory of her duplicity renewed the fight in him.

"I'm all ears now," he said with sarcasm.

Taking a deep breath, she rubbed her arms and shivered. "Before you came over Wednesday night, I read through some of my mom's old journals hoping to find something to help me with my trances. Instead I found out that my mom had been a psychic advisor for the FBI and had also been in love with a man named Ian."

Her mom had been in love with Ian? He couldn't imagine anyone loving Ian. Self-centered, egotistical, and a downright ass on most days, the man didn't have a sympathetic or compassionate bone in his body.

"Let's cut to the chase before steam starts coming out of his ears." Ian dropped into a chair. "Although I have to admit, I like seeing this side of you, John. It's good to know you've got more than ice running through your veins. You sometimes worried me."

"Worried," John echoed. "That must be why you didn't bother to return my calls this week, because you *worried* so much."

Ian chuckled. "In less than five days you've become not only insolent, but sarcastic. You're starting to remind me of someone else."

"Who's that?"

Ian glanced at Celeste, his eyes holding a glimmer of pride. "My daughter."

John jerked his head as if he'd been slapped. He hadn't seen that one coming, and turned to Celeste for confirmation.

She nodded. "I found out yesterday morning. I wanted to tell you—"

"But I asked her not to," Ian interrupted. "You needed to stay focused on the investigation, not concern yourself about the ramifications of dating the boss's daughter."

"Ramifications? You really thought I'd care one way or another?"

"I did, and stand by my decision."

"Of course, because you're a manipulative son of a bitch," he said to Ian, then looked to Celeste. "And you went along with him. After everything we'd talked about, after..." After he'd told her he'd loved her, that he wanted to be with her. "How could you keep this from me?"

"I didn't want to, and it was hard not to tell you after..." She blushed and tossed her hand in the air. "I know you have trust issues, and I planned on telling you everything once Ian left tomorrow. Please, let's go home and talk about this. I don't want what's happened tonight to come between us. I love you, John. I still want to come to Chicago with you."

"Chicago?" Ian smacked his hand on the table, and they both swung their gazes to him. "This is wonderful news. Does this mean you're considering joining CORE?" he asked, grinning at Celeste.

"He offered you a *job*?" John shoved his hands in his pockets to keep from knocking the grin off Ian's face. "You find out yesterday he's your dad, he offers you a job and you didn't think you should tell me?"

"I wanted to," she said, her voice rising. "I told you, he asked me not say anything to you and I didn't want to start our relationship off by betraying his trust."

"But you had no problem betraying mine?" He pushed a hand through his hair again. "I can't do this."

Tears swelled in her eyes as she frowned at him. "You can't do what?"

"Be with you."

Her breath caught on a sob. "John, you don't mean that. We can work through this. Please, come home with me and let's talk."

"You were more worried about starting off your relationship with Ian, than you were about *ours*." He shook his head. "You would have always come first, Celeste. *Always*. Over my family, my friends, my career." He took another step away, distancing himself, his heart, from her. "I need the same in return. You proved where your loyalties lie, and I'm not willing to take the chance that it won't happen again."

"Kain," Ian snapped, as Celeste covered a hand over her mouth and turned her back on him. "Walk it off. When you've cooled down, and have that logical, rational head of yours on straight, come talk to her. Don't say something you'll regret. Regret's an ugly thing. Trust me on that."

"I already regret," John shouted at him, letting the pain and anger free. "I regret coming to this shitty town, dealing with this shitty investigation and falling in love with a woman who..."

She whirled on him, her eyes narrowed, her cheeks flushed and wet with tears. "Who *what?*" she asked, her tone low, seething.

Was she actually mad at *him?* He hadn't done a damned thing wrong. She had. If she'd only had enough trust and faith in him, none of this would have been a big deal. He could give a shit if her dad was Charles Manson, and certainly could care less that Ian was her biological father. None of it would have made a difference to him, but her silence had. Without trust in a relationship, there was no relationship at all.

Ignoring her, he headed for the door. As he passed Ian he said, "You're right. I do need to walk away."

"No, I said walk it off," Ian corrected.

"Whatever."

"What about the investigation? Are you really going to walk away from that, too?"

John stopped and stared at his reflection in the glass. He could make out Celeste's and Ian's, too. Like father, like daughter, they both glared at his back.

He didn't want to quit the investigation. They'd come so far, and he knew they were close to catching Tobias Haney. He wanted to see this case through to the end. He wanted to see Haney dead or behind bars before he killed again. He also wanted to make sure they didn't miss anything that might allow Winston to serve a lesser sentence because of some bullshit technicality.

Winston.

Better watch out for her. My brother's got a thing for knives.

The crybaby killer's threat haunted him. He gazed at Celeste's reflection. He might be angry. He might not want anything else to do with her. But he didn't want to see anything happen to her, either.

A woman you'd die for, or die without.

343

He *would* die for her. He loved her. Despite what had happened tonight, a part of him would probably always love her. Although he could walk away from her, he couldn't allow himself to walk away from the investigation, knowing she could possibly become one of Haney's victims.

"No," he finally answered Ian. "You're right. I've never quit during a case. I'll finish this one out." He glanced over his shoulder. "But afterwards, expect my resignation."

"And Celeste?"

"Don't, Ian," Celeste yelled from across the room. "If he wants to walk away from me because he's too pigheaded to see past his black and white little world, let him. And don't you dare breathe a word of what happened tonight to Roy. I don't want either of you giving John attitude on my account. Let him finish what he's started so he could go back to his pitiful life in Chicago. Alone."

"Pitiful," John shouted back, as he swiveled. "Look who's talking. You've spent the past three years hiding in Hicksville avoiding your grief and your guilt."

"You're no better. How long has Renee been dead? Two years?"

He looked away. "I'm over that."

"Really? I don't think so. That bitch warped your trust, and two years later, she's still doing it. Only you don't see it that way," she said as she moved toward him. "You've taken a simple misunderstanding and blown it completely out of proportion. But you go ahead, finish this case then run back to your pathetic life where everything is nice and tidy."

"You're damn right I will. And by the way, look who's talking. From what I've seen, your best friend is a fifty-year-old man, and your idea of a good time is baking up a storm in your basement. Instead of living your own life, you've been living through everyone else. Don't talk to me about pathetic." He reached for the door handle, the acid reflux burning bad enough he wouldn't be surprised if smoke rose from his chest. "And you know what else?"

She folded her arms across her chest and cocked a brow.

"Do tell."

"I hate your fucking gnomes."

"Enough," Ian shouted. "Kain, get the hell out of here."

"I'm gone," he said as he turned his back on them and pulled open the door. Rain and wind whipped against him as he stalked to his car. Once inside the rental, he slammed the door shut, then sped away from The Sugar Shack.

From Celeste. From the only woman he'd ever loved.

Celeste locked the front door, then turned and leaned against the glass. Her heart breaking as the taillights from John's car disappeared into the night. How could he have just walked away from her, from them? And over a stupid misunderstanding?

A misunderstanding she could have prevented.

Through her tears she caught Ian's reflection in the glass as he moved toward her. "I'm sorry," he said. "This is my fault. If I'd known he would react this way..."

Cradling her upset stomach, she turned away from the door. "This isn't just your fault. I could have told John yesterday. I had plenty of opportunity." She shook her head. "It's probably best things happened the way they did. I'd rather find out now that we aren't compatible than when I'm moved into his condo."

"Do you really believe you're not compatible?"

"Yes. No." She wiped her cheek with the back of her hand. They were more than compatible. John was her soul mate. The only man she'd ever given her heart to. And damn him, he'd trampled it, along with the hopes and dreams of the future they'd share.

"It doesn't matter at this point. We'd both said some regrettable things that can't be taken back." Anger began to filter past the overwhelming sadness dampening her soul. "I mean, who is he to call me pathetic?" she asked, unable to stop her voice from rising as her temper continued to flare. "And he hates my gnomes? What is he, five going on thirty-five?"

Ian chuckled, and tucked a curl behind her ear. "Most men are, I'm afraid. I know I've done some stupid, childish things."

"Like asking me to keep this whole father-daughter thing secret?" she asked, unable to keep the bitterness from her tone. None of this would have happened if Ian hadn't waltzed into her life. Then again, none of this would have happened if she'd been upfront with John yesterday.

Ian gripped her shoulders. The anguish and misery in his eyes lessoning the resentment, the blame she wanted to lay at Ian's feet. "I'm sorry, honey. I was thinking more about myself than about you. But thank you for keeping your word. Roy said you were a loyal person. It humbles me that you'd remain loyal to me, even though you knew it might cause a problem between you and John."

"Well," she began with guilt niggling at her. "I was going to tell him after you left, so maybe I'm not as loyal as you think."

He laughed and hugged her to his side as they walked toward the counter. "What I think is that you might have some of me after all, because that's something I would have done. Don't worry. John's stubborn, but he'll come around once he has time to think."

"I don't know," she said as a sliver of hope pushed past the anger, the hurt. Then she squashed it. "Even if he does apologize, I'm not sure if I want to take another chance on him. I don't want a man who will walk out every time things don't go his way, or who isn't willing to set aside his pride and talk over a problem."

"Dump the jackass," the short order cook, Rick, said as he rounded the corner and took off his greasy apron.

Karen came around the other end of the counter. "Don't you listen to Rick, Celeste. Men say stupid things all the time. It's part of their nature." She looked at Ian. "No offense."

Ian grinned. "None taken."

"Well, *I'm* deeply offended," Rick said with a smile. "But I'll still give you a lift home. Unless you need anything else, Celeste."

"No thanks." She mustered a smile even though her heart and stomach ached. "You two head on out."

After they'd left, Ian tugged at her hand. "Come on, let me take you home."

During the short drive to her house, her thoughts remained on John. The anger had dissipated, leaving her miserable. For what could have been and for what would never be. And as Ian pulled into her driveway, a deep sadness swept through her as she stared at her empty home. John should have been here with her. Holding her, loving her. Now she'd walk into a quiet house, and crawl into bed with only her grief and her sorrow for company.

Realizing she didn't want to be alone, she turned to Ian. "Want to come in?" While she could have asked Will to keep her company, she didn't want him to know what had happened between her and John yet. Will would likely grab Lloyd and head to the Chippewa Inn prepared to kick John's ass for hurting her. She didn't want that. She wanted John to finish the investigation and leave. And after he was gone, she'd have to make some major decisions regarding her future. One thing John had proven to her, she'd been wasting her life in Wissota Falls and it was time for her to live for herself. Not everyone else.

"Really?" Ian asked. "I thought after…"

"We both screwed up," she said with a tired shrug. "And besides, I've got a left over pie that needs to be eaten before it becomes a science experiment."

He climbed out of the car, then opened the passenger door for her. "I love moldy pie."

She grinned. "It's not moldy yet." Then her smile fell when she stared at her gnomes and remembered John's parting remark.

Resting a hand on her shoulder, Ian pointed to the gnome bent over, with its pants down, mooning any critter or passerby. "You should let me drop that one off at John's motel room. Sort of a kiss my ass gesture."

"That wouldn't be *too* childish," she said with a half-smile, while tears filled her eyes again.

He put his arm around her and walked her to the door. "Don't worry, tomorrow will be a better day. Just wait and see."

Well, she thought, with a heavy heart, it couldn't be any worse than today.

Dr. Alex Trumane woke on the sofa with a jerk, dumping an open water bottle in his lap. He jumped and righted the bottle, then went into the bedroom to change. When he glanced at the clock and realized it was already after five in the morning, he decided to shower instead.

Although the water wakeup call had him alert and wide awake, he needed to clear the cobwebs from his head. If he hadn't known any better, he would have sworn he was hung over. His head pounded, his body ached, and the odor emanating from his mouth reeked enough to disintegrate his nostril hair.

But he hadn't had a drink. He'd stared at the computer screen for too many hours during the night, had pushed his body too hard during his run, and had eaten too many slices of lousy sausage and onion pizza, with way too much garlic in the sauce.

After brushing his teeth, he stepped into the hot, steamy shower. As the water pulsed against his head, he tried to come up with another way to find Miranda Gates. While he still hadn't reviewed any obituaries, after the daunting, and fruitless task of reviewing hundreds of death records, he didn't look forward to another long day of dead ends.

Maybe he should hire a PI.

Paper trails.

No.

He rinsed the soap from his body. He didn't have to work today or tomorrow. He'd review the obituaries. The PI would be a last resort, one he hoped he wouldn't have to use. If

Miranda had died of suspicious causes, he didn't want a PI butting into his business or threatening to tell the authorities. If anyone would go to the cops, it would be him. He'd created this mess, he'd own up to it.

Showered and dressed, yet exhausted after little sleep, he rubbed his eyes and headed into the kitchen to make a cup of coffee. His knee cracked. Damn he was growing old. He should probably start wearing a brace when he ran. The shin splints had been bad enough, but blowing out a knee—

Alex dropped the empty mug into the sink and raced back into the living room. "*Nee*. I can't believe I didn't think..." He sat in front of his computer. With renewed determination, he began to search through the Mississippi obituaries from five years ago. Miranda had been alive then, otherwise she wouldn't have been listed in her grandmother's will.

As he viewed one obituary after another, he grew restless and increasingly despondent. The words on the screen were beginning to blur together. Then he finally found her. He moved the arrow on the screen over Anna Lynn Gates's name, then hit enter.

"Come on, come on," he coaxed the computer as he waited for the website to produce her obituary. After a few more seconds, and enough toe tapping that if he had neighbors below him, they'd have thought he'd just taken up tap dancing, the screen went blank.

"What the...?" He checked the cord leading to his laptop, then quickly plugged it into the wall socket. He rebooted the computer, and sighed with relief when the screen instantly opened with Anna's obituary.

"Okay," he said, then began to read out loud. "Anna Lynn Gates, nee Hamilton, age 83. Beloved wife of Thomas J. Gates, deceased. Loving mother of Robert, deceased. Devoted grandmother of Miranda *Malvern*, nee Gates. Husband...Daniel."

Dan Malvern.

"Oh my God." He swiped a hand down his face. "She married a monster."

CHAPTER 27

THE NEXT MORNING, tired and in need of more caffeine after talking with Ian until nearly midnight, Celeste slowed her car and pulled into the Malvern's long, gravel driveway.

Decked out in his beige uniform, gun belt and all, Dan stepped onto the front stoop. "Mornin'." He gave her a big grin, his red mustache twitching over his upper lip as he walked toward her car. "Thanks for coming out and keeping an eye on Randa for me. I really appreciate it."

"I'm glad I can help," she said as she stepped out of the car carrying a fresh batch of kalachkis.

"Here, let me." He took the box, then led her into the house.

The moment she walked through the front door, the odor of bleach and antiseptics permeated her senses. The stale smell reminded her of sickness and death, of the hospital room they'd tried to force her mom to stay in when she'd been dying. The scent brought back painful memories, but she ignored them as she followed him into the living room.

Noon.

The hospice nurse would arrive by then, and she'd be free to leave. She could handle staying there, and keeping an eye on Miranda. Besides, if she couldn't be part of the actual search, at least she'd be helping in some capacity.

"Randa's asleep now." He placed the bakery box on the coffee table. "I told her you were coming over before she dozed off."

"Anything I need to know?"

"Well," he began. "She had a bad night again, but seemed to be okay this morning. Rest is what she needs." He blew out a breath, hitched his hips, then placed his hands on his gun belt. "I'm worried. I don't know how much more her body can take."

She didn't know what to say. His situation was too familiar, too close to her heart. She'd watched her own mother go from strong and healthy, to weak and sickly, and it hurt. It *still* hurt.

You've spent the past three years hiding in Hicksville avoiding your grief and your guilt.

John's words had stung, especially because she knew he was right. She *had* been hiding, using her grief and guilt as an excuse to not move on with her life. Too bad it had taken a heated argument with the man she loved to make her realize it.

"I know this is a difficult time for you." She did know, and wouldn't wish the pain and suffering on her worst enemy.

"Thanks." He glanced at his watch. "I have to get going. Let me show you her room before I leave."

She followed him down a short hallway. The carpet screamed circa 1975, yet was immaculate and clean, along with the stark white walls.

"Here we are," he said, and pushed open the door.

As he moved around the bed, she held back a gasp. She hadn't seen Miranda in nearly two years, and her physical condition shocked her. Her pale blond hair had thinned, likely from the medications. Her face was ashen, her cheeks hollow. She'd lost so much weight she appeared skeletal.

"Not how you remember her, huh?" Dan asked as he stroked Miranda's hair.

"No," she whispered as she fought back the tears. It pained her to see the results of this horrible disease, how it had robbed a vibrant woman of her life.

He placed a kiss on his wife's forehead, then moved toward

her. "I've already given Miranda her morning medication. It has a sedative in it." He stopped in front of her. "So she should sleep." He glanced over his shoulder at the bed, then shrugged. "Oh...forever."

She blinked and shook her head. Sure she'd misunderstood, even as her skin prickled with unease. "What are you—?"

His fist slammed into her jaw, knocking her back into the door, which bounced against the wall, pushing her into him. Seeing stars, she tried to right herself, but fell forward. He caught her, gripped her shoulder, then punched her again.

She dropped to the floor, her face hitting the carpet. She shook her head and spat blood as she pushed with all of her might to scramble away from him.

He caught her legs. She kicked out and made contact with his chin. As he toppled backward, deep satisfaction mixed with the fear seizing her chest and coating her skin in sweat. Taking advantage she twisted and lunged to her feet.

"Shouldn't have done that," he growled, and grabbed her legs again, then flipped her on her back and pounded his fist into her stomach.

Crying out, she cradled herself, but he flung her arms away and straddled her. Panic she'd never known ripped through her. Why was he doing this? "Why?" she whispered.

He leaned his body over her, pressing his erection against her aching belly and pinning her to the carpet. "Aww, honey, you haven't figured it out yet? Some psychic." His hot breath coated her cheek, and his rough mustache rasped against her as he licked her from her jaw to her temple.

She cringed and sobbed. "Stop, oh God, please stop," she wailed.

"No one's gonna stop me." He reached into his pocket with one hand, while keeping her arms confined with the other. "Not you. Not your *powers*." He held a rag above her. "Not your limp dick boyfriend. You're mine."

"Wait," she screamed, her breath coming in shallow pants.

"No time for talking."

"Please, just tell me why. I don't understand." She stared at the rag, not sure what he was going to do with it.

A slow smile crossed his lips. "Women should be obscene and not heard," he said mimicking Groucho Marx to a tee, down to the twitching mustache and wriggling eyebrows.

She stared at him as he laughed, realizing she didn't know this man. This demented, scary man who she'd once considered a friend.

"Still don't get it? Okay, okay." He sighed. "Time's a wasting, so let me set you straight. Those women you've been dreaming about? I killed them. Winston? He's my brother. Too bad he's such a fuck-up, because if he were free, we'd sure have some fun with you."

"Oh my God. No." Screaming as loud as she could, she fought him. Turning her head from side to side, trying desperately to avoid the rag he dangled over her face. Not Dan. He couldn't be Winston's partner. He couldn't be the masked man from her trances.

Laughing he held her still. "Fight me." He pressed his erection against her. "I love it when they fight."

She did fight, until her muscles burned with the exertion. Until her neck ached from trying to avoid the rag he teased in front of her face.

"I'd love to keep playing this game, but like I said, time's a-wasting." He clamped the rag over her mouth and nose. "Breathe. Take it."

Holding her breath, she knocked her body against his, refusing to give up the fight.

He only groaned with sexual gratification. "Yeah, keep fighting me," he encouraged, and pushed himself against her.

She went still. With fright. With horror. She wouldn't give him what he wanted. He wasn't going to rape or kill her now, she assured herself, but he would try later. She'd escape him then, or maybe John would...

Dread gripped her. No one knew she'd volunteered to help Dan today, except Ian and Will. But she'd told Will she wouldn't be at The Sugar Shack until around twelve thirty. As for Ian, he was supposed to leave for Chicago this morning.

Her lungs burned. She didn't know how much longer she could hold her breath. Would Will even suspect something was wrong if she didn't show? Would he call John?

John. Despite what had happened yesterday, she loved him so much. He'd blame himself for this. For all of the things he'd said last night. He'd never forgive himself if anything happened to her. She wished she could tell him she loved him, that none of this was his fault.

She pushed a few breaths out, still refusing to inhale. But her lungs demanded air. Her face grew hot as she stared up at Dan. The excitement in his eyes sickened her. Bile began to rise in her throat, and her airways opened instinctively.

"That a girl," he crooned as she drew in a deep, ragged breath. "Take it all."

Her head swam. Her eyes drooped.

Then everything went black.

"About fucking time," Dan muttered, then unable to resist, he ground his dick against Celeste's limp body. He'd prefer her awake for what he'd do to her, though. He did like when they fought, and she was a fighter. He couldn't wait to break her and show her who held the power, the control.

He lifted her into his arms, then carried her to her car. Racing back into the house, he grabbed the duffle bag he'd packed last night, her purse and keys, then paused at the front door.

Miranda had still been breathing when he'd bent down to kiss her. She should have been dead with the amount of morphine he'd pumped into her body. With his hand on the door knob, he fought the urge to go back and check if she'd finally died or not. Glancing at his watch, he realized he was already behind schedule.

Burn the place.

He could, but the fire would alert them to him. He needed to make sure he had hours between them and the time they discovered Celeste was missing.

The phone rang. He jumped and dashed into the living room for the receiver. If Roy or anybody else were calling, he'd have to play it cool. After all, he was the concerned, doting husband with the terminally ill wife.

He checked the caller ID, then relaxed.

Private Number.

Probably another solicitor. He tossed the phone on the couch, and without hesitation this time, slammed the door behind him.

Dr. Alex Trumane cradled the phone against his ear. When a computerized voice message came on the line, relaying the number he'd dialed and nothing more, he ended the call, then rested the phone in his lap.

It had been a stupid idea to call in the first place. If Miranda had answered, what would he have said? Worse yet, what if Dan Malvern had answered? The man was a walking nightmare.

Thank God he had an unlisted phone number. He didn't want Dan to know he'd called. Malvern had been a cop when he'd first blackmailed him, and now Alex wondered if he were still in law enforcement.

He quickly Googled: Dan Malvern, Wissota Falls, WI. The screen popped up with more links than he'd expected. None of them had to do with Dan, but with a serial killer plaguing the county. Frowning, yet curious, he opened the first link from the Chippewa Gazette's website, then jerked back with a gasp.

Garrett Winston. He stared at what was likely a photo taken from Winston's driver's license. He had a beard now, but those cold, arrogant eyes, the hard set of his mouth—he'd never forget that face.

Skimming through the article, he shook his head in disbelief. Winston had killed four women, and was suspected to have murdered two others.

In Wissota Falls.

Where Dan and Miranda Malvern lived.

Alex opened another article. This one reported that Winston had murdered a prison guard, and was now hospitalized after suffering severe injuries.

He clicked on several other links, hoping for more information, but they all told the same story. Then he found an article, dated two years ago, this one also from the Chippewa Gazette, and about *Deputy* Daniel Malvern. He read through it, then snorted.

The Wissota Falls mayor had honored Malvern for acts of bravery. Apparently the deputy had gone to a house because neighbors had complained about the traffic and noise that had been disturbing them during all hours of the day and night. Instead of handling a case of simple noise disturbance, Malvern had discovered a meth lab.

"What a prince," Alex muttered, then looked up the number for the Wissota Falls Sheriff's Department. They needed to know about Malvern and his connection to Winston. He knew they'd ask him questions, but he no longer cared. What he'd found today went beyond making amends with Miranda Malvern. If she were dead, he'd have to live with that. But what if, as a deputy with the means and the badge, Malvern tried to help Winston escape? What if Malvern had taken part in Winston's killing spree, or knew about it all along and had turned the other cheek?

He dialed the phone number that had popped up on his computer screen. A woman answered the call, and he froze. Damn, he should have rehearsed what he'd planned to say.

"Hello?" she asked. "Are you there?"

"Ah...yes, may I speak with the sheriff?"

"He's not in right now. Can I take a message and have him call you back?"

"I...just tell him that I have reason to believe Deputy Malvern is personally associated with Garrett Winston."

"Reason to believe? Who's calling?"

"Ma'am," he began. "I don't *just* have a reason to believe, I *know* for a fact that your deputy and Garrett Winston were friends, partners, when they lived in Mississippi."

There was a long pause before she finally spoke. "Did you say Mississippi?"

Sweat began to dampen his brow. Maybe this had been a stupid idea, too. Maybe he should have just chartered a plane to Eau Claire and met with the sheriff in person. He was dealing with a small community. What if she was good friends with Malvern? She could go to him first, rather than the sheriff. If she did, Malvern would know he'd been the one to place the call that would incriminate him. He wasn't ready to sign his own death warrant.

"Yes," he finally said his voice rising. "And I have urgent information the sheriff needs to know."

"Okay, okay. I'll patch you through to the sheriff. Before I do, give me your number in case I lose the connection."

"Malvern can't know about me," he said with vehemence, with fear. "He'll...I know what he's capable of and I have a family to protect."

"I understand, and I swear to you no one will know about this phone call except me and the sheriff. I'm assuming you've read about what's happening here."

"Why do you think I'm calling?"

"Then you know we could use any help we can get. *Please*, sir, give me your information and I'll patch you right through."

Paranoid that she might be lying, he almost gave her a false name and number. Then a thought occurred to him. "Before I do, I need to know something."

"Sure, what is it?"

"Is Malvern's wife, Miranda...alive?"

The woman's breath hitched. "She's...yes, but terminally ill. Why do you ask?"

He released a deep sigh of relief. She was still alive, there was still time.

"Because he's killing her. Slowly."

"Sir, do you know what you're implying? First—"

"My name is Dr. Alex Trumane," he interrupted, his chest

suddenly swelling with pride. He'd found Number Twenty-Two and he would save her. "And I know exactly what I'm *implying*. You have a monster on your hands, and I'm about to help you stop him."

John shuffled through the sodden, dead leaves, poking the wet ground with a wooden pole. Roy moved alongside him, keeping a five foot range and doing the same. Surprisingly, so did Ian. Ian had planned to leave for Chicago this morning, but he'd decided, since he had no other plans for the weekend and he hadn't been in the field for a while, he'd join the search.

John hadn't bought his excuses, not after last night. Instead, he suspected Ian had stuck around to ensure he had his manipulative nose right where he wanted it. Between he and Celeste.

In the distance, the rest of the search party, including all of Roy's deputies minus Dan, a half dozen State Troopers, and a few locals, moved through the woods. Roy had hoped to have a cadaver dog as part of the search, but the handler, who had been driving from Green Bay, had run into a pile-up on the interstate. Still, they had eighteen men looking for the third victim, and that was more than he'd expected given the short notice.

Radios squawked and men's voices echoed against the trees. The air already damp from last night's storm, grew thicker as they approached the river.

John stopped and closed his eyes. Listened. Even from here it *did* sound like the water was rushing in three different directions. Goose bumps rose over his skin as he remembered Celeste's trance and how she'd described the sounds.

Celeste.

God, he'd been such a stupid ass and he couldn't wait to tell her. To apologize.

After he'd gone back to the Chippewa Inn, he'd spoken with Rachel, who had assured him that all of Roy's deputies' backgrounds were in check. Then he'd sat in front of his laptop, opened the binder containing everything they had on Winston, and instead of focusing on the investigation, he'd thought about nothing but Celeste.

He'd already realized what a fool he'd been even before Ian had called around midnight to read him the riot act. He'd let him say his piece anyway, knowing he'd deserved every bit of it. Instead of considering how Celeste must have felt when she'd found out her dad wasn't really her dad, and that her mom had kept so many secrets from her, he'd only thought of himself. Instead of comforting her, he'd walked away. Childishly.

She had every right to be angry with him, but he'd grovel, explain himself away until he was blue in the face. Maybe he should buy her a gnome as a peace offering. A way to break the ice. Then he pictured her throwing the plaster bastard at his head, and winced.

"Heartburn?" Roy asked as he prodded the ground, and shoved the wet leaves aside.

Ian chuckled. "Safe to say."

John glared at him, then shook his head. "Not the kind you're thinking, Roy."

"Screwed up again, huh?" the sheriff asked.

"Big time."

"Right it when we're done here."

"I—"

The sheriff's radio chirped. "Hang on a sec. Roy," he answered.

"It's Bev, I've got a call I'm patching through to your cell phone. It's urgent," she said, sounding breathless.

Roy frowned and looked at him, then Ian. "Patch it through," he said as he pulled out his cell phone.

"I've got something," one of the men yelled out not more than fifty yards from them.

"Bev, hold the call," Roy said into his radio.

"No," she shouted loud enough Ian, who was ten feet away, turned and raised a brow. "It's *urgent.*"

"Go ahead, we'll check it out," John said, and nodded to Ian. They left the sheriff behind, and jogged to where they'd heard the commotion.

As they neared a clearing close to the river, John stopped dead.

"Oh my..." Ian turned away from the decomposing body tied to a tree.

One by one, the rest of the search party approached. When they'd glimpsed the nude, battered body of the third victim, they'd turned away as well.

He didn't. He wanted to, but remembering Celeste's trance, he knew this was the crime scene. Another woman murdered by Winston and Haney. "Everybody stay back," he ordered, then turned to Lloyd. "You've got the tape?"

The Viking nodded.

"Set up a fifty foot perimeter around the body, CSU is on call." He scanned the crowd, then called on Jesse, one of the only men that didn't look as if he was about to lose his breakfast. "Get these men out of here. Have Ed wait for CSU along the road and lead them back here."

While Lloyd began laying the crime scene tape, Jesse disbanded the search party, just as Roy ran toward them. Pale, his eyes bleak, he looked to the dead girl with disgust, then to Lloyd. "You're in charge. Wait for CSU."

"Sure, Roy."

"Jesse, I need you to gather the rest of my deputies, along with the state troopers and meet me at the highway. Be ready to move out."

"Got it."

Roy began to move, but John grabbed his arm. "Roy, what's going on?"

"That call...I don't know what to believe, but I've got a doctor from Mississippi claiming he can connect *Dan* to Winston."

"Who's Dan?" Ian asked.

"Dan Malvern's one of my deputies."

Ian frowned. "The one with the sick wife?"

Roy's brows skyrocketed. "How did you know about that?"

"I was with Celeste last night. She told me Will was opening the diner this morning because she was going to help your deputy by watching his—"

John took off in a sprint. Fear squeezed his chest.

Better watch out for her. My brother's got a thing for knives.

CHAPTER 28

FRANTIC, AFTER ROY and Ian had discovered Malvern's wife barely hanging on to life, and no sign of Celeste, John burst out the back kitchen door. As he ran across the driveway apron, Jesse staggered from the garage, his face white, his eyes round with horror.

He grabbed the deputy, as fear grabbed hold of his heart. "What is it? Celeste?"

"No, it's—"

Releasing the man, John raced inside the garage, aware Ian was now only a few steps behind him. He stopped cold when one of the state troopers stumbled out the door of another room attached to the garage. Without preamble, without a word, John shoved his way in through the door.

Ian gasped over his shoulder. "Oh...God."

John couldn't speak past the bile rising in his throat as he stared at the grotesque scene. Blood coated the floor, splattered one of the walls, a patch on the ceiling, and even the light bulb. A woman, duct taped to an overturned chair, lay half-naked and lifeless on the floor, blood coagulating around her. The small room stank, not only of the dead victim, but as if something had been burned.

"This just keeps getting better and better," Mitchell said as he walked into the room.

John turned, relieved the lead CSU investigator was here

rather than at the other crime scene. "He has her," he snarled. "That son of a bitch has her."

"Highly possible based on what I've been told." Mitchell gripped John's shoulder. "Keep it together."

"Keep it together?" John shouted, then pointed at the dead woman. "Look what he's capable of. Look at what he's done." Raw fury, fear, and guilt suffocated him. Needing fresh air, needing to think, he stormed from the room, until he made it outside.

Resting his hands on his knees, he drew in deep gulps of the brisk, Fall air, as his mind and heart raced. Malvern, rather Haney, had Celeste. The things the sick bastard could do to her...

God, he loved her so much, and had made a huge mistake last night. What if that was the last time he'd ever see her alive? What if he never had the chance to talk to her, hold her, tell her he loved her and what a fool he'd been?

"John," Ian said as he came from the garage.

He stood and ran a hand through his hair. "Not now. I need—"

"You need to do as Mitchell suggested. Keep it together," Ian insisted. "Look, I love her, too. You have no idea how scared I am. But right now, love isn't going to do us squat. Neither are our fears. Right now, we need to be investigators first, a lover and father second."

John wondered when he'd become such a self-centered bastard. Ian suffered, too. Roy as well. Hell, every man here knew Celeste. They were all worried, because they'd all seen what had happened to Winston and Malvern's victims.

"You're right, and I'm sorry. You've just finally met her and now..." He shook his head, unwilling to allow himself to think the worst. He was a good investigator. They'd search. They'd hunt. They'd find her. They had to.

"Let's consider what we do know," Ian suggested.

"Right." He began running the facts through his mind. "Malvern likely took her car, because he left his pickup truck and cruiser behind. Will said her car was gone by the time he'd left for the diner. Roy has already issued a BOLO for her vehicle. I've looked at the map of this county. There's lots of country roads winding all through the area."

"Too many," Deputy Ed Young added as he and Roy joined them. "And who's to say he doesn't have another car ready and waiting. He ditches Celeste's and we're left chasing our tails."

The sheriff nodded, but added nothing more. Instead, he turned and hung his head.

Roy had known Celeste since she'd been an infant. According to what Ian had told him last night, the sheriff had been placed in Wissota Falls to look out for her, to protect her, and yes, to keep Ian updated on her life. Still, Roy's love for Celeste had been obvious.

"Roy," John said. "We need your help on this. Don't shut down now."

"It's my fault. If I hadn't involved Celeste and...Dan was one of my deputies."

"I told you to use her on the investigation," Ian reminded him. "As for Malvern, if Rachel wasn't able to crack his background until it bled the truth, then we're dealing with a very smart individual. But even the smart ones make mistakes. We need to find his, and hope it will lead us to Celeste."

"Winston knows," Roy said. "That self-proclaimed born-again knows."

John thought the same thing. "We've used every threat against him and he still hasn't turned his brother over to us."

"Don't matter. We'll *make* him talk." Roy turned to John, his eyes wild with anger and bloodlust. "He's in a hospital. They can bandage his sorry ass when we're done with him."

"That's not the way to handle the situation," John snapped. "I want to talk with him, but let's take a look around here before we do. See if we can find anything we might be able to use as leverage."

"*Leverage?* We're wasting time bullshitting. We need to act. You know as well as I do that Winston's hiding something," Roy insisted.

"We *are* acting," John said, even if he still agreed with the sheriff. "We have state troopers on the road. That's the best we can do for now. Malvern already has over an hour on us. I'm not going to argue with you about this and waste *more* time. We comb the house, then talk to Winston. It's the logical—"

"I'm tired of your Mr. Spock *logical* bullshit," the sheriff growled.

Ian grabbed Roy's arm. "Let's walk this off. John, start the search."

While he understood Roy's frustration, just as Ian had said to him, the sheriff needed to keep his emotions out of the investigation.

They needed to be smarter than Malvern. Or else Celeste would end up like the others. Dead.

Dr. Alex Trumane parked his car outside the airstrip located on the outskirts of Jackson. Duffle bag in hand, he slammed the door shut and headed for the chartered plane that would take him straight to Eau Claire, where a deputy would be waiting for him.

He couldn't wait to see Miranda Malvern for himself. Talking to the county sheriff wasn't something he looked forward to, but was necessary to close this chapter of his life. How it would end, he didn't know. At this point he didn't care. As much as he wanted to move on, spend the rest of his days working his practice and loving Kira, what he was doing now would be a defining moment in his life.

Thoughts of Kira had him realizing he'd most definitely not make their date for tomorrow night. How he wished he could have pretended he'd never met Miranda Malvern, or Winston, or that monster. But he had, and he couldn't live with himself if he didn't do the right thing. Even if it meant losing Kira.

As he climbed on board the small plane, he withdrew his cell phone. He knew Kira was working, and was thankful his call would roll into voicemail. She was inquisitive, and while he loved that side of her, he wasn't sure he could honestly answer any questions she might ask.

After leaving a brief voice mail, he stowed his duffle bag, then buckled his seat belt.

"With the wind behind us, and clear weather, we should land in about two hours," the captain said with a smile before he ducked into the cockpit.

Two hours. He leaned into the seat and stared out the window.

Two hours would give him too much time to think. About the past, the present and the future.

Breathing hard, Dan dropped Celeste's limp body onto the old cot in the corner of the abandoned, decrepit hunting lodge he'd stumbled on a few years ago. After working a kink in his back, he grabbed a water bottle and drank half of it down in a few swallows. Although she didn't weigh much, hefting Celeste a few miles through the dense woods surrounding Chippewa Lake had been exhausting. He'd needed to bring her here, though. The cabin offered the privacy he'd need to fulfill his fantasy, plus it contained everything he'd need for his escape.

After he drained the rest of the water, he glanced at his watch. He'd given Celeste a hefty dose of chloroform back at his house, enough to knock her out for a few hours. Once he'd ditched her car at the mouth of the forest and camouflaged it with a tarp, he'd injected enough morphine to ensure she'd sleep the afternoon away. Worried he'd been wrong on the dosage, he decided he'd make sure she was restrained before he finished preparing for his escape.

Using his state-issue handcuffs, he cuffed Celeste's hands, then linked the chain through a hook he'd screwed into the wood above the cot. He then duct taped her ankles to the metal base of the cot. Once satisfied she'd be incapacitated should she wake while he was busy outside the cabin, he couldn't resist running his hands over her breasts.

So pretty.

He moved his hand lower, tempted to undo her jeans and finger her pussy. Just before he made contact with the enticing zipper, he shoved away from her.

Heart racing with excitement, he rushed from the cabin, dragging in deep breaths. Man, he wanted her bad. But he refused to take her while she was half-comatose. He thought back to how she'd reacted to him just before he'd knocked her out. The press of her body when she'd fought him, the total power and control he had over her. Just thinking about it had him hot and aroused.

Even if she was awake and fighting him, and he didn't have to finish preparing for his escape tonight, he would have still stayed away from her for at least a few hours. Primed, dick hard, he worried he'd climax too soon.

Ugly Evie crossed his mind. That little bitch had gone and died on him before he'd even had a chance to touch her. There was no way in hell he'd mess up what he had with Celeste.

He went to the side of the cabin and unbuckled his pants, then did the next best thing. Moments later, with images of what he'd do to Celeste racing through his head, he released himself with a harsh groan. Panting, he wiped his hand clean.

After righting his pants, he peered through the small cabin window. Celeste lay on the bed as he'd left her, ready for him and all the depraved things he would do to that hot body.

He pushed away from the cabin. Work before play. And he *would* play with her.

First, he had to make sure he had everything packed and ready to go. After he killed Celeste, he'd walk the Kawasaki he'd stolen a few years ago to the highway, then ride off into the night with over a dozen IDs, passports and credit cards. Plenty of cash, too.

He checked his watch again. By now, they probably knew about him and would be looking for Celeste's car. Idiots would likely think he'd driven her over the state line. If only they knew he was right under their noses. Waiting.

If only they knew the horror that awaited Celeste.

***

John stood outside Winston's hospital room, anxious to enter, but forced to wait. He shifted the *leverage* they'd discovered in Malvern's workshop, then popped an antacid in his mouth. "How much longer?" he asked Roy, and looked at his watch. At this point, Celeste had been missing for almost five hours.

Five hours. She could be...

Ian shoved off the wall. "I'm going to take a wild guess."

John turned his head as Lloyd approached with the man they'd been waiting for.

Dr. Alex Trumane.

Mid-forties, the doctor had curly, sandy blond hair, and an athletic build. Wearing a golf shirt and khakis, he looked ready to play eighteen holes instead of coming face-to-face with a serial killer.

"Dr. Trumane," Roy extended his hand.

"Please call me Alex. How is Miranda?"

"She's in ICU. When we're done here, you can go talk with her doctor. She'll be able to give you Miranda's prognosis."

Although Alex appeared disappointed, he nodded, then looked at the door to Winston's room. "Does he know I'm here?"

"No," Roy said, then introduced Alex to him and Ian. After a couple of quick handshakes, the sheriff latched onto the door knob, then nodded to the box, the *leverage* John carried. "Let's hope this works."

Without knocking, they barged into the room.

Winston looked up from the Bible he'd been reading. His silver eyes moved from one man to the other, then settled on Alex.

"I knew we should have killed you." Winston slammed the Bible closed. Dropping it next to him, on top of a bunch of used tissues, he leaned against the pillows with a heavy sigh. "Now that I've found God, I'm glad we didn't. Besides, the fact that you're here leads me to believe that killing you would have been too quick of a punishment. I'm betting you lie awake during the night thinking about what you could have done different, huh?"

"Trust me, there've been times that I wished you and Malvern had killed me," Alex said as he moved into the room. He shrugged when all eyes shifted to him. "I was at the bottom of the barrel when I met Garrett, he knew it, used it, then he and Malvern blackmailed me."

Winston chuckled. "So you found out who my brother is? Pretty big shock, eh Sheriff? Yeah, Toby's good at blackmailing. How do you think he ended up a deputy?"

"What do you mean?" Roy asked, and clenched his jaw.

"Check on that Tennessee sheriff that vouched for him." Winston's chin began to tremble as his smile faded. "You'll find that he's...dead."

Roy sucked in a breath and turned away.

"Consider yourself lucky," Winston said to Alex. "You're the only one he's never killed after a blackmail." He made the sign of the cross. "I told him to take you out, even offered to do it myself, but Toby thought he might need you in the future. If he didn't, he'd figured you'd either OD on drugs or you were too drunk to remember what you'd done anyway."

"I remember every fucking moment," Alex said, his voice rising. "That's why I'm here. That's why I'm sober."

"Five years later?" Winston shot back, tears streaming down his face. "Do you have any idea what you've put Miranda through?"

"Garrett," John began. "Dan...Toby has kidnapped a woman. We need to know—"

"I told you to watch out for her." He reached for a fresh tissue. "He took the psychic, right?"

John nodded. "We need you to help us."

"I'll help you once the good doctor atones for *his* sins." He blew his nose. "Maybe."

"*Maybe?*" Roy yelled. "Listen up, you piece of—"

"Stop," Alex shouted. "I'll atone. I was drunk, just had a fight with my wife when I went to some honky-tonk outside of Jackson. I was looking for more booze, coke, and a woman. I met Garrett, and he gave me what I'd needed. Only he and Malvern set me up. Took pictures of what I'd been doing. I didn't know until Malvern showed up at my practice telling me to purposefully diagnose his fiancé with some terminal disease."

Alex paced the room, shoving his hands in the pockets of his pressed khakis. "He had pictures, and I still had abuse issues. I gave him what he wanted and have regretted it ever since."

John shook his head in disbelief. Not that the good doctor had admitted to purposefully misdiagnosing Miranda Malvern, but that they were wasting precious time. "Garrett, he atoned, damn it. We need to know—"

"She stayed with him," Winston wailed, clutching a tissue to his nose. "Because he told her he loved her no matter what was wrong with her. And the whole time he'd been poisoning her, lying to her, using her for the inheritance he knew she'd get when Granny Gates died. He killed the old bag, too, especially when he found out she'd left a house and property in this bum-fucked part of the planet to her granddaughter. I blame *you* for all of this."

The room fell silent, until Winston blew his nose again.

Tired of the bullshit, John opened the box, then dumped dozens of snapshots—each one encased in plastic baggies—on top of Winston. "Can you blame him for *this*?"

Winston stared down at the pictures of him performing despicable acts to the women he'd likely killed alongside his brother. His mouth gaped open as he quickly sorted his hand through the plastic bags, then tears began spilling.

"He...he...Oh my God," he cried, and reached for another tissue.

"You've been more than a liability." John pulled a picture of Winston raping a woman from the pile of many and shoved it into his face. "You were his fall guy. He set *you* up, just like him." John pointed to Alex. "Are you going to lie there and do nothing to stop him?"

Winston averted his eyes from the photograph. The

crybaby killer, once again, lived up to his name, sobbing and blubbering to the point John worried Winston had been pushed too far.

"That bastard. That lying bastard," Winston repeated, this time with anger, with rage, and crossed himself again hard enough he left a red mark on his forehead.

Excitement boiled through John. He wanted Winston angry. He wanted his hatred for Malvern. "He'll get the death penalty for what he's done. If you help us, I'll do my best to make sure you're not extradited and serve your sentence here, in Wisconsin." Whether Winston was extradited or not would be up to the district attorney, but he'd make all sorts of promises and tell a million lies if it would help them find Celeste.

"What about the good doc over there?" Winston asked as he jerked his head toward Alex.

"What about me?"

"For what he did to Miranda, you should fry his ass, too."

"You knew what Malvern had been doing to her all along. Why didn't *you* stop him?" Alex asked. "You're as much to blame."

Worried the arguing between the doctor and the crybaby killer might cause Winston to derail and clam up, John said, "Dr. Trumane is in our custody, and will be dealt with for his crimes against Miranda Malvern."

John sent Alex a look, hoping the man realized he'd been bluffing. Then he turned to Lloyd. "Cuff him, and take him out in the hallway."

While Lloyd placed Alex in handcuffs, Winston stared at the doctor with a smug smile. After Lloyd led him into the hall, then shut the door, Winston turned his attention back to them.

"What do you want to know?"

"Where would Malvern run?"

"You got a map on ya?"

Roy pulled a county map from his back pocket, then spread it out and handed it to Winston. "The red dot indicates Malvern's house," the sheriff said.

"Okay." Winston ran his finger over the road leading from the Malvern residence. He zigged, then zagged over other roads, then stopped and tapped. "Here."

John and Roy stood on either side of the bed and stared at the map. "What are we looking at?" John asked. The road Winston had pointed to dead ended into nothing but forest, and lots of it.

"Toby found an abandoned hunting cabin a few years back. Since then, he's been storing stuff there, just in case the heat came down on us."

"Can you point out where this cabin is?" John asked, anxious to begin searching for Celeste. They'd already blown through another half hour with Winston. By the time they reached the area Winston indicated, another hour would be wasted.

"Not exactly. I've only been there once. But…" Winston ran his finger across the large section of forest, then pointed to the highway that ran parallel to the county road. "The plan had always been that if Toby had to hide out in his cabin, I was supposed to pick him up at mile marker one sixty-two. I'm not sure how far the highway is from the cabin, but I'm thinking no more than a half mile."

"How do you know?"

"Because Toby said he'd timed himself once, and he'd made it from the cabin to the highway in under ten minutes. That was with carrying a load on his back and dealing with running through the woods."

While it wasn't exactly a street address, it was better than what they'd had before now. John nodded, then looked to Roy and Ian. "Let's go."

As Roy took the map, Winston said, "How long has he had her?"

"Almost six hours," the sheriff answered with disgust.

Winston shook his head and released a low whistle. "Don't bother with an ambulance." He picked up his Bible. "If Toby's had her that long, you'll need a body bag."

CHAPTER 29

CELESTE WOKE SLOWLY, her head swimming. She shut her eyes and fought the nausea. Wanting to curl onto her side, she turned her head to cradle her stomach, then panicked when her numb arms didn't respond.

Eyes wide and now fully alert, she stared up, her heart and mind racing. *Dan.* "Oh my God," she whispered, and pulled against the handcuffs fastened to a hook on the wall.

She looked to her legs with increasing horror. He'd duct taped her ankles to the cot, leaving her lying spread eagle, her body stretched and vulnerable.

Craning her neck, she scanned the small, dank room. A battery-powered lamp sat on the floor casting eerie shadows along the supplies—canned food, bottled water—lining the wall. Her gaze stopped on a small window. No sunlight filtered inside, not even the shadows of dusk. How long had she been here? One day? Two? And where was here?

Wherever here was, she'd rather run free, into the unknown, than lie on a musty cot waiting for Dan to come back and kill her. Based on her visions, her trances, she knew he would do just that.

She looked up at her cuffed hands and yanked with all of her strength. Metal bit into her wrists. If she was going to die, she'd die fighting. And if she survived, she swore, no matter what happened with John, she'd start living for herself, not everyone else.

Her muscles burned and sweat coated her skin as she strained her body at odd angles, trying to either unhook the metal chain, or force it from the wall. Breathing hard, she stopped, gave her arms a moment's respite, then went at it again.

"Yes," she hissed when the hook wiggled. Tears of relief streamed down the side of her face, tickling her skin.

A motor revved outside. She froze, wondering once again where Dan had taken her. If she screamed, would there be neighbors nearby to hear her? No. He would have gagged her if that were the case. Not willing to risk allowing Dan to know she was awake and trying to escape, she ignored the ache in her shoulders and yanked against the hook. Small splinters of wood fell behind her head as the hook moved again. Another tug and she...

The motor died. She held her breath, then jumped when the door slammed against the wall.

"Hey, sleepy head. How was your nap?" Dan asked as he loomed over her, raking his eyes across her body.

She remained silent. Biding her time, and praying he'd leave the room again. If she had a few more moments alone, she could possibly free herself.

"What, no small talk? Okay then, maybe you just want to get at it."

He unsheathed a knife. A very long, very scary knife. Her skin crawled as the dim light gleamed off the blade. "What...what are you doing?"

He raised a red brow. "With this?" He fingered the knife's sharp edge. "Fulfilling my ultimate fantasy," he said, then sat on the edge of the cot.

Placing a hand on her leg, he ran the knife along the column of her throat. "You sure are pretty." He dipped the tip at the collar of her shirt, then ripped through the material.

She squeezed her eyes shut as the smooth side of the cold blade rested against her skin. Tears streamed down the sides of her face. She held her breath as he tore the shirt in half and cool air rushed over her exposed chest. He pushed the material aside, baring her cotton bra and stomach.

"So soft," he said, and ran the flat edge of the knife along her belly while he rubbed her breasts with his free hand.

She jerked with disgust and loathing.

"You like that?" He began unbuttoning her jeans. "Well, there's more where that came from."

Hysteria, terror and unnerving fright tore through her. "Why are you doing this?"

He unzipped her jeans. "C'mon, you're the psychic, you know why."

The visions. "You read the visions I gave to Roy."

"Yep," he said as he forced her jeans over her hips until they drooped around her calves. "I heard about your trances, too. And well, I honestly hadn't had you on my list of loose ends until then." He shook his head as he stared between her thighs. "But I should have. You're sexy, and hot, and so much better than those whores Garrett would bring me."

"You don't have to do this," she implored, careful not to tug too hard against the hook above her. She needed to be certain it would wrench loose. If that meant waiting until he raped her, at least she'd have the element of surprise on her side. "I'd never seen you in any of my visions."

"But you *did* see me. As the masked man," he finished with a wag of his brows as he played with the elastic of her panties.

"I didn't know it was you."

He dropped the knife on her stomach, then ripped her underwear in half with both of his hands. Panting, he retrieved the knife, then focused on her crotch. "Maybe not, but it was only a matter of time."

She had to act fast, had to keep him talking. Fighting her tears, her revulsion, she asked, "What about the fourth vision?"

He stopped and wrinkled his forehead. The menacing knife hung over her stomach. "What are you talking about?"

"I had *four* visions," she said, eyeing the jagged blade, and exerting her arms.

"Oh," he chuckled. "That's right. I almost forgot about that. You know, I thought it was odd at the time, but now..." He laughed, his entire body trembling and shaking. He wiped away a tear and smiled. "This is too funny not to share. See, there were only three."

She flinched, and her mind raced. She'd had *four* visions. Seen *four* women die.

"Okay. I see you're not gettin' it. Since it won't matter, I'll let you in on a little secret. My brother and I have been killing whores for years. Garrett would scrape up these disgusting lot lizards. Now, don't get me wrong." He ran the blade along her inner thigh. "They served their purpose, but I got tired of slutty, trailer trash."

"You didn't seem to have a problem killing those four women they found in the woods," she said, hoping her tone didn't come off as taunting. She just wanted to keep him talking, distracted from her naked body.

"That was all Garrett, that piece of shit. I didn't know about them. But the other three? The girl in the cranberry bog, she was *all* mine."

"The other two?"

"We did them together."

"And the fourth?"

He shook his head. "There *wasn't* a fourth."

"I had—"

"I know *Miz* Psychic," he said, and rolled his eyes as if she were obtuse. "I get it. You had four visions, but here's the deal. I killed one, Garrett and I killed two. Do the math. One plus two equals three. *Not* four."

"But I saw four," she insisted.

"Take a look at yourself and remember the little diary you wrote to Roy," he said with a sarcastic chuckle. "You *are* the fourth vision."

"Oh my God," she whispered, and tasted a new kind of fear as the images of the victims from her visions flashed through her mind.

"God ain't gonna help you now." He rose from the cot and

began unbuckling his pants. "When I was snooping through Roy's files and came across your visions, I'll admit, I got a little worried. When I found the fourth one and knew I had nothing to do with it, well, I hoped that I wouldn't have to hurt you. I like you Celeste, always have. You were always so sweet and friendly. Plus you made those kalachkis for the missus." He grinned. "You have no idea how them tasty pastries helped me. Mixing rat poison with powdered sugar kept my Randa's symptoms where I needed them."

She ignored the guilt, that she had somehow played a part in his wife's poisoning. While he was busy shoving his pants over his hips, she looked up at the hook and tugged as hard as possible.

Nothing happened. The defeat that ripped through her heightened her fear. All of her efforts had been for nothing.

When he settled himself between her outstretched thighs, she averted her gaze from his erection.

This was it.

He was going to rape and kill her.

She didn't bother to cry or struggle. He'd said he liked when they fought. She wouldn't give him the satisfaction. Instead, she lay still, accepting her fate, and praying for strength and a quick death.

When his flesh made contact with hers, rubbing against her inner thighs, she closed her eyes and sought a safe place in her mind and hid there. A place where happily-ever-after was real and sadistic killers didn't exist.

He slammed his fist into her jaw. Her head dangled, as stars shot through her skull.

"Bitch," he gritted, then hit her again. "Fight me."

Squeezing her eyes, she fought the bile rising in her throat, and forced herself to remain still even as her heart pounded. Even as the cold metal of the knife pressed against her stomach, even as he stabbed his erection against her thigh.

"Fine," he grunted, his breath labored. "No foreplay. We'll just get right to the good stuff."

With her eyes still closed, she brought John's strong,

handsome image to mind. She remembered his soothing touch, how it had always calmed her and given her strength. She honed in on that memory now as Dan licked a sloppy, wet path from below her bra, to her stomach. His mustache chafed, grated against her skin. Biting her lip to keep from screaming, she squeezed her eyes tighter.

"Look at me," he ordered, then ran the serrated edge of the blade along her torso.

Pain sliced through her. Snapping her eyes open, she screamed.

"That's what I'm talking about," he said. "Fight me."

She clenched her jaw. "Not much of a fight when I'm tied down, is it?"

Laughing, he punched her square in the stomach, then stilled.

She did, too, as the room began to rumble and shake.

Then she heard the unmistakable hum of helicopter blades. The sound, a beautiful symphony, as it thumped and hummed.

John.

"Mother fucker," Dan shouted, as he raised the knife high, his eyes wild with hate and anger.

She tensed, and cried out at the cruel twist of fate. With rescue in sight, she'd die anyway.

He brought the knife down with a hard stab, catching the skin along the side of her waist, then shoved off the cot. "Don't fucking move," he said as he righted his pants. He withdrew his gun, gave her one last glance, then left the cabin.

The moment the door slammed shut, she strained the handcuffs against the hook. Hoping the helicopter meant they were looking for her, she fought with renewed determination.

Pulling. Tugging.

The skin around her wrists broke against the metal cuffs. A thin stream of blood trickled down her arms as she continued to exert herself.

Something snapped, popped in her left shoulder. She bit her lip to keep from crying out in pain. Sweat soaked her skin, and she put her weight into her good arm. Small shards of wood fell against her forehead as the hook moved against the old plank.

Despite the pain, she pushed herself. The hum of the helicopter retreated. Dan could storm into the cabin at any second. Kill her and—

The hook fell, and bounced off her nose. She didn't give herself a moment to savor the small victory. Moving quickly, despite the cuffs, she wrenched the knife imbedded in the cot, cut through the duct tape surrounding her ankles, then hiked her jeans to her waist.

Free. But now what? She glanced around the room. Moving toward the door, she stopped and looked through the window. Other than empty cobwebs, the only thing she saw was her reflection in the dirty glass.

Giving up on the window, which was too small to crawl through, she moved to the door. She pressed her ear against it and listened.

Nothing, but the pounding of her own heart.

She clutched the knife in one hand. Her fingers tingled as she touched the rusted metal door handle with her other hand. She drew in a deep breath.

Dan had a gun.

She had a knife.

John—hopefully—was on his way.

And if he wasn't? She knew how the fourth vision ended.

As the memory of it ran through her mind, she whipped open the door, then ran into the darkness.

Fuck fate. She'd change hers tonight.

Dan lost sight of the helicopter's search light as it flew east, back toward the county road and where he'd hidden Celeste's car. While there wasn't enough room for a helicopter to land there, or even on the highway a half mile west of the cabin, he knew he'd just run out of time.

They could block him in, which would force him to run

north or south through over a thousand acres of dense forest. If that were the case, he'd have to leave the motorcycle behind, then steal a car later.

He sprinted for the cabin, mulling his options, then decided he would not deviate from his plan. The bike was packed, gassed and ready to go. Even pushing the bike, he could reach the highway in ten minutes.

Fuming over how fucked up the night had become, he ran faster. First he'd been denied Ugly Evie, now he'd be denied Celeste. His ultimate fantasy would have to wait until he started a new life.

Still, he considered as he slowed when a cramp seized his side, it *would* only take maybe a minute, two at the most to kill her. Not enough time to fuck and gut, but plenty of time to wrap a cord around her neck until he squeezed the life out of her. And what a fitting tribute using the cord would make. A kickass, fuck you farewell to Garrett, a way of coming full circle, if he believed in that shit. He bet Celeste did, and maybe he'd tell her about this whole full circle thing as he circled the cord around her neck.

Grinning at the prospect, that the night wasn't completely lost, he approached the cabin. Stopped. Drew his gun, then quickly crouched.

The door stood slightly ajar. He crept toward the cabin, and when he was certain an ambush wasn't awaiting him, he moved to the window.

Empty.

He raced inside. She was gone, and so was his precious knife.

"Fuck," he shouted and flipped the empty cot. Reining in his anger and disappointment, he rushed outside. Not having time to kill her infuriated him, but there'd be others. And they'd pay for what she'd denied him tonight.

He moved to the bike, knocked the kickstand back, ready to walk it to the highway, then froze. The bitch had taken the key. He'd locked his passports, IDs, credit cards, and cash in the side compartment. He needed that key.

He ran back into the cabin and grabbed the flashlight and cord.

The bitch was now as good as dead.

CHAPTER 30

CELESTE PRAYED THE night's shadows concealed and worked in her favor as she dashed between the trees. It had grown eerily darker the deeper she moved into the forest, but without knowing which direction she was heading she worried she might accidentally circle back to the cabin. To Dan.

She held onto a sliver of hope, though. With the helicopter still flying over the area, she assured herself that John and a search party were looking for her. Until they found her, though, she was on her own, continuing this fight alone.

She gripped the knife, wishing she'd spared a few minutes to search for the key to the handcuffs. She'd hoped it was on the key chain she'd swiped from the motorcycle, but apparently today wasn't her lucky day.

As she fumbled through a thicket of trees and thorny brush, a branch snapped across her swollen cheek. The sharp sting a lover's caress compared to Dan's ruthless fists.

She broke through the overgrowth of small spiky pines and entered a small clearing. Heavy clouds moved in the night sky. The moon's strong beam infiltrated through the trees and gleamed off the steel edge of the knife. The weapon gave her confidence. The moon's luster gave her light. The openness of the clearing gave her vulnerability.

Twigs snapped behind her, heavy footfall crunched through layers of brittle leaves. She held her breath, and glanced over her shoulder. The high beam of a flashlight danced and zigzagged.

Deep fear centered in her core. Had to be Dan. If it were someone searching for her, they'd call out, right? Not willing to take the chance, she fled from the clearing and moved for cover among the trees.

The beam of light grew stronger. The crackling twigs grew louder. She panicked and changed directions, then hesitated, twisted her body. If she went left, would it lead her back to the cabin? Or was it right...?

Damn it, she couldn't remember. No time to think, she ran straight ahead.

As she dodged trees and brush, she looked over her shoulder. The flashlight faded and diminished. Out of breath, she paused, crouched behind an immense pine and ran the back of her cuffed hands over her sweaty forehead, then stilled.

Her fourth vision filtered through her memory. Now that she thought about it, the clearing she'd run through had been similar to the one in her vision. The chirping crickets, the hollering of owls, the fluttering of bats as they whooshed amongst the treetops. These sounds were similar, too, only she swore she'd heard something else, something different from what she'd dreamed.

She crawled to the neighboring pine, and then the next. Flattening her back against the bark, she closed her eyes and concentrated, listened.

In her vision she thought she'd heard the hum of cars along a highway, and had even caught the scent of rubber and tar. The noises she thought she heard a moment ago didn't sound like traffic. They sounded like—there it was again.

Tears of relief streamed down her cheeks as the muffled shouts of men grew louder, the baying of a dog grew closer and more distinct. Spurred by hope, she took off toward the barking.

A hard crack smashed against her skull, jarring and fracturing her vision and equilibrium. She tripped over a large rock. Tumbling and unable to flail her arms, she threw her cuffed hands in front of her. Her efforts did little to help cushion the fall. Her chest hit the hard ground knocking the air from of her lungs. She panicked, gasping and wheezing, trying desperately to fill her lungs with air.

Blood oozed from her scalp and dripped into her eyes. Catching her breath, she wiped her face with the back of her hands, then gasped.

She stared at a pair of muddied, black boots. Fear broke and shattered. She gripped the knife as strong hands gripped her ankles.

With a sudden, hard yank, Dan dragged her. Her torn shirt flapped around her sides. The rugged ground scratched against the thin knife wound on her stomach. She tried to scream, from the pain, from the fear and outrage, but her jaw remained snapped shut as it scrapped the dirt.

He released a low, menacing, mocking chuckle as she struggled. Still clutching the blade in one hand, she dug her fingers into the dirt with the other. The red acrylics she'd had applied only days ago snapped back, a bitter reminder of her fourth vision, of its horrifying outcome.

She tamped down the increasing terror and fought. Clawed, scratched, searched for anything to halt her descent. Left with a fistful of dirt, she mule kicked. Twisted and thrashed.

"Goddamn bitch," he grunted, and tightening his hold on her ankles, flipped her onto her back.

A large tree root slammed into her shoulder blade and the shock to her system caused her to drop the knife. She ignored the pain.

What he had planned for her next was much worse.

John broke through a thicket of trees, then stopped when the search dog began moving in circles. Its handler had arrived hours ago, and had thankfully remained for the impending search. The same men they'd used to look for the third victim this morning were present, too, along with a dozen State Troopers and officers on loan from the Eau Claire PD. Lloyd had led half of the men into the forest from the county road, and had discovered Celeste's car, but nothing else. John had remained with Roy, Ian, and the other half of the search party and had entered the woods from the highway at mile marker one sixty-two.

When he'd first climbed out of the sheriff's cruiser and stared at the forest, with the way the sun quickly dipped into the horizon, the dense woods had appeared dark, ominous, and endless.

For over twenty minutes they'd been combing the forest. With each step, fear for Celeste had consumed him. When they'd found Malvern's cabin empty, the cot with a knife slice and shredded duct tape still attached to the metal legs, his fear had intensified. He'd hoped to God she'd somehow managed to escape, but considering Malvern had left his motorcycle behind, he'd immediately assumed the worst. Malvern was going after her.

He needed to find Celeste before it was too late. His chest tightened and his gut twisted with alarm and anxiety as the dog continued to circle and sniff. He loved her so much, and could no longer imagine life without Celeste in it.

"What's with the dog?" Jesse asked as he approached with Ian.

"Could be the trail your guy had used to reach the cabin," the German Shepherd's handler answered, then crouched down and petted the dog. Speaking low in its ear, he held a piece of Celeste's clothes under its nose. Tail wagging, the dog dropped its muzzle to the ground, then took off, back toward the cabin.

John reluctantly followed behind, beginning to think the dog unreliable. Minutes passed, then the dog stopped, put its nose to the ground again, then ran in a completely different direction.

"Up ahead," Ian called.

A faint beam of light broke through blackness, not moving

side to side as if being used to search. Instead it remained still.

Although difficult to gauge the distance, John figured the light came from at least a hundred yards away. Not far, but if Dan had Celeste?

Better watch out for her. My brother's got a thing for knives.

A woman's scream pierced the night, sending sharp shards of fear and terror straight into his heart. A hundred yards suddenly seemed as if it were a hundred miles.

Celeste released another scream, this time beneath the hand clamped over her mouth, as Dan dug his fingers into the thin cut lining her stomach, stretching and pulling at the tender skin. She cried and moaned, as waves of pain ricocheted throughout her body.

"Shut your mouth," he ordered, then grabbed her head with both hands, crushing her skull, digging his fingers into her temples and cheeks. With a grunt, he pulled her forward then slammed her head against the ground.

The impact rattled her jaw and shook her brain. Her vision blurred. The flashlight he'd dropped next to her dimmed, as her eyelids drooped and everything began to fade to black.

"You're not going to pull an Ugly Evie on me." He smacked her face. "Keep your eyes open and look at me."

He hit her a second time, the sharp sting jarring her from the blessed semiconscious state. When she met his gaze, a sick smile twisted beneath his mustache.

"Running from me was your first mistake." He settled his weight on top of her and reached into his back pocket. "Your second was taking my knife, which I see you've gone and lost." He stretched a thin cord taut. "Your third and biggest was taking the keys for my motorcycle."

A tear rolled down her cheek as she stared at the cord and sifted her hands through the leaves above her head. "I...I didn't take your keys," she lied, hoping to bide her time and find the knife. "Check your pockets. You could have already been on the road to freedom by now."

A deep scowl lined his face, as his eyes turned feral with shock and rage. "You're a lying bitch." He raised his hand to strike her again.

She turned her face away, searching for the knife with both her eyes and her fingers. "I swear, it's true."

He dug through her jeans pockets first, and she thanked God she'd tossed them when she realized the key to the handcuffs wasn't on the chain. "Better be," he warned, as he checked his pockets. "Or I swear to God I'll wrap this cord around your neck until you begin to die, then just when you think you're free to travel through those pearly gates, I'll stop. Revive you and do it all over again."

Stunned he'd fallen for such a stupid distraction, she continued to carefully sift her hands through the leaves. When the sharp edge of the blade nicked her right palm, she inched her fingers along the knife until she could wrap her hand around the handle. Her heart pounded, with adrenaline, with hope.

When he finished patting his pockets, he settled his full weight back on her stomach. Pulling the cord tight again, he raised it above her head. "You lied to me."

"I swear I didn't. The keys must have fallen out while you were chasing me," she said, keeping her cuffed hands and the knife under the dead leaves.

"Is that right?" he chuckled. "What did I tell you I'd do if you lied to me?"

She tightened her hold on the handle with her sweaty palms. "You don't have to do this. Just leave me here and run. Go. I won't tell. I won't—"

"I know you won't. You'll be dead," he whispered, with another low, mocking chuckle.

After all she'd gone through the bastard had the balls to laugh at her? Hate, pure and black, raged within her as the images of the other women he and his brother had murdered tore through her mind.

"Better make sure," she baited.

His face twisted into an ugly sneer. "Bitch," he muttered, then lunged, pressing the cord against her throat.

The dog she'd heard earlier barked. Maybe it was her imagination, her hope playing tricks on her, but she swore it grew louder, closer.

"You hear that?" he asked, his putrid breath hot against her cheek. "Somebody's looking for you. Maybe that boyfriend of yours. But guess what? When he finds you, you'll already be dead, and I'll be gone." He leaned in and shoved his tongue in her mouth.

She gagged, clamped her teeth and bit as hard as she could.

He jerked back and punched her in the head.

"Stupid bitch," he cried over his bloody tongue. Yanking her hair, he wrapped the cord around her neck and squeezed.

The thin cord closed off her windpipe. With hatred burning in her soul, she used every ounce of strength left in her, and plunged the knife into his back.

Dead leaves flew and settled around them as he released a harsh grunt. He dropped the cord, but replaced it with his hand, squeezing her throat as he reached for the knife with his other hand.

Kicking her legs, she clawed at the hand surrounding her throat. His grip slackened, while his face twisted in pain, as he wrenched the knife free.

Before he could use it against her, she slugged him in the jaw with her cuffed fists. The punch knocked his head back. She hit him again, and again, until he teetered to the side. Untwining her body from his, she kicked him in the forehead with the heel of her shoe, then jumped on top of him and hit him again.

His head lulled to the side as she grabbed the knife from his hand. "I found your fucking knife for you," she screamed. Gripping the handle with both hands, she raised it above her head then plunged the jagged steel square into his chest.

Howling with hatred, she rotated the handle, and thrust deeper, aiming for his cold, black heart.

He looked down at the knife imbedded in his chest, then

back to her. "Bitch," he coughed. Blood oozed from his mouth and dripped down his chin. He reached for the protruding handle, then surprised her with a hard upper cut to the chin.

The unexpected blow knocked her on her back. Her head bounced. Even with the blade still imbedded in his chest, he shifted, clambered and rushed on top of her.

"I'll haunt you," he whispered against her throat, his sweat, his blood coating and sticking to her skin. "I'll come to you in your fucking dreams, I'll..."

"I don't think so, *bitch*." She grasped the knife handle and rammed the blade deeper into his chest. "You'll be burning in hell."

He choked. Sputtering blood across her face, he leaned back, reaching for the knife buried in his chest.

A shot rang out and echoed off the trees.

She jumped and gasped, as a trickle of blood seeped from a small black hole in the center of Dan's forehead.

Then he fell forward.

The knife handle dug into her ribs as Dan draped over her body. Even dead, he suffocated her.

Bile rose in her throat. Sure she'd vomit, she kicked and screamed. She coiled her body, trying desperately to free herself from his vile, disgusting deadweight.

A booted foot kicked Dan off of her, then strong arms carrying a familiar scent were wrapping her in a cocoon of safety, security.

John.

"I've got you, baby," he said, and held her tight against his chest.

She clung to him and closed her eyes. As he ran his hands over her body, likely checking for injuries, she remained still, relieved to be alive and in his arms again. Even as dozens of men approached, their voices mingling together, none more distinct than the other, she didn't move. She couldn't. Exhausted, every inch of her body ached. And her head...she swore it suddenly weighed a hundred pounds. She couldn't lift it, move it. The voices around her grew tinny, distant. All but

John's.

"EMTs on their way with a stretcher. Just a few more minutes and we'll get you to the hospital."

"Stay...with...me," she managed to whisper against his chest.

He tightened his arms around her, which hurt, but at this point she didn't care. The pain had become a blessed reminder that she'd survived. That she'd changed her fate. Yet fate and murder had brought her and John together. Fate had also brought Ian into her life. Which had potentially destroyed what she had with John.

She would survive if she lost him. She'd go on, fulfill her own dreams, but knew in her heart, fulfilling those dreams would be so much sweeter if John was there beside her. She didn't want to lose him. And although her fingers ached, the tips numb from clawing at the dirt, she gripped the front of his coat. "John," she said thickly, keeping her eyes closed as her head grew dizzy.

"Shh." He kissed the top of her head. "They're almost here."

"I..." she began again, and on the verge of blacking out, she clung tighter. She had to finish, had to tell him. But her mouth wouldn't cooperate.

"Where are they?" he shouted, his tone desperate as he rocked her.

Mustering the last bit of strength she possessed, she whispered, "I love you," then everything went black.

She loved him.

John paced the hallway for the millionth time since Celeste had been brought to the hospital. At least he thought that's what she'd said before she'd lost consciousness. God, he hoped that's what she'd said, and not his mind playing tricks on him. He loved her and didn't want what they had together to end.

Today had been utter hell. More times than he could

remember, he'd feared the worst. And each time those thoughts crept in throughout the painful day, terrifying, desolate blackness swallowed his heart and soul. How he'd managed to roll through life without even knowing Celeste until days ago, he didn't know. Because now he couldn't picture his life without her.

The door to Celeste's room swung open as her doctor and a pair of nurses exited.

"How is she? Can I see her?" John asked anxiously.

The doctor nodded as the nurses moved down the hall. "She's dehydrated, suffered a concussion, and needed a half dozen stitches for the laceration she received on her left side. The wound on her stomach required a few stitches as well. Other than being pretty banged up, she's in good shape. She'll be free to leave in a few days." He glanced at his watch. "I've just given her a mild sedative, so if you plan on talking to her, you better do it now."

John thanked the doctor, then rushed into the room. He fought a wince when she looked up at him. Banged up didn't even come close to describing her appearance. It had been too dark in the woods for him to notice her swollen eyes, mouth and jaw, let alone the bruises marring her skin, the split lip, and cut on her forehead.

"That bad?" she asked with a tilt to her lips.

"You're still the most beautiful woman I've ever known."

She rolled her eyes. "Yeah, right."

He sat on the edge of the bed, and reached for her hand. With his thumb, he gently caressed the gauze around her wrist. "The doctor said you could go home in a few days."

Nodding she looked at him. "Are you?"

"Going home? That depends."

"On?"

"You." He leaned forward, careful of her stitches. Caressing her bruised face, he then fingered one of her curls. "I was such an ass last night. I'd actually planned on apologizing to you today, only not like this. When I found out Malvern had taken you, I...I'd never been more scared in my life."

She reached for his hand and gave him a small smile. "That makes two of us. Thank you for coming to my rescue. I'd bat my lashes and tell you that you're my hero, but my eyes are so swollen I'm afraid it will hurt too much."

"You did just fine on your own." He kissed her bandaged fingers. "You outwitted a very smart, very dangerous killer. Your strength and determination amazes me."

When she frowned, he moved closer. "I'm sorry for what I'd said about you hiding here. I didn't mean—"

"No, don't apologize for that. You were right. I stayed in Wissota Falls for all the wrong reasons. Nurturing is in my nature. I want to help whenever and wherever I can."

"That's one of the things I love about you."

"It's not a bad quality," she agreed. "But I also need to start putting myself first now and then. When I woke up, handcuffed and strapped to that cot..." She shivered. "As I tried to free myself, I swore that if I survived, I'd make sure I started living *my* dreams. For me, not someone else."

He stared at her battered face, into her blue eyes which held such conviction and strength. He'd never been more proud of anyone in his life. She'd taken a horrifying ordeal, and was determined to use it to better herself, whereas most people would use it as a crutch.

That last thought hit home. Celeste had accused him of using his past as a crutch. Not anymore. A strong woman deserved a strong man.

"I love you, Celeste. I'm sorry for everything. I said a lot of things—"

She placed a finger on his lips. "I love you. And we *both* said a lot of things. I'm sorry, too."

Relief burst inside him. "Will you still come to Chicago?"

"I've always loved the city. Plus my sister's there, and my brother will be in less than a month. Then there's Ian."

"So am I."

"That you are." She tilted her head against the pillow. "Only you hate my, ahem, gnomes. I'm not sure I can be with a man who has issues with—"

He silenced her with a gentle kiss. "Bring every gnome you own. I don't care, as long as you're with me. In less than a week, you taught me what it is to love, and to be loved. Last night I realized how right you were. That I *had* been living in the past and that dwelling there was only going to screw up my future. With you. I breached *your* trust when I walked out last night. When I saw Ian at the dinner, then learned about him being your father, I should have been holding you, asking how you were handling the situation. Instead, I—"

"Stop, you're rambling." She touched his cheek. "You had me at gnome."

Laughing, he kissed her again, not the way he wanted, but there would be plenty of time for that. God willing, for maybe the next fifty years.

A knock at the door had him pulling away with reluctance.

"It's probably Ian or Roy back from the cafeteria coffee run. You up for a few visitors?"

"Absolutely."

Only Ian and Roy hadn't entered the room, but Dr. Alex Trumane. "I'm sorry to disturb you," Alex said, as he cautiously approached, his eyes on Celeste. "But I thought Celeste might want to hear about Miranda."

"Are you her doctor?" she asked.

His face reddened. "I will be when she moves back to Jackson, Mississippi."

When she frowned, John explained how Alex knew Miranda, as well as how he'd led them to Malvern.

"You can't possibly blame yourself for this," she said adamantly.

He smiled. "That's what Miranda said, but I still do."

"Get over it and move on." She shifted her gaze from Alex back to him. "Guilt is an unnecessary emotion that only holds you back. From what you love, and those you love. Do you have someone you love in Jackson?" she asked, looking to Alex now.

"Her name's Kira. But she doesn't...know how I feel about her." He closed his eyes. "She doesn't know about any of this."

"Tell her," John said, and looked to Celeste. "Celeste is right. Guilt's an ugly thing, and the past can be, too. Quit living in it, and embrace the future."

"And buy her a gnome," Celeste added with a rueful smile.

Two days later, Dr. Alex Trumane rolled onto his side, bringing Kira with him. They'd made love twice already tonight, and despite pushing forty-six, he was ready to go again. He hadn't planned on sex. He'd just wanted to be honest and upfront with her, before they'd gone out to dinner.

They'd never made it to the posh, exclusive restaurant, though. After he'd given her every sordid detail, from the past all the way to the present, she'd pulled him into her arms and held him.

And when he prematurely told her he'd loved her, she'd held him tighter, and told him the same.

"Thank you for accepting me, faults and all," he said, and kissed the top of her head, as he caressed her back.

She shifted on top of him, and kissed him on the lips. "I love you, Alex. I swear from the moment I met you. But this sealed the deal for me." Straddling his arousal, she reached over to the nightstand.

Kira embraced the kissing gnomes Celeste had recommended. "I love these two," she said, then set the plaster couple on the bed next to them. "They're so cute, I think I might have to buy myself a few more."

He moved her onto her back, and kissed her. "I'll buy you as many as you want," he murmured, then tossed a pillow over the kissing gnome couple. "Let's just keep them out of the bedroom."

EPILOGUE

Three weeks later...

CELESTE SIPPED WINE and scanned the crowd. According to the owner of Zuko Art, an exclusive gallery located in the heart of downtown Chicago, over one hundred people were expected for Will's debut. Based on those waiting on the sidewalk to enter, and the shoulder-to-shoulder crowd inside, she believed him. She'd also never been more proud of her brother.

She smiled when she caught sight of him surrounded by a group of men and women. She couldn't ever remember seeing him so animated and happy. Still the artist, just no longer brooding, Will had finally accomplished his lifelong dream. Before the gallery had even opened, the owner allowed a select few to view Will's work. All of them had bought either a couple of paintings or one of his sculptures. One anonymous art aficionado had supposedly paid over twenty thousand dollars for one sculpture in particular. Yes, everything was right in Will's world—she met John's gaze from across the room—and in hers, too.

She broke eye contact with John, and looked to her dad, Hugh, who was laughing at something either Ian or Roy had said. The day she'd been released from the hospital, she'd spoken with her dad. When she'd told him she knew the truth about Ian, he'd sighed and said that it was about time. And when she told him about John, and her plans to move to Chicago, he hadn't mentioned the diner, or asked who would run it. Instead, he'd given her his blessing.

Between recuperating from her injuries and packing for the move, the next two weeks had flown by with a whirlwind of activity. Her dad had sold the diner to Karen, her assistant manager, and Rick, the short order cook, who had promptly eloped to Las Vegas after the transaction. How she hadn't caught on that the two were dating, she didn't know. Not that it mattered. Karen and Rick both loved The Sugar Shack and she knew they'd make sure the diner would prosper.

She'd sold her house to the young deputy, hired by Roy after CORE had done an extensive background check that went beyond the norm, and his wife who was expecting her first child. They, in turn, had decided to rent the studio apartment above her garage to the other deputy Roy had hired to replace Lloyd, who had moved to Chicago with Will and was now the newest member of the CORE team.

Yes, everything was right in her world. She loved John's condo and living with him. She loved waking up in his arms, dreaming *pleasant* dreams while lying beside him, laughing, loving, and planning for the future.

He snared her gaze, then smiled as he broke away from her dad, Ian and Roy. Carrying a fresh glass of wine, he moved next to her and kissed her cheek, where the bruises had finally faded.

"Isn't that your sister?" he asked, and nodded to the corner of the room.

She glanced around and spotted Eden on her cell phone. In the week that she'd been in Chicago, she'd only seen her sister once. While still beautiful, Eden's super thin figure and the tired smudges under her green eyes worried her.

"Yes, that's her. Probably following a hot lead or something. I swear she's a certifiable workaholic. My dad's been here for two days. Tonight's the first time he's had a chance to see her and instead of mingling she's on the phone."

"Bitter much?" he asked with a grin.

"That *did* sound bad. Don't get me wrong, I'm happy for her. Network is seducing her away from Chicago with the opportunity to have her own show. I'm so proud of both Eden and Will. They both had big dreams and are now living them."

"And I'm proud of you, and the way you're finally fulfilling *your* dreams," he said, and kissed her again.

She rolled her eyes. "Let's not get carried away. I'm a baker, not a famous reporter or artist."

"Once the people of Chicago taste your apple pie and chocolate chip cookies, you'll become the most famous baker this town has ever seen."

Thanks to the money she'd made off her house, and the unexpected cut her dad had given her from the sale of The Sugar Shack, she would open her own bakery/coffee shop in a few months. Ian had his lawyer negotiate the rent and renovations for the coveted space on Michigan Avenue. He hadn't been disappointed that she'd decided to not take his job offer at CORE, but instead made her promise he'd be her first sale once she opened the doors.

She nudged him with her shoulder. "You're biased."

"Because you're my fiancée?" He nipped her earlobe. "Or because I not only get to sample the baker, but her sweet treats, too?"

"Stop before my dad sees."

"Which one?" he asked.

"Does it matter?"

"After how they'd both grilled me when I asked each of them for their permission to be your husband? Not at all."

"They did say yes, though," she reminded him.

"True, but I could have done without the threat of bodily harm should I ever make their baby girl cry."

She laughed. "Then I guess you better make sure you keep me happy."

"Why don't we go home and let me get to work on making you happy enough we'll wake the neighbors."

"Mmm, sounds good, but you'll have to wait. I'm not about to leave in the middle of Will's big night."

"Your sister is," he said and nodded toward the door.

Celeste ignored her disappointment as Eden left without a word to anyone. But she couldn't fault her sister for living her dreams, not when her own were finally coming true.

"John," she said with a raised brow. "If you promise to exercise some patience, I'll let you—"

He cupped her rear. "Exercise this hot body?"

Warmth rushed through her, and settled between her thighs. "Yes," she said, fighting a moan, and wishing they really could leave. "You'll need it." She licked her lips and dropped her gaze to the bulge he was trying to hide against her hip. "After I do some serious sampling of my own, I have plans for that talented mouth of yours."

His hot breath fanned across her cheek as he released a chuckle. "I had no idea how demanding you could be."

"What can I say? If I'm fulfilling my dreams, I might as well fulfill my fantasies, too." She kissed his cheek and started to move toward her dad, Ian and Roy before he could sweet talk her into leaving. "Coming?" she asked, when she looked over her shoulder at him.

"Not soon enough," he said as he offered her his arm.

She pressed her breast against his bicep. "I'll make it up to you."

"Promise?"

"With all my heart. I promise to love you forever."

His smile melted her heart. "That wasn't the promise I was looking for, but I'm still going to hold you to it."

THE END

SHADOW OF PERCEPTION
BOOK TWO OF THE
CORE "SHADOW" TRILOGY

What happens when negligent plastic surgeons receive a taste of their own medicine...?

Chicago investigative reporter, Eden Risk, receives an unmarked envelope containing a postcard ordering her to watch the enclosed DVD...or someone else dies. No Police. After Eden watches the DVD, a gruesome, horrifying surgery, she turns to the private criminal investigation agency, CORE, for help. Only she hadn't expected that help to come with a catch. Her former lover, Hudson Patterson, has been assigned to the case.

Hudson would rather have another CORE agent handle the investigation. Two years ago, he'd screwed things up with Eden...bad. And as more DVDs arrive, Eden and Hudson find themselves not only knee-deep in a twisted investigation, but forced to deal with their past, and the love they'd tried to deny.

ENJOY AN EXCERPT FROM SHADOW OF PERCEPTION...IF YOU DARE.

SHADOW OF PERCEPTION

BY

KRISTINE MASON

PROLOGUE

"LOOK AT ME, Daddy."

Michael Morrison ignored the howling wind lashing against the metal building and concentrated on the old TV. A slow, bitter smile pulled at the corner of his mouth as his daughter moved across the screen. She'd just turned five and had looked so adorable and proud dancing and twirling for the camera in her lavender taffeta dress.

"Do you think I'll win, Daddy?" she asked as she paused to admire herself in the mirror. "Mommy says I'm sure to be crowned Little Miss Hanover." She frowned at her reflection and plucked at the puffy lace capping her slender shoulders. "But I saw the other girls during rehearsal and—"

"Don't you worry about those other girls," he reassured her as he'd held the camera steady. "And even if you don't win, no matter what, I think you're the most beautiful girl in the world."

He still did.

His eyes misted, with grief, with regret, with overwhelming sadness.

Another strong gust swept against the building. Howling and protesting, the wind angrily pelted the metal walls. Almost as if nature, the universe, God, or whatever higher powers there may be, understood and shared his pain. Approved of what he was about to do.

He wiped a hand across his damp forehead, a huff escaping from between his dry lips. If anyone had heard his inner thoughts they'd think he was crazy. Hell, if anyone had a clue of what he'd planned they'd lock him in a padded cell until his body rotted to dust and his soul slid to the bowels of hell. But he wasn't crazy. Angry, yes. Vindictive, you bet your ass.

Hardening his jaw, he returned his focus to the TV, where the DVD he'd created from old home movies segued to the next scene. The crowning of Little Miss Hanover. As her mother had predicted, Eliza had won. While the crowd had cheered and the judge placed a bejeweled crown on her head, Eliza had smiled for the camera, mouthing "I love you, Daddy" as she'd smoothed her tiny hands over the full skirt of that lavender dress.

Her proud, innocent smile faded from the screen as the film moved forward. Images of Eliza's many other beauty pageants—that she'd ultimately won or placed—flew by almost as quickly as her short life.

The wind barraged the building again, the TV screen suddenly flipped, blurring the frames into a Technicolor nightmare. The old picture tube protesting its use, he supposed as he stood and gave the top of the box a slap. After a second, the screen burst to life again, but in slapping the TV, he must have accidently rattled the DVD player, too. The images jerked to a screeching halt before jumping ahead. Past Eliza's cheerleading years, the night she'd been crowned homecoming queen, her first modeling shoot, and straight to the final scene.

He hit PAUSE and froze the image. No. Not a scene or a segment from the old home movie collection, but a still shot of his daughter lying on her bed.

Naked. Dead. Unrecognizable.

His throat thickened and his eyes filled with tears he couldn't afford to shed at the moment. Holding his grief at bay, he focused on the anger. And as he leaned forward and traced his fingers along the TV screen, along the gaping slashes across her wrists to the blood pooling at her sides, he allowed that anger to take root. Let the hatred numb his heart and blacken the soul that would eventually belong to the devil. The devil could have him. He could give a shit if he burned in hell for an eternity so long as he took the men who had destroyed his daughter along for the ride.

He would have added her mother, the woman he'd once loved fiercely, to what he liked to refer to as his "death wish list." But, Sarah had scratched herself off his list before he'd written a single name by putting a bullet through her head at their daughter's funeral. Not even in death could Sarah allow Eliza a moment to shine. No, the narcissistic bitch had to blow her brains all over the metal casket, making it about her. Always about her.

Now it was about Eliza. As it should have been from the beginning, as it would be now, and ever shall be, world without end. A-fucking-men.

The alarm on his watch beeped, reminding him what he'd already known. His patient would be waking soon, and by the low moan from the other room, Michael would have to act fast before the bastard regained full consciousness. Sure he'd strapped the man down, but he didn't want to miss the look on the shithead's face when his eyes fluttered open only to discover he'd just woken up in hell.

As he was about to exit the office, though, shame suddenly clouded his judgment. What he'd spent seven long years preparing for went beyond immoral and had his conscience battling with his anger and need for revenge. Sweat coated his skin and trickled down his back. His heart quickened and his head grew dizzy with the onslaught of a panic attack. Until he glanced at the letter he'd framed and hung on the wall. The final contact he'd ever have from his beloved daughter. While he'd memorized Eliza's words, each bold and bubbly stroke of her script, he honed in on one line in particular for encouragement.

Make them listen, Daddy.

Another moan, this time even louder, filtered into the office. His head cleared, his heart slowed to normal, and an eerie calm settled over him.

"They'll do more than listen, baby," he whispered, rage suddenly sweeping away any thoughts of immorality or ethics or principles. Screw those things. Screw those quacks who'd destroyed his daughter's life.

Without hesitation he left the office and entered the main section of the thirty by fifty steel garage. He hadn't needed the entire space and had chosen to fulfill his plans in the west corner of the building, where the lighting was best and the bathroom and utility sink were closest. Things would become messy after all.

When he reached the corner that housed his private operating room, he couldn't help a stab of pride. He'd worked half his life in the medical field and knew the space he'd created here rivaled most hospitals. Although, his OR did lack a heart monitor, he amended with a grin as he rounded the operating table and stared at the man strapped to it. His patients were here to suffer, not survive.

As he reached for his scrubs, the man on the table lolled his head and his eyes began to flutter. Grabbing a water bottle from the bench next to him, Michael opened it then splashed water on Doctor Thomas Elliot's face.

Coughing and sputtering, Elliot widened his eyes. Before the man could release a word, Michael pierced the doctor with a syringe, sending a paralytic rushing through the man's veins.

Elliot's eyes drifted shut and his body stilled. If someone were to walk into the room, they'd think he was dead. The drug paralyzed the body, but not the mind, or hearing, or...

Michael used masking tape to force the doctor's eyelids to remain open. "Can't let you off that easy, can I?" he asked Elliot, then turned the man's head toward the bench that held the medical instruments. He wanted him to see the tools. He wanted him scared out of his mind. Helpless and at his mercy.

Make them listen, Daddy.

Even though immobile and paralyzed, he'd guarantee he had the bastard's full attention.

"Good evening, Dr. Elliot. I'll be handling your surgery," he said as he shed his own clothes and reached for the scrubs again. Once dressed he pointed to the instruments on the bench.

"I'm sure these items are familiar to you considering you're a doctor. As you can see, I have everything needed to perform your procedure. I wouldn't want you to think I was a quack or anything."

He glanced at his watch. The paralytic would wear off in less than a minute. He'd love to give the good doc another dose, but didn't want to risk killing him before he had a chance to perform the surgery.

"I've got a schedule to meet, so let's get this show on the road." After slipping on his surgical cap and gloves, Michael reached for the Ziploc bags lying on the bench. He pretended to weigh the bags in his hands, fighting a grimace as the maggots inside moved. "Like you tend to do for your own patients, I took it upon myself to choose just the right size for you. With your height and build, I thought a D-cup would be perfect. Don't you think?"

He dangled the bags in front of Elliot's face. "No? Yes?" With an exasperated sigh, he set the bags on the man's bare chest. "I have to admit, I *am* a bit nervous. After all, you've performed hundreds of breast augmentations and this is my first." He shrugged. "But, gotta start somewhere, right? I just hope I don't botch this up. Not that you would know anything about botching up a surgery. I mean, you *are* the expert."

Michael noticed the bags on the man's chest begin to move, and it had nothing to do with the contents. The drug had started to wear off and within seconds, Elliot would regain control of his body. He leaned closer to the man's still paralyzed face. "This is truly an honor, Doctor. One I know I won't regret. Oh, and thanks so much for agreeing to do the surgery without anesthetic. It really saves on time and money, don't you think?"

Elliot answered with an audible wheeze. As he dragged in a deep breath, his eyes widened. He shifted and circled his gaze, the muscles around his eyes fighting against the tape holding his lids in place. "W-why...?"

Michael slapped a piece of duct tape over the doctor's mouth. "Really, Doc. You know how tight surgery schedules can be. But because you asked so nicely and you've been such a good patient so far, I'll give you a hint. Eliza Morrison. Ring a bell?"

Elliot groaned and shook his head. If he could have spoken, Michael suspected the doctor would have spewed lies to save his sorry ass. The bastard had known how Eliza had died. He'd known why. Abiding by his daughter's last wishes, Daddy had told them and tried to make them listen. They hadn't, though. Holding the scalpel high, Michael would bet his own sorry ass Elliot was ready to listen now.

Too little, too late.

Elliot screamed from beneath the duct tape, raised his head from the table and fought the straps holding his shoulders, waist and legs. He would need more restraints, Michael realized. But as he'd told the good doc, this was his first surgery. He'd just have to make note to purchase more restraints for his future patients.

"Hold still and we'll be done before you know it," Michael said as he hovered above the doctor, whose watery gaze darted from the metal blade to the bags. "Wait. You're not worried I'm going to screw up your breast implants like you did my daughter's are you?"

Elliot groaned, his breath quickening through his nostrils, tears and sweat coating his face.

"Or maybe you're worried about the implants themselves. If you are, don't be." Michael leaned closer, relishing the fear in the man's eyes, and whispered, "The coyotes will have torn the limbs from your body before the maggots ever have a chance to fester in your flesh."

Elliot screamed against the duct tape. Eyes bulging with terror, he pulled and thrashed against his bindings with renewed vigor.

Michael straightened. With a satisfied sigh, he tied his surgical mask, then turned and flipped the video camera he'd stationed in front of the operating table to RECORD.

Setting the disgusting bags aside, Michael raised the scalpel and smiled. "Let's begin. Shall we?"

OTHER CORE TITLES AVAILABLE BY KRISTINE MASON

SHADOW OF VENGEANCE
BOOK THREE OF THE
CORE "SHADOW" TRILOGY

Welcome to Hell Week. You have seven days to find him...

At Wexman University, male students will do anything to get into a top fraternity. They'll prove their worth during Hell Week by participating in various physical, psychological and even juvenile pranks. But those shenanigans aren't so funny when pledges start disappearing. What kind of evil has stalked this small Michigan university for the past two decades? Theories range from obscene scientific experiments to grotesque satanic killings...but they're all wrong. The murdered boys serve a single purpose...the ultimate revenge.

Rachel Davis, forensic computer analyst for the private investigation agency CORE, has been itching to leave her desk behind and work in the field. When her brother Sean, a student at Wexman, is found beaten and his roommate kidnapped during Hell Week, she gets her chance. Only her boss insists former U.S. Secret Service Agent, Owen Malcolm, helps her with the investigation. Owen is the last person she wants on this assignment. She'd been secretly half in love with him for over four years, until the night he'd crushed her ego and destroyed her hopes for any kind of future with him.

For his own reasons, Owen refuses to risk becoming involved with a coworker. Now that he and Rachel are stuck working side-by-side to solve this perverse investigation, he's having a hard time fighting his attraction to her...an attraction he's tried to deny from the moment they met. But time is ticking. They have seven days to find the missing pledge and catch a killer. Seven days before the body count rises and the pledge ends up another victim of Hell Week.

ULTIMATE KILL
BOOK ONE OF THE ULTIMATE CORE TRILOGY

When the past collides with the present, the only way to ensure the future lies in the ultimate kill...

Naomi McCall is a woman of many secrets. Her family has been murdered and she's been forced into hiding. No one knows her past or her real name, not even the man she loves.

Jake Tyler, former Marine and the newest recruit to the private criminal investigation agency, CORE, has been in love with a woman who never existed. When he learns about the lies Naomi has weaved, he's ready to leave her—until an obsessed madman begins sending her explosive messages every hour on the hour.

Innocent people are dying. With their deaths, Naomi's secrets are revealed and the truth is thrust into the open. All but one. Naomi's not sure if Jake can handle a truth that will change their lives. But she is certain of one thing—the only way to stop the killer before he takes more lives is to make herself his next victim.

CONTEMPORARY ROMANCES BY KRISTINE MASON

KISS ME

When is a kiss...

After a series of bad relationships, Jenna Cooper wants a sex buddy—no-strings, no emotional involvement, and absolutely no expectations of commitment. She sets her sights on Luke Sinclair. A player and commitment-phobe, he'd make the perfect boy toy. Only Luke's tired of playing the scene and wants a serious relationship with Jenna, not a series of one-night stands.

...More than a kiss?

When Luke makes Jenna an offer she can't refuse, the sexual tension between them combusts and their emotional chemistry becomes too hard for Jenna to ignore. They both end up with more than either bargained for, especially when Jenna's wild past is exposed and threatens to tear their relationship apart. Now Luke will do anything to make things right between them, but knows it's going to take more than a kiss...

PICK ME
BOOK ONE OF THE
REALITY TV ROMANCE SERIES

For the chance of a lifetime...

To help save the TV reality show, *Pick Me,* from cancellation, Valentina Bonasera swaps her position as the show's Production Assistant, to play the role of Bachelorette, only to discover Bachelor Number One, rancher and sports agent, Colt Walker, happens to be her one and only one-night stand she'd snuck away from six months ago.

...Pick me.

Colt had never forgotten the hot, sensual night he'd shared with Valentina, or how she'd left him without so much as a note or her contact information. He'd spent months searching for the woman who'd given him a night he couldn't forget and thought he'd never see again. Now that she's in Dallas, he's determined to make her his...

LOVE ME OR LEAVE ME
BOOK TWO OF THE
REALITY TV ROMANCE SERIES

Love me...

Carter James, real estate agent for the hit reality show, *Renovate or Relocate*, has been crazy about the show's designer, Brynn Dawson, for years. He's been aching to take their friendship to a new level and when he gets his chance to spend a hot, sensual night with her and fulfill his wildest fantasies, he falls hard for Brynn. When the director of the show reveals that Brynn could possibly be fired, Carter knows he has to act fast before she's booted from the show. He'll not only jeopardize his reputation, but he'll go behind her back to help her keep her job. Knowing Brynn's pride is also at stake, he hopes his deception doesn't come back to haunt him in the end. He can't imagine life without the woman he loves.

...or leave me.

Brynn has been aware of Carter for years. How good he smells, his sexy smile, his lean, muscular body, his big, rough hands and what she'd like him to do with them. When she takes a chance by going from friends to lovers, she risks both her heart and their friendship, but discovers it's the best decision she could have ever made. Despite having her job on the line, she also knows that as long as she has Carter by her side, she can get through anything. Until she finds out what Carter's been up to. Hurt and betrayed, her emotions raw and her love for him tested, she'll have to decide whether she can move past the deceit and love him or if his lack of faith in her will force her to leave him.

ABOUT KRISTINE MASON

I didn't pick up my first romance novel until I was in my late twenties. Immediately hooked, I read a bazillion books before deciding to write one of my own. After the birth of my first son I needed something to keep my mind from turning to mush, and Sesame Street wasn't cutting it. While that first book will never see the light of day, something good came from writing it. I realized my passion and found a career I love.

When I'm not writing contemporary romances and dark, romantic suspense novels (or reading them!) I'm chasing after my four kids and two neurotic dogs.

You can email me at authorkristinemason@gmail.com, visit my website at www.kristinemason.net or find me on Facebook https://www.facebook.com/kristinemasonauthor and https://twitter.com/KristineMason7 to connect with me on Twitter!

KRISTINE MASON

Made in the USA
Columbia, SC
30 June 2020

12710218R00226